THE

HUNCHBACK OF OLD ST. PAUL'S;

h

OR,

A ROMANCE OF MYSTERY.

COMPLETE.

BEAUTIFULLY ILLUSTRATED.

LONDON:

"BOYS OF ENGLAND" OFFICE, 173, FLEET STREET, E.C.,

AND ALL BOOKSELLERS.

THE
HUNCHBACK OF OLD ST. PAUL'S;
OR, A ROMANCE OF MYSTERY.

"'SOH, WE HAVE YOU NOW!' CRIED BLACKMORE."

No. 1

THE
HUNCHBACK OF OLD ST. PAUL'S;

OR, A ROMANCE OF MYSTERY.

By the Author of " The Armourer's Son," " Bravos of Alsatia," &c.

Book 1.—Lord Blackmore.

CHAPTER I.

OF WHAT OCCURRED IN THE VAULTS OF OLD ST. PAUL'S—OF HOW THE CATHEDRAL WAS BESIEGED, AND OF HOW THE HUNCHBACK HELD IN CHECK A THOUSAND SOLDIERS.

Old St. Paul's.

WHAT a long, long train of historical recollections does the very name awaken!

What terrible deeds were committed within its sacred walls ere it fell a prey to the Great Fire!

With the reign of every monarch, Old St. Paul's became the scene of some event, which has been duly handed down to posterity by the pens of historians, ancient and modern.

Old St. Paul's was a very different building to the St. Paul's of our day.

It was nothing to be compared to the present structure—London's landmark, the pride of the wealthiest city of the world.

It was, in fact, nothing whatever like it either in shape, size, or magnificence.

In the earlier years of the "Virgin Queen Elizabeth"—the period at which this romance opens—Old St. Paul's, besides being a house of prayer, was also the rendezvous of the scum of London.

In the very middle aisle of the sacred edifice money-lenders, dealers in birds, beasts, and fishes, and indeed, "domestic pets" of almost every description, including white mice—which, by the way, were sold by a man with whom we shall have to deal anon—openly transacted their business.

Thieves and assassins congregated there—" by appointment or otherwise "—and in the sacred building arranged their vile business with villainous and disappointed men, who were eager to engage the bully's sword or the assassin's knife.

It is on the night of the 5th of June of the year 1564 that our story commences.

It had been a terribly hot day, and yet the sun had not poured its full rays upon the City.

It was one of those dull, hazy days, when the air is still and suffocating.

When night came on, the air seemed hotter and more oppressive, and the general cry was—

"Oh, for a strong breeze!"

The sky was black, and not a single star shone forth.

It was evident that a storm—and a storm of no common kind—was brewing.

In anticipation of this, the shopkeepers hastily closed their shops, and persons whose business called them out, hastened through the streets with all possible speed.

Soon every thoroughfare became silent and deserted.

Not even a drunken gallant, strange to say, was to be seen.

But hour after hour passed, and the threatened storm did not burst.

For one person the threatening weather had no terrors.

On the leaden roof of Old St. Paul's stood the black figure of a man.

We say "black," for no other colour could have been discerned even by the sharpest of eyes.

It was a *curious*-looking figure—short, thick, and of singular shape.

To look at it sideways, one might have thought that it bore a very strong resemblance to a pedlar having a pack on his back, over which a long thick cloak was thrown.

Motionless this figure stood against one of the huge coping-stones.

Presently it came forth and looked—first at the west, and then at the east.

While thus looking, a bright flash of lightning darted across the heavens, and for an instant lit up the face of this mysterious person on the roof of the old cathedral.

A remarkable face! A face once seen, never to be forgotten.

A long, thin, pale face, with high cheek-bones and a large mouth—a mouth which, though certainly ugly, showed great firmness and resolution.

The eyes were large, black, and glittering.

The head was covered with a mass of thick, almost straight hair, but on the face itself, not a vestige of hair grew.

The arms were long and muscular, and the same may be said of the hands.

The legs were short, and slightly "bowed," the feet of enormous size, while between the shoulders was a large hump.

This strange mis-shapen being was none other than the

Ibunchback of Old St. Paul's.

A mysterious, wonderful man in every way was the Hunchback.

A gloomy-looking person, who was said to be the possessor of a dark, dreadful history over which he was ever pondering and brooding.

He was a man who never smiled—at least, no one remembered to have seen him smile—and who never took part in amusements.

What had he to do with Old St. Paul's at this hour?

Ah, that was a mystery!

He was perpetually haunting the old cathedral. For years he had been continually coming and going.

Regarded at first with suspicion, this gradually wore away, and he was eventually taken but little notice of.

But at last the citizens—everyone was more or less superstitious in those days—began to look upon him as a man in league with the Evil One.

They thought him a professor of the "black arts," and it was very well known indeed that he was able to appear and disappear in the most remarkable manner.

He was very rarely seen in the day-time, but, like the owls, came out at night.

His history was—a mystery.

The flash of lightning was instantaneously followed by the low, sullen muttering of thunder.

"Just as I thought!" muttered the Hunchback. "Good—good! excellent! The storm-fiend is emerging. He will rave, howl, flash, hiss, and then the air will be purified, and I shall be able to move in the vaults without suffocation.

"Holy Virgin!" he cried, as he moved slowly round and surveyed the City, "how silent everything is. Ha!" he added, as another flash of lightning, followed this time by a crashing, deafening peal of thunder, crossed the heavens. "Ha! 'tis dangerous here. I will descend. Since the streets are so silent there is little fear of molestation. I will depart for Westminster, where I may see Lord Whitmore."

Disappearing from the roof, in the space of a few minutes he emerged from a little door by the side of the vestry entrance, and closing it, looked cautiously round.

Not a human soul was to be seen.

Drawing his long cloak closely about him, and his broad-brimmed hat well over his heavy brows, the Hunchback went cautiously forth.

Suddenly loud shouts fell upon his ears, and the Hunchback caught the sound as of the rapid beating of horses' hoofs on the hard road.

Stepping back into the roadway he looked eagerly ahead.

He was surprised to see—for the flashes of lightning, now dazzlingly brilliant, followed each other in rapid succession—three horsemen galloping furiously down Fleet Street.

Just as Lud Gate was reached, the foremost rider turned in his saddle and raised his right hand.

There was a flash, bright and rapid as the lightning itself, followed by a sharp report, and one of the other two riders, throwing up his arms, fell from his saddle, his foot catching in the stirrup.

The shot was followed by a really appalling flash of lightning, and the report of the thunder which followed it can only be compared to the simultaneous discharge of a whole park of artillery.

The horse, maddened with terror, and having no guiding or restraining hand upon the reins, turned and dashed back the way he had come, dragging his late unfortunate rider with him.

Up the hill came the other two horsemen.

Each was urging his steed, by dint of spur, whip, and voice, to its utmost speed.

Just in front of the cathedral door, and close beside the huge steps, the foremost horse fell, throwing its rider clean out of the saddle.

But the man was quickly upon his feet again, and drawing his sword, stood on the defensive.

The second horseman drew up at his side, threw himself from the saddle, and also drawing his blade, cried—

"Yield, my lord of Whitmore—yield!"

"Never!" was the firm and stern reply; "never with life will I yield to you!"

"Then will I compel you. And you know that if I fail to capture you a thousand troops are following, and that escape is impossible."

"Not to twenty thousand would I yield with life."

In another instant the weapons of the two men met in deadly strife.

In the meantime the Hunchback had drawn close, but he took care to keep in such a position that there was little likelihood of his being seen.

Suddenly a startled exclamation left his lips.

"Lord Whitmore!" he muttered. "Whitmore! Heavens! what can this mean? And the one he fights with? Methinks I recognise his voice. Oh, for one more flash of lightning that I might see his face."

As if in answer to this, a flash of lightning leapt from the black heavens, and seemed to tremble for an instant on the naked blades of the combatants.

It lit up the faces of both men with wonderful distinctness.

"Lord Blackmore!" muttered the Hunchback; "on his evil errands again, the villain! May Whitmore's sword find its sheath in his black heart."

Now, above the clash of the swords, was heard the steady tramp, tramp of many feet.

Looking down the hill, the Hunchback saw a huge blaze of light, and soon made out that it was produced by a large number of links.

He saw, too, that these flaming links were reflected in hundreds of glittering steel spikes, breastplates, and helmets.

There could be no mistake made in the men who were so steadily advancing.

They were the queen's troops.

The surrounding inhabitants heard the rattle of steel and the steady tramping, and throwing up their windows, gazed in astonishment on the scene.

Lord Blackmore, knowing that troops were behind his back, increased the rapidity of his passes.

At the same time he shouted—

"Yield, I tell you! Yield—yield in the name of the queen."

But no answer did Whitmore return.

Suddenly a dark figure crept behind Lord Blackmore.

A large, heavy stone was upraised, and fell with a crash on his head.

His lordship, without a cry, fell heavily to the ground.

So startled was Whitmore, that for an instant he seemed unable to speak or move.

A heavy hand was laid upon his arm, and a low, harsh, peculiar voice said—

"Come, follow me—quick, or you are lost!"

Recovering himself by a great effort, Whitmore gasped—

"The Hunchback!"

"Aye," was the calm reply; "'tis I, my lord. Come," he added, as he pressed Whitmore's arm, "follow me, and you will be safe. See, the troops are rapidly advancing. Another moment's hesitation and you are lost. Quick, my lord, for your life!"

He led Lord Whitmore to the little door by the side of the vestry entrance, which he opened without the assistance of a key, and thrusting him in, closed the door again.

"Wait but an instant, my lord," said the Hunchback, "and I will light the passage which we must traverse."

By means of flint and steel, a light was procured, and a link which was thrust into a bracket beside the door lighted.

Taking it in his hands, the Hunchback said—

"Follow me, but be careful, for the stone flooring and steps are full of great inequalities, and a fall may prove dangerous."

So saying, he again went on, followed closely by Lord Whitmore.

Several narrow, curious passages were traversed, and several flights of dark stone steps descended, and at last the crypt was reached.

Here the Hunchback paused, and looked into the face of his companion.

"You do not fear?" he asked.

"Fear? Nay. But where go we? To the vaults of the dead?"

"Even so."

"What dark, solemn, and gloomy place is this?"

"The crypt of Old St. Paul's."

"Ah! Your dwelling-place?"

"At times—yes."

"Then where— Ha! what noise was that?"

A loud roar, which seemed to shake the crypt, was heard.

"'Tis naught but the thunder," replied the Hunchback. "You have nothing to fear. Come."

"Nay; 'twould be far better did I return," answered Lord Whitmore, shaking his head. "The troops you saw advancing seek me. They will force an entrance into the cathedral, and then—"

"Tush! Who saw ye enter?" asked the Hunchback.

"I know not, but—"

"Let not that trouble ye, my lord. They will search the exterior of the cathedral, and, likely enough, some of the surrounding houses, but when they find that they cannot trace you, they will return whence they came. Come."

"You are wrong," replied Lord Whitmore, as they once more proceeded. "All my plans have failed. False news has been conveyed to the queen by that dastard Lord Blackmore, and it was by her majesty's orders that he, at the head of a host of soldiers, set out after me. A messenger came to me at Westminster, and warned me. I had just time to fly. But, as you see, I barely escaped with my life."

The Hunchback looked startled.

"All lost!" he muttered. "All lost! I was about setting out to seek your lordship when the sound of your horse's hoofs fell upon my ears."

"'Tis well you did not go to Westminster," said Whitmore, "for had you been found at my house you would have been charged with complicity in this so-called plot, and the instruments of torture at the accursed Tower would have wrung from you a full confession of the great efforts we have of late been making."

"The torture should never force a confession from me," answered the Hunchback.

Stopping at the further end of the crypt, the Hunchback held the link above his head.

Pointing to one of the huge pillars, he said—

"No one would dream that that pillar is the entrance to the place you, a few moments ago, were pleased to call my dwelling. Behold!"

The Hunchback placed his hand on the stonework—and solid enough it looked; but as he did so, the distant shouting of hundreds of voices fell upon his ears.

"They have entered the cathedral," cried Whitmore. "Hark!"

The sound as of heavy hammering was now distinctly heard.

Whether the Hunchback thought that the troops, having discovered that Whitmore had entered the cathedral, had forced an entrance, we know not. If such was his thought he did not communicate it to his lordship.

"Fear not," he said ; "they cannot enter. Here, my lord, you are quite safe."

"And you in danger. Blackmore will soon recover from the blow you dealt him, and remembering that you have been seen with me, and that this cathedral is almost your home, he would naturally conclude that I had made my escape by your assistance. Hark ! Hear the shouts and cries !"

"Stay here, and I will ascend to the cathedral, and see that the bolts and bars are properly secured," said the Hunchback.

"Do so. I shall then feel easier, for, though I care little for myself, I do not wish to entangle you, or anyone else connected with me, in the net which has been thrown around me."

" You do not fear to stay here alone and in darkness ? "

Whitmore smiled sadly.

"No," he said. " The dead cannot harm me ; I fear the living. Go quickly ; I will stay here and not move from where I now stand. But are you well armed ? "

"I am," answered the Hunchback, grimly. "I am always well armed, and on more than one occasion I have found it greatly to my advantage."

With this he departed, leaving Lord Whitmore alone in this dark and dreary spot, alone with the dead.

In a short time the Hunchback was in the cathedral aisle.

He carefully examined the ponderous bolts, bars, and chains, and uttered an exclamation of satisfaction as he found they were all secure.

They could not be opened from the outside.

As he looked, the hammering upon the door became louder than ever, and shouts of " Surrender ! Surrender in the queen's name ! " were wafted to his ears.

The Hunchback now feared that Lord Blackmore had recovered.

He knew that no time was to be lost, for the danger was great.

Hastening to the principal door, the Hunchback, after blowing out the link, placed his ear near the keyhole, and now he heard a voice giving orders in a loud commanding tone.

He instantly recognised the voice as that of Lord Blackmore.

"He has recovered," he muttered. "Ha, it would have been well had I driven my dagger through his heart. But what says he ? "

Blackmore was addressing one of the commanding officers.

"Do you proceed to the surrounding houses, and in the name of the queen demand to be supplied with axes and hammers," he cried.

"But, your lordship," was the reply, "do you not observe the threatening attitude of the people ? "

" What causes them to be threatening ? "

"Your lordship's pardon—your presence."

"Heaven's mercy ! " shouted Blackmore. "Who did ye hear say so ? "

" The mutterings of the citizens are plain enough, your lordship. " If you will give ear to them, you —"

"Silence ! On your life, sirrah—silence ! I am here by the queen's orders, to effect the arrest of Lord Whitmore, who, aided unquestionably by that ugly brute, the Hunchback, has contrived to gain an entrance to this cathedral. In the name of all the infernal fiends, how *did* he find his way into the building ? "

"The Hunchback, your lordship," was the reply, "is supposed to be in league with the Evil One."

"Bah ! Go, do as I command you. And at your peril, fail not."

"They will force the inhabitants to give them axes and hammers," muttered the Hunchback, "and in time the woodwork will be hewn away. Ha, I have it ! I will *scare* them from the top of the cathedral."

Rushing to the end of the aisle, he pulled open a small door near the choir, darted through it, rushed up a long flight of steps, and entered a small room.

All this had been done without the aid of a light, for the Hunchback was familiar with every inch of the ground.

But in this little room, the Hunchback once more produced his tinder box, and striking a light, rekindled his torch.

The light revealed the contents of the room.

It was filled with an extraordinary and miscellaneous collection.

On one side were a number of barrels of various sizes. These contained oil for filling the church lamps.

On another side were bundles of links, several thousand torches altogether.

On another side, in a state of utter confusion, were books, hassocks, carpets —in fact, all sorts of things.

It was a place which, if it once took fire, would burst into a fierce blaze, and no doubt be the means of engulfing the whole cathedral in flames.

Placing the end of his lighted link between his enormous teeth, the Hunchback lifted up a couple of bundles of torches, and leaving the room, ascended a few more flights of stairs.

He presently emerged on the roof of the cathedral.

Sticking the link in a bracket which was placed on an iron support, he laid the bundles on the leads.

Then, dropping on his hands and knees, he crept to the parapet, and looked over.

He saw that the whole space in front of the principal entrance was absolutely swarming with soldiers.

The storm, it must be borne in mind, was still raging, but the presence of the soldiers had so excited the citizens, that they had ventured from their houses; and crowds of them now stood at a respectful distance from the troops, regarding their movements with great interest.

The Hunchback's keen eyes soon discovered that a few axes and hammers had been procured, for as he looked he saw several soldiers hurrying through the ranks of their comrades, holding them in their hands.

Creeping back, with his dagger he severed the cord which held the links, and, lighting three or four, waved them about until they were burning fiercely.

Then he again advanced to the parapet, and hurled the flaming torches below.

This done, he returned and lighted more.

A wild, terrified shout rose on the air as the burning brands fell upon the men below.

An instantaneous rush to the door was made, but not before several more flaming links fell among the men.

The noise and the confusion below were terrific, and they were increased by the loud exultant shouts and roars of laughter of the citizens.

Lord Blackmore, though surprised, became furious with rage. Sword in hand he endeavoured to incite the soldiers to advance, and batter down the doors.

But they hesitated. A burning link, thrown from such a height, did not fall lightly—a burning link in the face was something to be fearful of.

For some few moments they refused to advance, but at last Blackmore's threat to report their conduct to the queen, and also the cries of the citizens, " Cowards ! cowards ! " caused them, after a short consultation, to dash forward.

Just as a few hundred of the soldiers reached the cathedral door, another blinding flash of lightning shot out of the heavens, and lit up the whole of the sacred pile.

The weird-looking figure of the Hunchback was observed on the roof.

His long arms were raised high above his head.

All who saw him observed that he held some object in his hands, and instantly they uttered a loud cry of warning.

Too late !

In another moment a tremendous piece of coping-stone came crashing down the cathedral walls, smiting off various portions of the iron and stone-work in its descent.

It fell with fearful force on the head of one of the captains in command, killing him on the spot.

Once again the soldiers, with loud cries of dismay, retreated ; but before they could get out of the way, a perfect volley of flaming links was hurled into their midst.

Another pause now ensued, during

which the troops, to their great mortification, were subjected to the jeers and laughter of the citizens.

For one man to defy a whole regiment of the queen's soldiers was certainly a novelty to them.

But though the soldiers moved back, Blackmore did not.

He stood within the doorway, sword in hand, urging the troops to advance to the attack.

While he stood there, a little shrivelled-up old man—an individual employed by a wool-mercer opposite as "odd man"—crept round to his lordship.

"Your pardon, your honour," he said, "I would whisper to ye."

"Whisper away then," cried Blackmore.

"Your honour, just at the side of the vestry, and at about twelve feet from the ground, there's a little window. If I had a ladder I could enter it, and, dropping within the church, unfasten the door."

"Ha! is such a thing possible?"

"Quite. I can do it with the assistance of a soldier or two—for a consideration."

"It shall be done, then," replied Lord Blackmore. "Follow me."

And leaving the cathedral door, followed by the man, he gave directions to the soldiers.

Two of the men then accompanied the old man to a yard attached to his master's house.

Here a ladder was found, and at once carried to the spot pointed out by the old man.

It was placed against the window, and the man ascended it, hammer in hand.

In the meantime, to cover these movements, Blackmore had again led his men to the attack.

But the Hunchback made the place too hot for them.

The flaming torches were now flying among the soldiers with extraordinary rapidity.

Everyone naturally began to wonder where on earth he got them all from.

But it was not only torches he sent flying among the men.

Huge pieces of stone and iron were thrown upon them, and many were seriously injured.

Some of the best marksmen among the troops were placed in the best positions, and ordered to fire at the black figure above.

They did so, but it was quite evident, since the Hunchback, in defiance of the shots, continued to move about, that he was not struck by any of the missiles.

The old man, having ascended the ladder, set to work upon the window with the hammer, and had soon hacked away the frame.

A hole, sufficiently large to allow of the passage of his skinny carcase, was soon made, and being assisted by one of the soldiers, he got through the window and dropped to the floor.

Five minutes passed.

Blackmore, now in a towering rage, stood at the head of the soldiers.

On the roof, with several flaming torches clutched in his huge hand, stood the Hunchback.

He was, of course, awaiting another opportunity to send the dangerous brands among the troops.

But the motionless attitude of Lord Blackmore and his men surprised him, and, in fact, made him feel somewhat alarmed.

He was beginning to wonder whether Blackmore would have the audacity to attempt to set fire to the cathedral, when a loud shout arose.

The Hunchback leaned further over the coping-stone, at the risk of receiving several shots.

He saw the little old man we have mentioned dart rapidly away, and mingle with the soldiers.

At the same moment Blackmore raised his sword.

The troops—now giving vent to a ringing cheer—dashed forward.

Both of the large cathedral doors were wide open, and they dashed through pell-mell, making the interior of the sacred edifice ring with their loud, fierce cries.

The torches hurled upon them by the Hunchback were picked up by the soldiers and lighted—thus the cathedral was filled with a great blaze of light, and also by a huge mass of thick smoke.

"Upon the leads with you," roared Blackmore. "Away—and drag down that accursed Hunchback! S'death! I have a mind to have him torn limb from limb in this building—aye, even in Old St. Paul's."

There were many doors which led to the roof, and every one that could be found was forced violently open.

The Hunchback by this time had become aware of the fact that the soldiers had contrived to enter the cathedral.

But even now he did not despair of saving Lord Whitmore.

Having listened for some few moments, he decided to return to Lord Whitmore by means of a door which he knew could not be discovered by the troops.

Drawing his sword and gathering his cloak about him, he hastened towards it.

But the soldiers had poured up to the roof, and just as he was within half-a-dozen paces of the door he intended to use, a torch was suddenly thrust almost in his face, and a loud, harsh voice exclaimed—

"Hold there! Ho! The Hunchback! Accursed ugly brute, surrender."

"Never!" replied the Hunchback. "Never will I surrender to such vile worms as ye are!"

"Vile worms!" cried the soldier, now backed up by a dozen others. "Vile worms, eh? Take that, you—"

He had levelled his pike and aimed a terrific thrust at the Hunchback.

But the soldier had no idea of the wonderful strength of this singular being.

As he made the thrust, the Hunchback stepped nimbly aside and seized the staff of the pike in a firm, iron-like grip.

Then, ere the soldier could step back, the Hunchback's sword passed completely through his body.

The man fell, with a fierce cry of rage.

His companions hesitated to avenge his fall.

For a few moments they stood looking upon the Hunchback's deathly pale face, and from his face their eyes wandered to the long, glittering sword raised to strike.

The Hunchback's left foot rested upon the body of their companion; and, in this position, he certainly looked a most formidable and fearful opponent.

And yet the face of this strange being was wonderfully calm, but full of determination.

Suddenly Blackmore's voice was heard.

"Have you got the Hunchback?"

"Aye, aye; he is here," was the reply.

"Then seize the wretch—seize him, I say. On my soul he shall pay dearly for this night's work."

The Hunchback saw that escape was hopeless, and that further resistance would be useless.

He threw down his sword, folded his arms across his broad chest, and waited to be seized.

A dozen rough, violent hands were placed upon him, and he was dragged through the doorway, and down the narrow stairs.

At almost every step he received a heavy kick or cuff, either from Lord Blackmore or his men.

By the time he reached the aisle his hands and face were bleeding.

His appearance was hailed with loud shouts of revenge.

"Stand the ugly brute in the very centre of the aisle," said Blackmore, "so that we shall be able to look upon him."

This having been done, Blackmore advanced savagely towards him.

CHAPTER II.

OF THE AWFUL TRAGEDY COMMITTED IN THE "GREEN ROOM" AT BLACK-
MORE HALL—OF WHAT BEFELL THE HUNCHBACK, AND HOW HE WAS SAVED.

"FIRST," said his lordship, "bind his hands firmly behind his back."

But no rope was to be found, and so one of the soldier's belts was used.

"Now," continued Blackmore, "where have you hidden the conspirator, Lord Whitmore?"

No answer.

"Where have you hidden Lord Whitmore, I repeat?" thundered Blackmore. Still no answer.

Lord Blackmore snatched a flaming link from the hand of a soldier, and raised it threateningly.

"Answer, knave, or you shall die!" he said.

As the Hunchback answered not, Blackmore dashed the torch into his face.

"That is a taste of what you have given my men," he said. "Now answer me—where is Lord Whitmore? You still refuse to answer? Well, you shall be tortured."

"Your lordship," said one of the captains, "since he is not on the roof, or concealed hereabouts, it is certain that he must be *below*."

"Aye," said his lordship, "such must be the case. Find the entrance to the crypt, then. Haste, or perchance his lordship may find some hole by which he may escape."

The whole place was searched by the troops; but for some time the entrance was not discovered.

It was not the door by which the Hunchback and Lord Whitmore had entered the vault, however; still, it led to the same place.

The door was fast closed, and as it did not yield to the blows from the soldiers' pikes, hammers were brought to bear upon it.

In a short time it was burst open.

Addressing Blackmore, one of the captains said—

"Your lordship, the entrance to the vaults below is open; but it is almost a certainty that whoever goes first will soon be a dead man?"

"How so?"

"Lord Whitmore is provided with firearms, and is a most determined man. He will fire upon the first man he sets eyes upon."

"Maybe you are right," replied Blackmore.

"And that being so, the first man who shall descend will be the Hunchback. Now lead the wretch to the stairs, and force him to descend."

Fiercely they threw themselves upon the Hunchback, dragged him to the stairs, and bade him descend to what they hoped would be a sharp and certain death.

The Hunchback commenced the descent fearlessly.

How anxiously did Lord Blackmore and his men wait.

They were, of course, certain that Lord Whitmore *would* fire.

Did they hope he would?

Most decidedly. Did Whitmore fire and slay the Hunchback, the deed would have been hailed with loud shouts of delight.

Down, down, slowly, and without the least sign of fear, did this strange being proceed.

The bottom was reached at last.

A strange, terrible silence seemed to prevail.

"We are simply walking into the vaults of the dead," said one of the captains.

"What of that?" growled Lord Blackmore. "If these are the vaults of the dead, they are also the vaults of the *living*—for Whitmore will be found here."

So it proved.

In the centre of the crypt stood his lordship.

Calm, stern, and erect he stood, his arms folded across his chest.

There was no sign of fear on that fine noble face.

Nay, but a look of deadly hatred rested upon it directly Lord Whitmore saw Blackmore.

Pushing his way through the soldiers, Blackmore stalked in front of him.

"Soh!" he hissed, "we have you now, Lord Whitmore; *and— Stand back!*" he roared, turning sharply to his men.

The soldiers slunk back, a look of wonder on their faces.

"Now," he continued in low tones to Whitmore, "you are in my power. I have the queen's warrant for your arrest. You know that."

"Oh, yes, I know it, black-hearted ruffian that you are," answered Whitmore.

"Hum!" chuckled Blackmore, with a ghastly grin. "Ruffian! Ha! you shall eat your words ere long. But let me proceed. I could arrest you under the queen's warrant, but—"

"*Could?*" said Whitmore; "and you intend to do so."

"I do *not*."

"You do not?"

"No, my lord," and here Lord Blackmore looked carefully round; "you will never be taken to the Tower of London. You will meet with your death at the hands of the *Cowled Eleven!*"

Whitmore shuddered at these words —shuddered visibly, despite his efforts to remain calm.

Lord Blackmore saw that shudder, and his ugly countenance became again distorted with a ghastly grin.

"You will never dare—" commenced Lord Whitmore.

But Blackmore interrupted him.

"Dare!" he sneered; "*dare!* Have I not often told you that did I once get you in my power, I would dare anything? I have said that many times, and you have laughed scornfully in my face. But now—ha, ha!—you have no heart to laugh!"

"I cannot laugh at present, I must admit," answered Whitmore, proudly. "But yonder friend of mine I have brought into serious trouble and danger. And—"

"*Friend?*" shouted Blackmore, turning and pointing his finger at the Hunchback. "Friend—eh? Is that ugly lump of humanity one of your friends? Bah! I should have thought that a member of such a proud and haughty family as the Whitmores

would have scorned to call a brute like that his *friend*. But fear it not, he will share the same fate as yourself."

So saying, Blackmore stepped back to speak to one of the officers.

At the same moment loud voices were heard crying out—

"Stand back! Stand back!"

"What now?" asked Blackmore.

One of the captains, hurrying through the ranks, said—

"Your lordship, two gentlemen desire an audience with you."

Blackmore started.

Without asking whether they had given their names, he said—

"Show them here."

A few seconds elapsed, and then there stalked down the stairs and into the crypt two tall persons, wearing long cloaks and masked, so that no one could see their features.

Blackmore eagerly advanced towards them, and, for the space of a few moments, they conversed in whispers.

Then the two masked individuals took their departure as hurriedly as they had come.

Blackmore called to one of his captains, and taking him by the arm, led him out of earshot.

"Coningsby," he said, "you have often told me that you are a poor man."

"Aye," was the reply, "and that unfortunately is only too true, and I should be even poorer were it not for the fact that your lordship has been pleased, at one time and the other, to place in my hands sums—"

"Hist! don't speak of so paltry an action, Coningsby. I know what you are worth. I know you to be a brave man, and, moreover, a man who can keep a secret, even when—er—er— when you've been drinking, Coningsby —eh?"

Coningsby bowed.

"Well, now an opportunity occurs by which you may easily pocket the sum of five hundred crowns."

Her majesty's captain of the guard started.

"Five hundred crowns!" he gasped. "Do I hear aright?"

"Aye, you do. Five hun—"

"But hasten, your lordship," interrupted Coningsby, "and let me know how I can become the possessor of this large sum of money?"

"Listen, then. We have the queen's warrant for the arrest of Lord Whitmore on a charge of treason."

Coningsby nodded.

"Well, I do not want Whitmore to be taken to the Tower."

"Not taken to the Tower? Hum! Well, your lordship, where do you want him to be taken?"

"To Blackmore Hall."

"Ha! Such a thing is out of all question, your lordship. If the soldiers knew—"

"They must *not* know."

"What does your lordship suggest? But first let me ask—you wish to get Lord Whitmore entirely in your power?"

"Precisely," replied Lord Blackmore, coolly, "and this is what I suggest. Do you take charge of Lord Whitmore and the Hunchback, and with half-a-dozen men proceed towards the Tower. Instead of going to the Tower, turn down the steps at London Bridge. There you will find a wherry awaiting you. Enter it, and you will be rowed to Wapping Stairs. Landing there, you will be conducted to—"

"Your pardon," interrupted Coningsby, "*who* will conduct us?"

"An individual you will meet in the wherry."

"One of the gentlemen who were here but a few moments ago?"

"Nay; quite another person."

"Proceed then, my lord."

"You will be conducted to 'The Wapping Arms.'"

"I know it."

"The prisoners will there be provided with rooms, and you can entertain your men right merrily until my arrival."

"All this sounds plausible enough, your lordship," answered Coningsby, in uneasy tones, "but the whole affair is exceedingly risky. By Heaven, your lordship, do you know what, if all happened to be discovered—what all this would end in?"

"Perfectly," replied Blackmore, still in cool, deliberate tones. "The block for me, and the halter for you."

"You speak of these matters lightly, my lord."

"And so should you, since five hundred crowns are to be yours. There is no risk whatever attached to this business, Coningsby—none whatever, I swear. If you follow my simple directions all will go well."

"But you see, your lordship, the men will know all about it, and when in their cups they might—nay, are almost certain to mention the circumstance."

"*I will place that beyond the bounds of possibility*," replied Blackmore, grimly.

Coningsby looked into Lord Blackmore's face as he said this, and he noticed how fiendish was the expression upon it, but he had not the slightest idea as to what Blackmore's significant words meant.

Coningsby hesitated.

What to do he knew not.

Five hundred crowns was a lot of money—a fortune to him.

Should he refuse to become the possessor of it?

No, he thought he would have it, and determined to risk anything for it.

Besides, he knew only too well what sort of man Lord Blackmore was.

He knew that if he refused to aid Lord Blackmore in his dastardly schemes, his lordship had plenty of ways and means at his command to amply avenge himself.

"I will do as you propose," said Coningsby.

"Good; and the five hundred crowns shall be yours immediately Lord Whitmore is within Blackmore Hall. In the meantime, here are a dozen pieces," and he slipped the coins into Coningsby's ready hand. "They will enable you to entertain the men as I suggested. Now the officers can march the troops back to Whitehall."

Lord Whitmore and the Hunchback had watched these proceedings very closely, the latter having tried, but in vain, to overhear something of what had been said.

In a few minutes loud orders of command were issued by Coningsby, and the soldiers hurried up to the cathedral, whence they were marched into the streets.

They were met with loud howls of derision by the citizens, who seemed only prevented from attacking them by the fact that the soldiers were well armed.

Coningsby and six of the men remained behind.

It was a long time ere they ventured forth.

Lord Blackmore took care to see that the majority of the citizens had returned to their homes.

Then they left the cathedral by a side door.

Between two soldiers walked Lord Whitmore, his hands tied behind his back, while between two others walked the Hunchback, similarly secured.

Lord Blackmore and the others, who brought up the rear, were greeted with a few yells, but beyond this no demonstration was made, and the soldiers took their way in the direction of the Tower.

When within sight of London Bridge Blackmore whispered in Coningsby's ear—

"Remember my instructions."

"Aye, aye," was the reply; "I shall make no mistake."

"I shall join you soon after your arrival at 'The Wapping Arms.'"

Another instant, and Blackmore had disappeared.

On marched the soldiers, carefully guarding their prisoners, and at last London Bridge was reached.

Whitmore suddenly halted.

"This is not the Tower," he said.

"I am aware of it," replied Coningsby.

"Why are we being taken in this direction?"

"That is my business, your lordship."

"I shall refuse to go any further."

"My instructions, my lord," said Coningsby, savagely, "are to the effect that if you do not proceed quietly and without resistance I am to give orders for the men to fire upon you."

"Whose instructions are those? Do you mean to tell me that such instructions are in the warrant?"

"I mean to tell you absolutely nothing, my lord. But I repeat what I have just said."

"You say that if I hesitate to proceed you will order your men to fire on me?"

"I shall, my lord."

"And I a helpless prisoner?"

"Aye, my orders are imperative."

Up to this moment the Hunchback had remained perfectly silent.

Through the streets he had gone with downcast head—never once looking up or around him.

But more than one bitter groan left his lips.

Now that Whitmore hesitated, he, looking up, said in his harsh, peculiar tones—

"My lord, I pray you do not hesitate. Let us obey the instructions of this man, who, although in the pay of the queen, accepts the bribe of one of the queen's most bitter and most determined enemies."

"You had better keep a still tongue in your head," cried Coningsby, fiercely. "Who told you I had received a bribe —eh? If you fancy that I have received such a thing, let me tell you you are most grievously mistaken."

But the Hunchback had formed his own conclusions.

Again addressing Lord Whitmore, the Hunchback said—

"My lord, I beg of you to hesitate no longer. Think of those you love. Even now, my lord, we may escape."

Whitmore no longer hesitated.

With a firm step he advanced.

Down the steps of Old London Bridge went the party, Coningsby urging on his men in case Whitmore might change his mind and appeal to whoever happened to be passing for assistance.

The storm by this time had entirely passed away, but though the clouds had apparently exhausted themselves in discharging their lightning, thunder, and torrents of rain, they appeared to be still black and heavy.

The river seemed also to be as black as pitch.

Overcharged as it had suddenly become by the torrents from above, the waters rushed through the archways of the old bridge with frightful velocity.

It was some time ere Coningsby could make out a boat near the steps.

But it was evident that he and his men were heard by those in waiting, for before they reached the bottom a light was struck, and a torch kindled and held on high by a person standing in the bows of a large wherry, which the three watermen who manned it had the greatest difficulty in keeping from being swept away by the violence of the waters.

The torch threw a lurid glow over the boat, its occupants, the old, rotten, slime-covered steps, the outline of the old bridge, and the black, swift-rushing river.

The individual in the bows of the boat, a tall, slender, sinister-looking youth of about twenty, shouted out—

"Hasten, hasten, or we shall be swept away, and dashed to pieces against one of yonder buttresses."

In a few moments all were on board the little vessel, which was at once pushed from the steps.

For a moment it seemed as if all on board stood a good chance of being drowned by the rushing waters.

It was righted at last, however, and by skilful handling, got safely through one of the arches.

Wapping Stairs being reached, the party landed, and were taken by the youth who had held the torch, not up the steps, but to a little door let in the side of them, and which was much higher than the boat.

Taking his dagger from his belt, he knocked three times upon the narrow, nail-studded door, and the call was almost instantaneously answered by a short, withered-up old scarecrow of a man, who, in tones which seemed to proceed from his long hooked nose, bade them enter.

At the same time he detached a lantern from his belt, and handed it to the youth, who unceremoniously pushed him on one side, and strode into the low and most horrible-smelling passage.

"Follow, captain," he said, in authoritative tones, "and hasten, for I feel somewhat damp, and my stomach craves for that which has been denied it many hours."

Coningsby, who was evidently only too anxious to see his two prisoners safely placed somewhere, hurried his men along.

The passage was of brick and stone, and had evidently been in existence for generations.

It was filthy in the extreme, and it had that peculiar smell about it which can only be caused by continual damp.

In about the centre of the passage, the youth paused, and producing a small key, inserted it in the lock of a small iron door.

"In *here*," he said.

"What, *both* of them?" asked Coningsby.

"Aye, both of them. There is but one vault, and out of that they could not get. Quick, man—in with them."

With their hands still behind their backs, the two unfortunate prisoners were thrust, like a couple of dogs, into the vault.

But ere the door closed, Whitmore said—

"Remember, I well know where we are. We are in the vault below 'The Wapping Arms.'"

"May the knowledge be of service to you," replied the youth, with a loud laugh, as he banged the door to, locked it, and placed the key in his pocket.

Turning to Coningsby, he said—

"Now, captain, since the first part of our work is over, let us enjoy ourselves, and that right merrily. Do you follow me, and we shall soon find ourselves in most comfortable quarters."

Coningsby obeyed him, and after many flights of steps had been ascended, they reached a large hall, a hall which was brilliantly illuminated.

"This is the back of 'The Wapping Arms,'" said the youth; "no doubt you have been here before?"

"Nay," replied Coningsby, "I have not, though I have been in the front of the hostelry."

"We will go upstairs," continued the youth, "and you will find that everything has been prepared for our reception."

"Pardon me," said Coningsby, in low tones, "may I inquire your name?"

"Oh, certainly. Did not Lord Blackmore tell you?"

"No."

"He did not tell you, or *hint* to you as to the person whom you would meet in the boat?"

"Nay."

"Ah!" ejaculated the youth; then he muttered, "He is still ashamed of me—my most bitter curse on him! But if *he* wants to keep it a secret I don't, and, moreover, I will not."

Then turning to Coningsby, he said,

as he patted him familiarly on the back—

"My friend, though you may not think it, I am Lord Blackmore's *son*."

Coningsby stepped back a pace and looked hard into the face of the youth.

A low, cunning, brutal face it was, and a savage face withal.

But as he looked, a broad grin of incredulity spread over his face, and he said, as he shook his head—

"That will not do, my lad. No, no, that will not do. Lord Blackmore is not married—never was married."

"I never said he *was*," was the reply ; "but still I am his son."

"Oh, I see—I see—you are his illegitimate son—eh ? "

"That is just so."

"Ah, then, of course, *you* can never hope to inherit the title."

"Nay, but unless I am mistaken, I shall inherit some of the money, which is quite as good."

"Aye, aye. But your name ? "

"I am known as Dacre Deadman."

"Deadman ! " repeated Coningsby ; "then I have heard of you before—aye, often—very often. Why, now I come to remember, I have been told that Lord Blackmore's principal *catspaw* was a person of the name of Deadman. But then I thought that his principal catspaw must be a man as old as I am myself."

"Well, my friend Coningsby—for you see I know your name well enough—you are, as you observe, most grievously mistaken in what you had supposed. But let us proceed, for you see your men are mighty thirsty, and they look very suspicious."

The room in which the men were to stay was reached, and it was quite evident that all had been prepared for them hours before.

The soldiers, who, of course, had been entirely in the dark as to why they had proceeded by water to this mysterious house, and who had become sullen and impatient, uttered grunts of satisfaction as they saw the huge oaken table in the centre of the room full of liquors of all descriptions.

They flung their weapons into a corner of the room, and without awaiting their captain's or anyone else's permission, proceeded to fill the goblets with the sparkling wine from the bottles.

"Here, my man," said Coningsby, "observe these pieces. You will see that I have enough to pay for whatever you may choose to eat."

"Three cheers for our noble captain," cried one of the men.

And three cheers were given.

"I will go below and give orders for the supply of the men," said Deadman ; "and," he whispered, "do you follow me."

"No, no," replied Coningsby—"no, no. I will stay and see that they do not get too drunk."

"But we shall have a far better—"

"No, no," interrupted Coningsby ; "I will stay with them."

"Well, if I cannot persuade you—"

"No, I yield to no persuasion. I *will* stay with my men."

"Then you are a fool."

"Aye, maybe ; but still I will stay with my men."

Seeing that to attempt to persuade Coningsby was useless, Deadman descended the stairs to give orders.

Soon the table was groaning beneath the weight of all kinds of eatables, and the soldiers prepared to do full justice to the food set before them.

Coningsby pretended to share the meal with them, but it was *only* pretence, for hardly a mouthful did he swallow.

He was thinking of the promised reward, and was wishing—oh, how fervently—that the two prisoners were already at Blackmore Hall.

Yes, the soldiers ate, and drank, and laughed, and joked, but they little thought what a horrible net was slowly but surely closing round them !

* * * *

To return to Lord Blackmore.

He proceeded with all speed to St. Paul's Chain, descended the steps leading to the river, and shouted for a sculler.

But he was answered only by the echo of his own voice.

Not a solitary boat or a human being was to be seen anywhere.

His lordship returned and hurried along Fleet Street, and through the Strand to the Savoy.

"'VILLAIN! WHAT IS YOUR INTENTION?' CRIED FELTON.'"

No. 2

Near here stood a large stone building, half house, half palace.

That it was an ancient structure could be seen by a single glance at its walls, blackened as they were by the hand of time, and by its battlements, now, however, partly decayed.

It was approached by a long flight of stone steps, which on either side were ornamented by two enormous crouching lions made of bronze.

This mansion was one of the family residences of the Whitmores.

Drawing his long cloak closely about him, and his plumed hat over his brows, Lord Blackmore ascended the steps of this mansion and knocked on the ponderous door.

The sleepy porter, leaving his huge armchair in the hall, proceeded to unfasten the bolts and chains.

One of the latter he kept up in case of surprise.

"Well," he growled, "what want ye?"

"Entrance," replied Blackmore, sternly.

"Entrance, eh? At this late hour—"

"The hour," interrupted Blackmore, "is a matter of no importance to me. Open."

"If it is of no importance to you," said the porter, "let me tell you that it is of importance to those within this house."

"Know ye not who I am, sirrah?"

"Eh? Know? Why, 'tis Lord Blackmore."

"It is. You are expecting your master, are you not?"

"We are."

"I have news from him."

"Ah, her ladyship received news that the troops had been sent to capture him. I trust they have not succeeded?"

"They have not. But admit me."

"I will first say—"

"Say nothing, my friend," interrupted Lord Blackmore, as suddenly placing his hand round he unfastened the chain, pushed open the door, and strode into the hall. "Say nothing, but take this piece of gold and close your mouth."

The porter drew back.

"Touch *your* gold!" he cried. "No, I would not touch it were I starving! Listen to me, Lord Blackmore. Ye

are no welcome visitor, and you know it. Had Lord Whitmore been here you would not have dared to cross the threshold of this door. But I thank Heaven her ladyship is not alone. Her son is with her, and he will assuredly protect his mother from insults."

"Who taught you to give utterance to such pompous words?" sneered Blackmore. "Mark it well, there is an old proverb, 'A still tongue makes a wise head.' And remember to what fate you may be doomed if you insult me."

"Do not think your threats will terrify me," exclaimed the porter.

Lord Blackmore bestowed a fierce look on the man, and, without further talk, strode through the splendid hall and up the broad staircase to the first floor, on which was one of the reception rooms.

Into this room we will precede him.

Standing before the magnificent oaken fireplace, was a tall, graceful, and remarkably handsome lady of some forty summers.

Her hair was arranged in that high fashion peculiar to the reign of Elizabeth.

Her beautiful face was deathly pale, and the nervous twitching of her lips showed that she was undergoing some severe mental agitation.

By her side stood a tall, gracefully-formed, slender youth of some twenty years.

Though slender, it was quite evident that he was a powerful youth—a youth, indeed, who well knew how to protect himself; aye, and also those who might be entrusted to his care.

It did not require more than one glance to see that this youth was the son of the lady we have described. The likeness was simply extraordinary.

Our readers have already guessed that the lady was Lady Whitmore, and the youth was Stanley, Lord Whitmore's only son and heir, and the hero of this romance—a youth destined to experience most extraordinary adventures.

"Since we have received no further news, Stanley," said Lady Whitmore, in tremulous tones, "I take it for granted that the troops have not succeeded in effecting the capture of your unhappy father."

"I know not what to think," replied Stanley. "I know this, however—that it would have been far better had I gone forth, and so learned all the particulars."

"Oh, no, no, my son! I cannot bear you out of my sight. Have I not already enough to think of? If you went forth, Stanley, the abandoned Lord Blackmore, who for years has sworn vengeance on our house, might set his hounds after you, and—"

"Tush!" interrupted Stanley. "I thank Heaven that I have the power to defend myself. Lord Blackmore, if he cause one hair of my father's head to be injured, shall answer for it to me."

"He is here to answer any questions which may be put to him," said a low, deep voice.

Both turned with a cry towards the door.

There, on the threshold, was the well-known figure of Lord Blackmore.

He had thrown back his cloak, thereby revealing a magnificent dress, adorned with costly ornaments.

He held his plumed hat in his hand, and, as Lady Whitmore and her son turned towards him, he bowed. It was a mocking bow, and was not lost either upon Lady Whitmore or Stanley, who placed his hand on his sword-hilt.

"What!" said Blackmore, in feigned surprise; "draw your blade on a friend?"

"Friend!" cried Stanley, contemptuously. "Do you dare to call yourself a friend?"

"I do. Come—"

"Hold!" interrupted Stanley. "Let us hear what has caused you to enter this house uninvited."

"Certainly. Your ladyship—"

"Address yourself to *me*," said Stanley, drawing his fine figure to its full height. "Address yourself to *me*. It is her ladyship's wish that she may not pass a word with you."

Again Lord Blackmore bowed.

"Well, then," he said, "I will address myself to you. Allow me to say that Lord Whitmore has not been captured by the queen's troops. By my aid he escaped."

"By *your* aid?" cried Stanley. "By *your* aid?"

"I repeat, by my aid he escaped. I am here to tell you so, and also to inform you of the place where his lordship may be seen. He is on the road to Blackmore Hall, and if you set out in about six hours from now, you will reach Blackmore Hall in time to obtain a last interview with him."

"A *last* interview!" gasped Lady Whitmore.

"What mean you?" asked Stanley.

"This. Lord Whitmore must immediately leave the country, otherwise the queen will cause him to be hunted down. Of course, you both are well aware of the fact that he is accused of high treason?"

"Aye," answered Stanley. "*And who, my lord, is his accuser?*"

"That I know not. But I can see, by the way you glare at me, that you have considered me the accuser Never were you more mistaken."

"By Heaven!" exclaimed Stanley, turning swiftly on his heel, "I doubt you!"

"You can prove what I say. If you depart from this house for Blackmore Hall in six hours' time, you will reach it to-morrow night, and in time to see Lord Whitmore before his departure."

"It cannot be," replied Stanley. "I, my lord, am about to go to her majesty and demand from her the proofs of my father's guilt, and therefore I cannot undertake the journey at present."

Lord Blackmore was only too well aware of this intention; had he not been, he would never have made the proposal he had.

"But I, my son—I might go," said Lady Whitmore. "Oh, Stanley, perhaps his lordship speaks the truth. I will go."

"Such a thing may not be," he said. "I value you too much, my dear mother, to give my consent to your undertaking a journey from which you may never return."

"Again you are wrong," said Blackmore. "Her ladyship has nothing to fear in seeking her *last* interview with her unfortunate husband."

Lady Whitmore turned to her son.

"Stanley," she said, "Markham and

Loveridge could accompany me. With them I should be perfectly safe."

"Ah," replied Stanley, "yes, with them you would be safe. Well, you can test the truth of Lord Blackmore's words. But I charge you, my dear mother, go not with Lord Blackmore."

"I am about to set off at once," said Blackmore, "and could not possibly accompany her ladyship if desired."

"Very well," answered Stanley, who now, swiftly turning, stalked right before Lord Blackmore.

"Listen to me," he said. "Her ladyship believes what you have just said, and therefore I will say nothing further in respect to it. But, bear this in mind: if anything should happen to her, I will call you to account for it with my good sword."

"Take my advice, and—"

"Do not pretend to give *me* advice," interrupted Stanley, scornfully and proudly. "If I were asked to give you a little advice, it would be this: *Do not pose as a saint, while the dagger of the assassin is grasped in your hand!*"

"What!" thundered Blackmore, starting forward, "these words, from you?"

"Stay where you are, my lord," said Stanley, laying his hand on his sword-hilt; "stay where you are, or I may forget where I am, and at the sword's point, force you to say whether you have not been *lying* to us."

"Oh, Stanley, Stanley," cried Lady Whitmore, clasping her hands, "I implore you, do not be rash."

"Well, I bear him no ill-will," replied Blackmore. "And you, my lady, ere many hours have passed, will be assured from your husband's own lips that I am not the enemy he for so long has considered me—nay, but that I have proved his friend when all had deserted him."

"Not all," said Stanley. "There is one who would never desert him—one who, though a mysterious being—a man isolated from his fellow-creatures, is nevertheless a most powerful friend—this man would never desert my father, Lord Blackmore."

"And the name of this devoted friend?" queried Blackmore.

"*The Hunchback of Old St. Paul's.*"

Lord Blackmore started, but he had trained himself too well to express surprise when he thought he should not do so.

His face, too, underwent no change.

"Ah," he said, "I have heard of him. My lady, I bid you adieu."

Lady Whitmore stiffly returned his bow, and Lord Blackmore, without another word, left the room.

"She is in my power!" he muttered, as he descended the stairs. "The son will come next. By Heaven!" he hissed, through his clenched teeth, "that boy has inherited all the haughtiness and daring of his father. Oh, I will crush them—I will crush them. But yet he is a splendid youth. How unlike the wretch who calls himself my son."

The porter stood aside as Lord Blackmore strode through the hall.

He made not the slightest attempt to open the door.

Blackmore stood still a moment, and fixed his flashing eyes on the man.

It was such a terrible, fiendish look that the porter fairly trembled.

Blackmore, uttering a low, scornful chuckle, turned swiftly and strode from the house.

What passed between mother and son after Blackmore's departure it is not necessary to repeat here.

But we may say that Stanley tried his hardest to persuade his mother from setting out on the proposed journey. But he found it useless.

Her ladyship hoped that Blackmore had told the truth, and that she should see her husband.

Oh, had she known the truth, she would not have set out upon that journey, and so she would have been spared being a witness to one of the most dreadful tragedies which ever disgraced English history.

* * * *

We must now, for the time being, return to that mysterious "house of entertainment for man and beast," "The Wapping Arms."

"The Wapping Arms" was kept by a man of the name of Simon Silex, a big, burly fellow, considerably over six feet in height.

Some two years before our story opens, Simon Silex had sold himself to Lord Blackmore.

He had at one time been a warder in the Tower of London, but he disgraced himself while in that position, and was dismissed, and for some time after that obtained a living in many questionable ways, lending his sword or knife to the highest bidder.

Having proved himself useful to Blackmore, his lordship—no doubt in order to find him whenever he required his services—purchased "The Wapping Arms," and installed him there.

Simon Silex was unquestionably a thorough scoundrel—a brutal, depraved ruffian, who was ever ready to do the bidding of the titled wretch whom he was compelled to acknowledge as "master," and his wife was always ready to aid him in whatever he undertook.

Some two hours had elapsed since Coningsby and his men had arrived, and so well had they been supplied with liquors, that they were very nearly drunk.

There was, however, one exception.

This was an old soldier of the name of Felton, a man who had grown grey in the service of his country.

While his comrades thought of nothing but the articles with which they were being supplied free of charge, Felton sat in a corner of the room, a jorum of punch before him, thinking of the extraordinary circumstances which had brought him and the other men there.

A dim suspicion that some foul play was intended for him and his comrades hovered in his mind, and so he determined that, whatever condition his comrades might get in, he, at least, would remain sober.

By-and-by the laughter and the jokes grew less and less—one by one the soldiers leaned their heads on their arms, and dropped off to sleep.

Felton did, or rather pretended to do likewise.

His head rested on his arms, but his eyes were fixed upon his officer.

Coningsby—who had been particularly careful that he did not take too much—as soon as he saw the soldiers slept, rose.

"Curse this delay!" he muttered ; "how long will his lordship be? I—Ha ! here is Dacre."

Cautiously Dacre entered the room.

Seeing that the men slept, a hideous grin overspread his ugly face.

Placing his fingers on his lips, he said—

"Hist ! his lordship has arrived and has given the necessary instructions. Do you go to him and ask whether you are to get ready at once."

"Then I had better rouse the men, eh ? "

"No, no, not yet ; for 'tis not certain when his lordship will set out. Haste to him ; he is in the parlour of the house with Simon Silex."

Coningsby did as desired, and when the sound of his footsteps had died away, Dacre advanced and blew out the lamp hanging above the table.

The place was now illuminated only with one small taper, which flickered on the sideboard.

This taper Dacre took and stood upon the table.

Next he turned a punch-bowl upside down, and then took from his pocket a small packet wrapped in blue silk.

This he placed on the punch-bowl.

Of course, his movements had been minutely watched by the soldier, Felton, whose suspicions of foul play now amounted to a certainty.

Just as Dacre was about to untie the packet, Felton started up.

"Villain ! " he cried, "what is your intention ? I see, monster, you have a packet of *poison* on that bowl."

The soldier sprang forward, and at the same instant, Dacre, snatching his dagger from his girdle, rushed towards him.

Felton clutched the table, his intention being to overturn it, and thus arouse his comrades, but he was too late.

The long, keen blade was upraised, and the next moment was buried to the hilt in the unfortunate man's breast.

With the reeking blade in his hand, Dacre turned only to come face to face with Coningsby.

That officer stood petrified with astonishment and horror.

He strode forward, but Dacre pushed him back, and seizing the taper, set light to the packet.

So intoxicated were the soldiers that

they slept that sleep which only comes after a night's debauch, and the noise of the fall of Felton's somewhat heavy body had not aroused them.

The packet commenced to burn with a blue light, in which there was just a speck of white.

Slowly and steadily it burned, the smoke ascending in one long, graceful volume.

"In the name of Heaven, what is the meaning of this?" gasped Coningsby, again striding forward. "Tell me, I say, what is the—"

"Silence!" interrupted Dacre. "Silence! or I shall summon Simon, and you will share their fate. Hist! for one or two of your men move. Come."

"No, no; let me—"

"Come on! Do you want to lose your life?"

"Murderer!"

"Aye, if you will. And I am no worse than you. You want to know the meaning of my movements, eh? Then I will tell you. Those men are the holders of a secret—a secret which, if revealed, would bring Lord Blackmore to the block. They are asleep now, and asleep they will remain—for ever!"

With this Dacre closed the door and drew a heavy mat across the bottom.

"When I say asleep," continued Dacre, "I mean that they will never issue from this room alive. Yet but little blood has been shed—that you must admit.

"Here," he added, calmly and coldly, "—here—look, and you will see the last of your men."

So saying, he led Coningsby (who verily was now so thunderstricken that he could have been led anywhere)—he led Coningsby, we say, to a small hole some distance from the door, in which a piece of glass had been let in.

Looking through this, the terror-stricken and trembling officer saw the dim outlines of his men.

The room was now filled with a deep blue vapour.

A curious, ghastly effect was produced by the taper, which still dimly burned on the table.

Presently one of the soldiers lifted his head, then slowly stood upright.

His action was followed by the others.

But as quickly as they stood as quickly did they drop like logs into their seats.

Never, never had Coningsby looked upon so horrible a sight.

No sound whatever could be heard as the soldiers resumed their seats.

They had the appearance of phantoms, and as their heads fell once more upon their arms, each man seemed to direct an awful stare upon the little hole through which Coningsby was looking.

Presently the fumes from the packet became so dense that the taper was extinguished.

Darkness took the place of the bluish light, and Coningsby fancied that he could see a ghastly white face stalk through the room and halt in front of the hole.

Uttering a loud, fearful shriek he staggered back, and fell at the feet of Dacre.

"The accursed fool!" hissed Dacre, as he bent over and turned his face upward, "I am afraid that he will be more in our way than otherwise."

The fall had been heard below, and as Dacre bent over the rigid figure of the queen's officer, Simon Silex and Lord Blackmore came up.

"What is this?" said Blackmore. "How came this man in this position?"

"He has seen what he didn't expect."

"What mean you?"

"I mean in reference to your instructions concerning the soldiers."

"Ha! Well, Simon, see that he is revived, and at once. No further delay must there be; we must be on the road immediately."

Simon Silex stooped, and seizing Coningsby by the chest and legs, picked him up, and carried him below, where brandy was administered to him. He recovered after a while, and the first person on whom his eyes rested was Lord Blackmore.

"Do you feel fit to attempt once more the earning of the sum I promised you?" asked his lordship.

"Aye, I do," answered Coningsby, looking wildly around as though he expected one of the ghastly faces he saw at the table to suddenly stand before him.

"Then get ready," said Lord Blackmore, sternly, "and conduct yourself more like a man. Gad's mercy! where are your nerves, eh?"

Coningsby groaned distinctly.

"Where are your nerves, I say?" repeated his lordship. "Are you afraid?"

"No, no; but the sight I saw, your lordship—the sight I saw was enough to make one's very blood turn to ice."

"Bah! You will see worse sights than that if—if you live long enough."

Coningsby caught the significance of these words.

Looking up, he said, anxiously—

"If I live long enough! You mean that I am to be served in the way my men were?"

"I mean to say nothing. But it will be all the better for you if you express no surprise and no emotion at whatever you might see. You are now in my power, Coningsby. I have purchased you at a price—purchased you, body and soul! Henceforth you are in my hands."

Coningsby again groaned.

Only too well did he know he was in the power of this fiend in human form.

"Ere you leave this house," continued Lord Blackmore, "you will be provided with a suit of clothes more becoming, under the circumstances, than the uniform you now wear. In that you will not be recognised, and it would appear to her majesty and everyone else that on the way to the Tower Lord Whitmore escaped, and you and your men were so terrified that you have left the country. Do you see all this?"

"I do."

"Then," thundered Blackmore, "no longer affect surprise. You would rather be in my pay or *power* with plenty of money in your pocket, than in the service of the queen with little or *none?* Again I say, rouse yourself. Ah, Simon—Simon Silex, I say."

"Here, your *lud*-ship," replied that worthy, skipping up.

"The dark suit, for my friend Coningsby."

"Friend—eh, your *lud*-ship—eh?"

"Aye, friend. Away with you, you grinning ape."

Simon Silex ran off, a broad grin on his ugly, blotched face, and in a few moments he returned, carrying on his arm a suit of clothes.

At the same moment Dacre came up.

Coningsby looked at him in surprise; and well he might, for Dacre had changed his attire completely.

From head to foot he was altered.

A pair of silken wove shoes, fastened with silver buckles, adorned his feet.

He wore a broad, Italian-shaped hat, ornamented with an enormous black feather, fastened with a diamond star; a thick, massive, and costly cloak was thrown completely round him, but the slit in the centre did not conceal his attire beneath, *which was all of a deep black, and fitted tightly to the skin.*

A suit of clothes of a most peculiar cut was handed to Coningsby by Silex with a mock bow.

"Now," said Blackmore, "don these clothes, my friend Coningsby, and then Simon will bring you to the vault."

Turning to Dacre, his lordship made a rapid sign with his forefinger and thumb.

Dacre nodded, and the pair separated.

Simon assisted Coningsby to don the fresh attire, at the same time urging him, as he valued his life, to hurry.

In a few moments Coningsby was clothed in the new suit, and Simon, leading him to a looking-glass, bade him examine himself.

"You see nothing to grumble at, eh?" grinned Simon.

"Nay, nothing," answered Coningsby, who knew that he must express himself as satisfied whether he was so or not.

"Now, sir," said Simon, as he handed him his weapons, "buckle these on, and you are complete. That's right. Now will you take just one glass of brandy?"

"I will."

Simon soon procured the liquid, which Coningsby swiftly poured down his throat.

"I will now take you to the 'lock-up,'" said Simon; then having looked cautiously around to see that he was not overheard, said, as he clapped his finger to the side of his enormous nose—

"Take the advice of a man of the world: do as Blackmore bids you. He is wealthy and all-powerful. Moreover, he is one of the heads of a society which could sentence you to death; and the sentence once pronounced, there is no revoking it. Blackmore is a cunning, bloodthirsty villain—like I am, so they say—but, nevertheless, while you do as he says, you are safe, and you are rolling in money. I might have starved, my friend—one of the queen's ex-captains—but I accepted his lordship's offer, joined him, did as I was bid, and—heigh, presto!—what am I now? Proprietor of one of the busiest hostelries in London."

"I will take your advice, my friend," said Coningsby.

"Right, and you will not regret it. But what I have said of Lord Blackmore applies also to the—er—hem!—the son. Oh, he's a nice youth! a nice youth! *Beware of him.* Now come."

In a brief space the "lock-up," as Simon called it, the vile hole in which Whitmore and the Hunchback had been confined, was reached.

Lord Blackmore and his son were already there.

The door was unlocked, and Simon, lighting a torch, entered, stuck the torch in a bracket, and led the Hunchback forth.

When he was on the threshold of the door, Simon suddenly drew a gag from his pocket, and in an instant it was securely fastened to Lord Whitmore's mouth.

Then Simon brutally flung him to the ground, unbuckled several straps from his waist, and securely tied his lordship's legs.

It was a cruel, cruel way to treat one of England's purest and gentlest nobles.

His lordship's eyes looked what he would have spoken.

The Hunchback fixed *his* eyes fiercely upon Simon Silex.

Oh, had his hands been free!

Though surrounded with the swords of his enemies, he would have sprung at the villain's throat, and it would have been strange had he left him ere he had strangled him.

"That's settled," growled Simon.

"Now the other," said Blackmore.

Simon turned to the Hunchback, but the look in his great eyes was so fiercely threatening, that even this big, brutal ruffian paused.

"Proceed!" thundered Dacre, "or I will have you punished. Be quick, for we even now stand a good chance of being captured. The coach waits, Simon—rascal!—the coach waits."

"Aye, aye," growled Simon, "I know it does, and so do the horses. Look you, sirrah," he said to the Hunchback, "look you, thou ugly lump of humanity, look you—down you go!"

And with a sudden push he thrust the Hunchback backwards.

With his hands tied so securely behind his back, he could make no effort to prevent himself from falling, and as he fell he struck his head a terrific blow against the wall, which apparently had the effect of amusing Dacre, for he laughed loudly.

The Hunchback having been served in the same way as Lord Whitmore, he was seized by Simon and Dacre, and carried, not by the door which led to the water, but through another passage, up two small flights of steps, and out into the courtyard of the house.

Here stood a coach—one of those lumbering, awry old things then just coming into general use—and it was painted black.

Four powerful black horses were attached to it, but only one postilion.

On either side of the coach stood a powerful grey horse.

These were for the use of Lord Blackmore and his son.

The coach-door was opened, and the Hunchback flung in.

Then they returned, fetched up Lord Whitmore, and thrust him into the coach beside the Hunchback.

The door was thereupon closed, Dacre and his father sprang into their saddles, and away went the party at terrific speed.

* * * *

At the expiration of six hours, Lady Whitmore set out.

The journey she had determined to undertake had to be performed on horseback.

Though her face wore a careworn expression, and her eyes showed unmistakable signs of weeping, not many would think, to look at her, that she was the mother of a youth fast attaining manhood's estate.

She was plainly attired in a riding-habit of black velvet, slashed with blue, and she wore no jewellery or ornaments of any description, except an ivory and gold cross, with a pair of tassels at her waist.

Her two faithful men-servants, Markham and Loveridge—men who had been in the service of Lord Whitmore for years and years—were well armed and mounted on strong horses.

Stanley's last words to his mother were—

"Farewell, dearest mother. Remember how I tried to dissuade you from this journey. If aught happens I pray you to remember it. I would sooner trust to the shifty temper of her majesty, or the uncertain action of the Privy Council, than believe one word Lord Blackmore uttered. Once more, farewell."

"If I should see your father, Stanley?"

No answer was returned.

Stanley seemed to be thinking of something else.

"Stanley," pleaded her ladyship, "Stanley, my dear boy—Stanley, if I should see your father?"

"Tell him," answered Stanley, in low, but fierce tones—tones which cut his mother to the heart—"tell him *that I will avenge his death!*"

"Oh, Heaven!" cried Lady Whitmore, clasping her small, snow-white hands together, "his mind wanders."

Stanley smiled bitterly.

Shaking his curly head, he said—

"Nay, mother, my mind wanders not. I am in full possession of all my faculties."

Here he suddenly strode up to the men-servants.

"Loveridge—Markham," he said, "you will guard your mistress—guard her well—guard her with your lives."

"Oh, your worship," exclaimed Loveridge, raising his hat, "you must know that we will guard her with our lives. If harm come to her— But, no, no! fear it not—fear it not! Her ladyship will be safe."

"Farewell," cried Stanley, once more, as he abruptly stepped aside.

"Farewell, my son," whispered Lady Whitmore. "Heaven guard ye, as I hope Heaven will guard me and your unhappy father."

The great gates rolled back, and the impatient horses trotted forth.

Stanley stood with bowed head, his hat clasped in his hand, listening to the clang of the iron hoofs.

Presently they died away, and then our hero, with a deep sigh, turned and slowly re-entered the mansion.

Blackmore Hall, the country residence of the Blackmore family for generations, was a large, rambling old mansion, built partly of brick, and partly of stone.

It was surrounded by a deep moat, and by several acres of ground—ground which never, by any chance, got attended to by the hand of man.

The old Hall stood just off the high road leading to, and within a couple of miles of the town (now the city) of Oxford.

In its time it had been the scene of festivities on a grand scale, festivities which had repeatedly been graced by the presence of royalty ; but this was, of course, long before Elizabeth came to the throne.

Since the title and the estates had fallen to the present Lord Blackmore, no festivities whatever had been given at Blackmore Hall.

No ; it had sunk very low indeed in the estimation of everybody, and it was looked upon at the period of which we write as a very mysterious place indeed.

Many and many a night the surrounding neighbours—nearly all of the very poorer class, and many of them tenants of his lordship—had been awakened by loud yells of terror, groans of agony, and heart-rending cries of despair.

In the dead of night, on several occasions, the neighbours had ascended the roofs of their houses, which overlooked the grounds, and had witnessed a strange scene—a weird and extraordinary scene.

They had seen the grounds suddenly illuminated with a strange, brilliant light—a light so powerful, that the dark heavens were illuminated with a dull, red glow ; they had heard strange sounds—sounds which bore a striking resemblance to the somewhat monotonous chant for the dead; and then they had seen several strange figures wend their way in single file round the grounds.

Each carried a lighted taper, but the light did not show up the faces of those who carried them.

Nay, nothing of their faces, or any other part was to be seen, for they were clothed from head to foot in black, and even their faces were so covered, but not the eyes.

Nay, the eyes glared out through two little holes—glared (so said those who saw them) with supernatural brilliancy.

The wondering, startled neighbours watched this line of dark, mysterious figures as it slowly wended its way in and out the various paths of the grounds —listened to the slow, monotonous chant until the figures had vanished, and the chant had died away.

The neighbours spoke of these strange things with bated breath.

What did it all mean?"

Who was the chief of all this?

Why, who else but the *owner* of the house?

Was he the chief?

At present we cannot satisfy our readers on that score.

The neighbours considered that these mysterious beings, these black figures who chanted after the style of a number of monks, must be members of a secret society.

They were not far wrong here.

But then, if a "secret society," of what class was it?

Was it *for* or *against* Church or State?

No one could venture to offer an opinion. If anyone thought that something was surely wrong, then he or she had the wisdom to keep it to him or herself; for all knew only too well what a dangerous and most determined and deadly enemy this Blackmore could be.

But we must make our readers acquainted with *this* fact—that is to say—

Of these mysterious beings there were never seen more nor less than eleven, and they were known to the members of their own class as

"The Cowled Eleven."

And each man wore on his breast three diamond daggers arranged thus—

"To Traitors, Death!"

Nothing of any importance occurred on the road from London to High Wycombe, which was reached when once more darkness was just gathering over the country.

The journey had been slow—very slow, for the road was rough, and it is not to be expected that so gentle a lady as Lady Whitmore could travel so fast as a man, or even a woman accustomed to the roads.

Several stoppages were necessarily made for refreshment, both for themselves and horses.

Just before passing out of the pretty village (it was a village then) of High Wycombe, Loveridge respectfully suggested that he should be given authority to hire—say half-a-dozen men, in case they might be attacked by robbers, who, it was said, occasionally prowled about that part of the country.

But so deep in thought was her ladyship that it was some time ere she heard him, or if she heard him she did not for some time understand him.

But when she did, she said—

"Nay, an increased escort I will not take, lest Lord Blackmore may think I am come to his house in a hostile manner. Nay, nay; let us proceed alone. I trust to you—to you, my faithful servants."

So on they went.

When about a mile past High Wycombe it had become quite dark.

But Markham was well acquainted with the road, having travelled it many a score of times when a soldier, so they were not afraid of losing themselves.

By-and-by they came to a broad sheet of water, which was known as "Miriam's Pool," and which was crossed by a small rustic bridge.

When her ladyship reached this, Markham cried out—

"Hold, my lady; though we can see fairly well what we are doing *here*, and can see the water and the bridge, we cannot see what is on *the other side*. So let us get our arms ready."

"Heavens!" gasped her ladyship, shading her eyes with her hands and looking ahead, "you do not mean that our progress is to be stayed?"

"Nay," replied Markham, "I do not mean that, my lady, but I mean this: this bridge is not strong enough to hold more than one at a time, so while your ladyship crosses we will watch you with arms ready."

So Lady Whitmore proceeded.

Slowly and carefully she went, the horse's hoofs making a loud, hollow noise as it proceeded.

The opposite side was reached. But no sooner had the hoofs of her ladyship's horse touched the ground, than a swift, rushing sound was heard, and a loud, gruff voice shouted—

"Hold! But gently—gently."

Lady Whitmore uttered a loud, terrified shriek as she found her horse's bridle seized by a couple of masked men.

Forgetting the frailness of the bridge, Markham, with a loud cry of rage and terror—terror, as he thought of the danger into which his beloved mistress had rushed—urged his horse onwards, Loveridge being close behind.

But ere Markham's horse had taken half-a-dozen strides, a bright flash lit up the darkness, a sharp report rang out, and Markham, raising himself in his stirrups, and throwing up his arms, cried—

"My mistress! Oh, Heaven, guard her and receive my soul!"

Back sank the man—back, right across the haunches of his terrified horse.

For one instant Loveridge stood motionless; then giving utterance to a loud cry, he plunged his spurs into his horse's flanks and dashed forward, pistol in hand.

But at what was he to fire?

He could not make out.

Nothing could he see but a mass of trees; but he concluded that the assailants were between these trees.

He plunged forward, and as he reached his now dead comrade, an ominous crackling of the wooden bridge warned him of the danger of proceeding.

If he turned back and went round he had a mile to traverse.

And his mistress was already in the hands of the robbers; for such he, of course, thought the assailants must be.

He clutched his pistol firmly in his hand, and raising himself in his stirrups, endeavoured to penetrate the intense darkness.

Useless— oh, useless task.

"My lady," he frantically cried, "my lady—where are you? Speak! Speak!" and a couple of tears—tears of agony—rolled down the rugged face of the old soldier. "My lady, speak."

It was not her ladyship who spoke, but the iron mouth of a pistol.

Crack it went, and the bullet had found its billet, for Loveridge, with only one terrible groan, fell from his saddle to the ground, shot through the heart.

Another instant, and a couple of dark, masked figures rushed upon the bridge, seized upon the bodies of the unfortunate servants, and, without ceremony, flung them into the pool.

Then they cut all the trappings from the horses, except the bridles, flung them into the pool, and then led the animals away.

All this was done in an incredibly short space of time—much faster, in fact, than we can drive our pen along the paper.

While this terrible scene had been enacted, Lady Whitmore had remained silent.

The masked men who had seized the bridle released not their hold for one second.

Neither had spoken except to say—

"Silence, and be still, as you value your life!"

The murderous scene over, a tall personage, clothed in black, and, like the others, wearing a mask, and who was evidently the leader, and the man who first cried, "Hold!" came forward.

"Lead her ladyship's horse, and carefully," he said; "and let silence prevail."

The men did as desired, but ere they had proceeded far, Lady Whitmore's tongue was loosened, and she said—

"Oh, tell me—tell me, I entreat, whither do you lead me? I implore you to tell me? What ransom do you require? What——"

"Hist!" interrupted the tall personage, "hist! We require no ransom."

"You are robbers?"

"No, lady."

"Then what are you? Why am I stopped, my faithful servants murdered, my——"

"We can give you no explanations," was the impatient interruption; "but I can tell you that we are merely obeying orders, and so far as we are concerned, your person and your valuables, whatever they may be, are safe."

"You say you are obeying orders?"

"I do."

"Whose orders?"

"If you will but be patient you will see."

"Sirrah!" cried her ladyship, "were your orders to murder my servants?"

No reply was made to this.

Again and again her ladyship spoke to the man, endeavouring to learn from whom he had received his "orders."

It did not strike her that those orders were from Blackmore.

Mile after mile was traversed, and at last a halt was made.

Her ladyship looked, and she saw, lying off the road, the black outlines of a huge mansion.

"What house is this?" she cried. "What house is this? I demand to know?"

"Listen!" said the tall individual; "I will tell you—this is Blackmore Hall. Now preserve silence, my lady, for I swear that whatever you may say, whatever questions you may ask me, I will not answer you."

Neither of the men knocked or rang at the gate, neither did they make any signal, but nevertheless, almost as soon as the party arrived, the massive oaken gate rolled noiselessly back.

When all had entered, the tall individual said—

"To the right."

Suddenly they stopped, and at the same instant Lady Whitmore uttered a cry of alarm.

But neither of the men expressed surprise at what was before them.

A bright light had suddenly burst upon the scene, and a number of black figures carrying tapers were advancing slowly towards them.

Round and round they wound all the while keeping up a low, monotonous chant, a chant which was calculated to freeze one's blood.

It might have been thought that Lady Whitmore would have placed her hands over her face to shut out the weird and extraordinary sight, but she did not.

Erect she sat upon her horse.

In a few seconds the strange party of men reached Lady Whitmore's side, but they took not the slightest notice either of her or of the men.

With startled eyes, Lady Whitmore watched them.

She saw that they were completely enveloped in black, and that only their eyes were visible.

And those eyes!

Her ladyship saw how fiercely they glittered through their masks; also the glitter of the diamond daggers affixed to their breasts.

Presently the last man went by, and instantly darkness prevailed.

A deep groan left Lady Whitmore's lips.

In low tones she said—

"I pray you, relieve my mind. Tell me that you have made a mistake and that this is *not* Blackmore Hall."

Whether her ladyship would or would not have received an answer to this appeal we know not, but hardly had she spoken, ere a long and narrow door opened at her side, and a flood of light burst forth, the said light being produced by a number of masked men, who, ranged on either side of the passage, held aloft a small silver lamp.

Lady Whitmore was forced to dismount, and she was conducted through a vaulted passage.

Poor lady! Though the weather was warm enough, she shivered as though it were the middle of winter.

Having entered, the door was closed, and the tall individual, approaching her ladyship, took from his pocket a delicate silken kerchief.

"Your ladyship will forgive me for being compelled to use this," he said; "but my orders are that your ladyship is to be blindfolded."

"Blindfolded!" gasped Lady Whitmore, whose face now was white with terror, "blindfolded! Wherefore? Oh," she cried, starting back, and placing her hands in front of her as if to shut out some horrid sight, " I am in a trap. I am betrayed."

The tall individual made no reply, but advanced, holding out the kerchief.

Lady Whitmore, after giving utterance to a little sigh, stood firm while the kerchief was bound about her eyes.

" Oh, Stanley!" she muttered—" oh, Stanley! thou wert right, my son! Lord Blackmore is the villain you warned me against. I see it all. My darling husband is to die, and I—I am to die with him."

" Let me take your hand, my lady," said the tall personage, " and I will safely conduct you to the room in which you are to meet—"

He paused abruptly.

" To meet whom? Quickly—am I to meet Lord Blackmore ?"

The man impatiently took Lady Whitmore's hand.

" Come! I will not answer questions," he said.

Ere two paces had been taken, a loud voice at the extremity of the vaulted passage cried out—

" March!"

Instantly Lady Whitmore heard the rattle of arms on all sides of her, and knew that the masked and armed men who had stood in the passage had formed up behind her.

So the strange party proceeded.

A most extraordinary sight they presented—a sight which many a brilliant painter would have seized upon for a wonderful picture.

If the party, with her ladyship at the head, and the tall, masked man at her side, made one think of anything, it was Tower Hill and the procession to the fatal block.

Up several flights of stairs Lady Whitmore was led—how many, however, she knew not—and at last she was taken through several apartments.

These apartments were, save for the lamps carried by the men, in total darkness she also knew, for though she could not distinguish objects through the kerchief, she could light and shade.

Presently the word " Halt!" was called, the party came to a standstill, and the kerchief was instantly taken from her ladyship's eyes.

Lady Whitmore now found that she was in a small ante-room, which was only illuminated by a small lamp hanging from the ceiling.

The masked men no longer carried silver lamps.

Instead, they held drawn swords.

After a few seconds' pause, Lady Whitmore turned to the tall person, who still stood at her side, and said—

" Tell me, where am I ?"

" Hush!" was the whispered reply, "hush! Your life depends upon your silence."

* * * *

We must now for a time leave this mysterious scene, and return to Lord Whitmore and the Hunchback.

They reached Blackmore Hall some hours before Lady Whitmore, and were immediately conducted to vaults below the moat.

There, after a time, they were supplied with " refreshments " in the shape of pitchers of water, not over clean, and small loaves of bread, and were informed by a bullet-headed, greasy-looking scoundrel, who acted as gaoler, that they could either consume them or leave them alone.

In the vaults they remained until the arrival of Lady Whitmore.

Lord Whitmore heard sounds as of some fresh arrival, but of course he had not the slightest idea as to who it was.

He had no more idea of his devoted wife's presence than of the presence of her majesty herself.

By-and-by the doors of the vaults were thrown open, and a flood of light illuminated the damp, mouldy-smelling cells—terrible dungeons, with not even a pallet or a wisp of straw to serve as bed, or a stool to sit upon.

Lord Whitmore, who, like the Hunchback, was now quite released from gag and bonds, was half standing, half leaning in a corner of the dungeon.

He looked up as the door opened, and for some few moments was dazed by the brilliancy of the torches and the lamps held aloft by a regular crowd of masked and armed men.

As the door was opened, one of them —it was Coningsby—stepped forward.

" You are to follow me, my lord," he said.

" I am ready," replied Whitmore; " I am ready, traitor—vile traitor that you are. For, despite your mask, I can recognise you. Aye, you cannot mask your voice."

"Silence!" roared Coningsby—"silence, and come forth!"

Whitmore folded his arms and stepped forth, when he was instantly surrounded by half-a-dozen men.

The Hunchback was next directed to come forth, and he came in precisely the same attitude as his lordship.

He was also at once surrounded by a number of armed men.

Coningsby now gave the order, and the party moved on.

They traversed a long, subterranean passage, and ascended a broad flight of stone steps, at the sides of which a number of men were placed.

Whitmore and the Hunchback—who, of course, knew where they were—were now thoroughly astonished at the number of men.

It seemed as if the building fairly swarmed with them.

Presently a large archway was reached.

On the other side of it hung a pair of heavy curtains—curtains as black as jet.

Over them hung a representation of the daggers the Cowled Eleven carried on their breasts.

As the party reached the archway the curtains were drawn aside, and a deep, solemn-sounding voice said—

"Enter!"

The whole party entered, but halted on the threshold.

And now, for the first time, Lord Whitmore allowed a great cry of astonishment to escape his lips.

But no cry escaped the Hunchback.

Not a muscle of that pale, watchful face moved.

For one instant there was a strange glitter in his eyes, but the next it had disappeared.

Was it any wonder that his lordship should utter a cry of astonishment?

No.

He found himself in a large, lofty apartment, the walls of which were draped in black, yet this apartment was called the "Green Room."

At each corner of the room stood a model of a man in a complete suit of black armour, and by the side of each helmet was stuck a link.

At the farther end, in the form of a half circle, was a bench or table, also draped in black, and around this sat eleven cowled figures—the same we have previously described.

But this was not all.

At the other end of the room stood a peculiar-looking object.

In shape it was like a huge box placed on end and covered with black drapery.

In front of this burned a silver lamp.

After the lapse of a few moments, the centre cowled figure slowly rose, and as it rose, the prisoners were brought into the centre of the apartment, around which the armed men arranged themselves.

Coningsby, answering to an arranged signal, cried out—

"Lord Whitmore and the Hunchback, known as the Hunchback of St. Paul's."

The central figure took up a sheet of parchment, looked at it, and said—

"Lord Whitmore, after investigation, you have been found guilty of treachery, and—"

"Liar!" cried Whitmore, starting forward—"liar! *You*, Lord Blackmore—for, despite your disguise, I recognise you—*you*, I say, are the traitor. You are at the head of a dangerous society—a society having for its object the overthrow of her majesty Queen Elizabeth. I knew of the working of this accursed society—a society which has already many a dastardly murder to answer for—I knew it, and had I been allowed time, I would have rooted it out and so have saved the queen many an hour of bitter agony. But you, vile traitors that you are, obtained her majesty's ear, and denounced *me* as a traitor—me, who have always been one of her greatest friends. You, and your vile associates there—they who conceal their identity beneath those cowls—managed to produce forged proofs of my supposed treachery, and telling the queen that I had a small army at my back, managed to persuade the queen to send a whole troop of her soldiers to effect my capture. Oh, fool that I was to fly from them. But I did so only because I thought I should thus gain time to have the circumstances investigated by her majesty herself. 'Tis now too late. But my revenge will yet follow you—"

"Lord Whitmore," interrupted Blackmore, in what he intended to be calm tones, but which were very far from it, "Lord Whitmore, you have been allowed to say more than we had agreed to allow you. I say again that you have been found guilty of treachery—"

"Fool!" again interrupted Whitmore. "If it be treachery to attempt to uproot a society having for its object the overthrow of the reigning monarch, then indeed I am guilty."

"Aye," said the Hunchback, in cold tones, "and I am also guilty."

"You, Lord Whitmore," continued Blackmore, "are sentenced to *death*. Torture and poison were proposed, but you will die not by either. By my influence you are to meet your death in a manner befitting a peer of the realm, that is, *death by the axe!* As for you, you who are one of his lordship's friends, and commonly known as a mysterious being, the Hunchback of St. Paul's, we have not come to any conclusion respecting you. You might save your life by answering certain questions we shall put to you hereafter."

The Hunchback bestowed upon Lord Blackmore a withering look of contempt.

"Wretch!" he hissed, "wretch! base-minded villain that you are, nothing, not even the most horrible torture ever devised by man for man, would cause me to answer one question you or anyone else might put to me. Death! *Death!* I have faced death hundreds of times, in every shape. Do I fear death? No. But let me tell you this, my lord. Though both of us are sentenced to death, and though you carry out that sentence, you will not rend in pieces the net which is gradually but surely being drawn about you and your co-conspirators. By Heaven, no! You are watched, and by those whom you least suspect."

"Lord Whitmore," said Blackmore, without pretending to notice what the Hunchback had said, "you are to *die*—at once. Our motto is—"

Here the other cowled ten suddenly leapt to their feet, and cried, simultaneously—

"*To traitors, death!*"

"I have no fear of death," replied Lord Whitmore, calmly. "Unlike you, Lord Blackmore, I shall die with my soul unstained by the blood of my fellow-man. But oh," he suddenly added, as he pressed his hands fervently to his brow, "I should like to wish an eternal adieu to my dear wife and my son."

"Lord Whitmore," interrupted Blackmore, "I am aware how you love your wife—how she loves you. She shall see the last of you—*behold!*"

And he brought his hand down with a crash on a bell on the table.

Hardly had its echoes died away ere the curtains were drawn aside, and Lady Whitmore dashed wildly into the room.

A pause of an instant, a wild, passionate cry, and her ladyship, holding forth her hands, was about to precipitate herself into the arms of her thunder-stricken husband, when Blackmore, a tone of triumph in his voice, cried—

"Hold!"

Coningsby instantly strode forward, and, seizing her ladyship's arm, drew her back.

"Let there be no sobbing and sighing here," said Blackmore, scowling fiercely.

"Ha!" gasped Lady Whitmore, pressing her hands upon her snow-white brow, "that voice—'tis Blackmore who speaks. Husband, tell me, is it not so?"

Lord Whitmore bowed his head.

"Oh, Heaven!" moaned her ladyship, as her beautiful eyes ran rapidly round the gloomy-looking apartment, and finally rested upon the eleven grim, mysterious figures.

"Oh, I now see it all. Stanley was right—Stanley was right."

"What said he?" asked Whitmore, eagerly.

"That Blackmore was a villain. That you, if you were at Blackmore Hall, would never leave it alive; and he bade me say—"

"Yes—yes."

"That he would avenge your death."

"HER LADYSHIP, HOLDING FORTH HER HANDS, WAS ABOUT TO PRECIPITATE HERSELF INTO THE ARMS OF HER THUNDER-STRICKEN HUSBAND."

No. 3

"I am satisfied," replied Whitmore. "I know him too well to fancy that he will break his word."

"This scene can be no further prolonged," hissed Blackmore. "Your time has come, Lord Whitmore. Here in this room—at once—you die. And her ladyship is here to see our sentence carried out."

And again Blackmore's hand descended on the bell.

This time a noise was heard at the further end of the room.

All turned and saw that the drapery, which had covered the something that had looked like a box turned on end, had fallen off.

What was revealed?

A small, square platform, in the centre of which was a block, and leaning on his axe was the headsman.

Truly it was a frightful sight, and no wonder Lady Whitmore gave a fearful shriek of terror.

Neither Whitmore nor his wife knew to whom that black figure on the platform belonged.

But the Hunchback did.

Despite the black mask he had penetrated the disguise.

Turning to Whitmore, he said, in loud tones—

"Do not die without knowing who your executioner is. That wretch is Dacre Deadman, Blackmore's illegitimate son."

"Thou art a liar!" roared Blackmore, now more excited than he had previously shown himself.

"If I am a liar, prove it before those present—order the wretch to take off his mask."

"Nay, not to please you or anyone else. Lord Whitmore, prepare to die."

With a terrible cry Lady Whitmore broke from those who held her, and, rushing forward, she threw herself on her knees before the mysterious council.

"Oh, hold!" she cried; "hold! Have mercy! Mercy, Lord Blackmore —have mercy! He is innocent. Have not I—his wife—had the opportunity of looking into his inmost soul—of knowing his every thought—his every action? Oh, my Lord Blackmore—oh, gentlemen, gentlemen!" she frantically cried, "have mercy. Have mercy on him and on me!"

"Lady Whitmore," replied Blackmore, in his cold tones, "I have eagerly waited for this moment. I wanted to see you on your knees pleading to me for your husband's life. But no supplication on your part will have the effect of causing us to alter our decision. Once a sentence is pronounced by this society, there is no altering it."

"Then," cried her ladyship, starting up, "since blood must be shed to satisfy you, let an exchange be effected. Take *my* life, and let him live. I am willing to die for him—yes, let me—"

"Stay, stay!" interrupted Blackmore; "such a thing cannot be."

"Even if *you* consented to such an arrangement," said Whitmore, scornfully, as he drew himself proudly erect, "I would never consent to it. Monster! Remember that my wife is a witness to my murder."

"True—to your *execution*. But then she will never have the power of giving evidence as to what she saw. We have not yet decided what we shall do with her. That will command our attention hereafter, but 'tis certain that she will never be free again."

Blackmore now motioned with his hand.

Several soldiers strode forward.

Some of them seized the Hunchback, while others caught hold of Whitmore, whose hands were instantly tied behind his back, and his neck bared.

Lady Whitmore would have flung her arms about her unfortunate husband's neck, but she was not allowed.

A couple of men held her with a brutal grip.

Another signal was given, and Lord Whitmore was conducted to the platform.

There he turned and fixed his eyes upon his now nearly distracted wife.

Oh, what volumes did that look speak!

"Mercy!" shrieked Lady Whitmore, as she frantically endeavoured to release herself. "Mercy—mercy! Oh, Heaven, mercy! Oh, will Heaven allow such an infamous deed to be done? Murder, murder!" she shrieked, her voice ringing throughout the building —aye, and it was heard in the grounds.

Wild shrieks such as this were the

sounds often heard by the terror-stricken peasants.

"Beloved wife," said Whitmore, in low, sad tones, "we part for ever. We—"

"Oh, no, no!" cried her ladyship; "oh, no! Oh, my darling, my own! Oh, I shall go mad—mad!"

Whitmore, terribly affected, turned to Blackmore, and in proud tones, said—

"I am compelled to make one appeal to you. Will you grant me the favour of a parting embrace with my wife?"

"No!" was the fierce reply.

Whitmore bowed, saying—

"When your time comes no mercy will be shown to you."

Then turning to his wife, he said—

"Farewell! Be firm, dear wife, that I may die—that *I* may die firmly. Remember me to my dear son; tell him that you told me what he has said; tell him that with my last breath I blessed him, and that I bade him farewell, farewell until we all meet in Heaven. Once more, my beloved wife, I bid thee farewell. Heaven guard you and our son."

Then sinking upon his knees he raised his pale face, and cried, in tones which were never forgotten by those who heard them—

"O Father, receive into Thy bosom one of Thy faithful servants, one who has never willingly injured his fellow-man. Thou wilt bring comfort to my sorrowing wife and son. Thou wilt avenge this most foul murder."

Again and again Lady Whitmore's appalling shrieks rung out, again and again did she frantically struggle to rush to her husband.

But such a thing was out of all question.

She was held too securely.

Rising, Whitmore turned to the Hunchback.

"Farewell, friend," he said; "farewell! You will remember me?"

"Fear it not," was the low reply; "fear it not. Heaven will spare me to assist thy son—or if not, then *my* son and thy son shall go hand-in-hand."

"I cannot embrace thee," said Whitmore—"I cannot embrace thee as I would were my hands free. But I can bid thee a loving farewell."

The Hunchback would have replied, but he found it impossible.

His head fell upon his breast, and the tears stole down his cheeks.

One more loving look Whitmore fixed upon his devoted wife, then he was hastened forward.

Now for the first time the headsman moved himself.

Drawing to one side, he drew himself erect.

"Art thou ready?" he said.

"I am, knave," answered Lord Whitmore, as, kneeling down, he placed his head upon the block.

Another shriek left Lady Whitmore's lips, and it was the last.

A merciful Heaven came to her assistance, and deprived her of her senses.

She slid through the hands of her guards, and fell in a heap to the floor.

Almost at the same moment Blackmore gave another signal.

Round with a "whizz!" flew the broad-bladed axe.

The blow was most truly aimed, for the head of Lord Whitmore was instantly severed from his body.

The fearful tragedy—a tragedy unparalleled in the annals of history—was over.

The eyes of the Hunchback had been fixed upon the scene on the platform, and he never once removed them.

Even when the axe severed the head, he moved not.

"Listen to me," said Blackmore to the Hunchback. "A worse fate than has befallen Lord Whitmore will be yours if, on the morrow, you do not answer our questions. Your bravado is well enough, but you will alter your tones anon. For the present, though you will be a prisoner, you will be provided with a better apartment than the vault below, and you will also have some good food and drink. You will think over what we have said, and no doubt, on the morrow, you will be prepared to answer our questions."

The Hunchback smiled scornfully, but made no reply.

At a word from Blackmore he was seized and conducted from the room.

He had therefore no opportunity of knowing what became of her ladyship.

Instead of taking him downstairs, he

was conducted to the top of the mansion.

Here, on the landing, was a small room.

It had no door, but in place of it a number of immense iron bars, which reached from the floor to the ceiling, and formed a gate.

This, no doubt, was so that whoever was placed on guard could watch every movement of the person confined.

This iron gate moved in and out of the wall by means of a spring, which was acted upon by treading on a knob fixed in the flooring near the stairs.

The apartment was fairly well furnished, but nevertheless it looked gloomy, damp, and cheerless.

" Here is your room," said Coningsby, " and I hope you will like it. You ought to think yourself highly honoured by being provided with so excellent an apartment."

The Hunchback moved and looked into the speaker's face.

So *withering* was the look, that the traitorous officer of her majesty's guard quailed before it.

" I would they had beheaded this man," muttered Coningsby, " for somehow or other I verily believe I shall meet with something at his hands which I shall not like. And he and Lord Whitmore have friends who will avenge their deaths—that is, punish those who had any hand in the business. Well, I must be on my guard."

Never, in the whole course of his life, had Coningsby a truer thought.

The Hunchback having entered his apartment, the gate was closed, and over it a small lamp was hung.

Coningsby now told off two men as guards, their instructions being that they were to remain at their post six hours, and that they were to keep on the move the whole of the time.

Did the traitors fear that if the guards slept, only for a few minutes, that the Hunchback might effect his escape?

Should he do so, too well they knew that the strange being would never rest till he had brought down upon the guilty heads of Lord Blackmore and his vile associates a swift and a terrible revenge.

* * * *

At three o'clock in the morning, a solitary horseman rode at a terrific pace down the hill overlooking High Wycombe.

With whip and spur he was urging on his horse, but it was evident that the poor creature could go but little farther.

His foam-covered mouth, forelegs, and flanks, his trembling nostrils and glaring eyes, showed that for many a long mile his pace had been tremendous, and that now he was exhausted.

Just as he reached the hostelry at which Lady Whitmore and her unfortunate servants had partaken of their last refreshments, the host, who had caught the rapid sound of the horse's hoofs, popped his head out of the window.

Truly this was a most welcome sight to the traveller.

" What ho ! Is that you, master host ? " he cried, as he reined in his steaming animal.

" It is, your worship," was the reply. " What want you ? "

" Refreshment for myself and horse. I am aware that this is the hour when host and hostess should be sleeping quietly in their beds, but, master host, if you will supply me with what I require, I shall take it as a favour."

" As you are so civil," replied the host, " I will descend to ye, and attend to your wants."

The traveller dismounted and patted his horse, praising him for the tremendous pace at which he had been going, and saying—

" Not much farther, old boy—not much farther."

In a few moments the host appeared, carrying a lamp.

This he held high over his head, and the light fell full upon the traveller.

Never, in the whole course of his life, had the eyes of the host rested upon a more splendid specimen of a young man.

He stood considerably over six feet in height, and was possessed of a powerful frame—a frame of the most perfect description.

His face was simply perfection itself, though it was now exceedingly pale ; but this served to set off to great advantage the large black eyes, shaded with heavy eye-lashes, the slight moustache, and the heavy black ringlets which fell about his broad shoulders.

However strange it may appear, this fine young man—his age was about twenty—*was the son of that mysterious being, the Hunchback of Old St. Paul's!*

His name—or the name he was known by—was Ronald Rockley.

He was attired in a tight-fitting black costume, unadorned with a single ornament, and over his shoulders was thrown a short cloak.

He was well armed, a long dagger hanging on his right side, while a long sword hung at his left. In his belt were a pair of pistols.

From his appearance the host took him to be a person of some importance, and therefore felt glad that he had replied to his summons.

"What do you need, young master?" he asked.

"I require a small bottle of your best wine, and a half-gallon of ale, with a small loaf, for my horse."

"You shall have it immediately. Do you not require anything else?"

"Nothing, thank you—yet, stay, a wisp of hay to rub down my horse."

"Aye, aye, sir. Have you much farther to go?"

"Nay. Why?"

"Because, young sir, your horse looks thoroughly worn out. I have a horse in my stable which you could have for a—"

"No, no," interrupted Ronald, testily; "go with me he must. Some ale, a loaf, and a rub down will do him good, and I shall not travel so fast for the remainder of my journey."

The host soon procured the desired refreshments, and while Ronald rubbed down his horse, he put several questions to the host.

With this result:

He learned how Lady Whitmore—for he recognised the description—had put up there with her servants, of the time she departed, and so on.

"I fancy," said the host, "that the lady was going to pay a visit to Blackmore Hall. If so, I don't admire her taste. You are a stranger hereabouts, young sir?"

"Yes. I am from London. I am now on the road to Oxford."

"Ah! Then you will pass this Blackmore Hall. 'Tis a strange place, young sir, and it has a strange master. There is frequently some awful goings-on at the Hall—so I have heard some of my customers say. Some few hours before the lady I speak of put up here, the whole village was in an uproar for a moment. A coach drawn by four powerful horses was seen descending the hill. I ran to the door, of course. Lor'! the way it rattled down the hill. It came and vanished like a flash of lightning. What it contained, or who the two horsemen were who rode at the side of the coach, I know not, but some people said that one of them was Lord Blackmore himself."

"The villain! Simon Silex told me the truth then," muttered Ronald; "and 'tis well for him that he did so. Had he told me a falsehood I would have run my blade through his carcase directly I again saw him."

Looking up, he said, indifferently—

"Ah, master host, these are strange times, eh?"

"Very; and wicked times also."

"And one has to be careful, eh?"

"No doubt."

"If not, one may meet one's death at a time and in a manner one least expects, eh?"

"True—very true. But I should think there's not many who would attempt to play tricks with a young man of your build. No doubt you can use a sword to some tune, if it so please you, for attack or defence?"

"True, host," was the reply of Ronald Rockley, as, having seen that his horse had consumed the loaf and ale, he drank off the remains of the small bottle of wine, and once more sprang into the saddle. "Well, I bid ye adieu, and good luck, master host."

"And I wish ye the same, young sir," was the reply.

"You are satisfied with what I paid ye?"

"Oh, your worship, *more* than satisfied."

Ronald nodded and rode away.

The host stood on the threshold and watched until horse and rider had disappeared in the darkness, then turning, he muttered—

"I think I can guess the true character of that young man. He has a kind, a tender heart, but upset him and he is a very devil."

Master host was not far wrong.

The ale and the loaf had unquestionably had a very beneficial effect on the horse, for after leaving the hostelry he went on at a very fair pace.

It seems quite certain that Ronald was acquainted with the road he travelled, for he hesitated not one instant.

At last his destination was reached.

Blackmore Hall.

When Ronald came in sight of the black, grim-looking building, he turned his horse sharp off to the left, plunging through a mass of brushwood.

His noble animal found great difficulty in getting through this, so Ronald dismounted, and taking him by the bridle, assisted him to clamber over the many obstructions which beset his path.

A small, dilapidated gate was reached at last, and here Ronald dropped the bridle, and patting his steed affectionately, he said—

"Await me here, old friend—await me here. Move not, and make no noise. I go on a risky errand, but I pray Heaven it may prove successful."

With this he opened the gate, and was in the grounds of Blackmore Hall.

Creeping cautiously along, careful that the dry twigs did not crack too loudly beneath his spurred boots, he went onward to the back of the mansion.

It was soon reached.

Standing in the shadow of a mighty oak, he surveyed the house very carefully.

Save for a solitary light, the mansion was in profound darkness.

Silence, too—silence the most profound—reigned, though occasionally it was broken by the hoot of the owl, or the sudden rush of a hare or rabbit through the brushwood.

In the shadow of the oak Ronald Rockley stood erect, his hands behind his back, nervously clutching his heavy riding-whip, watching that light, and wondering who was in the room.

"I have been told that men are always on guard in the grounds of this accursed mansion," he muttered, "but as yet I have not seen one of them. My father is here—*unless*," he said, in deep, solemn tones, "*unless* he has been murdered. Great Heaven! what a strange, terrible feeling seems to have suddenly crept over me! My blood seems to have turned to ice! And my brow—'tis like marble exposed to the snow!

"If my father has not been murdered, in what part of the house has he been placed? Ah, that is the question. And Lord Whitmore? What has happened to him? He has met his doom—he has been murdered. Aye, aye; more has come to my ears than my father thought for.

"They sentenced Whitmore to death long ago—they got him at last into their power. He is dead. But if they have injured my father, I will pull the house about their ears—I will never rest until I have spilt the blood of every man who was concerned in injuring him. If they have slain Whitmore, I will help his son—though as yet we have met but as strangers—I will assist his son, I say, to accomplish a most terrible vengeance. I will devote my whole time and attention to vengeance. I will, so help me Heaven!

"And what of poor Lady Whitmore? Oh, who could have persuaded her to set out on such a journey? Not her son? No, not—not her son. Let me—Ah, who comes?"

Hastily placing himself behind the tree, Ronald waited the approach of a man.

From the way he was armed—with pike and sword—it was evident that he was one of the men on guard in the grounds.

Considering it certain that he could obtain any information he desired from this man, he determined to get it, and silently drew his long blade.

On came the fellow, and when he reached the huge trunk of the old oak he took a flask from his pocket, and placed it to his lips.

Instantaneously Ronald started in front of him.

With one hand he snatched the flask from the man's lips, then raised his sword on a level with the man's breast.

The man, with a cry of rage, clutched

his pike and prepared to strike, but Ronald was much too quick for him.

He seized the pike by the handle, and tearing it from the man's grasp, flung it aside.

Then suddenly he struck him down.

"Make no noise," said Ronald, "or you will lose your life! Observe—my sword's point is at your throat."

"Aye, I see it is," interrupted the man, with a bitter curse; "I see it is. Who, in the name of the foul fiend, are you?"

"A stranger to you."

"So I should say. Are you always in the habit of treating people in this fashion, may I ask?"

"Always when they are persons in the pay of a scoundrel like Lord Blackmore, as you are."

"Hem! Well, will you inform me when you will take your heavy foot off my chest?"

"At once, if you will swear that you will stand up while I bind you to this tree. Quick! I have no time to waste on you."

"Of course I must do as you ask, owing to the fact that I do not at present wish to be spitted like a piece of meat."

"Now unbuckle your sword, and hand it to me."

The man did this at once.

He was brave, but he saw that this young man had him at a disadvantage, and was very determined in all his actions, and that if he did not do as he was told, he would most likely lose his life.

He unbuckled his sword, and handed it to Ronald, who placed it by the side of the tree.

Ronald now allowed the man to rise.

Then, still holding his weapons ready for action, he told him to place his hands behind his back, and the man obeyed with almost laughable promptitude.

"You need not fancy that I should be such a fool as to do this had I not been taken unawares," he growled; "but I have another reason. Coningsby —that is our leader's name, and he has only just now been placed over us— Coningsby, I say, fancies that one man is quite sufficient to guard these large grounds; so when he comes and finds me like this, he will see how *tre*-mendously mistaken he is."

"You are a humourist," said Ronald, grimly, "and no doubt a drunkard."

"Oh, well—fairly," answered the man.

Ronald tied his hands behind his back, and then fastened them to the tree in such a way that there was no chance of his getting free unaided.

"Now," said the man, "as I have obliged you, perhaps you will oblige me by placing the nozzle of my flask to my parched lips."

Ronald could not refuse so moderate a request, so he did as desired.

"And now," he said, "I shall be compelled to gag you, for I have learned never to trust such as you. I will, however, gag you lightly if you will first answer my questions faithfully. But if I find that your answers are lying ones, I will drive my steel in your lying heart."

So fiercely did Ronald say this, that for the first time the man was thoroughly terrified.

"I will answer you truly, then," he said.

And from the questions Ronald put to him he learned nearly all the facts which we have placed before our readers.

"Then," he said, "the Hunchback is not now in the vault below the moat?"

"He is not. Observe yonder light— there, high up on the topmost floor?"

"Aye, I see it."

"That light is burning outside the apartment in which he is confined. I see now that it is your intention to attempt his rescue."

"You are right; such is my intention."

"Well, there are a thousand chances against one that in making the attempt you will lose your life. However, try it. For my part, I bear Lord Blackmore no good will. He is a lying and a tyrant master, and his hands, like the hands of his infamous son, Dacre Deadman, who beheaded Lord Whitmore, are deeply stained with blood. And since I bear neither good service, I will tell you how you may easily effect an entrance to the house if—"

"Go on—fear nothing."

"If you agree to compensate me."

"I have little money with me; but if you will tell me how to effect an entrance, and where I may obtain a horse, I will give you this."

And Ronald took from beneath his doublet a diamond cross.

The man's eyes fairly glittered at the sight of the beautiful object.

"It will enable me to leave the country," he thought.

Aloud he said—

"That will satisfy me. Kindly place it in my doublet."

Ronald did so.

"Now," said the man, "turn off sharp to the left, following that narrow path you see close beside you. Keep straight along and you will reach a shed; in that you will find six horses. You may easily obtain one or the whole six, since the place is always unlocked. Then at the back of the shed you will find a large stone or slab; 'tis a monstrous thing, weighing over two tons. If you approach the right of it, stoop, then draw your hand along the ground, and you will touch a brass handle. Pull that up and the stone will roll back, revealing a dark aperture. Get down backwards, and your feet will touch a flight of stone steps. At the bottom of them is the passage of the vault in which Lord Whitmore and the Hunchback were confined immediately they arrived here. Thus you will have gained an entrance."

"And after that?"

"Ah, there I am lost. I swear that I know no more. But, of course, the vaults lead to the upper part of the house, and so you will not have very great difficulty in finding your way. Now, young sir, pray do as you said— that is, gag me. I shall then be found gagged and bound, and it will thus be seen that I could not have told you anything."

"You are a shrewd fellow," observed Ronald, as he gagged the man. "'Tis a thousand pities you should have taken service under such a villain as my Lord Blackmore."

Ronald now followed the path and soon discovered the shed.

He tried the door, which yielded instantly, and pushing it wide open, Ronald saw, though of course indistinctly, six horses.

Five were lying down, but the sixth was quietly chewing some hay which hung over his head.

On the stall hung bridle and saddle.

Ronald hesitated not an instant, but backing the animal from the stable, he quickly saddled him, then shut the door, and returning the way he had come, he had soon placed the steed beside his own.

Little did he dream that that horse was one of the two ridden by the servants of Lord Whitmore, who, by order of Lord Blackmore, had been so foully murdered.

Ronald had no difficulty in discovering the stone—a huge, solid slab of granite.

Acting as the man had said, he found the handle and pulled it.

Instantly the stone rolled back, and a dark aperture was revealed.

Ronald looked down.

All was most profoundly dark and silent.

"So far the man's words are true," muttered Ronald; "and I will now risk the remainder."

He descended backwards as he had been told, and suddenly gave a sharp, suppressed cry, for he found the third stone quickly move.

Ere he could raise his foot, however, he heard a rumbling noise overhead.

He soon made out what this meant. The third stair acted upon the stone as the handle above had done, and caused it to roll again into its place, so that it was quite evident to Ronald that whoever got *in* that way could not get *out* without learning the secret.

However, the circumstance was not calculated to alarm the fearless Ronald.

Turning, he prepared to descend.

Drawing his long dagger, he clutched it firmly in his right hand, and then stooping, he proceeded to cautiously feel his way.

Thus he descended at least thirty steps.

At last the bottom was reached, and now placing his hand on the right and the left, he found he was in the passage.

Slowly and noiselessly he went onward, being careful to feel the ground with his feet; for he was only too well aware of the numerous unexpected death-traps in mansions of this description.

Ere he had proceeded far, a light suddenly appeared.

Dim it was at first, but as it advanced it grew brighter and brighter, and in a few moments the figure of a man—a short, bullet-headed, ugly wretch—appeared, carrying a lantern.

It was the fellow who had been Lord Whitmore and the Hunchbacks' gaoler on their first arrival.

He seemed to be about to traverse a passage running parallel with the one in which Ronald stood.

Ronald drew as far back as possible.

It was a most unlucky move, for his head touched an unlighted lantern slung on the wall, and he knocked it off the hook.

It fell to the ground with a loud crash.

Of course the noise had the effect of alarming the man.

He started back with an exclamation of terror.

Ronald moved not.

The man raised the lantern on high, and waved it to and fro.

But he saw nothing.

"What can that noise mean?—perhaps rats!" he muttered.

Again and again he waved aloft his lantern, but seeing nothing, he drew his sword and advanced up the passage.

Now it was certain that he would discover Ronald.

"'Tis my life or his," muttered Ronald, grimly; "aye, my life or his! Should I hesitate? Should I pause when *one* has already been murdered, and my father simply awaits his doom? No! I have sworn that nothing shall stop me, and by Heaven, nothing shall!"

On came the man, and when within three feet of him, Ronald dashed forward.

A great—a fearful, unearthly cry of terror escaped the man's lips as this tall, dark figure started before him.

That cry was his last.

High aloft the long blade was raised for one second, the next it was buried deep in the heart of the man, and Ronald never slew a more brutal ruffian.

The man fell—fell like a piece of lead —fell with his eyes, glassy, staring, fixed upon Ronald's face.

It was a deed which could not be avoided, if he would save his father from a horrible death.

The brutal villain—alive one moment, dead the next!

Fortunately the lamp was not extinguished.

Ronald took it from the fast stiffening fingers of the man—this really brutal ruffian, who acted in such a terrible way towards whoever was placed under his charge, not only because he was paid for it, but because he *gloried* in murderous actions—and concealing the light with his cloak, again went on.

Fortunately the farther he went he found the ground to be of a more sandy nature, and therefore there was less likelihood of his being heard should there happen to be any more men about.

But there were not. Evidently the man he had slain was the master of these filthy underground dungeons.

At last he reached a flight of stone stairs.

Ascending these, he came to a small landing.

Before him were three small archways.

Here for an instant he paused.

Which one should he enter?

This was a most important question.

Half-a-dozen wrong steps, and he might find himself surrounded by a host of armed men.

Having thought as to the construction of the house, he decided to pass through the centre arch.

As he crossed the threshold he chanced to look to the left, and saw through the archway into a small room.

A dim light beamed within it, and by its aid Ronald was enabled to see the figures of at least twenty men.

They were sitting or lying about the room fast asleep—no doubt they slept the sleep of drunkards.

In the centre of the group, with his face resting upon his right hand, and his left resting upon the hilt of a huge pistol, sat a figure our readers know well—Coningsby.

Officer and men were evidently supposed to be on guard, or ready to change the guard in the various parts of the mansion, but the god MORPHEUS and the demon DRINK had stolen from them all sense of their responsibility, and they slept and snored.

Ronald was struck with a sudden thought.

"If I turn the key on these men," he considered, "they would be powerless—at least for a time—to give any assistance in case of alarm. I will attempt it."

He cautiously crept to the massive oaken door and examined it.

There was no lock to be seen, but on the other side was a monstrous iron bar.

It weighed at least a hundredweight, and was for use either on the one side or the other, the sockets being affixed to both sides.

Placing the lantern on the floor, Ronald took the bar in his arms, carried it to the outside, closed the door, and placed the bar in position.

Thus Coningsby and his men were as securely fastened in that room as rats in a trap.

Now, through the centre archway strode Ronald.

It is unnecessary to follow him every step of the way.

We may say, however, that the centre arch was the right one, and after he had traversed several more flights of stairs, he reached the landing on which was the "cage" in which the Hunchback was confined.

He saw the place the man had described, for the lamp hanging over the gate showed it to him plainly enough.

Close by the side of it stood one of the men who had been placed on guard.

He was leaning on his pike, his face towards the gate, and was apparently half asleep.

His comrade had sat himself upon the landing, and, leaning his back against the wall, had fallen also off to sleep.

For an instant Ronald held the dagger in his hand, and seemed about to dash forward.

But presently he checked the impulse, and took from his pocket a small phial.

It contained a most powerful sleeping draught.

Taking the cork out, he advanced to the sleeping man and placed the phial for a few seconds against his nose.

The stuff made no perceptible alteration in the man's breathing, but the effect of it was that in that position he would remain for at least hours, and not even the thunder of cannon would awaken him.

Pocketing the phial, Ronald drew a pistol, set down the lantern, and delivered on the shoulder of the other man a mighty thwack.

The man turned to find the cold barrel of a pistol almost touching his face.

So astonished and terrified was he, that he made no effort to cry out.

He felt certain that if he uttered a sound the pistol would be discharged, and while it would alarm everyone in the mansion, it would also be the cause of his death.

"Make no noise," whispered Ronald, "and your life will be spared ; attempt to cry out, and I will shoot you like a dog!"

"In the name of the foul fiend," gasped the man, "who are you ?"

"No matter who I am. The Hunchback is confined in the room there, is he not ?"

"He is."

"Open that gate."

The man moved back, Ronald following.

Another moment and he stood exactly in front of the cage.

The Hunchback was seated at no great distance from the gate.

His attitude was that of a person in deep and painful thought.

A cry of joy rose to Ronald's lips, but it was soon stifled.

He seized one of the bars and shook it.

The Hunchback turned, and instantly recognising his son, a prolonged exclamation of astonishment escaped him.

"Ronald!" he gasped.

"Father!" was the joyful reply ; "father! Thou art uninjured ?"

"Up to the present, my son, yes," was the reply.

"You are surprised to see me here ?"

"I was for the moment, but *only* for a moment. I well know your daring, my son, and your great love for me."

"You are right, father. For you I would risk my life a thousand times."

"Aye, my dear son, I believe you. But, Ronald, you have thrust yourself into the lion's den. 'Tis easy for you to get within it, perhaps, but to get out is another matter."

"No, no," said Ronald, emphatically.

Turning to the man, whose body during this time he had covered with his pistol, he said—

"Open this gate."

The man pressed the spring, the gate flew open, and Ronald rushed into his father's arms.

Instantly the man saw his opportunity.

He snatched his sword from its sheath, and attempted to run Ronald through the body.

But the Hunchback took the long dagger from his son's side, threw himself upon the man, and buried the weapon in his body.

But he died not like the man Ronald had been compelled to slay.

A fearful cry for help left his lips—a cry which penetrated into every nook and corner of that large mansion.

"Follow me—quick, father!" cried Ronald.

"'Tis useless, my son," replied the Hunchback. "Close here there are a large number of armed men."

"I have secured them," replied Ronald, snatching up the lantern. "Here," he said, taking a pistol from his belt and handing it to the Hunchback, "take this; you well know how to use it, and, if necessity arise, don't hesitate."

"You may depend upon that," was the Hunchback's grim reply.

The pair set off almost at a run, Ronald leading the way.

As they traversed the various landings and stairs, loud shouts fell upon their ears, but they sounded somewhat distant.

It was certain that the inmates had been aroused, and were hurrying to the spot whence the fearful cry had proceeded.

The guard had been aroused, and were hammering furiously on the door which Ronald had closed.

But they might hammer for a month on that solid piece of oak—it would not yield unless axes were brought to bear upon it.

Onward rushed father and son at terrific speed, their movements being considerably hastened by the shouts they heard.

It suddenly seemed to Ronald that, though he had got into the vault, he could not find the secret of exit.

So reaching the first-floor landing, he essayed to pull up the window.

Vain effort! It was most securely fastened.

"This must be the way, my son," said the Hunchback.

And he thereupon raised his pistol, and, with the butt-end, smashed the lock.

There was a wide ledge outside, and Ronald, getting upon it, saw that the jump to the ground was easy.

He at once took the leap, and the Hunchback followed him.

Then away they sped, side by side, pistol in hand, and ready for any surprise.

But they were not interrupted.

They looked back again and again, and saw lights appearing at almost every window.

Loud shouts and cries rang out on the night air, but as they ran they grew fainter and fainter.

At last the horses were reached.

"Thank Heaven—thank Heaven!" cried the Hunchback, fervently. "Safe once more—safe once more. Oh, my Lord Blackmore, wait, wait. But, alas! poor Lady Whitmore — poor, unhappy—"

"Hist, I pray you!" interrupted Ronald. "Let us converse respecting her anon. Now no time is to be lost. Quick! The saddle."

Ronald flung the lantern away and leapt into the saddle, his action being followed by his father.

Another second and they were speeding like the wind across the country.

The escape of the Hunchback was a terrible blow to Lord Blackmore and his associates.

The former knew only too well that the Hunchback was the bosom-friend of the murdered Lord Whitmore, and would never rest until he had avenged the murder of his friend.

CHAPTER III.

OF WHAT HAPPENED TO STANLEY AT SMITHFIELD.

SIX days passed away, and during this time, Stanley, after many attempts, had secured an audience with the queen.

But so well had Lord Blackmore worked his cards, that he got no satisfaction.

Elizabeth informed him that she had had ample proof of Lord Whitmore's treachery.

"But," she said, "since we are informed that he has left the country, no more need be said about the matter until he shall think proper to return, and then we will not forget that Lord Whitmore has to answer to his queen and his country for his treachery."

Stanley told her that Lord Whitmore had been at Blackmore Hall, and that his mother had gone there to bid him adieu.

The queen opened wide her eyes at this extraordinary announcement, then she laughed outright.

"Who put such a thing into your head?" she asked.

"Who, your majesty?" replied Stanley. "Lord Blackmore himself. If your majesty will ask him—"

The queen interrupted him with an impatient wave of her hand.

The interview thereupon terminated.

Oh, if Stanley had but waited! Had he even returned to his home just before that interview!

He would have learned all the terrible tidings—of his father's strange murder, of his mother's detention.

For the Hunchback had written a letter to him, and had despatched a special messenger with it to the Savoy.

He received it some hours after his interview with the queen.

Imagine his horror, his despair, when he read it!

Could he believe it? Was such a fearful thing really possible?

Should he at once take the letter to the queen?

All these questions rushed like wild-fire through his brain.

He was for a long time in a state of utter distraction and despair, and with his hands clasped upon his brow, he wandered from one room to another like a madman.

"Aye," he moaned, "this letter was written by the Hunchback, and it is therefore true. Yes, true! Oh, Almighty Powers! what a fate—what a fate! And my mother—what is *her* fate to be? I shudder to think of it! To take this letter to the queen—but 'twould be worse than madness. She would not see me. Nay, and if she did? She would never believe what is here stated. Why, it reads more like the wildest romance. Let me think! Let me think what is to be done. Soon, no doubt, I shall have no home, for all my unfortunate father's property will certainly be confiscated. I will go to the—but, no; I cannot go to the Hunchback, for he affixes no address to this document.

"And the reason of that is because he must keep his whereabouts secret. What did her majesty say? I remember her words : ' Your father's friend—this mysterious individual who is known as the Hunchback of St. Paul's—has managed to effect his escape from my soldiers. Or, no doubt, Lord Whitmore paid the soldiers for his release as well as his own—those soldiers, with an officer named Coningsby at their head.' Yes, they were her very words. But since I have this letter in my possession, 'tis hardly likely that the Hunchback can have left England. I must wait. Wait! But while I am waiting I will watch for Lord Blackmore, and for Dacre Deadman. Oh, my heart seems bursting."

By degrees Stanley calmed down.

He walked to the apartment which had been his mother's favourite room, but the sight of the many little things which had been her favourite objects was too painful for him, and he hastily left it.

On the threshold of the door, he was

met by a large mastiff, his father's favourite dog, by name Swift.

The poor creature seemed to have as much sorrow at its heart as our hero himself.

He raised his massive head, and his large eyes looked sorrowfully into Stanley's face.

"Poor Swift!" said Stanley, sadly—"poor Swift! They who loved you so have gone never to return."

Swift seemed to understand, for he uttered a low, pitiful howl.

"But," continued Stanley, "you shall go with me, Swift. You shall share my fortunes."

Suddenly a servant handed him a letter, securely bound with silken thread, and heavily sealed.

"Who waits?" asked Stanley.

"No one, your worship," was the reply.

"No one! What sort of person brought it?"

"A short, well-attired man, whose face I could not see."

Stanley broke open the seal, spread open the parchment, and read these words—

"Vengeance! vengeance! Come, Stanley Whitmore, this evening to Smithfield, where a well-tried friend of thy father's will meet thee. Thou must come on foot and unaccompanied. Come to 'The Three Spies,' where a friend who knows thee will meet thee, and conduct thee to the writer. Fear nothing, but come, if you would have vengeance on those who have so deeply injured thee.—THY FRIEND, WHO DARES NOT SIGN HIS NAME."

Several times Stanley read this.

"From whom can this be?" he muttered. "It is from someone who is acquainted with all that has transpired. That is certain enough. It cannot be another letter from the Hunchback. Nay, for the writing is nothing like it. Let me see. Ah, can this be from the Hunchback's son? That he *has* a son I know—a hunchback, I presume, like his father, so there would be but little difficulty in recognising him. 'The Three Spies' at Smithfield—there a friend will meet me. But 'tis now midnight. No matter, I will set out."

Having thus resolved, he attired and well armed himself, and set out for Smithfield, as directed, on foot.

Several of the men-servants endeavoured to persuade him to allow one of them to go with him.

But Stanley refused.

He, however, took with him the mastiff—Swift.

Nothing occurred on the road, and as St. Paul's was tolling the hour of one, he reached the large and most peculiar-shaped hostelry, called "The Three Spies," a house well known to almost every traveller who journeyed to the City of London.

He found the place in total darkness, but nevertheless he walked boldly up, and paused on the threshold.

Almost instantly the door opened—so it was evident someone had been on the watch for him—and a man appeared.

"Are you Master Stanley Whitmore?" he whispered.

"You are correct," answered Stanley. "And your name?"

"That I am forbidden to tell at present. I am sent here by the gentleman who dispatched a letter to you."

"His name?"

"That I am also forbidden to tell," was the firm answer.

"Well, my friend," said Stanley, who really thought that this mysterious "friend" must be the Hunchback's son—"well, is the gentleman who made the appointment within this hostelry?"

"He is not. If you will follow me, I will conduct you to—"

"His residence?"

"Nay, to the house of a person with whom he is staying. Let me whisper in your ear. The friend who desires to see you dare not show his face in the public street."

"Ah, for fear of arrest?"

"Precisely."

"I understand," answered Stanley; "and I can guess who this friend is. So lead on, and I will follow."

Swift sniffed at the man's legs, looked into his young master's face, and uttered a low, threatening growl.

"Hush!" said Stanley, placing his hand on the animal's head—"hush, Swift, make no noise!"

"I hope the dog is not dangerous?"

said the man, looking uneasily at the animal.

"Nay," said Stanley, "he is as gentle as a child—with a friend ; but he is different with an enemy. Swift has been well trained to pull down by the throat an enemy of our house."

The man turned slightly pale on hearing this, and started off at a quick pace, saying, as he bowed very low—

"Follow me, your worship."

Stanley kept pretty close to him.

Through several narrow turnings went the man, and at last he reached Cloth Fair—then really a "cloth fair."

In about the centre of the market-place stood a little tumble-down wooden building, over the doorway of which was written this peculiar name—

"SHILOH SEPTESSION."

And beneath that—

"APOTHECARY TO HER MOST GRACIOUS AND WELL-BELOVED MAJESTY, **Queen Elizabeth.**"

Though it was a somewhat dark night, there was little difficulty in deciphering all this, for the words were written in gold.

It at once struck Stanley that it was a peculiar thing that a Court apothecary should carry on business and live in such a dirty old house, and in such a questionable neighbourhood as Cloth Fair.

At this time our hero had had no experience of the villainy of some of these apothecaries.

His conductor rapped softly on a little window-sill in the door, and the summons was at once answered by an old woman.

"Enter !" she grunted.

"One moment," said Stanley. "The person I am to see is not the apothecary ? "

"You will see him first; he will direct you how to act," replied the man. "Come this way."

"And what of this monstrous animal ? " said the old woman, pointing to Swift.

"He will go with me," replied Stanley.

On through the narrow passage went the man, and at last our hero was ushered into a small, low-roofed apart-ment, which, judging from the hundreds of bottles of all shapes, sizes, and colours which were arranged round the room, was the apothecary's "making-up" room.

His conductor offered him a seat, and barely had Stanley taken it when the apothecary, Shiloh Septession, entered.

He was an old—a very old man—age having bent him nearly double.

A more benevolent-looking person could not have been found.

Waving his hand, Stanley's conductor withdrew.

Our hero rose and bowed.

The apothecary bowed himself almost to the ground in response to Stanley's salutation.

"*Be* seated, my young and most unfortunate friend," he croaked ; "*be* seated. I will shift your chair. There —so—that is more comfortable, and your dog will seat himself at your side."

And the apothecary took hold of the chair and placed it on a large black rug near the fireplace.

"Now, sir," said Stanley, "will you inform me as to the friend who wrote me this letter ? " taking it from his pocket. "Will you tell me his name —and can I see him at once ? "

"You can. And I will tell you his name. This friend is acting under instructions received."

"Ah ! From whom ? "

The apothecary took two rapid steps backward, crying—

"*The Cowled Eleven !* "

As he uttered these words a loud crash was heard, the black rug disappeared below, and down went Stanley and the chair into the trap beneath!

But as he fell our hero's presence of mind did not leave him.

He clutched the edge of the trap and clung frantically to it, calling aloud for help.

The apothecary rushed towards him, raised his heavily-shod foot, and again and again stamped upon our hero's fingers.

At the same moment, the villain who had been his conductor rushed into the room from the other end.

Just as he reached the apothecary's side, Swift, who had not fallen, leapt forward with a growl of rage, and fastened his huge teeth in his throat.

The man's cries were frightful.

In vain he tried to draw a dagger which hung at his side.

Swift bore the wretch to the ground, his fangs tearing the flesh from his throat.

All the while his fierce growls filled the apartment, and struck terror in the heart of the apothecary.

Stanley could hold on but little longer.

Suddenly the curtains at the end of the room were again drawn back, and a young and remarkably pretty girl, a look of terror on her face, rushed in.

"What is this?" she cried, frantically. "What is this? Oh, look—look! The dog tearing Bradley to pieces—and here— Oh, Heaven! 'tis murder! 'tis murder! Away," she shrieked, as she rushed upon the apothecary, and seizing him by the waist, attempted to pull him from the trap, where he was still stamping on the fingers of Stanley.

But Stanley was exhausted, and was compelled to let go.

Down he went into the dark abyss below.

But not before he had had a good look at the girl who would, had it been possible, have been his saviour.

Turning fiercely upon her, the apothecary, with a most foul and bitter curse, seized her by the shoulders and brutally pushed her from the room.

"Go!" he hissed, "go! lest I may be tempted to kill thee. Go—go, I say, and be cursed to you—you, who so many times have spoiled my plans, and would do so now."

With all his power he thrust the pretty girl from the room through the doorway, and closed the door with a crash.

Turning, he found that the huge beast had still a firm hold of the man who had decoyed Stanley into this den of imfamy.

The apothecary, with trembling hands, opened a drawer and took out a huge pistol. At the same time he screamed out at the top of his voice for the old woman who had opened the door.

She at length made her appearance.

But she expressed no surprise at what she saw.

Perhaps she was used to scenes of bloodshed and murder.

"Open the street door!" yelled the apothecary. "Open it. Quick!"

The old woman very quickly did as directed, and then rushed up the stairs with all speed.

The apothecary took aim at Swift and fired.

The noise and the crashing which followed the shot were terrific.

Whole rows of phials and bottles came to the floor with remarkable haste, and the place was instantly filled with all sorts of most abominable smells.

Added to this, the apartment was filled with smoke and vapours of one kind and another, so that for some few minutes it was utterly impossible for the apothecary to see anything in the room.

But, fearful that the dog would spring upon him, he bundled his doubled body under the table, and with a speed that would not have been discreditable to an experienced acrobat.

He had not placed himself in this position, however, more than a couple of minutes ere a loud voice cried out—

"Ho! Here! Ho! What the devil is the meaning of all this? Is the house on fire? Shiloh! Shiloh! Where are you, old villain, eh? Where are you?"

"Who speaks?" whined the apothecary. "Who speaks?"

And he came from beneath the table.

The smoke and the vapours had by this time somewhat cleared off.

In the centre of the room stood a well-known figure.

It was no less a person than Dacre Deadman.

"*You* here!" cried the apothecary.

"Aye—me," was the reply. "And what is the meaning of this, you murderous old villain?"

And Dacre pointed to the dead body of the wretch who had acted as our hero's conductor.

Torn and mangled almost beyond recognition it was, and the flooring beside it was covered with blood.

"HE SNATCHED THE FLASK FROM THE MAN'S LIPS, THEN RAISED HIS SWORD ON A LEVEL WITH HIS BREAST."

No. 4

"This is no ordinary murder, at any rate," said Dacre; "for never in all my life did I behold a man in such a state. How did you—"

"Hist, hist!" interrupted the apothecary. "Accuse me not of such a deed. You know well enough that, though I have done many things for Lord Blackmore and yourself, I have never stained my hands with *blood*."

"You are right," answered Dacre, with a hideous grin. "Poison is your weapon—and a good one, too, sometimes."

"I will tell you how this occurred," continued the apothecary. "Acting on your instructions, which were taken from the *Cowled Eleven*, eh?"

Dacre nodded.

"Well, I caused the letter to be written. It proved effective, which shows that Lord Whitmore's son is but little acquainted with the world's ways, and he came to 'The Three Spies,' at which hostelry my man—now, alas! dead—met him, and—"

"But," interrupted Dacre, excitedly, "where is Stanley?"

"Down there," replied the apothecary, pointing with his thumb to the trap through which our hero had disappeared, and which had now assumed its former position, the black rug looking as though it had never been disturbed.

"Thank you, old poisoner," exclaimed Dacre, "that he is in our power."

"*My* power," corrected the apothecary, with a leer.

"Go on," said Dacre, haughtily.

"He brought a dog with him," continued the apothecary, "a monstrous and most ferocious mastiff, which, so soon as Stanley Whitmore disappeared down there, flew upon my man, and, as you see, worried him to death. Had I not fired a pistol at him, no doubt he would have torn him all to pieces."

"Aye," replied Dacre, "and then he would have fastened his fangs on you; but since you have no flesh on your bones, he could not tear it, eh?"

"Precisely," said the apothecary, with a meek bow.

"And where is the dog?" queried Dacre, casting a suspicious glance about him.

"That is exactly what I should like to know," replied the old man; and he, too, cast more than one cautious glance around him.

"One might fancy," said Dacre, "that you had blown the animal all to powder, since there is not a bit of him left. But now let us proceed to business."

"Just so—to business," repeated the apothecary. "I trust that you have brought the—the money?"

"The money, you old money-grubber?" said Dacre. "Well, no; but I have brought a part. Behold it."

And placing his hand beneath his cloak, he brought out a bag of money, and flung it at the apothecary's feet.

"That will do for the present," replied the apothecary, as he stooped and picked up the bag. "And now let me ask you—will you see Stanley at once?"

"No, no; not now—not now," replied Dacre. "I shall return in the course of an hour in company with Lord Blackmore."

"Good. Then you do not wish to see him die?"

"Nay; I wish to see him *dead*."

"Yes, yes. And what is to be done with his body? *To be placed in the box?*"

"Yes, and given up to us. By us it will be taken to 'The Wapping Arms,' and thence it will be taken to Blackmore Hall, where it will be shown to Lady Whitmore."

"Oh, the lady is *still* there?"

"She is."

"Under the charge of the Cowled Eleven?"

"Mind your own accursed business," replied Dacre, furiously, "and do not endeavour to pry into ours. Remember, in one hour. And remember this also: you are to administer to him a poison of such a nature that not the slightest distortion of the features will take place. He must appear as if simply asleep."

"Fear it not," chuckled the vile apothecary; "these instructions shall be well and truly carried out."

Dacre turned and strode haughtily from the rotten old house, while the apothecary shouted for the old woman.

But it was some few moments ere she condescended to descend the stairs.

At last, however, she came cautiously

down, and in surly tones asked the apothecary what he required.

"Take Beatrice with you," growled the old man, "and go below into the cellar. You will there find a young man ! he has *accidentally* fallen through the flooring."

"He, he !" chuckled the old woman ; "dessay, dessay."

"You will attend to him, mark you," continued the apothecary, "and while Beatrice can assist you, see that she comes none of her nonsense."

"Aye, aye."

"And look, if you will help me over this job I will give you five crowns."

"Ye will ? "

"I will—I swear it."

"Then I'll help you. But suppose the young man is dead ? "

"In that case he will not require so much of your attention, and I shall not pay you so much. Now go."

Off went the old woman, muttering—

"Five crowns — five crowns — five crowns ! fifteen bottles of Rochalla—good."

The old woman tottered down the stairs to the cellar, and her astonishment can be better imagined than described when she saw Beatrice already there.

The poor girl, shedding bitter tears, bent over the prostrate figure of our hero, endeavouring to staunch the blood flowing from a great wound on his head.

By her side stood a water jug.

Brandy she could not have procured in that house.

"Ah," cried the old woman, as she snatched up a lantern which was standing at Beatrice's side, " ah, what are you doing, hussy ? Who told you to come here and attend to this youth ? "

"My own conscience, woman," replied Beatrice.

"Woman ! Wretch ! How dare you call me woman in so offensive a tone ? By the Virgin, I will tell your guardian of your impertinence ! You shall rue it—yes, you shall rue it Give me that cloth."

And she snatched the cloth from Beatrice's hands.

"Fiend !" cried Beatrice, passionately, as she started up, " have you come to finish the work my guardian has commenced ? "

"Mind your own business," snapped the old woman. " Do you stand there, and be ready to lend me any assistance I may require."

"What is to be done with him ? "

" Eh ? "

"What is to be done with him ? "

"Same as has been done with others, I suppose," grinned the old hag.

"Oh, Heaven !" moaned Beatrice, wringing her hands, " how long will these dreadful tragedies continue ? "

After a brief pause, during which the old woman made a careful examination of our hero, the young girl said, as a sudden thought struck her—

"Listen to me. My guardian, no doubt, has offered you a sum of money to assist him in this dastardly work. Now tell me, what sum has he offered you ? "

No answer.

"Has he offered you ten crowns ? " asked the young girl.

The old woman shook her head.

"More—or less ? "

"Less."

"Five crowns ? "

"Aye."

"Then I will tell you what I will do. Look, you have often admired this ? "

And Beatrice took a beautiful diamond cluster ring from her finger and held it before the old woman's wicked-looking eyes.

"Aye," grunted the hag, " I have often admired it. 'Tis a bonny ring. What is it worth, wench ? "

"Five hundred crowns."

"Five hundred crowns, eh ? Ah, five hundred crowns ! Holy Virgin ! that would buy sufficient Rochalla to last me all my days."

"Assist me to foil my guardian," continued the young girl, excitedly, " and this is yours."

The old woman greedily snapped at the offer.

"I will," she said ; " aye, aye, I will."

"Then," said the young girl, " help me to lift him upon this pallet, and then we will endeavour to bring him to his senses."

So Stanley, totally unconscious, and bleeding profusely, was lifted and placed upon a low pallet ; this, with the exception of a box and a small square table, which stood against the wall, and was covered with phials and bottles, being the only article of furniture the stone kitchen contained.

But though this young girl had succeeded in securing the assistance of the old woman, they would have the greatest difficulty in foiling the apothecary—a man who had been accustomed for many, many long years to acts of villainy.

But for a few moments we must return to the dog Swift.

The faithful creature was not struck by the shot aimed at him by the apothecary.

But, knowing now that all hope of saving his young master was at an end, he turned, and, the door being open, fled, his intention being to return to the Savoy, where his presence, unaccompanied by Stanley, would create alarm, and inquiries would take place.

But the poor brute took a wrong turning, and instead of crossing Smithfield and getting to the Fleet, turned the other way and went down Aldersgate.

At a breakneck pace he went, sending over more than one person in his haste, and at last he reached St. Paul's.

Here, in front of the grand old church, solemn, silent, and deserted as it now looked, the dog stopped.

He looked piteously at the black outlines of the old pile, as much as to say, " Where am I now ? "

The dog has ever been credited with the most wonderful sagacity, and in the case of the dog of our romance, plenty of proof of this was forthcoming.

Swift continued for some few seconds to look at the building.

In a few more moments, the animal, giving utterance to a joyful yelp, commenced to pace the front of the cathedral.

At every crack and corner he paused and sniffed.

But only for a moment or two.

That he had been to this building before was certain.

At last he reached the door by the side of the vestry.

All about this he carefully sniffed, and with every sniff he became more and more exultant.

Eventually his excitement found vent in a series of loud, prolonged growls.

Suddenly the door was cautiously opened about an inch, and a deep voice said—

" Swift."

The faithful animal now capered and bounded about as if he had suddenly gone mad.

Further open the door was drawn, and then a well-known figure stood on the threshold.

It was closely muffled up certainly, but there was no mistaking it.

It was the Hunchback.

Close behind him was another muffled figure, and there was little difficulty in recognising the owner of it—Ronald Rockley.

" As I live," said the Hunchback, " here indeed is a great mystery. Behold, look at this dog. You know him ? "

" I," replied Ronald, " I have seen him with Lord Whitmore, and with Stanley, the son."

" You are right. It is Swift, a beautiful, noble, and faithful creature, the pride of Lord Whitmore, the pet of his unfortunate lady, and the frequent companion of the son Stanley. Why, Swift, Swift, what ails thee ? See, Ronald, how he remembers me. Aye, he would speak if he could, and tell me a story. Maybe something has happened to his young master, Stanley."

As the Hunchback uttered these last words, Swift growled pitifully, and then seizing the Hunchback by the end of his cloak, endeavoured to pull him out.

" Something has certainly happened,' said Ronald, excitedly ; " for, see, he desires to lead you somewhere."

" Truly," replied the Hunchback. " Come, come, let us hasten, or, should his young master be in danger, we may arrive too late to render him any assistance."

The door being cautiously closed, the Hunchback said—

" Go on, good dog—go on."

Swift turned, and with a joyful bark, retraced his steps.

Back to Cloth Fair he went, almost step for step.

*   *   *   *

In less than a quarter of an hour the apothecary, who had been mixing in the most careful fashion a draught from various bottles, descended the steps leading to the cellar.

To his surprise he saw Stanley had recovered consciousness, and was in the act of warmly thanking his young friend for what she had done.

He had just asked her in faint tones, "And your name, fair maiden?" and the young girl had answered, "Beatrice Bevan, young sir," when the apothecary, his face showing the rage he was in, crossed the threshold.

One look convinced him that the old woman had proved treacherous, for the hag was in the act of gloating over the diamond ring Beatrice had given her.

With a couple of rapid strides he was upon the old woman, and, raising his clenched fist, he dealt her a stunning blow on the face, sending her with a crash to the ground.

"Vile hypocrite," he yelled; "you, whom I feed and clothe, to turn like this at the bidding of a brat like her. Away," he shouted, turning to Beatrice and frantically stamping his foot. "Away—away, lest I be tempted to make away with you."

"As you have my money," replied Beatrice.

"Go, go! lest—"

"Yes, I will go; but mark it well, Shiloh Septession: injure that young man, and I will proclaim your infamy throughout the City of London. From wall to wall of this city it shall be proclaimed that the humble, cringing, harmless-looking apothecary of Cloth Fair is nothing less than a plunderer and a poisoner."

"Away," screamed the apothecary. "Away!"

And seizing a huge piece of stone which was displaced from the flooring, he raised it high and threateningly over his head.

Beatrice, knowing the apothecary's terrible temper, drew back, and hastily left the cellar.

But she did not ascend the stairs.

Nay, close by the door she stood, and watched the operations of the murderous dealer in drugs.

During this scene, Stanley had not spoken.

But when Beatrice had retired, and the apothecary approached the pallet, he said—

"Thou infamous scoundrel. In whose pay are you?"

"Silence," replied the apothecary. "Silence! whatever you may ask will meet with no reply."

At this instant the old woman rose, and Stanley, who felt parched with thirst, said—

"Oh, I pray you, if you have one spark of humanity left in your breast, give me a draught of water."

The apothecary's eyes sparkled at this request.

"Do you hear, woman?" he said. "Do you hear? Give water—water."

There it stood, in a small blue jug, on the table—there, where Beatrice had placed it.

As the apothecary pointed his bony finger at it, his right hand slightly stole to his girdle, from which protruded the fatal phial.

The old woman saw the movement, and she hesitated.

Had she not already received the present of the valuable diamond ring to "go over on the other side?"

Aye, that was so, but she knew that she dared not hesitate, for the apothecary was a man she had sufficient cause to dread.

If she disobeyed him, he had many and various ways of speedily terminating her existence.

She approached the table, and with a hand that trembled as with the ague, poured out a glassful.

At the same time the apothecary took the phial from his girdle and dropped into the glass its contents.

But still the water in the glass continued clear, though the contents of the phial were of a bluish colour.

Stanley's head was towards the apothecary, but so rapid had been this miscreant's movements, that our hero had not observed what he had done.

"The water," thundered the apothecary; "the water — curse you—the water! Don't you see that the youth's lips are parched? Quick, or he may faint."

The old woman attempted to raise the glass, but her hand trembled so violently that the apothecary, fearful that the liquid should be spilt, pushed her on one side, and, picking up the glass, he advanced to the side of the pallet.

"I am acting on instructions received," he said, "and I have no business to offer you a draught of water or anything else. However, drink, and I will then inform you under whose orders I am acting."

Stanley with difficulty raised his head, and held out his hand for the glass.

But ere he could take it, the cellar door was pushed open and Beatrice dashed in.

With a wild, passionate cry she ran to the pallet's side.

"Hold!" she said; "hold! Touch it not, youth. That glass contains a deadly poison."

"Away with you!" shouted the apothecary. "Away with you! Heed her not, young sir; she is simply one of my patients, and is suffering from a disordered brain. Take and drink this, while I thrust her from your presence."

"No, no!" cried Beatrice. "No, no! You will heed me, young sir—you will heed me; you are here to be murdered —mark it!—to be murdered. For some reason you are not to meet your death by pistol or the assassin's knife, but by the aid of a powerful poison, and that poison is, I swear, in that glass. I saw—"

"Wretch!" interrupted the apothecary, with a fearful oath; "silence your infernal tongue, or— What was that? Hark! Ah, the door has been left open, and someone has entered. Hasten up," he cried to the old woman— "hasten up and see who it is."

But the woman moved not.

Suddenly a loud, hasty pattering was heard on the stairs, and in a few seconds a huge dog bounded through the doorway.

The apothecary, with a loud yell, started back.

Of course he made certain that the animal — our readers have already guessed that it was Swift —would make a spring and fasten his fangs in his throat, as he had served the man who had decoyed Stanley to this house.

But no. He scented his beloved young master, and with a wild, joyful yelp he sprang to the pallet, raised himself on his hind legs, and frantically licked his young master's face.

Before the apothecary had time to think whence the dog had so suddenly sprung, two dark figures crossed the threshold.

Each figure carried in his right hand a long, bright sword.

No sooner did the apothecary behold the first comer, than a loud, startled cry escaped his lips.

"*The Hunchback!*" he whispered.

"Saved!" murmured Stanley, as he returned the caresses of his faithful four-footed friend. "Saved! and through you, my noble Swift."

"Aye," said the Hunchback, advancing to within a few paces of the apothecary; "aye, 'tis I—'tis I! Wretch! I am not too late. Thank Heaven for that."

It was evident that the Hunchback had taken everything in at a glance.

"I heard you, my pretty maiden," he said, in kindly tones, as he turned to Beatrice, "and I thank you. Ronald, we are not too late. Behold! see what the wretch has in his hands. Behold the Cloth Fair poisoner, though so few know him as such. Nay, villain! do not attempt to throw away the stuff you hold in your hand. Place it upon the table. Place it there upon the table, I say, or my good sword shall pierce your vile heart."

The apothecary hesitated.

Advancing close to him, the Hunchback placed the point of his sword to his breast, saying—

"Place that glass and its contents upon the table, and spill one drop at your peril."

"There's nothing but water in the glass," whined the apothecary.

"We shall see that in a moment," replied the Hunchback, sternly. "Place it upon the table," and he placed his sword close to the old villain's throat.

The apothecary, seeing that there was no help for it, did as directed.

"Sheathe your blade, Ronald," said the Hunchback. "Such a wretch as this is not worthy the sword of an honest man."

Turning to Beatrice, he said—

"Fair maiden, I pray you retire while I converse with this man. Though I have been here on many occasions, I have never before had the pleasure of seeing you. Is Shiloh Septession any relation of yours?"

"No, sir; though he has, on more than one occasion, passed himself off as a relative. He was appointed my guardian by my parents, who are now abroad. A large sum of money was left in his hands for my benefit, all of which has been dissipated by him."

"Oh, of that I have no doubt at all," replied the Hunchback, grimly, "for 'plunder and poison' has ever been the motto of this eminent *Court* physician. Well, I pray you retire while I speak with him, and with my unfortunate young friend yonder. And do you take this old woman with you, for we do not require *her* presence."

Beatrice retired, the old woman hastily shuffling off after her, and the Hunchback shut the door.

Then he turned to the apothecary.

"By whose instructions were you acting in this case, villain?" he asked.

No answer.

Now thoroughly terrified, the apothecary was shifting uneasily from foot to foot, and his bony hands toyed nervously with the phial concealed in his girdle.

"You do not answer me," said the Hunchback, "and so I will answer for you. You are acting under the instructions of the Cowled Eleven."

"True."

"And you received your orders direct from Dacre Deadman?"

The apothecary bowed his head.

"And money from that wretch?"

Again the apothecary bowed his head.

"Your instructions were to poison this youth—this noble youth who has never in all his life harmed man, woman, or child—your instructions were to poison him, I say."

"No, no. I—"

"Tell me no lies!" thundered the Hunchback, his large eyes flashing fire. "Wretch that you are, I can read now what is passing in your black heart. Answer me—but stay. Stanley, my dear, unfortunate young friend — Stanley, are you strong enough to tell me how you were decoyed here, and in what manner you received that wound on your head?"

"Aye, my dear, kind friend," an-swered Stanley, "I will endeavour to do what you ask, but I feel so weak that—"

"Wait but a moment," interrupted Ronald, as he hastily took a flask of spirits from the folds of his cloak; "drink a portion of this. It will revive you."

Stanley took the flask with thanks.

Then his eyes became riveted upon the handsome face bending over him.

"I have seen you before, many times," he said, "and have wondered who you were. Your face is not easily forgotten. Who are you?"

"I am called Ronald Rockley, and I am the son of the Hunchback."

"Heavens!" cried Stanley, "can this be really possible?"

"Aye, 'tis so."

"The Hunchback's son?"

"Aye, the Hunchback's own son. His only child."

"And yet you are tall—taller than I, *and your body is perfectly straight.*"

At these words the Hunchback started, then a deep sigh escaped his lips, but it was not heard either by Ronald or Stanley.

"Nevertheless, I am the Hunchback's son," said Ronald, with a smile.

"Aye, 'tis so," said the Hunchback; "and you two are destined to go hand-in-hand—hand-in-hand for a purpose—revenge. But let me no longer keep this wretch waiting. Shiloh Septession, for what reason was this youth to be *poisoned?* I ask this, because I bear in mind the fact that the Cowled Eleven and their emissaries prefer the pistol, the dagger, *and the axe* in carrying out their sentences."

"If I answer you truly, you will spare me?" whined the apothecary.

"I promise nothing—absolutely nothing," answered the Hunchback.

And now Stanley briefly told his story.

Whether the apothecary thought that the Hunchback or Ronald would take his life, we know not, but no doubt he did.

Though the scheming, murderous old villain—the scoundrel who had sent many an innocent and unsuspecting victim suddenly to their long home—though the villain, at the instigation of whoever thought proper to pay him the sum he asked, never hesitated to give the cup of poison to man or woman—he was himself afraid of death.

He well knew the character of the mysterious being before him, and he feared him—feared him now more than he had ever done, because he had learned of his connection with Lord Whitmore, and because he had heard that the Hunchback was at the head of a society which was gradually, but surely, becoming more—far more powerful than the "society" which had as its chief Lord Blackmore.

After a brief pause, during which great drops of perspiration poured down his wrinkled face, he said—

"The reason he was to be poisoned was because Lord Blackmore had conceived the idea of having him conveyed to his country residence, and required him to be in no way disfigured."

"Ah! The depraved villain! Then you have received a visit from him?"

"No. From the—from Dacre Deadman."

"And he is to return again?"

"Aye; in a short time he will be here, accompanied by Lord Blackmore. Do what you like with *them*, but think of my great age, and spare *me*."

Oh, what a look of withering scorn did the Hunchback direct upon the vile old poisoner as he said this.

"And this box?" he said, as he advanced to a box—long, but very narrow—which was standing on end in the farthest corner of the cellar, and, catching hold of it, pulled it with a crash to the ground.

The lid came off, and a number of cloths, white and black, were seen within the box.

"What of this, I say?" repeated the Hunchback. "It was in this box that this youth's body was to be placed for conveyance, was it not?"

"It was. But, oh, I do assure you most solemnly that the suggestion was not mine."

"No matter by whom it was suggested," replied the Hunchback. "It is a matter of no importance at all, since the body of Stanley Whitmore will not be placed within it. *Now*," he thundered, drawing a pistol from his belt, and pointing it direct at Shiloh's head—"*now*, take up that glass."

The apothecary stared, and gave a gasping cry of terror.

"Take up that glass!" again thundered the Hunchback.

"Oh, spare me—spare me!" howled the apothecary.

"Take up that glass," the Hunchback once more repeated. "Are you afraid of it? Did you not, but a few moments ago, say that it contained only *water?* Take it up. But spill any of its contents, and this pistol shall end your wretched life."

At last the apothecary took up the glass.

His hand trembled so much that he had the greatest difficulty in keeping the glass in position.

"Now," continued the Hunchback, grimly, "*drink it!*"

Another howl of dismay left the parched lips of the wretched man.

His body was still covered with the pistol, and besides that, Swift was crouching directly before him, and was eyeing him in anything but a friendly manner.

The apothecary's face was a sight to behold.

The twitching of the muscles, the working of the eyes and brows made him look absolutely awful.

"*Drink the contents of that glass!*" continued the Hunchback; "for here on this spot you die. But you can, if you will, choose the *manner* of your death. Poison, the bullet, or the *dog*."

The apothecary fell upon his knees, and in loud, horror-stricken tones begged for his life.

But he might just as well have pleaded to a stone wall.

The Hunchback was totally deaf to his entreaties.

The apothecary turned his eyes towards Stanley and Ronald.

But he saw no pity in their faces.

Both considered that the villain deserved to die.

"Hasten," said the Hunchback, "and choose the manner of your death. If you delay much longer, Lord Blackmore and Dacre Deadman will arrive, though we have no fear should we happen to meet them. Quick, I say.

If you have not drunk the contents of that glass in two seconds, I will fire."

With a piercing yell of despair, the apothecary raised the glass and swallowed the contents.

Starting wildly to his feet, he raised his clenched hands, and would have given utterance to the curse which rose to his lips, had not the powerful compound he had drunk prevented him.

Waving his hands once or twice over his head, he suddenly fell.

The Hunchback turned him over.

"He is dead," he said—"quite dead, which proves the power of his own concoction. Thus the poisoner has died by his own poison, and by his own hand. Now, Stanley, do you feel able to walk as far as St. Paul's?"

"Yes, yes; I can manage that distance," replied Stanley.

Ronald lent his assistance, and Stanley got upon his feet.

Deathly pale he looked certainly, and no wonder.

He had lost a lot of blood.

The wonder was that he had not broken his neck.

"Lend me now your assistance, Ronald," said the Hunchback. "I will show you what is to be done with the apothecary's body."

Ronald lent his father the desired assistance, and in a few moments the body of the apothecary was placed within the box and covered over with the cloths.

"There Lord Blackmore will, no doubt, find him," said the Hunchback, "and much good may the sight do him."

Leaving the cellar the three ascended the stairs.

On the landing they found Beatrice and the old woman.

"The apothecary is no more," said the Hunchback to Beatrice; "he has met a fate which he most richly deserved, for I have compelled him to drink the poison he prepared for my young friend here."

"Heavens!" exclaimed Beatrice, clasping her hands, "what a fearful fate."

"But deserved."

"Yes—yes, deserved."

"Is this old woman any relation of yours?"

"No—none whatever."

"Then you desire no further connection with her?"

"Oh, no, no!" replied Beatrice, with a shudder.

"Then let me tell you," said the Hunchback to the old woman, "you had better begone at once. If Lord Blackmore finds you here it may go hard with you. Begone."

He did not have to say "Begone" twice.

The old woman turned and ran off as hard as she was able.

"You have no longer a home here," continued the Hunchback to Beatrice. "Come with me. I will find you a home in return for your kindness to my young friend here. Will you come?"

"Oh, sir, willingly. I feel sure I can trust you."

"Aye, my child, you are right. You *can* trust me. Come."

A cloak was hanging on a stand near the door, and Ronald, taking it down, placed it about Beatrice's shoulders.

Thus the four departed, Swift following and jumping with joy.

*   *   *   *

It must have been about half-an-hour after the departure of our friends that Lord Blackmore—like his son, disguised—arrived at the house in Cloth Fair.

The door was wide open, and Dacre was the first to enter.

He was quickly followed by Lord Blackmore.

Both were surprised to find the door wide open, and they did not hesitate to say so in tones which were sufficiently loud to have been heard all over the house.

"Hi! Hillo!" roared Dacre, stamping his foot. "Ho! I say. Where the— Ho! Shiloh—Shiloh."

No answer, save the echo of his own voice.

"The wretch is evidently absent," growled Blackmore, as he glared savagely about him.

"Absent?" echoed Dacre; "absent? That is hardly likely. But then if he is absent, where the devil is the old woman and the pretty girl, of whom I have more than once caught a glimpse?'

"The foul fiend take the pretty girl! Call the wretch again."

Dacre did so, and, of course, got no answer.

Thereupon he led the way down-stairs.

Our readers know how the cellar looked.

The lamp still burned, though but very dimly, on the table.

"No one here," said Dacre, looking about him in astonishment. "Not a single— Ha, but look. Ho, ho! The apothecary has done his work well and truly, for see—that box contains the body of the accursed son of Lord Whitmore."

And advancing a few paces, Dacre snatched off the cloths.

For some seconds he stood looking wildly into the box, then, with a loud shriek, he darted back, his action being followed by Lord Blackmore.

Truly these two villains had never in the whole course of their lives been more thunder-stricken.

Blackmore stood clutching the table, and trembling violently.

At last Dacre, in low, hoarse tones, said—

"The apothecary!"

"Dead—murdered!" gasped Blackmore. "And the youth — he has escaped."

"No doubt of it," replied Dacre. "By all the saints, this is indeed a most awful mystery."

"No mystery at all," cried Blackmore, "now I consider. This is the first blow struck at me by the accursed Hunchback."

"Yes, yes," said Dacre; "I fancy you must be right. And he has been assisted by Ronald Rockley, who, so it is said, is the Hunchback's son."

"Ah," exclaimed Blackmore, through his clenched teeth, "let them not think they can overcome us. By all the fiends, we will quickly show them how powerful we are. We will show them that our power does not commence and finish at Blackmore Hall. We will show them that we have agents in every part of London—agents ready and willing to do all we require of them. Oh, and I thought to show young Stanley's body to his mother! I looked forward to the hour when I should see her terrible agony, and gloat —*gloat* over it."

"You must wait, my lord," said Dacre; "wait. And you will not have to wait long. But now let us consider what is to be done here."

"Done here!" answered Blackmore. "What can be done here? Let us hasten away from the vile spot, and—"

"What!" interrupted Dacre, "hasten away and leave this place as it is?"

"Aye, what is it to do with us?"

"I will tell you," replied Dacre. "It is a good job that I am almost continually at your side, ready to give you good suggestions. If I were not, my lord, it would go hard with you."

"Fool!" cried Blackmore.

"Gently, gently!" grinned Dacre. "I will tell you what I was about to say. You said hasten away from this place and leave it as it is. Good. Does your lordship forget that on many occasions you sent Shiloh Septession documents, containing instructions which are highly treasonable and murderous? Where are those documents? Why, in this house! Suppose they were found by enemies—and Heaven knows you have enough enemies at this present moment—if found by enemies, what would happen?"

While Dacre thus spoke, Blackmore turned deathly pale.

"You are right, Dacre; you are right. We must immediately institute a careful search for these documents. Though do you not think it possible that Shiloh would have destroyed them as soon as received?"

"Most certainly not. And why? Because in the event of your not paying him any sum or sums due to him, he would threaten you with them. But as to search for them, such a thing is entirely out of the question. We may take hours—precious hours—over them, and to no purpose."

"What, then, do you propose?"

"*Fire the house*, and thus destroy all evidences of our connection with this man."

This cold-blooded proposal did not surprise his lordship, nor did it meet with his disapproval.

On the contrary, he, no doubt, considered it a most excellent idea.

"We should be certain, then, that all

evidence was destroyed," said Blackmore. "So let us at once proceed to carry out the plan."

"Do not endanger yourself, my lord," smirked Dacre; "let *me* have the carrying out of all this. Your lordship's horse awaits you at Aldgate. Do you go, mount, and away to Wapping, whither I will follow you as soon as I see (from a safe distance) that the fire burns briskly."

"Very well," answered Blackmore. " I will do as you suggest. Farewell."

As he crossed the threshold of the cellar he muttered—

" I wish to Heaven that as soon as you have fired the place, you may fall down some trap and so be burnt alive. By the Virgin! I should thus be released from you."

When Blackmore was gone, Dacre gave utterance to a low, but prolonged chuckle.

"The consummate fool!" he said. "Though I reminded him of *one* matter, I did not remind him of the other, which, according to my thinking, is the most important of the two, and that is the apothecary's *money*. Ha! he must have a lot in this house, and it will go hard if I do not find it. And now let me commence the task, for, should anyone gain an entrance, I might be taken for a thief, aye, and a murderer."

Taking the lamp in his hand, he made a thorough search from top to bottom.

But, singular to say, not a piece could he see.

In the apothecary's bedroom was a ponderous iron box.

Its four sides and bottom were cast in one piece, while the lid and the steel lock were affixed to it in a most ingenious, nay, marvellous style of workmanship.

Dacre examined this and found it locked.

An exclamation of rage escaped his lips when he saw this.

But at last an idea struck him.

He would attempt to *smash* it open.

So he descended to the lower regions once more, and, after searching for some time, found a large hammer.

With this he again ascended the stairs.

"If that box can resist my strength, and this," he muttered, "well, my name is not—ahem!—Dacre Deadman."

He brought the ponderous weight of metal to bear on the box.

But it did not even make the slightest impression on it.

Dacre rained blows on the box until his arm ached, and the perspiration ran in streams down his face.

But eventually he arrived at the conclusion that he was only wasting time, and exhausting himself, in endeavouring to smash this mass of iron, and so relinquished the task.

Leaning on the handle of the hammer, he gave utterance to several bitter curses. Then he turned to depart, but again a thought struck him.

He was loth to leave the box, but, of course, he could not take it with him.

Had he been able to carry it he would have taken it, and have obtained the services of a blacksmith to open it.

" If I can move the box backwards and forwards," he thought, " I shall be able to tell whether there is money within it."

Then getting on his knees, he pushed the iron box violently backwards and forwards.

No welcome chink of precious gold pieces met his expectant ears.

Dacre started up with a loud cry of rage.

" The old, miserly scarecrow! Where can he have hidden his accursed gold ? Perhaps he has turned it into goldsmith's notes, and hidden them behind the wainscoting. Well, if that is so, they will be consumed. I must abandon the search. But, lor'! how I would have liked to clutch his gold. Heaps he had from Lord Blackmore. Now I cannot even find the bag I brought this evening."

After throwing the bedclothes about, and the place generally into a state of confusion, he descended the stairs for the last time.

In a little room, which for some considerable time had been allotted to Beatrice, he found a couple of straw mattresses.

These he dragged into the cellar, and placed them in the centre.

On the top of them he placed the pallet, and on the top of that, the box containing the body of the murderous old poisoner.

"A funeral pile!" he muttered, as he surveyed his handiwork; "a glorious funeral pile."

Then, with a wild, fiendish laugh, he applied the flame of the lamp to the mattresses.

Instantly the dry straw took fire, and began to burn furiously.

Dacre stood and laughed as he watched the long tongues of flame writhing, and twisting, and licking the sides of the box containing all that was mortal of the vile apothecary.

But so quickly did the flames assume gigantic proportions, that Dacre was soon up the stairs.

Closing the door with a crash, he crept round the house, and then made his escape.

And the "questionable characters" who made Cloth Fair their abiding-place, slept on, all unconscious that in the cellar of the "Apothecary to the Court," a deliberately-planned fire was making rapid headway.

But they were soon made aware of it.

In less than a quarter of an hour the smoke and flames rushed out in volumes, threatening the houses on all sides.

The watchman on duty was the first to observe the fire, and he was so overcome with astonishment and horror, that for some few moments the fool stood gaping at it, unable to sound his rattle, or cry "Fire!"

Soon windows and doors were flung open in every direction, and the faces of terrified men, women, and children appeared at them.

But only for a few minutes did they stay at the windows.

Down the stairs into the narrow thoroughfares they rushed, forgetting in their fright everything but their own safety.

The dark, gloomy courts and alleys were quickly illuminated by the fire.

And every now and then a phial or a case containing some explosive spirit went off with a loud report, sending the windows flying about in every direction.

In those days there were no appliances for the extinguishing of fires, except the bucket, and a thousand buckets would never have checked the flames which, in an incredibly short space of time, had penetrated the roof, and rose high into the star-studded sky.

So alarming did the fire become that the authorities feared that the whole of the quarter would be destroyed.

So the church bells were set ringing.

Steeple after steeple took up the call, and very soon almost every church in the City was ringing out the alarm.

But, amid the din of hundreds of bells, the deep, solemn boom of the ponderous alarm bell in "London's Great Church" made itself most distinctly heard.

This was considered strange by the inhabitants of Ludgate and the churchyard, who were well aware that, for some considerable time past, the sexton had been ill.

Who was ringing the bell, and in so regular a manner?

Ronald and the Hunchback had reached the cathedral in safety, and when the alarm of fire was given, Ronald ascended to the roof.

He told his father of the direction and nature of the fire with this result—the bell was rung by the hands of the Hunchback of Old St. Paul's.

CHAPTER IV.

IS OF HOW LADY WHITMORE ESCAPES FROM HER PLACE OF CONFINEMENT.

WE are anxious to return to the unfortunate and most unhappy Lady Whitmore, and no doubt our readers are just as anxious to learn what befell her after the tragedy enacted at Blackmore Hall.

By Blackmore's orders she was taken to an apartment on the ground floor.

It was a poorly-furnished and most gloomy place, and well calculated to make her more miserable and unhappy than ever.

That the apartment was but little used was evident from the enormous cobwebs which the busy insects had spun in every direction, the massive curtains covered with dust, and the bedstead, which contained not an atom of bed-linen.

The carpet also was covered with dust, and in such a dreadful state had the windows got, that to see out of them was out of all question.

At the time she was thrust into this place, poor Lady Whitmore, of course, was too agitated with what had already transpired to pay much attention to the room.

With a wild, piercing cry—a cry which came direct from her over-charged heart—Lady Whitmore threw herself by the bedside, and, burying her face in her hands, gave way to a passionate fit of sobbing.

That fit continued, without cessation, for at least an hour.

At last she became calmer, and took a survey of the apartment.

She had been provided with one small lamp, the light of which was of so tiny a character that her ladyship, in order to view her apartment, had to carry it with her.

"Horrible! horrible!" muttered Lady Whitmore; "truly horrible! And here I shall remain until—until—Oh, I shudder—I tremble to think of the dreadful fate in store for me. And the Hunchback, what is in store for *him*? Ah, but he has powerful friends, I have heard my husband say—powerful friends who, if they discover his whereabouts, will move Heaven and earth to effect his release. Oh, that he may escape. I should not then fear for the safety of my son. Oh, Stanley, Stanley," she moaned, "what a fate is thine! I fear like thy poor murdered father's."

Throwing herself into a chair, Lady Whitmore gave way to reflection.

She tried hard enough, Heaven knows, to shut out the dreadful vision of what had happened in the Green Room, when her noble husband was beheaded.

But the effort was in vain.

In the midst of other thoughts the horrible picture floated before her eyes, and the agonised groan she uttered told only too well the story of what was passing in her mind.

Morning came, and the bright sun tried to struggle through the windows, but the dirt effectually shut it out.

Lady Whitmore was glad of it.

She would rather remain as she was —in darkness.

And her wish in this respect was nearly gratified, for, despite the sun, the apartment remained in a state of semi-darkness.

Hour after hour passed, and presently, loud shouts and the rattle of arms were heard in all parts of the mansion.

It was evident that something of great importance had happened.

What it was, however, her ladyship could not even guess.

Oh, how glad she would have been had she known that this noise was owing to the fact that the daring escape of the Hunchback had become known to Lord Blackmore.

By-and-by she was startled by a small trap fixed in the door of her apartment being let down.

The face of Lord Blackmore appeared at it.

"Ah," he said, fiercely, "you, at any rate, are safe. For you there will be no chance of escape. None—none."

And the trap was closed with a crash.

"No escape?" muttered her ladyship. "No. He speaks only too truly. It might be within the power of a man to escape, but a woman—no. Then, from what he says, someone has effected their escape. Can it be the Hunchback? Alas! I have no means of knowing, for there can be but little doubt that in this gloomy old pile there are some dozens of prisoners—martyrs to a desperate and murderous secret society."

Within an hour the trap was again let down, and this time the face of the traitor Coningsby appeared at it.

Behind him stood a score of armed men.

"*Now* then," cried Coningsby, in brutal tones, "come hither and take your refreshments for the day."

"Wretch!" replied Lady Whitmore, in scornful tones, as she drew her beautiful figure erect—"wretch! How dare you keep me a prisoner?"

"How *dare* I ?" answered Coningsby. "Because here, in this building, I am master—at least, I am at present—and by Heaven, you shall find such to be the case."

Her ladyship was turning haughtily away, when again Coningsby shouted to her.

"Take this. That's my orders," cried the villain.

Gracefully the shamefully ill-treated lady glided towards the trap.

Lady Whitmore took the pitcher of water offered her, but suddenly drawing back her arm, she hurled the contents clean into Coningsby's face.

The wretch fell back among his fellows, spluttering and hissing.

"'Tis what you deserve, sirrah !" said Lady Whitmore ; "and now I pray you come not near me again."

Coningsby once more advanced to the trap, and shaking his fist through it, said, in furious tones—

"Your time is coming."

"Aye," answered her ladyship, "let it come. But *your* time may come first."

Her words proved prophetic.

Her ladyship picked up the loaf that had been thrown in with the intention of hurling it back through the trap, but it was closed ere she had an opportunity of doing so.

Oh, how lucky it was for her that she did not do so.

Seating herself in the chair, Lady Whitmore once again gave way to her painful reflections.

And while she reflected, she mechanically picked to pieces the loaf.

Suddenly a low cry of surprise left her lips.

She started up in a state of intense agitation.

"What is this I see ?" she muttered. "What is this? A paper— yes, a slip of paper !"

She pulled it forth.

It had been rolled up, and a hole having been bored in the loaf, the paper had been thrust in and the hole re-filled.

With feverish haste she unrolled the scrap, and saw a few lines of writing.

It was written in a bold hand, and, moreover, it was written in French.

Fortunately, Lady Whitmore was a first-class French scholar, and she had no difficulty in translating the words as follows—

"Keep up your spirits. I, a friend, am near you. Though I cannot write English, I speak it. At midnight I will be with you.

"DESARGE, the French Page."

Lady Whitmore re-rolled the paper, and thrust it within her bodice.

"Desarge—the French page," she muttered—"the French page ! Page to whom ? Is he servant to his horrible lordship, or is he, like me, a prisoner ? Nay, that cannot be. Oh," she thought, as she clasped her hands fervently together, "Heaven, then, has raised up a friend, and beneath the very roof of this most terrible and determined enemy. But can I believe this ? It seems too good to be true. 'At midnight I will be with you,' so runs the note. How will he get here ? Has he a duplicate key of this room ? Oh, I must wait—wait, as patiently as I can. Midnight ! Alas ! how many, many hours have to come and go ere the hour of midnight strikes ? "

Throughout the whole day the trap was not again opened.

The only sound which fell upon her ladyship's ears was the tramping of men, and the clink of arms.

Midnight came at last, and her ladyship was in total darkness.

The lamp had long since burned itself out, and it was certainly not Coningsby's intention to have it relit.

The hour of twelve struck.

Lady Whitmore counted the hours as the clock struck them, and our readers may guess what her feelings were as the echo of the last stroke died away.

She glided to the door and listened.

She heard similar sounds to those she had heard all day—the monotonous tramp, tramp, tramp of the men on guard.

While her ladyship was listening at the door, she heard a peculiar noise at the other end of the apartment, behind the head of the bed.

Most intently did her ladyship listen. Her heart beat wildly the while.

In a few seconds Lady Whitmore

felt a draught, just as if a door had been suddenly opened.

Then a low, sweet voice, with a strong French accent, said—

"Madame, where are you?"

"Here—here!" gasped Lady Whitmore, stretching forth her hands.

She found them grasped by a pair of hands as soft and as white as her own.

"Hist!" continued the voice. "Not a word, as you value your life—as you value the life of one who serves you. Hist! I have a dark lantern beneath my cloak, but will not turn on the light until I am assured that the men are not guarding the passage. Listen."

"I can tell you," said Lady Whitmore, "that the men are at the further end of the corridor. I, myself, have been listening intently for some time."

"Then that is well," was the reply. "Behold!"

The mysterious visitor lifted its cloak, brought out a lantern, and turned on its light.

Curiously did Lady Whitmore look at her visitor.

She saw before her a slight figure clad in male attire, wearing a long, gold-embroidered cloak, and closely masked.

"You are the French page?" said Lady Whitmore, eagerly.

"Yes—yes. But fear nothing; I am of your sex."

"You are a woman?"

"I am. Yes—yes; a woman, despite all I have gone through. Yes, I remain a woman—at your service. But let me tell you, no time is to be lost. Follow me, without hesitation, and I will set you free. Will you do this?"

"I will—I will; oh, how gladly."

"'Tis well. But let me warn you—the slightest hesitation may cost you your life, for the orders of the men on guard here are to fire upon anyone attempting to escape. Come."

Desarge took Lady Whitmore's hand and led her behind the bed.

Imagine her ladyship's astonishment when she saw that a long, narrow portion of the wainscoting had been drawn back.

"A secret door," said Desarge, observing her astonishment; "but only used by Lord Blackmore. No doubt, had he been here to-day, he would

have entered your apartment by its means."

"Blackmore, then, is away?"

"He is in London."

"And those dreadful beings, the Cowled Eleven?"

"They also are away, seeking fresh victims, for aught I know," replied the French page, closing the door.

Her ladyship now found herself in a lofty, but exceedingly narrow passage.

"'Tis safe to talk here," continued Desarge, "though we have no time for conversation. We—"

"But," pleaded her ladyship, "you will—you cannot refuse me the favour of letting me see your face."

Desarge started, and was silent for some few seconds.

Presently she said, sadly—

"My face? Ah, *my* face! Lady, there is little to see in *my* face. Why do you wish to behold it? I am delivering you—it is enough, is it not?"

"Oh, pardon me—pardon me! It was an impulse which I could not resist—"

Desarge interrupted her.

Snatching off the mask, she said—

"There, lady, behold my face. Look, I pray you, closely. What see you?"

"Oh, I see a beautiful face—a very beautiful face."

"Beautiful, lady—beautiful? Oh, *mon Dieu—beautiful!* No, no; you are jesting. *Once* I was beautiful, they said; but now—*now*, lady, my beauty is but a mockery of what it was."

"But in your face," said Lady Whitmore, "I can trace much sorrow, much suffering."

"Oh, hush!" interrupted Desarge, in agonised tones; "hush!" Oh, lady, in my face you cannot read my history. No, no! My history is a horrible one —most horrible. Yesterday you suffered. But yet what happened was as nothing compared with what has happened to me. My husband was slain, stabbed to the heart, and my four children poisoned."

"Oh, Heaven!" gasped Lady Whitmore, her pale face peering into that of Desarge. "By whose orders?"

"*The Cowled Eleven!*"

"SWIFT FASTENED HIS TEETH IN HIS THROAT."

"Ah! and Blackmore at their head. And you—you are under the same roof! *His* page?"

"His *slave!*" said Desarge, calmly, but nevertheless, in tones which spoke volumes. "His *slave!* I am to do his bidding — to obey orders, however horrible—however loathsome they may be."

"He has you in his power, then?"

Desarge bowed.

"But suppose you refused to obey his orders?" asked Lady Whitmore.

"Aye."

"What would be the alternative?"

"Death."

"If you escaped—what then? I mean, if, after having escaped, you were captured?"

"He holds documents written by me at my misguided husband's dictation, which would procure me death at the hands of the State. Your queen is cruel, madame; she would not hear me."

"And so you wait here. But you have some object in view."

"I *have* had. But I wait here no longer."

"You will escape with me?" asked her ladyship, joyfully.

"Aye, with you."

Lady Whitmore bent over and kissed the pale, beautiful face.

Desarge shuddered as she did so, and tears started into her eyes.

But quickly recovering herself, she said—

"Again, I say, do not hesitate."

"I will not."

"Yet you will pass a trying time."

"Yet I will not hesitate."

"Good, madame. Now I am about to lead you through this passage, and down a flight of stairs into the 'Blue Chapel.' Have you ever heard of it, madame?"

"The Blue Chapel! Never. This is the first, and I hope the last, time I have been to Blackmore Hall."

"Well, the Blue Chapel is so called," said Desarge, "because the roof is painted blue, and because the hangings are blue. It is a pretty chapel—something like the one your queen uses at Windsor Castle—but I need hardly say that Lord Blackmore prays not within it. No, no; the villain uses it as a *graveyard*."

"A graveyard?"

"Aye. Under the stone flooring of the chapel repose the mutilated bodies of those who have had the misfortune to receive the sentence of the bloodthirsty Cowled Eleven. Well, madame, I shall lead you through this chapel, because it is our only way. No doubt we shall be unobserved, for the cowardly wretches who take the pay of Blackmore shudder when the Blue Chapel is spoken of. But we *may* meet one of them. If we do, *strike*—strike for life and liberty. See, here is your weapon—'tis all I could find."

And stooping, Desarge picked up a small, but heavy battle-axe.

It glittered and flashed as she presented it to her ladyship, who for an instant shrank from it.

But the next she took it firmly in her grasp.

"For life and liberty," she thought. "*Life?* Ah, how little I value my life *now*—now that *he*, the partner of my joys and sorrows, is no more. But liberty! Liberty for Stanley's sake!"

"Madame," said Desarge, "you are ready?"

"Quite."

"Then follow."

Desarge stepped boldly forward.

The passage was traversed, and the flight of stairs noiselessly descended.

Desarge had resumed her mask, but she did not conceal the rays of the lantern.

A few short passages were now traversed, Desarge being apparently perfectly acquainted with every step of the way, and a low-arched doorway was reached.

Before it a pair of massive curtains were drawn.

These Desarge pulled aside, whispering, as she she did so—

"The Blue Chapel."

"Ha!" said Lady Whitmore, "and a light burns within it."

"That is so. In this chapel a single taper is always burning. Now we must cross it. Come."

Lady Whitmore followed Desarge across the threshold, and was thus quite within this singular chapel.

It was very small, but singularly lofty, with beautiful Gothic windows; the vaulted roof was painted a light blue with deep shading, and the hangings in every direction were blue.

The flooring was of beautiful white marble, so exquisitely laid that the centre of the chapel looked as if it was one solid piece.

The furniture was of dark oak, most richly carved, and surmounted with the arms of the Blackmore family.

The dim, uncertain light of the taper shed a strange, ghastly glimmer around the gloomy structure, which, as Lady Whitmore became aware of in a few moments, smelt like the interior of a charnel-house.

Desarge placed the lantern beneath her cloak, whispering, as she did so—

"Come. And tread lightly."

She had to repeat her words twice, however, for Lady Whitmore appeared as if spellbound.

Firmly grasped in her delicate right hand, the small battle-axe which Desarge had given her, saying, "*Strike for life and liberty!*" glittered and flashed in the rays of the taper, as would a mirror in the rays of the moon.

"Come," Desarge again whispered, "come—the moments are precious."

She went forward, and Lady Whitmore followed, gliding rather than walking across the marble floor.

Two of the massive pillars were passed, and the third one was reached. Desarge rapidly rounded it, Lady Whitmore being close at her heels.

Suddenly Lady Whitmore stopped and uttered a sharp, piercing shriek.

Desarge turned; the lantern trembled violently in her hand.

"What is it?" she gasped.

But she instantly saw what had caused her ladyship to utter so startling a cry.

Lady Whitmore pointed her finger to an object lying upon the floor.

Strange to say, the light from the lantern was full upon it.

What was this object?

The decapitated figure of a man.

The head was lying close to the body, the pale, ghastly face was turned up, and the eyes were wide open; and as Lady Whitmore bent over, they seemed to be looking into her face.

"My husband!" gasped her ladyship.

"It is," replied Desarge. "I had thought you would have missed the sight. See, the ground is opened here —shortly, Lord Whitmore will be placed in his grave. But I implore you—"

"Ha!" cried a loud voice, "what is this? An escape, as I live! An escape! Surrender yourselves."

Desarge turned the rays of the lantern on the speaker.

It was Coningsby!

He had drawn his sword and held it threateningly before him.

But his attitude did not terrify Desarge.

"Stand back!" she said, as she laid her hand upon her dagger. "Stand out of our path!"

"Surrender!" repeated Coningsby, who, no doubt, thought this was a fine opportunity for distinguishing himself. "Do you hear me? Surrender!"

"Aye, we hear you," answered Desarge; "and I say again, stand back!"

"Attempt to advance, and your life pays the forfeit—you, Desarge, the French page. You see I know you. Your mask does not hide your French figure."

"If you do not stand back," replied Desarge, snatching her dagger from its sheath, "*your* life may pay the forfeit. Ah, madame," she said to Lady Whitmore, "behold the wretch who helped in the capture of your husband."

"Yes, I have seen him before," replied Lady Whitmore, "and the word 'scoundrel' was never more clearly written upon a man's face than on his."

"Stand back, I repeat!" said Desarge.

"Nay, not I," replied Coningsby. "I will advance."

Raising his voice, he shouted—

"What ho! what ho! An escape— an escape."

Instantly Desarge, with upraised dagger, rushed forward, but Coningsby was not off his guard.

With a terrible oath, he, with his left hand, seized Desarge's arm as it descended, and, raising his sword, he plunged it into Desarge's body.

But the wound did not appear to be very deep—at any rate, Desarge did not fall.

Coningsby now rushed upon Lady Whitmore.

But she was ready for him.

With a little cry of despair she flung herself upon the traitor.

So tightly did she seize him by the throat, that the villain, gasping for breath, staggered back, his helmet falling off.

"Strike—strike!" shouted Desarge.

Her ladyship required no urging.

Maddened at the thought of being again captured—now, when escape seemed so near—she raised the glittering battle-axe over her head.

Within the space of a second it descended with terrible force on Coningsby's head.

It clove his skull completely in twain, and, bathed in his blood, he fell, a lifeless mass, close to the body of Lord Whitmore, in whose capture and subsequent death he had taken so prominent a part.

The reaction then took place, and the gentle lady stood appalled at the dreadful deed she had committed.

"Keep the axe in your hand, lady," said Desarge. "Another wretch may stand in our path."

The voice of Desarge was so changed that Lady Whitmore instantly noticed it.

The soft tones had gone; her voice was now low and hoarse—in fact, it was the voice of one undergoing great pain.

"You are severely wounded," said Lady Whitmore, "and I am the cause of it. Oh," she added, recoiling, "you are smothered in blood."

"True," answered Desarge, calmly. "My life's blood is fast flowing away. Hasten—hasten! I will put you on the road to liberty. As to myself, my dream is over. I struck for liberty, but I lose my life. I am dying. My wound is mortal; no human skill could save me. But welcome, death; it relieves me of all my sorrows. But yet," she added, excitedly, as she placed her hand over the dreadful wound—for that it *was* a dreadful wound was now quite evident—"but yet, *he* lives—*he* lives. You or yours will avenge me and mine now in recognition of my services?"

"Aye, I promise that; and the promise shall be most sacredly kept. But you may not be so seriously wounded as you imagine. Some—"

"Say no more, lady," interrupted Desarge. "You will escape, **and I** shall surely die. I thought that, did I succeed in escaping with you, you would have taken compassion on me, and have provided a home for me until —until—"

Here she broke off abruptly, and burst into tears.

But there was no time to give way to emotion.

On went Desarge, her ladyship being close to her side.

Again several passages were traversed, but in a few moments Lady Whitmore saw, from her tottering gait, that Desarge was becoming weaker every moment.

"Alas!" cried her ladyship, who, at the dreadful fate which had overtaken her most beautiful, but unfortunate companion, felt inclined to burst into a passionate flood of tears.

Suddenly Desarge paused, drew herself erect, and tore the mask from her ghastly face.

Then placing her hand on her heart, she said, in terrible tones of anguish—

"Oh, Heaven, spare me but for a few moments, that I may see that this lady has escaped from this house of assassination. Oh, my heart. Stand back! Touch me not. Listen to me, lady! We shall now pass through a passage that leads to the open air—to the grounds. As soon as you touch the ground, lady, turn sharply to the left. You cannot mistake the way, for it is between two rows of elms. Soon you will reach a ruined lodge, and at the side of it you will see two horses saddled and bridled. One is for you; the other was for me, but the dream is over. Come, come, or it will be too late."

Staggering on, rather than walking, Desarge led her ladyship through several strange and dreadfully smelling passages, and at last they came out at the very spot where Ronald Rockley had slain the man who would have stayed his progress.

Desarge almost stumbled over the body of the man, as he lay stiff and cold on the ground.

"Ah!" cried Lady Whitmore, pointing to the body and recoiling a pace, "behold the dead body of a man. Oh, this is indeed a house of blood."

Desarge flashed her lantern in the man's face.

"I recognise the wretch," she said, "and his death is most richly deserved. He was a vile wretch. This is the man I have heard gloating over the tortures inflicted on others. See the expression on his brutal face, observe the staring eyes, the clenched hands. This shows the nature of his death. But look."

Desarge pointed ahead.

Her ladyship looked, but she saw nothing beyond a flight of steps.

All appeared dark and forbidding.

"Come," said Desarge, whose voice could now hardly be heard.

She led Lady Whitmore to the steps.

"Look here," she said, "you see this flight of stone steps? They contain a secret—a secret known but to a very few. Do you ascend them. I shall tread upon one in a peculiar fashion, and the effect will be that a huge stone above will roll back. Then you are free—free!"

Lady Whitmore, whose nerves were now strung up to a fearful pitch, ascended them as rapidly as she could.

Desarge followed, but it was with the greatest difficulty.

Just as Lady Whitmore reached the last step, the huge stone above rolled slowly aside, and the star-studded sky—oh, welcome sight!—was revealed.

Desarge had caused the spring, about which we spoke some time back, to act, but she still kept her foot upon the step.

Extinguishing her lantern, she said—

"Go, lady—go to the very top. That is right—now you are indeed safe."

"Oh," exclaimed her ladyship, "I do most earnestly entreat you to attempt to accompany me. If you can only get out into the open air, you might be revived, or you might conceal yourself under one of the bushes here while I hasten and procure assistance."

Desarge solemnly shook her pretty head.

"You are kind, lady," she said, "but such a thing is out of all question. It is too late—too late! I bid you—farewell!"

She raised her face, and at the same instant the moon's rays shone full upon it.

A very striking figure she presented as she stood there—so striking, indeed, that Lady Whitmore never forgot it to the day of her death.

"Ah," said Lady Whitmore, as she clasped her white hands fervently together, "what would I not give could I take you with me!"

"It has been my dream," said Desarge, sadly, "but it was not to be. Of course, I knew that I could never again be happy, but still I thought I might live to see vengeance overtake the wretch who was the destroyer of my husband and my children. Oh, madame, once I was happy. But my husband would dabble in affairs which he should have left to the traitor and the assassin. I repeatedly warned him, but of what use was it? My voice was not heard; it was like the cry of the swallow in the storm—lost."

She paused an instant, gasping for breath; then again she spoke, and this time her voice was nothing more than a low whisper—

"Go, lady—go at once. On the morrow my dead body will be found here, and it will be seen that it was I who aided you in your escape. Go! I can speak no more."

Uttering a startled cry, Lady Whitmore sprang forward, as if to clutch Desarge by the arm.

But she was too late.

Grim Death had fastened his dreadful fingers about the beautiful, but most unfortunate woman; her foot released the spring, the ponderous stone noiselessly resumed its position, but not before Lady Whitmore had caught sight of a white face falling backwards down the long flight of slimy stairs.

Instantly Lady Whitmore fell upon her knees, and offered up a short prayer for the repose of the soul of the hapless Frenchwoman; then rising, she ran swiftly in the direction which Desarge had indicated.

Sure enough she found the horses awaiting her, and a couple of splendid animals they were.

One was a grey, the other black.

Lady Whitmore, after a brief examination of the horses, selected the grey, and mounted him.

Though she prayed Heaven that she should have no occasion to use them, she was overjoyed to find in the holsters a pair of pistols.

The horse, finding the reins grasped, set off at a sharp walk.

He found the path, and in a few seconds Lady Whitmore was able to say—

"I am free for vengeance!"

CHAPTER V.

IS OF THE STARTLING EVENTS WHICH TOOK PLACE AT THE "ROVER'S ARMS."

THE day after his arrival at St. Paul's, Stanley's injuries took a serious turn.

So seriously ill indeed did he become, that the Hunchback deemed it advisable to secure the services of a very old friend of his, a man skilled in the study of all kinds of ailments.

This gentleman consented to attend upon our hero, but in order to do so he had to be smuggled into the vaults.

This, as may be supposed, was dangerous to everyone, for it might have led to the discovery of the Hunchback —for whose arrest the warrant still held good—and all his friends.

"It passes my comprehension," said Ronald, "why you smuggle Master Lang in this way, when the subterranean vault could be used without a chance of discovery."

"My son," replied the Hunchback, as he laid his hands on his son's shoulders, and looked tenderly into his face, "I have my reasons; is not that sufficient?"

"It is. Pardon my impertinence."

"Nay, nay; thou wert not impertinent, but curious—only curious. Ronald, that subterranean passage—which was discovered so many years ago by myself—is left to be used by *The Avengers*, and by them alone. Shortly —indeed, in two nights from now—the meeting will be held in the crypt, and you— But you must wait. At present you have never seen any of these men?"

"Never."

"But you know that they were agents of Lord Whitmore?"

"I have heard you say so. Agents of Lord Whitmore and yourself."

"I—through Whitmore—have directed them—that is all. Up to the

present, their station has been in all parts of London."

"And you will swear to me, my dear father, that the only object they have in view is—"

"The welfare of the English crown. Aye, I swear before high Heaven that that is their only object."

"Oh, that Lord Whitmore had laid all before her majesty!"

"He *would* have done so, but the queen is at present blind, as it were, to her own interest, and perhaps death from the hands of the assassin will be her fate. The Cowled Eleven and their agents are slowly but surely drawing together the strings of their plot, and unless the queen—aye, and her favourites, are guarded, they will fall."

"And you have no means of finding out the real names of the Cowled Eleven, with the exception of Lord Blackmore?"

"I cannot answer that, my son."

"'Tis well. I seek not to know. I was born to obey you—and obey you I will."

"Ay, you are a true son. Do you know, Ronald, before you were born, I met with so many misfortunes that I no longer trusted in Heaven. But oh, do I not well remember the night when a merciful Providence, taking compassion on me, sent you into the world."

"And my mother—you do not speak to me of her."

"She was a gentle lady," replied the Hunchback, whose voice suddenly became husky.

"And she is dead?"

"Yes, she is dead."

"Has she been dead many years?"

"Yes—many, many years."

"How— But, no, I see that I have

pained you — pained you deeply. Pardon me, but I have so longed to hear of my mother."

The Hunchback was most violently agitated.

His lips trembled, his hands opened and shut nervously, and his large eyes glittered fiercely.

Ronald saw that some memory of the past was agitating him in no ordinary manner.

"I have nothing to pardon," said the mysterious being, in low, deep tones— "nothing—it is but natural that you should wish to know something of your mother. I have often been about to tell you, now that you have reached manhood's estate; but my heart has failed me, because you bear so striking a resemblance to her. I will tell you the story, but you must remember that it *will not be complete. The missing link will be supplied by-and-by.*

"Listen. Twenty years ago—nay, it is now twenty-one years ago—I first met your mother. She was then a young, light-hearted girl of twenty or thereabouts, and was the orphan child of a couple who were at one time well known in England and abroad, the father having been a sculptor.

"The father and I were friends— great, staunch, honest friends; but until his and his wife's death, I never saw the daughter. You see, I was appointed her guardian.

"The first time I saw her I was struck, not merely with her loveliness, which was simply perfection, but with her winning ways, and above all, with her superior education and intelligence.

"She knew very little of the world and its ways—very little. She was like a little child in simplicity. About three months after I first made her acquaintance I offered her my hand.

"She at once accepted me, just as a child might accept a present, and we were married. We were happy together—very happy. She loved me, but whether her love was as great as it should have been towards me I hesitate to say.

"I know that I idolised her. I loved the very ground she walked upon, Ronald. But by-and-by a change came over her. For some time I could not understand it—indeed I knew nothing until some time after your birth.

"I must tell you that I was frequently away from home on business, and by-and-by my confidential servant, a man named Dasson, who had been my father's servant before he became mine, wrote me several letters, which he despatched to London by special messenger.

"Those letters were intended to place me on my guard, and they did so. But I had then a deal of business at Court (for I was a great favourite of Henry VIII.), and consequently, could not devote that time and attention to the matter which otherwise I should have done.

"I have lived to regret it.

"One day a special messenger reached me with a letter. The contents I found of so urgent a character that I at once took horse and hastened to my home, which was at Norwich.

"I arrived there at night, unexpected and unseen. Oh, that night—that fatal night!" moaned the Hunchback, as he placed his hand for a moment across his eyes. "Never—never will the remembrance be shut out—never.

"With the assistance of the servant I have mentioned, I entered the house, and cautiously advanced to my wife's apartments.

"You, my son, were in your little cot fast asleep, while your mother was in the arms of— But his name you shall hereafter know.

"I burst the door open and stood on the threshold.

"The guilty pair, with a loud cry, started back, glaring at me as though I had been some foul fiend preparing to pounce upon them.

"I snatched my blade from its scabbard and made for the wretch who had weaned my wife's affection from me.

"But she—she rushed towards me and seized me by the arm, while her paramour, smashing the window to pieces, dashed through it and escaped.

"My rage knew no bounds. I was mad—mad. My brain was on fire. I could not pause to reason. No, I snatched my dagger from its sheath, and plunged it to the haft in your mother's breast.

"Instantly she ran to the cot,

snatched you up, and placed you in my arms. 'Your child,' she said, 'yours, as Heaven shall judge me.'

"Just as I took you she staggered back and fell.

"Her last words were, 'I am guilty—I am guilty. I deserve my fate, but spare him—spare him."

"Oh, Heaven!" gasped Ronald, "what a fearful story. My poor, misguided mother."

"'Spare *him!*'" she said, continued the Hunchback, "'spare *him!*' No, no, no; I would not spare him did I find him—but I failed. I relinquished my profession to hunt for him—to track him down. But 'twas useless.

"Then I learned that he had left the country and was residing in Spain. To that country I went and searched for him, but I found him not.

"It was on my return to England that I commenced to be known as the Hunchback. Occasionally I heard of the man who destroyed my happiness—I hear of him now, and I await him.

"He not long ago inherited a vast property in England, and one of these days he will return—yes, he will return—and I shall meet him face to face; and then my good sword will be eager for his heart's blood."

"He will deserve his fate," said Ronald.

"Yes, he will well deserve it. Years have not erased from *my* mind the foul wrong he did. The day will come, and I shall meet him, I say, and—"

"This man is no connection of Lord Blackmore, I suppose?"

"Not of the *present* Blackmore, but of the present Blackmore's *father* he was. But still, their connection, so far as I am aware, has nothing whatever to do with the matter. Now, my son, you must wait for the sequel, and until the time comes for that, let us not again refer to the matter."

Ronald bowed his head.

"I am content," he said. "I find no fault with what you did, for I should act in the same manner."

On the day after the medical gentleman was called in, the Hunchback, having seen that Stanley was being carefully tended by Ronald and Beatrice, set out on a journey.

Ronald knew whither he was bound, but he was the only one who possessed this knowledge.

Beatrice, who had now learned all about the affairs of our friends—at least, so much as the Hunchback deemed it advisable she *should* know—was not informed as to the destination of the Hunchback, in case she might inadvertently mention the matter to Stanley.

Our readers, no doubt, have guessed to what place the Hunchback was bound?

To Blackmore Hall.

Leaving St. Paul's by a subterranean passage (to which we shall have occasion to refer anon), he entered a boat just below Paul's Chain, and was rowed to the other side of London Bridge.

Here was situated a small street or alley, called "Caleb's Walk."

It consisted of a row of tumble-down wooden houses—or what had once been houses—and the footway in the centre of the passage was blocked with huge pieces of stone, wood, and so on, and to such an extent that the casual observer might have thought that they were the ruins of some building which had fallen.

But such was not the case.

These monstrous pieces of wood and stone had been placed there intentionally.

The object was to prevent the entry of anything like a large body of troops.

To the last of the houses went the Hunchback.

Passing round to the back, he instantly, and in the most mysterious manner, vanished.

What transpired within that miserable-looking house we need not say, but in less than an hour the Hunchback and two companions came forth, each mounted on a powerful horse.

Yet to look at the house one would have been prepared to lay a wager of a thousand crowns to one that there was no accommodation for *one* horse, let alone two or three.

Again, the Hunchback was attired in a totally different dress to the one he was wearing when he entered.

His attire was now rich in the extreme, and so also were the costumes of his companions.

Fine, tall, brawny fellows they were.

Each was well armed, though, with the exception of the pistols in the holsters, the weapons were concealed from view.

"One moment," said the Hunchback, as they reached the end of the Walk— "one moment. There can be no doubt but that we are setting out on a most dangerous journey. Before we go let us take a solemn vow that we will rescue the Lady Whitmore or perish in the attempt."

To this the Hunchback's companions agreed, and swore a vow, which was dictated to them by the Hunchback.

"You know my intention besides the rescue of this unfortunate lady," said the Hunchback. "It is to attempt to recover the body of the murdered lord, in order to give it decent burial beneath the roof of Old St. Paul's. But in that we might fail—circumstances might prevent us. Should such be the case, there will be plenty of time, and, no doubt, more opportunity in the future."

So the three set off.

Their journey was a long one.

*   *   *   *

The horse upon which Lady Whitmore was mounted was very fresh he not having been out of his stable for several days, and the consequence was that, directly he began to "feel his feet," he went along, in the manner of speaking, with the speed of a whirlwind.

Lady Whitmore soon found that she had lost all control of the steed.

Away, away he dashed, paying not the least heed to the rein.

Whither she was being taken, her ladyship could form no idea.

Though it was a beautiful moonlight night, and the roads in almost every part were light enough, she could not tell their names, nor recognise either of them as the road by which she and her murdered servants had travelled.

Danger appeared to be threatening her on all sides, for she considered (remembering that Lord Blackmore, Dacre Deadman, and the Cowled Eleven were absent) that it was not unlikely that she might fall into the hands of the enemy, and then, would they allow an opportunity for a second escape to occur? No.

Presently her ladyship heard a rushing sound, as of the falling of a heavy body of water.

Before she had time to think of what it might be, the horse plunged headlong into a mill-stream.

Fortunately, as it plunged—or *fell*, would be the more correct way of describing it—Lady Whitmore had the presence of mind to clutch at the overhanging bough of a stout willow.

Clinging frantically to this with both hands, she saved herself, for the horse fell bodily into the stream, leaving her partly in the water and partly in the air.

The swift, rushing stream carried the horse away like a straw.

He had no chance of swimming— away he went with wonderful rapidity, and was soon lost to sight.

Her ladyship, knowing that she could not, for any length of time, retain her position, cried as loud as she was able for help.

Again and again did she cry, but was only mocked by the echo of her own voice.

She looked about her on all sides, but saw not the least sign of a house.

On her left, though she saw it not, she could hear the unmistakable clatter of a mill-wheel; so that though she saw no signs of a dwelling-house, she knew that there must be one close to the wheel.

Again her voice rang over the rushing waters, and at last she saw, at some distance on the opposite side of her, the lattice of a window slowly open.

Oh, how eagerly, how intently did she fix her longing eyes on the spot.

She made out that a figure stood at the window, and that it was the figure of a woman.

Again she cried—

"Help! Oh, in the Virgin's name, I pray you, help!"

An answer was returned—

"Are you in the water?"

"Aye, here—here."

"Keep up your courage then, and I will come to your assistance."

Presently a light appeared directly opposite to her, and her ladyship now saw a young woman carrying in her right hand a lantern, and in her left a coil of stout rope.

Holding the former high over her

head, she flashed its rays over the water, and made out the black outline of Lady Whitmore.

"Save me?" cried her ladyship.

"I will save you." was the reply, "if you will do as I direct."

The young woman placed the lantern on the ground, and holding the coil of rope, swung it backwards and forwards a few seconds, and then let it go.

One end of it fell on the branch to which Lady Whitmore was clinging.

Lady Whitmore clutched at it.

When she had it firmly in both hands, she released her hold of the branch and dropped into the stream.

"Hold tight!" cried the young woman—"hold tight! or you will surely be swept away by the stream."

So saying, she commenced to draw in the rope.

She was a powerful young woman—a person evidently used to hard work—and very soon Lady Whitmore was hauled to the bank on which she stood.

Then stooping, she lifted her ladyship out of the water as easily as she would have lifted a child.

Not a moment too soon, for Lady Whitmore at once lapsed into unconsciousness.

When she recovered, she found herself in bed in a small, comfortably-furnished apartment.

A bright fire burned upon the hearth, before which her clothes were drying.

At a small table sat the young woman who had rescued her from certain death.

She appeared to be buried in deep thought, and from the expression on her face, her thoughts were not of the best.

Lady Whitmore raised herself, and her action at once aroused the young woman, who approached her, bearing a lamp.

"Let me look at you," she whispered.

Lady Whitmore held up her beautiful, but ghastly pale, sorrow-laden face.

"Ah," said the young woman, with a sigh of relief, "you are, or will soon be, all right if you take care of yourself. I thought an illness might overtake you, which would last a long time. I am glad such is not the case, for if you were confined here for any length of time, discovery would be certain, and death might follow—death to both of us."

"Heavens! what mean you?"

"What I say, lady."

"How long have I been here?"

"This is the third night You remember all? How you were in the water—"

"Yes, yes," interrupted Lady Whitmore, with a great sob. "I remember all. Heaven pity me!"

"Amen. You are an unhappy woman. I have gathered as much from what you have uttered in your unconsciousness. 'Unhappy' is hardly the word. I would not stand in your shoes, though you are Lady Whitmore."

"Ha! How know you this?"

"Your clothes told me as much."

"Yes, I am indeed Lady Whitmore, and an unhappy woman. Oh, so unhappy, so miserable. Pity me! Pity me!"

"I do pity you from the bottom of my heart. But I am the only one in this house who would pity you."

"Where am I?"

"You are at 'The Rover's Arms,' which is the property of my father, Elias Ellis, who also owns the adjoining flour mill."

"Then why am I in danger here, for I presume from what you say that I am in danger?"

"Aye, in great danger. Listen, lady"—and the young woman bent over her ladyship, and whispered in her ear—"I heard you talk of the Cowled Eleven and their leader, Lord Blackmore—of what bitter enemies they were towards you. Know then, lady, that this house is one of their secret places of meeting, that my father is the slave of these dreadful men, and that some of them will be here this very night."

"Then I am lost!" exclaimed Lady Whitmore, starting up still farther.

"Not yet—not yet! Silence! On your life—silence! See, I have washed out all your clothes and dried them. They are now airing for you, and will be ready in a few moments. Oh, lady, I would not send you from the house until you had fully recovered—but I must—I must."

"Help me out," said Lady Whitmore —"help me out, I pray you. I will at once leave. One kind friend lost her life through me—a *second* shall not fall. Never."

"Be guarded! Speak softly; servants are about, and those servants are my father's spies—and they would betray even me, if they thought it would bring a few miserable pieces to their pockets."

The kind-hearted young woman lifted Lady Whitmore from the bed and commenced to assist her to dress.

"I have had to resort to all sorts of extraordinary devices to conceal you," said the young woman, "and I trust that now— Hist!" she added, holding up her hand.

Loud conversation fell upon their ears, as well as loud laughter, and the rattle of arms and spurs.

The young woman rushed to the door, pulled it ajar, and listened.

And as she listened her face assumed a terrified expression.

Lady Whitmore watched her narrowly, and she instantly made out that something of an alarming character had occurred.

"What is it?" whispered her ladyship.

"They are here," replied the young woman, wildly; "they are here. Oh, lady, if you should be discovered, I shall surely lose my life, and so will my father, for they will adjudge him a traitor."

"It may not be too late to effect my escape," said Lady Whitmore. "Quick, I pray you. Let me finish dressing, and I will attempt it."

"'Tis useless, lady—'tis useless to attempt to descend those stairs until these wretches have departed."

"But the window?"

"The distance to the ground is too great. You would assuredly kill yourself did you attempt escape by this window. Listen, lady. You shall re-enter the bed, dressed as you are, and I will place the clothes over you in such a manner that it will appear as if the bed is simply in a state of disorder. Then if the—"

"But," interrupted her ladyship, "have these men authority to rove about the house just as it suits them?"

"Yes, they go and do just as it so pleases them. Though this house is my father's, those in whose pay he is can do just as it suits them. More than once I have found one of their number in this room."

"The persons below, you say, are those forming the council called the Cowled Eleven?"

"Aye."

"All of them?"

"No, perhaps one or two; the rest are the men they frequently take with them as a body-guard. But hasten, lady. Remain motionless as I shall place you, and good fortune may yet attend you. From time to time I will creep up and tell you how matters are progressing."

Lady Whitmore was soon fully attired and placed in bed, which the young woman so arranged that it really looked as if the clothes had only been thrown on the bed in a state of disorder.

This done the young woman opened a drawer on the table and took out a long, bright-bladed knife.

"Behold!" she said. "This is the only weapon I have to offer you. If unfortunately you *should* be discovered, I pray you, for the time being, to forget your sex and strike! It will not be murder, lady, to kill a man who forms one of this dreadful secret society."

"Fear it not—I will strike. But one moment. Do you know the names or the titles of either of those forming this society?"

"I do not. And I do not believe that my father does, except it is Lord Blackmore. If either of the names were told me, no doubt I should instantly forget them."

"And why?"

"Because all these foreigners have such strange-sounding names."

"Ha, these men are foreigners, then?"

"Aye, Spaniards."

"*Spaniards!* Ah, *now* I understand the meaning of my husband's oft-repeated, significant words: '*Spain and her emissaries will cause the Crown great uneasiness in the time to come.*' Spaniards! Heaven shield us."

Shortly after, Lady Whitmore was

alone, and, save for the small fire in the grate, in darkness.

Every now and then she heard shouts of boisterous laughter, and the most appalling oaths and curses.

The time passed, but oh, how slowly —how fearfully slow it seemed to her ladyship!

One hour seemed like ten.

Would she at last contrive to escape, or would it be her fate to be murdered as she lay?

With these thoughts agitating her, she was forced to think also of all the dreadful past.

From time to time, the kind-hearted young woman, as she had promised, made her appearance, and informed her of affairs below.

Once she said—

"There are two of them Spanish nobles, and men, according to my father, who think nothing of exercising at all times the utmost brutality towards both human beings and animals. At present, however, they do not seem inclined to stir from where they are. Still, be cautious. It will be quite unsafe to stir until they have taken their departure."

It was not, of course, only the "two of them" her ladyship had to fear.

It was also the numerous body-guard with which these two "Spanish nobles" were surrounded.

With these nobles were two Spaniards, named respectively Cholotto and Pedro.

Both were men of about forty years of age, and both were short and fearfully deformed.

They were the possessors of enormous heads.

Certainly no masks ever painted could have been more hideous than the faces of these two men.

These two individuals were tolerated —nay, not only tolerated, but paid good money—on account of the services rendered.

One did duty as secretary, and the other officiated as valet.

The secretary was Cholotto.

Both professed the blindest devotion to their masters, and—robbed them whenever they got the opportunity.

Not only did they rob their masters, however, but everyone else they could.

Their thieving fingers were never at rest, and the pair were always "knocking their heads together" in the concoction of plans for the swindling of anyone they considered likely to be in the possession of funds.

So they considered that Elias Ellis, being an innkeeper and a miller, was a bird worth plucking, and they resolved to pluck him accordingly—that is, of course, if they found the opportunity.

The two Spanish nobles, with Elias, were in one room, the guard in another, and the secretary and valet in a third.

The pair could therefore form their plans with little fear of interruption.

And the result of their deliberations was, that it was decided to make "an inspection" of the apartments above.

So while their masters and the guard were drinking and card-playing, the two very cautiously prepared to leave their room, which was on the same floor as the place where the liquors were drawn.

"I think," said Pedro, as he placed his finger to the side of his nose, and winked significantly at his companion, "it would be a wise thing to bar this door. You may not have observed that the old man's daughter has been going and coming pretty frequently since we have been sitting here."

"Oh, but little escapes *my* notice," grunted Cholotto, "and I *have* observed her. Yes, yes; as you say, it will be a wise plan to *accidentally* drop the bar."

The young woman who had been so kind and so thoughtful towards her ladyship, was at this moment engaged in drawing a tankard of wine from one of the many huge barrels, and her back was towards the door to which the Spanish blackguards referred.

Though it seemed that her attention was entirely fixed on what she was doing, such was not the case.

Her thoughts were entirely of the unfortunate lady upstairs.

So lost in thought was she that, as Pedro dropped the bar into the socket, she did not observe the slight noise it made.

Having thus secured the only person whom they considered likely to impede their movements, the two men crept cautiously along the passages, and commenced to ascend the stairs.

On the first landing they stopped,

and in the most unconcerned and audacious manner, entered one room after the other to search for valuables.

But Elias Ellis was not the kind of man to lay articles of value about, as though they were things worthy of little or no consideration.

The Spaniards found little or nothing—certainly nothing of value.

So they proceeded still farther upstairs.

At last they reached the room in which Lady Whitmore was concealed.

Oh, how the poor lady's heart beat as she heard them cautiously cross the threshold.

"Ah," said Pedro, "every room in the house, you see, is—"

"Ah!" interrupted Cholotto, as he pointed at the bedstead. "As I am alive I saw the bedclothes move."

"Bah!" replied Pedro, incredulously; "since no one is in the bed, how can the clothes move?"

"Nevertheless—"

"Let us see," said Pedro, who thereupon advanced to the bedside, seized the clothes and pulled them down.

Instantly Lady Whitmore started from the bed to the floor, the large, glittering blade clutched nervously in her hand.

For some few seconds no word was spoken by one or the other.

The Spaniards appeared thunder-stricken at this sudden and totally unexpected appearance, and they could only look idiotically into her ladyship's beautiful face.

But at last Cholotto recovered himself, and giving utterance to an ear-piercing yell, he started off downstairs, shouting "Murder!" at the top of his voice.

His companion was quick to follow, and in such a hurry was he to get down the stairs that he missed his footing and fell.

Coming in contact with Cholotto he sent him on his face, and over and over to the very bottom rolled the pair.

The noise made caused the guards to rush from their room in frantic haste.

There were about twenty of the guards, and they were led by a man nicknamed "Bald Bannister," on account of his having no hair either on his head or face.

The two Spaniards hastily informed him of their discovery, and the nobles, as well as Elias Ellis, were immediately on the scene.

"It's all nonsense!" cried Ellis. "They have seen nothing. There is not a woman in the whole house except my daughter, and she— Why, who has barred her in? I suppose the bar has dropped."

Here Elias Ellis pushed up the bar, and opened the door.

His daughter appeared, pale and trembling. She knew that her ladyship had been discovered.

Her father did not notice her paleness or agitation.

"Here, girl!" he said, sternly—"here! These men say that there is a woman upstairs, dressed in black, and holding a long dagger in her hand. And from what they say, this woman is in *your* room. Now contradict it, and so save the guard the trouble of going up."

The young woman turned first to one and then the other in an eager, nervous fashion, but she made no answer.

A cold perspiration broke out all over Elias' body.

Surely his daughter could not be deceiving him? he thought. Surely she understood the danger he and she stood in?

For if these two members of the dreaded council found that their men were speaking the truth, they would put him down as a traitor, and his death, he knew, would follow.

"Speak!" thundered Elias, grasping his daughter tightly by the wrist; "speak! I tell you—"

"Don't trouble her," said one of the noblemen, in an offhand, haughty manner; "don't trouble her. Though her tongue speaks not, her eyes do. The men are right. There *is* someone upstairs who should not be there. Elias Ellis, you know more of this matter than you choose to say."

On his knees fell Elias, and, raising his hands, he cried—

"Oh, gentlemen, gentlemen! believe me—believe me! I know nothing. I am in total ignorance of—"

The nobles waved their hands, as much as to say—

"We disbelieve you. Away!"

Turning to Bald Bannister, one of them said –

"You have our instructions. Proceed."

Bannister did not require to be told a second time.

He took the lead, and the whole of the men swarmed up the rickety old stairs.

Bald Bannister was the first to enter the room, and he instantly saw that the lady before him was a person of some importance.

He had seen her many times before, but where, or when, he could not call to mind.

Advancing further into the apartment, and allowing his men to swarm around him, Bald Bannister said, as he drew his sword—

"Lady—er—whoever you may be, I call upon you to lay aside that weapon and surrender."

No answer did her ladyship return.

Erect she stood, looking as one fascinated at the men before her.

She looked firm, but she was not so.

Her strength and her determination had alike forsaken her.

"Throw down that weapon!" shouted Bannister. "Do you hear me, madam? Throw it down instantly."

"I pray—I entreat of you—leave me in peace," replied her ladyship.

"A very likely request!" sneered Bannister. "Madame, we have orders to escort you below, so that you may be examined by persons in authority as to how and why you are in this apartment. So put down that weapon."

And he advanced a few paces.

"Stand back!" cried Lady Whitmore. "Stand back—lest I be tempted to drive this blade into your heart!"

"Oh, that's it, is it? Men, *present*."

Those of the guard who had their firearms with them, at once presented them.

They covered her ladyship's body, but she never stirred one inch.

Bannister looked at her, turned once more to the men, and again hesitated.

Whether he would have been brute and coward enough to order the men to fire, we are unable to say.

But before he could *give* another order, a slight commotion was heard— a slight figure bounded through the men, and in another second the innkeeper's brave young daughter stood before them.

Her eyes fairly blazed with passion as she stood, with clenched hands, confronting the men.

"Cowards!" she cried. "Monsters! —for you cannot call yourselves *men* —you who stand thus covering the body of a lady with loaded weapons— down with them! *Down* with them, I say."

And suddenly raising her hands, she dashed the muzzles of the weapons aside.

"Look you, my sweet maiden," sneered Bannister, "you had better take my advice, and not interfere with my business. You had—"

"You are in *my* apartment," interrupted the young woman.

"Very well," was Bannister's reply. "If we are, we shan't steal anything, nor stay very long. Now, will you have the goodness to request yonder lady to throw down that ugly-looking knife?"

"The hour has come," said Lady Whitmore, sadly, as she allowed the knife to fall from her hand. "The hour has come! I am fated to die a dreadful and ignominious death, and 'tis useless to struggle against my fate any longer."

"Oh, lady!" exclaimed the young woman, who was now wringing her hands in despair, "if any good could come of it I would defend you with my very life."

"I know it," answered her ladyship. "If—but no, I can give no promises— 'tis not in my power. But, let me see —did you give me your name?"

"I think so. It is Ruth Ellis."

"I will not forget. Oh," she said, in a whisper, "I do most fervently hope that this will not be the cause of your getting into serious difficulties."

"Do not trouble," answered Ruth. "I have already formed a plan of escape."

"Now then," cried Bannister, "you know well enough that the gentlemen are waiting."

Lady Whitmore, her white hands clasped on her bosom, walked slowly forward.

Bannister went first, and Lady Whitmore followed between two of the guard, the rest of the men bringing up the rear.

No sooner did she enter the room in which the nobles (who had each assumed a mask) awaited her, than a great cry escaped both.

"Lady Whitmore!" cried one.

"It is!" exclaimed the other. "Truly, this is most marvellous."

"And most fortunate," said the other.

"This wonderful discovery must be at once made a note of. Elias Ellis, procure pens, ink, and paper, so that a memorandum of the circumstances under which Lady Whitmore was found may be written down. Such a document will be required at the next meeting of the council. Holy Virgin! what news for the frantic Lord Blackmore."

Pens, ink, and paper were instantly produced by the host, who was now so terribly frightened that he fairly shook in his shoes, and Cholotto having been called, he was directed to seat himself and write what was dictated.

* * * *

While this was being done, Ruth Ellis, who knew perfectly well what was in store for her, had taken possession of what articles of jewellery she could lay her hands upon, and wrapping herself in a cloak, left the house by the back way, and fled across the fields, and so on into the high road.

Whither she would go, she knew not, but anywhere was better than to remain in her father's house, now that Lady Whitmore had been captured.

Along the dark, deserted road she sped, but when she had completed a mile, fatigue and the weight of her own thoughts overcame her, and flinging herself on the turf by the roadside, she burst into a passionate flood of tears.

Suddenly, however, she raised her head.

Were those horses' hoofs she heard?

She listened intently.

Yes, there was no doubt of it—she did hear horses' hoofs, and from their rapid beating it was evident that the animals were coming along at a swift pace.

She, however, made no attempt to rise, for she considered that the riders might be more of those in connection with Lord Blackmore—or it might be Blackmore himself.

In a few seconds she made out three horsemen riding abreast.

Two appeared very tall, while the centre was a much shorter man.

She crouched back, as if seeking to escape their observation.

But she was not successful, for, when opposite to her, a deep voice called out—

"Halt!"

The horses came to a standstill.

Ruth rose and turned her frightened eyes towards the horsemen.

They were masked.

Our readers have no doubt guessed that the horsemen were the Hunchback and his two companions.

"The hour is late," said the Hunchback, fixing his eyes upon the face of the innkeeper's daughter, "and young women should be in their beds."

Ruth cowered still further back, but suddenly she sprang forward, and standing directly before the Hunchback, looked steadily at his strange-looking figure.

"Ha!" she said, "I cannot, *cannot* be mistaken! You are he of whom *she* spoke—you are the Hunchback of Old St. Paul's?"

"True," answered the Hunchback; "and you? I have seen you before, but I cannot call your name to mind."

"Ruth Eilis."

"The daughter of Elias Ellis?"

"The same. Oh, quick, quick! Save her—save Lady Whitmore. She is now at my father's house, in the hands of two of the Cowled Eleven."

And Ruth hurriedly told them of her ladyship's escape from Blackmore Hall, and how she came to be at "The Rover's Arms."

"You must haste if you would save her," she concluded, in excited tones, "for she will be at once taken away. If you would follow me I can take you across the fields to the back. If you proceed on horseback along the road, the noise of your horses' hoofs will alarm the guard, and they will be ready for you."

"You speak truly," replied the Hunchback. "Lead on, and as fast as you can."

"SMASHING THE WINDOW TO PIECES, HE DASHED THROUGH IT AND ESCAPED."

No. 6

The three dismounted, and leading their horses, they turned after Ruth.

The Hunchback and his companions had to be extremely cautious, for, though the ploughed fields would bear the weight of a man, in many places a horse would sink almost to his knees.

But at last the back of the premises was reached without mishap.

*　　*　　*　　*

In slow and pompous tones the nobles dictated to their "scribe" the circumstances under which Lady Whitmore was found in the house.

Their tones were occasionally exultant, for they knew that a most important discovery had been made.

We may here mention that the horse on which her ladyship escaped from Blackmore Hall, and which plunged into the mill-stream, was found—drowned, of course—on the following morning, some couple of miles below the spot where it had plunged into the stream, and being recognised by one of the men at the Hall, the idea had gained ground that her ladyship had also met her death by drowning.

The writing being finished, the guard were ordered to prepare for departure.

"Where am I to be taken?" asked Lady Whitmore.

"To Blackmore Hall," was the reply. "And we will take particular care that you do not again escape."

"Blackmore Hall!" exclaimed her ladyship, as she clasped her hands convulsively together. "Blackmore Hall! Oh, the very name—"

"Silence!" shouted Bannister. "Keep what you have to say until you are before the council."

"You made sure of being able to escape to London," sneered one of the nobles, "but you see you are foiled."

"Ah, that I had," replied Lady Whitmore. "There I have friends who would protect me; there—"

"And may we venture to ask who is your *principal* friend?" asked one of the Spanish nobles, with an insulting sneer.

"The Hunchback of Old St. Paul's!"

In tones of thunder the words were spoken. The door at the further end of the apartment was burst open with such violence that it came partly off its hinges, and three masked men dashed in.

Each carried in his right hand a long, bright sword, and in the left a pistol.

"*Mark your men!*" cried the Hunchback.

Barely had these words left his lips, ere three shots rang out.

For some few seconds the apartment was completely filled with smoke.

When it lifted, Bannister, Cholotto, and one of the men forming the guard were found dead on the floor.

Again the Hunchback shouted—

"Fire!"

And three more shots rang out, each bullet finding a billet.

With wild yells the nobles and the men, who seemed so paralyzed with terror that they were unable to use their weapons, made a frantic rush to the door—we do not mean the door by which the merciless Hunchback and his mysterious companions had entered, but by the door *usually* used as an entrance to the apartment.

They flung all their weight upon it, but it yielded not.

And why?

Because Ruth Ellis had barred it on the outside.

"We will take care no harm comes to your father," the Hunchback had said. "He is part and parcel of Lord Blackmore's miscreants, but for your sake we will do him no injury. But let none of the others escape."

And Ruth accordingly had taken care that they did *not* escape.

The Spanish nobles, finding escape impossible, in despair ordered the men to fire, and they fired certainly, but with no effect.

The Hunchback started towards Lady Whitmore, and, taking her by the wrist, he said—

"Get behind us, my lady. No further harm shall happen to you."

"In the name of the Virgin, is it your intention to slay all of us?" roared the Spaniards, as they drew their rapiers.

"It is," was the Hunchback's grim reply. "The avengers spare no one."

So saying, the Hunchback and his companions strode forward, and attacked the nobles and the men with extraordinary fury.

Their blades seemed like flashes of lightning darting hither and thither, and dealing death on every side.

In less time almost than it takes us to write the account, the Spanish nobles were stretched lifeless upon the floor.

The fight became nothing more or less than a frightful slaughter.

Had the men properly defended themselves, it is a certainty that the fight would have lasted for a long time, and no doubt the Hunchback and his friends would have been wounded, if not killed.

But the men were so thunderstricken at the way in which they were being attacked, that instead of fighting, in the strict meaning of the word, they attempted to force the door.

But this was out of all question.

The ponderous oak bar resisted all their efforts.

Twice or thrice did Lady Whitmore, horror-stricken at what was being done, cry aloud for mercy on the villains.

And what was the Hunchback's reply?

"My lady, ask not for mercy for those who *show* none. Remember your husband. No mercy must be shown to these men, or the wretch who leads them—Lord Blackmore. Nothing but their deaths will satisfy us. No mercy will we show now, or at a future time!"

The fight did not last very long.

And not one of Lady Whitmore's enemies was left to tell the tale.

"Except Elias Ellis," the reader says.

No; he would never tell the tale.

And why?

While the fight was in progress, the old man had been crouching in a corner, crying and wringing his hands.

No doubt he expected every moment would be his last.

Into such a state did he work himself that his appearance became absolutely terrible.

When the fight was over the Hunchback turned to him.

He looked closely at him, and for a few moments listened to his mutterings. Then turning to his companions, he said—

"The man is mad! He raves—hearken to him! From his rambling statements no one will ever get to know what has occurred here."

Knocking on the other door, it was at once opened by Ruth.

Poor young woman!

What a dreadful shriek escaped her when her eyes rested upon the distorted face of her father.

"Mad!" she gasped. "He is mad!"

"He is," replied the Hunchback. "I pray you speak to him, and let us see whether he will recognise you."

Ruth did so.

She took him by the shoulders, and looking into his face, cried—

"Father!"

But it was useless.

His mind had gone.

"You will stay here with him," said the Hunchback, "and in a few hours assistance shall be sent to you. And let me impress this upon you—neither Lady Whitmore nor myself are likely to forget your great kindness. Now, do you know where we can obtain picks and spades?"

"There are many in the shed at the back of the house," replied Ruth.

One of the Hunchback's companions proceeded to the back, and having found the implements, the three set to work.

A large trench was dug by the side of the water, and in it the bodies of the slain were placed.

"This is but the commencement," said the Hunchback, grimly; "more of them will, I trust, soon follow."

Rejoining her ladyship, he said—

"And now, my lady, prepare for London. No further harm will happen to you while we are with you, for we will defend you with our lives."

"I know it," answered her ladyship; "and from the bottom of my heart I thank you. And my son, you say—"

"Is safe!"

"I thank Heaven!"

In less than half-an-hour, Lady Whitmore was mounted on a horse from Elias' stables, and the road to London was taken.

Her ladyship rode between the two mysterious friends of the Hunchback, while he brought up the rear.

On the road Lady Whitmore several times tried to converse with the Hunchback, but it was useless.

So deeply buried in thought was he, that it is questionable whether he heard her ladyship's voice.

CHAPTER VI.

IS OF THE MEETING IN THE CRYPT OF OLD ST. PAUL'S, AND OF THE TAKING OF THE OATH OF VENGEANCE—OF HOW STANLEY AND RONALD ARE ACCEPTED AS LEADERS OF THE PARTY—OF HOW THE HUNCHBACK SURPRISES THE FORMER, AND OF THE DEATH OF LORD BLACKMORE.

ANOTHER two days passed away.

Under the skilful treatment of the Hunchback's medical friend, Stanley recovered his usual health.

But not his spirits.

That, however, was not to be wondered at.

Several times he declared his intention to set out for Blackmore Hall, for not a word had he heard respecting the Hunchback's journey; but he was restrained by Ronald, who urged him to wait patiently.

During the interval, Swift had amused himself with exploring every hole and corner of the gloomy old crypt, and he succeeded in discovering several treasures, in the shape of books, small altar ornaments, and the like.

And Ronald had made good use of *his* time—for he most successfully made love to the pretty Beatrice—so successfully indeed, that, at the end of the fifth day, there was a very distinct understanding between them.

We return to the crypt on the night of the sixth day after the departure of the Hunchback.

The hour of eleven was striking, and the City might have been taken for a city of the dead, so silent was it.

In a bracket attached to one of the massive pillars in the crypt a link was burning, and by its light we are enabled to see two figures.

Stanley and Ronald.

Backwards and forwards they had been pacing for a length of time.

Stanley at last paused, and looking Ronald in the face, he said—

"And now, Ronald, answer me truly, do you not think something has happened to your father?"

Ronald's face was certainly very grave, but if he had any doubts as to his father's safety, he certainly did not show it to Stanley.

"No," was his reply; "I do not fear that anything has happened to him."

"Ronald, you are concealing something from me."

"I? No."

"Yes, yes, you are; I am certain of it. Did not that strange doctor who has been attending upon me bring you a letter early in the evening?"

"A slip of paper—that was all."

"Ah, from your father?"

"Nay, from someone else; but *who* I know not."

"You surprise me."

"No doubt. But here is the slip—read it yourself."

And Ronald took a slip of paper from his doublet and handed it to Stanley, who read as follows—

"The Avengers meet to-night in the vault below the crypt. Water."

"I understand it not," said Stanley: "do you?"

"Aye, quite well."

"Who are the Avengers?"

"A secret society."

"By whom directed?"

"By my father, or partly by him." .

"And their purpose?"

"You will hear anon."

"And what is the meaning of '*Water*'?"

"I was a long time ere I discovered what was meant. It evidently means that the members of this society will reach the crypt by water—by the Thames."

"Heaven above!" exclaimed Stanley, "how can that be, since the Thames is a long way from the cathedral?"

"From the crypt—or, rather, below this crypt—runs a subterranean passage."

"Ah, I understand. Well, well, all this is most mysterious. Your father was always a man of mystery, Ronald."

"I believe so," answered Ronald, gravely; "and he has his reasons for being mysterious."

"No doubt—no doubt. Well, though you think no accident has happened to him, I do. And listen to this, Ronald: I am now well enough to depart, and to-morrow I shall proceed to Blackmore Hall."

Ronald made no answer.

The time passed on, and very slowly to both Stanley and Ronald.

The hour of twelve commenced to strike, and ere the hammer had twice descended, both Ronald and Stanley heard a peculiar noise close to them.

It sounded like the gentle tapping of a hammer on iron.

Our readers are, of course, perfectly aware of the fact that Ronald was not acquainted with one quarter of the secrets of Old St. Paul's.

Imagine his and Stanley's intense astonishment when, the noise having suddenly ceased, a brilliant light appeared in the darkest part of the crypt, and from a square hole—made by the removal of a solid stone slab—a dark figure appeared.

In a second or two the light shone upon the face of this figure, and there were revealed the well-known features of—the Hunchback!

"Father!" cried Ronald, starting forward, "returned at last!"

"At last, my son—at last."

"No accident has happened to you? You are safe?"

"Aye, aye—safe and sound, my son. And how has Stanley fared?"

"I am now, thanks to your kindness and forethought, rapidly recovering my usual health. Oh, how thankful I am to see you again," said Stanley.

The Hunchback took his hand and warmly pressed it.

"But," continued Stanley, looking into his face, "you appear worried—agitated; something of importance has occurred?"

"True," answered the Hunchback, gravely, "something of vast importance has occurred. Stanley, this night, you will find, will be one of vast importance to you. But come, I have a long, long story to tell you. Ronald, do you accompany us."

"But will you not partake of some refreshment?" asked Ronald.

"Nay, I will partake of nothing but a glass of strong wine. No time is to be lost."

"No time is to be lost so far as *I* am concerned," said Stanley; "for I am determined to set off in search of my mother."

The Hunchback started.

"I have your interests at heart. You may rely upon that," he said; "and after all I have done for you, you cannot do less than grant me a favour."

"That is?"

"That you will allow six hours to pass ere you leave this cathedral."

"Well, I will do as you wish."

"Come then—quickly."

Down into the vaults went the three.

The Hunchback's "den," as he himself called it, was a stone apartment, in size about twelve feet by eight.

The roof, which was somewhat low, was supported by six pillars—three on each side; and around these, and on the walls, arms—intended for use, not for ornament—were hung.

In the centre of the apartment was a large and curiously-carved oak table, and at the further end a couch.

Beyond these and a number of blocks of wood, which did duty for chairs, the apartment could boast of but little furniture.

A large number of books and documents were scattered about in a state of indescribable confusion, and at one end was a small recess, in which was a bed.

Our readers may feel inclined to ask—

"And did the proper authorities know of the existence of this place?"

We cannot say that it was known to many, but that it was known to the verger of the cathedral was a positive fact, as also that the Hunchback had been in the habit of using it for years.

This apartment was the one bright spot among the host of gloomy and damp-smelling vaults, and though so small, it contained half-a-dozen secret doors leading in various directions.

There can be hardly any doubt but that the architect of this cathedral had accepted the suggestions of many interested persons as to the construction of these secret places, but it must have been left to his own powerful brain to have thought of and constructed the subterranean passage which was discovered by the Hunchback.

It was a masterpiece.

The entrance to it was *beneath the table!*

The close observer might have noticed that there were twenty-four blocks of wood, and that each block was of exactly the same size as the others, with the exception of one, and that this one was at the head of the table.

Now this particular block was the Hunchback's seat, and it also held the secret of moving the massive stone beneath the table.

Our readers will see how it acted anon, and they will agree with us that its construction, and the construction of the vault below—whither we shall conduct them—were alike marvellous.

When our three friends entered they found Beatrice seated on one of the blocks, attentively perusing a ponderous volume.

Swift was at her side, his noble head in her lap.

"What do you read, sweet maiden?" asked the Hunchback.

"I am reading 'Grafton's Stories of Mighty Wrongs,' which I discovered among yonder books."

"No doubt you find them interesting," replied the Hunchback, with a sigh; "but put it aside now and listen to the story *I* will tell. You will find it far more interesting than anything you can find there."

"Since I know at least one of the characters," replied Beatrice, "it must, of course, prove far more interesting."

The Hunchback and our friends seated themselves at the table, and the former repeated the story he had told Ronald, and then Stanley learned *all*—*except his mother's rescue.*

Oh, his terrible agony—his frantic and awful vows of vengeance.

But by-and-by a calmness took the place of his ravings, and he placed himself in the hands of the Hunchback.

* * * *

The hour of one struck, and the Hunchback, rising, took the lamp from the table, and going from pillar to pillar, lit several links which were affixed to them.

The vault was thus brilliantly illuminated, and such a weird appearance did it present, that Stanley felt a strange chill creeping over him.

"The time has come," said the Hunchback, "and you will now see the persons who are known among themselves as the Avengers. You will not see their features, because each man will be masked. Now listen."

Silence reigned for some minutes.

Suddenly the distant sound as of a gong being struck was heard.

It seemed to Stanley as if the sound came up from the very bowels of the earth.

The Hunchback started up, and removed the top portion of the block of wood on which he had been seated.

A steel handle was exposed to view.

This the Hunchback pulled.

A sharp crack rang out, and Stanley darted back as he felt that the stone on which his feet had been resting had been drawn suddenly back.

"Now," said the Hunchback, as he pushed the table aside and took down a link, "follow me."

Stanley looked down the dark hole, and by the aid of the torch saw a number of stone steps.

"This, then," he said, "is the subterranean passage of which you have spoken?"

"It is; but you need not descend unless you think proper," replied the Hunchback.

"I am not afraid, and will follow you."

"This passage might be of service to you and my son some day, and it will be just as well if you make yourselves acquainted with it. Be careful how you go, for the steps are very slippery."

Raising his torch high over his head, the Hunchback commenced the descent, followed by Stanley and Ronald.

Down, down they went.

The distance to the passage was not so great as one might have thought.

In a few moments the three stood in it.

"What think ye of this?" asked the

Hunchback. "What think ye of this for human ingenuity? Behold the massive supports! Is it not wonderful?"

"Extraordinary!" exclaimed Stanley.

"And, so far as I am aware," said the Hunchback, "the existence of this passage is only known to me and, through me, to my friends. I discovered it some years ago, but it took me a long, long time to discover the secret of *this*. Now—"

"But," interrupted Stanley, "since this passage leads to the Thames, does not the water flood in at high tide?"

"That is precisely what I am about to show you," replied the Hunchback. "Come."

Two hundred yards were covered, and then the Hunchback came to a sudden standstill.

"Look here," he said.

Stanley and Ronald looked.

The passage appeared to have terminated, but such was not the case.

"This looks like a solid wall, does it not?" said the Hunchback, as he pointed to what looked like a wall right across the passage.

Stanley nodded.

"But," continued the Hunchback, "I will show you that such is not the case."

So saying, he handed Ronald the torch, went to the wall on the left side, and removed a piece of stone.

A dark recess was revealed.

Plunging his hand in this, the Hunchback brought out a large iron handle.

This he placed on a steel knob, and then commenced to turn.

Lo! what appeared to be a wall began to move.

Slowly— almost imperceptibly — it moved back, and as it receded not the slightest sound was heard.

At last the wall had moved right back, and the passage was open.

The Hunchback, with a smile of triumph, turned to Stanley.

"There," he said, "now you are acquainted with one of my greatest secrets. That which appears a wall is no wall at all, but a solid piece of iron painted to *resemble* a wall. When I discovered it it was nothing but a rusty door."

"Then whoever restored and painted it so marvellously true to nature was a clever painter," said Stanley.

"Ay, so men said," answered the Hunchback, with a sigh. "So men called me years ago—years ago."

"Do you mean to say that *you* painted it, father?" asked Ronald.

"Yes, my son, I do," was the reply. "But now the passage is clear. You see now, Stanley, that it is this door which shuts off the water when the tide is high."

"I do."

"This is as far as you will go. I need only say that this passage is about five hundred yards long, and that the end of it resembles the entrance to a sewer, and no doubt that is what it has been taken for. Now, Ronald, conduct Stanley above while I receive our friends."

*   *   *   *

In five minutes the Hunchback returned.

Hardly had he crept from the aperture leading to the vault, than he was followed by a tall, cloaked, and masked figure.

Another and another followed, until at last no less than twenty mysterious-looking figures stood within the vault.

Stanley and Ronald surveyed them in wonder.

As for Beatrice, she had risen and cowered behind a pair of heavy curtains which concealed the recess in which was the bed sometimes, but very rarely, used by the Hunchback.

Swift, too, had become very uneasy at the appearance of these strange figures, and growling threateningly, he stood watching them as one by one they came up the aperture.

When all had come up, the spring was set in motion, the stone at once resumed its position, and the table was placed straight.

The masked men then ranged themselves around the table.

The Hunchback took his position on the block we have described, Stanley a position on his right hand, and Ronald one on the left.

The Hunchback, after a brief pause, called to Beatrice.

Tremblingly she came forward.

"You need fear nothing, sweet

Beatrice," said Ronald. "All these gentlemen are our friends. Is it not so, father?"

"Aye—firm friends. Fear nothing, my girl. There is not a man here who would injure you. Is this not so, gentlemen?"

The mysterious individuals murmured an assent.

Beatrice was reassured, but she felt very far from easy; and this was not to be wondered at—the appearance of these men was enough to inspire terror to the stoutest heart.

"Beatrice," said the Hunchback, "fetch me the basket which stands behind the curtains."

Beatrice did as desired, and placed it on the table.

The Hunchback opened and took from it a large silver flask, a couple of dozen small silver goblets, and a golden crucifix.

Opening the flask, he filled every goblet to the brim with its contents, and these were passed round.

The crucifix was next placed in the centre of the table.

"Hats off!" cried the Hunchback.

Every head was instantly uncovered.

And now, amid solemn silence, the Hunchback said—

"Health, long life, and happiness to Queen Elizabeth, and confusion to her enemies!"

The toast was drunk with great enthusiasm.

If Stanley had any doubts as to the loyalty of these men, they were now removed.

Again the goblets were filled and handed round.

The Hunchback's face now assumed a fearful expression—an expression of terrible hate—and, raising his glass in his left hand, he drew his sword, and in tones of thunder, shouted—

"Vengeance on the Cowled Eleven, and their fiendish leader—Blackmore."

Instantly twenty bright blades flashed in the glare of the torches, and twenty voices fiercely shouted—

"Vengeance!"

The goblets were raised on high, and the points of the swords touched the crucifix.

So heartily did Stanley and Ronald agree with this vow that they, too, drew their blades and mingled the points with the others.

A more stirring and striking picture than the party now presented was surely never imagined.

There was no mistake about this terrible vow.

The Hunchback and his friends meant to carry out what they had sworn; their determination was apparent in their flashing eyes and compressed lips.

Amid another cry of "Vengeance!" the goblets were drained.

"Gentlemen," said the Hunchback, "two members of this infamous council are wiped off the face of the earth, but others remain, and the leader, Blackmore, is becoming more powerful in a place where by rights he has no business to be—I mean at Court. I cannot understand what influence it is he has brought to bear upon the queen, but it is certain that she listens, and with great attention, to all he pours into her ear. But even if this were not so he should die.

"Oh, the monster—the atrocious ruffian! What sort of heart must the man possess who puts a fellow-creature to a dreadful death, and drags his wife to witness it?"

Again a loud cry of "Vengeance!" left the lips of everyone present.

"Since proceedings must be commenced at once," resumed the Hunchback, "it becomes us to select a leader. I know you will say that I am the proper person, but I am not so young as I was. Lately I have found that I am not so well able to withstand fatigue as I once was. So, gentlemen, I will make a proposal. Who so fitting to be the one to lead in this mission of vengeance, than the son of him who was for so long our guiding star—he who tried so hard to put down a society which he saw was becoming dangerous to his queen and country? I mean Stanley Whitmore."

"We accept him—we accept him!" was the cry.

"And will obey him?"

"In anything honourable."

"Hold!" cried Stanley; "you have not consulted me. I feel quite unable to lead men who are my elders—men who have had far greater experience of the world than have I."

"I will second you," said Ronald; "I am with you whenever and where-ever you may require me."

"If that is so," replied Stanley, "I hesitate no longer."

"You accept?" asked the Hunch-back.

"With all my heart. And were my dear mother here," said Stanley, with trembling lips, "I am sure she would approve of my resolution."

"You shall see her—*at once!*"

"What!" almost shrieked Stanley; "see her—here—at once! Oh, impos-sible! You are a mysterious man—a man possessed of wonderful powers, but you do not possess the power to snatch my mother from the clutches of a murderous villain, and transport her here!"

The reader, of course, remembers that the Hunchback had not told him of his mother's rescue.

"You will see," was the Hunchback's reply.

Stanley trembled, and it was with the greatest difficulty that he con-trolled himself.

Ronald's friendly voice served him in good stead.

It was Ronald who urged him to be patient for a few moments.

Raising his voice, the Hunchback said—

"Come forth, my friend."

A curtain at the extreme end of the vault was drawn aside, and the figure of the physician who had attended Stanley came into view.

Straight up the vault he walked, simply bowing as he passed, and entered the recess which contained the bed whereon the Hunchback sometimes rested.

This recess communicated with the subterranean passage, but no one had ever been that way except the Hunch-back.

In a few moments the physician re-appeared.

"Well?" queried the Hunchback.

"All is well," was the answer.

Then, leaning over, the physician whispered something in the Hunch-back's ear.

What he said appeared to be very satisfactory to the Hunchback, who, heaving a sigh of relief, turned to Stanley.

"You are agitated," he said, "and 'tis not to be wondered at. Come."

Stanley and Ronald, and, indeed, every man present, followed the Hunch-back to the recess.

The Hunchback seized a silken rope, pulled it, and the curtains moved back.

And now a great cry of astonishment and joy escaped our hero's lips as he looked at the wondrous sight before him.

To the ceiling of the recess was affixed a silver lamp.

Its rays, protected and softened by a shade, were thrown upon the bed be-neath.

It was a small bed of black oak, and hung with dark, heavy curtains.

Lying upon it was the figure of a beautiful woman.

Lady Whitmore.

Her head was raised upon a richly-worked pillow, her white hands were crossed upon her heaving bosom.

She was sleeping—calmly, peace-fully.

Stanley was about to rush forward, but the Hunchback restrained him.

"Hush!" he said. "Wake her not, or you destroy the labour of hours! This is the first calm sleep your mother has had for many days."

"In the name of Heaven!" cried Stanley, "tell me, how did she get here?"

"*I* brought her here," was the calm reply. "I and two of my friends rescued her from certain death. This is the other part of the story which I shall tell you."

Stanley threw his arms about the Hunchback, and, with the tears falling down his cheeks, blessed him again and again.

The Hunchback's eyes glistened with delight, and as to Ronald—well, he considered his father one of the bravest and best of men.

The whole party now seated them-selves at the table, and the subject under discussion was the capture of Lord Blackmore.

"That is the first thing," said the Hunchback, "and that we shall easily get hold of him there can be no doubt.

But though we slay him, Dacre Dead-man would at once jump into his place, and I believe that he would prove a greater fiend than Lord Blackmore. In securing the capture of Dacre Deadman we shall have to be ex-ceedingly cautious, for he is as cunning as a fox, and can smell the hunters afar off. I have ascertained that to-morrow night Lord Blackmore will be at Rox-burgh House at Hampton Court. I can guess his business with Lord Roxburgh —aye, only too well."

"Stay!" said Stanley, excitedly; "stay! Lord Blackmore is answerable to *me* for my father's death. I will seek him out—I alone—"

"Stop one moment," interrupted the Hunchback. "Since it is your desire, you *shall* seek him out—but not alone. Nay, that will never do. Blackmore will be surrounded by his friends, for to-morrow night my lord of Roxburgh is pleased to give another of his brilliant entertainments ; and so, you see, there will be plenty of his and Blackmore's friends present. If you go, you will take Ronald and ten men with you. With Ronald and ten avengers at your call you need not fear anything."

"It is well," answered Stanley. "Only too readily do I consent to their accompanying me, though I should not have asked for their assist-ance, considering it my duty alone to—"

"You are mistaken," interrupted the Hunchback ; "you have been chosen leader—Ronald is your second. You have but to command—we to obey."

Stanley bowed.

"I cannot understand even now," he said, "why it is I have been chosen leader."

"You are higher in the social scale than any of us," was the Hunchback's reply, "and some day, when all the facts and circumstances are laid before the queen, you—who no doubt, by this time, are deprived of your estates and the title rightfully yours—will be *re-stored* to your rights, and you will then see more clearly why you were chosen leader."

Before the party separated the ten men—fine, tall, powerful fellows, two of them being the couple who accom-panied the Hunchback on his journey,

and dealt death on all sides of them—were selected, and they were to meet Ronald and Stanley at Charing Cross on the morrow.

Stanley and Ronald remained at the cathedral until it was time to set out.

Lady Whitmore, after having en-joyed at least twelve hours' sleep, awoke to find the loving eyes of her son fixed upon her.

Oh, the rapturous joy of that re-union.

The Hunchback informed her lady-ship that it would not be safe for her to leave the cathedral, and that she was to make herself as comfortable as possible, and this her ladyship at once agreed to do.

"You need not fear that anything will happen to you here," said the Hunchback. "Beatrice will be your companion, and Swift will be your protector. But should anything alarm you, Beatrice knows the secret of the subterranean passage. I would not leave you, *but I have most important business with the queen.*"

"The queen!" exclaimed her lady-ship ; "will the queen see you?"

"Aye."

"Oh, should she grant you an audience," cried Lady Whitmore, fer-vently, clasping her hands and raising her tearful eyes, "you will remember me? You will lay before her majesty the terrible wrongs I have suffered—my husband's awful death—my own—"

The Hunchback raised his hand.

A grim smile rested upon his face as he said—

"Your ladyship knows that the war-rant for my arrest still holds good; therefore it is out of all character that the queen would *grant* me an interview. But I shall see her, nevertheless, and you need not fear that I shall forget you. It is upon your business, and the business of your son, that I am bound."

That night Lady Whitmore and Beatrice found themselves alone in the vaults of Old St. Paul's, with Swift as a protector.

* * * *

Lord Lionel Roxburgh was a mighty personage.

At least he was so considered by the majority of people, owing to the fact that he was the possessor of enormous wealth.

Some few months before our story commences, his father died, leaving him in full possession of everything.

Lord Lionel had then just turned his twenty-fifth birthday.

For some five years he had lived in London, and had been allowed a fine income by his father, who, being an invalid, was always confined to the mansion at Hampton Court, which was known, and is still known, as "Roxburgh House."

Lord Lionel was supposed to be a worthy successor to the Roxburgh estates, because it was said he possessed all the splendid qualities of his father, who was a soldier, a scholar, a courtier, and, moreover, a perfect gentleman.

But to speak the truth, young Lionel possessed none of these excellent qualities.

Though he had had the most competent teachers, he was a thorough dunce at twenty.

As to soldier-like qualities, he possessed not an atom, and he was very far indeed from being a perfect gentleman.

In London, according to his father's information, he was "studying State papers and affairs ;" but then this information was supplied to his father by those in the pay of the son.

Under the name of Waldeck, he carried on a terrible game in London.

The name of "Waldeck," in fact, became a household word.

Lord Roxburgh heard of the doings of this person and shuddered.

Little did he dream that this very individual was his own son.

When the old lord died, and young Lionel came into possession of the property, he immediately set about making "ducks and drakes" of it.

The old steward, who had been on the estate for many years, and who had the entire control of it, happened to speak to Lord Lionel in reference to his reckless waste, and ventured to warn him as to what would follow if he persisted in giving magnificent banquets to his friends, and finding apartments and expensive clothing and jewellery for a dozen or so "ladies," who each fought for the exclusive

right to the extravagant young lord, and was dismissed.

One of Roxburgh's principal friends was Lord Blackmore.

He was old enough to be Lionel's father, it was true ; but, according to the thoughtless young lord's idea, he was a splendid "guide," and as such was to be valued.

Lord Lionel agreed with him in everything, and, though he did not form one of Blackmore's terrible council, he supplied them with a large amount of money for "current expenses."

On the particular night of which we write, a banquet—or perhaps we should be more correct in saying a mad debauch—was to take place, and the "nobility and gentry" had been invited in such numbers, that the servants wondered how they were to be accommodated.

For the first time, rooms which had been used only as libraries, studies, and picture-galleries were thrown open, and books, objects of art—everything in the way, in fact—had been unceremoniously thrown out, and tables laden with plate and glass took their place.

Lord Lionel had caused the grounds, for a space of some ten acres, to be cleared, so that dancing might be indulged in by those who liked the amusement.

Enormous oaks and elms, the pride of the old lord, were mercilessly cut down to make more room, and the most beautiful flower-beds were destroyed wherever they "stood in the way."

The trees, bushes, summer-houses at the side and in the centre of the two ornamental lakes, were brilliantly illuminated with small lamps of various colours.

On the edge of one of these lakes was posted a band of musicians.

The night was a beautiful one, and the scene in the grounds was of the most brilliant description, and the brilliancy was added to as the guests, attired in all the colours of the rainbow, commenced to arrive.

If the cards of invitation had been sent only to members of the nobility and gentry, it is certain that other individuals of far less importance not only presented themselves, but were admitted.

It was close upon the hour of ten, when a horseman, beautifully attired, and who was distinguished by wearing a very long silken cloak, fastened with a golden eagle adorned with brilliants, drew up before that portion of the grounds where the admission tickets were being taken.

There was a small crowd of ladies and gentlemen, eager to gain admission, and so the horseman drew his beautiful steed aside, and waited until all had entered.

Then he advanced.

"Your ticket, my lord!" exclaimed the man on duty at the gate.

"I have none," was the reply.

"Then you can't be admitted. I have strict orders not to allow any but those with tickets signed by his lordship to pass this gate. So if you have mislaid your ticket, you had better find it, your worship."

"Does your master teach you to be insolent to his guests?"

"You are *not* a guest if you have no ticket," chuckled the man, "and you might have *guessed* that. But, oh, what is this? Stand aside—stand aside!" shouted the man, as he rudely pushed aside several persons who at this moment made their appearance; "stand aside — Lord Blackmore's coach."

As he said this a ponderous coach, drawn by four spanking grey horses, rumbled up.

The horseman instantly backed his steed and sprang to the ground.

He was none other than Stanley Whitmore.

Backing his horse in the shadow of one of the trees, he crept forward and saw within the coach two figures, and he at once recognised them as Lord Blackmore and Dacre Deadman.

Both were beautifully dressed, and profusely decorated with jewels.

As soon as the carriage rolled on, the crowd pressed forward, and Stanley pushed his way among them.

The man took the tickets as fast as he was able, grumbling the while because the people appeared to be in such haste.

Stanley, watching his opportunity, gave one of the people a violent push.

The effect was to cause the man to topple over, and in his fall he brought half-a-dozen others to the ground, including the ticket-collector.

While they were struggling to regain their feet, Stanley stooped, stretched out his hand, and, placing it within the ticket-taker's bag, which hung at his side, he took out a handful of tickets, and, transferring them to his own pocket, quietly returned to his horse, mounted, and rode off.

At a distance of a hundred yards, eleven horsemen awaited him.

All were remarkably well attired, their persons being decorated with gold chains and diamonds.

Though they wore no masks, and though their attire was altogether different to what we saw them wearing in the vaults of Old St. Paul's, there was little difficulty in guessing who they were.

A more determined-looking set of men could not have been met with.

Each, like Stanley, was remarkably well mounted.

As Stanley joined this group Ronald rode forward.

"I have succeeded," said Stanley, who thereupon described how he had got possession of the tickets.

"No doubt," said he, "we have a strange collection of names. Lord This, Lady That, the Earl of This or the Other, and so on; but that is a matter of no importance, for the man at the gate does not read the cards. Indeed, 'tis doubtful whether he can read at all."

"So much the better for us," replied Ronald. "And now what do you suggest?"

"This," answered Stanley: "We must present our cards one at a time, and at intervals. Thus we shall disarm suspicion. While I stood at the gate I observed, some distance down the avenue of trees, a pavilion, on which is floating the standard of England. It is at that spot that we will meet. I should not be surprised if the persons who form the council are with Lord Blackmore. If they are, we have no means of ascertaining whether they are members of the Cowled Eleven, for to-night, of course, they will not be wearing the dress and the diamond daggers with which they choose to distinguish themselves at Blackmore Hall. We must watch our opportunity to strike. And, by Heaven's grace, we *will* strike. Lord Blackmore does not see the dawn of another day, if Heaven guides my hand."

"Let us at once push on," said Ronald.

"Aye, on," cried Stanley ; "and I will go first."

The cards were distributed among the men, who, setting spurs to their horses, galloped off in various directions, the idea being to approach the entrance by different routes.

Stanley was the first at the gate.

The man instantly recognised him, and said—

"Have you found the pass, worshipful sir ? "

"I have," answered Stanley, as he presented his card.

The man took it, and allowed our hero to pass.

In a few more moments Ronald rode up, presented his card, and was admitted.

For an instant, however, he thought that discovery was inevitable, for the man, taking the card to a lantern, looked curiously, as Ronald thought, at it.

But it was not to read it that the man looked at it, but to see its colour, there being two colours issued—pink and blue, the former for the nobility, and the latter for the gentry.

Ronald soon saw that the man could *not* read, for the card he presented was inscribed—

"The Earl of Glendowry."

Ronald passed on, and at intervals of a few moments, the mysterious individuals who had taken the ominous name of the Avengers, came up.

Unquestioned, they passed on and mingled with the crowds of gaily-attired men and women.

It was soon apparent as to what sort of carnival this banquet would turn out, for on every side the most costly wines and spirits were dispensed with a liberal hand by the lacqueys in the pay of the profligate young lord.

Lord Blackmore's coach was driven up to the front of the mansion.

Standing on the broad marble steps was Lord Lionel Roxburgh.

He was surrounded by a host of titled friends and admirers (?), the ladies by no means forming the minority.

The coach having drawn up, the door was opened by lacqueys in attendance, and Blackmore stepped from it.

He was quickly followed by Dacre Deadman.

But though Blackmore was "heartily" greeted by the assembled ladies and gentlemen, and warmly welcomed by the host, Dacre Deadman was not so received.

We have previously remarked that he was beautifully dressed.

He was, but it was in the colour he was so much at home in—black.

On this occasion it was black velvet, fitting tightly almost to the skin.

It was relieved only at the throat and wrists by cream-coloured lace.

The jewels he wore must have been worth an enormous amount.

These had been lent to him by Lord Blackmore, who, if ever he kept an eye on his illegitimate son, did on this particular night, for he was perfectly well acquainted with the fact that no eel was so slippery as Dacre Deadman.

"My lord ! " cried Lionel, "I am delighted to welcome you—and—and —er—and *you*, Master Deadman."

"No doubt," replied Dacre, with an ill-disguised sneer ; "but from your hesitating manner you might lead other people to think differently."

Lord Blackmore bent over to Dacre, and whispered in his ear—

"Beware ! Remember what I told you. Disobey my orders again, and you will rue it."

Dacre uttered a growl, and slunk back.

He thought there was something fresh between Blackmore and Roxburgh.

Determined to find out what it was, he kept his eyes on the pair.

"You see I responded to your invitation," said Blackmore, "and Dacre— But did you really intend the invitation to extend to Dacre ? "

"No—emphatically no ! I inserted that in the note purely as a matter of form."

"Bad form then," said Blackmore, shaking his head—"remarkably bad form. I should not advise you to do the like again."

"I would I had been aware that it was not your lordship's wish that Dacre should accompany you on every occasion. You may rely upon it that I should not have mentioned him. It is a sad thing that your lordship should be so saddled."

"True, Roxburgh—true," answered Blackmore, in moody tones; "but I made the yoke and must wear it. He has been very useful though, Roxburgh —*very* useful. You see he is my *broom*, and for the scrapings which I occasionally throw to him he is willing to *sweep away all dirt* which I point out."

These words were overheard by Dacre.

He gnashed his teeth with rage, and looked ready to spring upon the pair.

As Roxburgh accompanied Blackmore up the stairs, the latter continued—

"He has done a lot of work for me in the past, and he will do a *little* more; then—"

"Then?" queried Roxburgh.

"Then," resumed Blackmore, calmly, "there will no longer be a Dacre Deadman."

"I understand," said Roxburgh, laughing softly. "By-and-by, when he has decapitated all your enemies, he will himself be decapitated?"

"I am not prepared to say how he will die," smiled Blackmore, "but die he will. He knows too much, Roxburgh."

"So I have often thought."

"And though I trust him in many things, he knows not one fourth part of my concerns. It would be the height of folly to trust him with all."

"So I have often thought," repeated Lord Lionel, who, as a matter of fact, had thought nothing at all of the matter. "But have you heard aught of Lady Whitmore?"

"Nothing," answered Blackmore, knitting his brows fiercely.

"Nor the Hunchback?"

"I have heard something of his and his son's proceedings. Let them wait. I will tell you what it is, Roxburgh—

though at Court I am creeping up the ladder, though I am so lucky in everything I undertake in that direction, I am unlucky in every other."

"I am sorry to hear it."

"Yes; two of the council, Don Ferdinand Gaspard and Siro Saveaux have in the most unaccountable manner disappeared."

Our readers will, of course, see that Blackmore referred to the two individuals slain by the Hunchback and his friends.

"You surprise me!" exclaimed Lord Lionel.

"No doubt. But not only have they disappeared, but a number of men who acted as their guard, together with a couple of Spaniards who acted as scribe and valet respectively, also."

"Wonderful! Probably this mysterious Hunchback could say something about it?"

"I have thought the matter over, but I cannot connect him with their disappearance; but there is still *another* surprising thing. Elias Ellis, who kept 'The Rover's Arms'—you have heard me speak of him?—has suddenly gone mad! Now he and his house were very useful to us. So that is another advantage lost."

"What caused him to lose his reason?"

"Heaven alone can tell—at least, that is what his daughter says."

"You have seen him?"

"Oh, yes—and questioned him. All to no purpose, however. The man's mind appears to be a perfect blank."

"But don't you think that if you engaged the services of a couple of the most skilful physicians, reason might be restored to him?"

Blackmore shook his head.

"Hopeless," he muttered—"hopeless! I have seen many lunatics, but never knew a more hopeless-looking case."

By this time they had arrived on the landing at the top of the grand staircase.

Here was another crowd of ladies and gentlemen.

Lord Lionel hastily led Blackmore through the throng, passed through one of the rooms set out for the supper, and thence into an ante-room.

It was a small, beautifully-furnished apartment.

At the farther end was a small recess, concealed by a pair of heavy Oriental curtains.

Over it, on a gold shield, was a silver dice-box with dice, and around that were several cards.

This was the profligate and eccentric young lord's idea of showing that this apartment was the "gaming saloon."

The room was brilliantly illuminated by a large silver globe, from which sprang a number of graceful cherubs holding lamps.

Around the centre table were a number of gentlemen, who from their dress and general appearance were persons of importance.

As soon as Blackmore entered the apartment, the game which they were interested in stopped, and each individual, hastily rising, bowed low.

Blackmore returned the bow.

"My lords and gentlemen," he said, "I need not say how pleased I am to see you here. I was thinking that our young friend Roxburgh, though he did not intend it, has done us a great favour in holding this banquet, inasmuch as it has brought us together at a most opportune moment, and under circumstances which cannot possibly command the slightest suspicion. In the midst of a great company of persons within and without this noble old mansion, we ostensibly play a game of cards or dice, whichever it so pleases us—*in reality we play a much deeper game.*"

A murmur of approval was the reply.

Blackmore glanced round the apartment.

"Is the *youth* here?" he asked.

"Aye," answered Lord Lionel; "and he has been ready for hours. I did not consider that it would be wise to let him remain in this apartment during the discussion and arrangement of affairs. Was I right or wrong?"

"Right," answered Blackmore.

"What you have to order Silex to do can be ordered on paper."

"Just so. You are more shrewd and careful than I thought you were. Simon Silex has previously been made acquainted with all the facts; he now only awaits instructions to proceed. But where is the youth?"

"In the grounds. I thought he might as well amuse himself."

"You had better watch him," replied Blackmore; "for being such a handsome lad, he might be taken a fancy to by some of your young lady guests, many of whom, I fancy, do not look as if they would be over particular as to whom they ran away with."

Lionel laughed, saying—

"I will myself see that he does not ramble too for."

"How long has he been your page?" asked one of the gentlemen.

"Two years."

"You can trust him with anything?"

"Aye—with anything."

"He has no weaknesses?"

"None."

"Will you not join us, Roxburgh?" said Blackmore.

"Nay, thanks," answered Lord Lionel, hastily; "but I shall not be far away if I am required. And after your deliberations have come to a conclusion, gentlemen, you will join us at supper?"

"Oh, certainly," was the reply of all present.

Off went Lionel, and the "lords and gentlemen" seated themselves at the table.

They took the cards in their hands, and anyone looking in upon them would certainly have been under the impression that they were intent upon a game in which some hundreds of crowns were at stake.

They conversed in low tones, as, slowly and carefully, the cards were handled.

The subject they were discussing was *the assassination of Queen Elizabeth!*

But now we will return to Stanley and those who accompanied him.

They met at the pavilion.

The pavilion itself—in which the musicians were placed—was crowded to excess, and there was a huge crowd without it.

So the presence of Stanley and his companions attracted but little attention.

Bidding Ronald wait, Stanley went off on foot at a rapid pace, and mingled with the crowd about the broad steps.

"'COWARDS! DOWN WITH YOUR WEAPONS!' CRIED RUTH."

No. 7

Oh, when his eyes rested upon Lord Blackmore and Dacre Deadman! The feelings which agitated his breast—can we describe them? No!

His trembling hand nervously clutched his dagger.

It was a wonder that he did not dash through that gay, dissipated throng and fall upon either the one or the other of these bloodthirsty wretches who had murdered his father in such a terrible manner.

But it was lucky for him that he did not allow his feelings to get the upperhand of him.

Had he rushed forward, he might have plunged his dagger either into the heart of Blackmore, or that of Dacre Deadman, but he would himself have been instantly cut down.

He watched Dacre listening to what was being said about himself—watched the terrible, revengeful expression upon his face—watched him slink away among the crowd after the manner of a whipped cur—watched Blackmore and young Roxburgh ascend the grand staircase arm-in-arm, and wondered to what apartment they were bound—wondered whether they were about to meet certain persons, and whom these persons might be.

As to where they were going he was soon satisfied.

Stanley was standing in the shadow of an enormous bronze eagle, two of which stood on huge pedestals at the foot of the stairs; and as he stood thus he heard one lady say to another—

"Now where can they be bound? It would be more polite did Roxburgh place himself at the disposal of his guests."

"Ah!" laughed the other, "they go to the gaming-saloon. Blackmore, they say, is a confirmed gambler."

"Then it is no wonder to whom Roxburgh loses his money," was the significant rejoinder.

In a few moments the ladies separated. Stanley followed the last speaker, and politely raising his hat, said—

"Madame, may I crave one moment's conversation?"

The lady turned, and observing that the gentleman addressing her was handsome, as well as most beautifully attired, replied, as she bowed very low—

"Oh, sir, I shall be delighted to converse with you on any—"

"I was simply about to ask," interrupted Stanley, "whether you could tell me where the card-room is situated?"

The lady was evidently surprised.

"Why should you ask me such a question?" she said—

"Pardon me. I happened to overhear you mention the gaming-saloon. To tell you the truth, I am quite a stranger in this house, never having been here before; but as I have heard a great deal of the gaming-saloon, I should like to see it. Again, lady, I ask your pardon."

"It is granted, sir. But the gaming-saloon is always closed to strangers on a night such as this. It is used only by Roxburgh and his personal friends."

"Ah! But I do assure you that I am only anxious to *see* it."

The lady looked full into Stanley's face; then her eyes ran over his elaborate attire.

No doubt she mentally exclaimed—

"I should have thought that you were a person of some importance, and could have obtained admission to the saloon elsewhere."

Aloud she said—

"Well, sir, I can show you how you may gratify your curiosity. You see it is out of all question for you to approach the room by the grand entrance. If you have no objection to accompany me, I will take you to a back staircase.

"By ascending the first flight you will come to a landing; on the right you will find a recess; enter that and you will come to a small room. If you walk across that you will come to another recess, shut off by a pair of heavy curtains. Approach cautiously, look through the chink in the curtains, and you will see the room; and," she added, with a laugh, "those within it."

"I am sure I thank you most sincerely," replied Stanley.

The lady thereupon led him through some curious passages, and at last the back of the mansion was reached.

She then led him to the staircase she had mentioned, and then left him with the remark—

"Be careful, young sir, for some of these people are very suspicious."

So saying, she hurried away, and Stanley entered the doorway, but he did not ascend the stairs.

He waited until he considered the lady had got some considerable distance, then he emerged into the open.

He looked carefully about on all sides.

But he could not see a soul.

Everyone was too busy in the front to pay any attention to the back.

Stanley went back the same way as he had come.

After some difficulty, he succeeded in reaching the pavilion.

He informed Ronald of what had transpired, and that brave young man was overjoyed.

"This is excellent—excellent!" he said. "And now what do you propose?"

"My idea is this," replied Stanley. "We two will reach the gaming-room by the back way, while our friends will loiter in the front. When they hear this whistle blown"—producing a silver whistle—"the time will have come. They will instantly dash up the terrace stairs, bolt and bar the front door, and then, while two of them guard the door on the inside, the others will join us."

"The idea is good. So now, as we all know what to do, let us at once commence."

"Let us not forget," said Stanley, "that we are bent upon the destruction of Lord Blackmore—aye, and the fiend Dacre Deadman. But remember this—by my hand alone Blackmore falls."

With this they once more separated, Ronald accompanying Stanley.

In safety, and without being observed, they reached the back, and ascended the stairs.

The curtains which divided the ante-room from the gaming-saloon were at last reached, and, looking through them, our hero and Ronald were surprised to see a dozen "gentlemen" besides Blackmore present.

That most of them were foreigners they could tell from their accent, but they could not tell, as a matter of certainty, whether any of them belonged to the secret society of which Blackmore was the head.

"Gentlemen," said Blackmore, as he dealt out some cards, "as soon as her majesty has met with the punishment she deserves, we will proceed with the provinces. This is Norwich"—and here he threw a card to a gentleman at the farther end of the table,—"and this is Winchester"—down went a card before a gentleman on his left,—"and at these two places the regiments which are already disaffected will be placed. Then—"

"But," interrupted one of the gentlemen, "would it not be as well to despatch the note to Simon Silex? If her majesty moves from Esher, an opportunity may not occur for a length of time. In her palaces she is so well guarded that to get at her is almost out of the question."

"Now I think of it," answered Blackmore, "it will be as well to send the youth off at once."

Pens, ink, and paper were procured, as well as Lord Lionel's seal.

In a few moments Blackmore had written a message, and this he read aloud.

It was as follows—

"Proceed at once to the house of the Earl of Normanton, prepared to carry out *previous instructions*. Be careful—do the deed cleanly, and your fortune is made.

"To Simon Silex, at 'The Wapping Arms,' Wapping."

This document Blackmore folded, and sealed it *with the Roxburgh seal.*

Those around the table noticed this, and smiled grimly.

It meant a great deal.

After being securely sealed, the letter was tied with silken thread; and just before Blackmore had fastened it off, in walked Lord Lionel, flushed and excited, as if he had been imbibing some strong wine.

Behind him came a tall and very handsome youth, not more than seventeen years of age.

This was Lord Lionel's page.

"My lord," said Roxburgh, "after some difficulty I succeeded in hunting up my truant page, and have brought him to you, thinking that perhaps you might be ready for him. His horse awaits him at the stables, ready saddled and bridled."

"Good!" answered Blackmore; "it is most fortunate you have brought him now, for the message is ready. Here it is," beckoning to the page; "take it, and place it securely in your wallet—so! That's right."

"I do assure you that I will take every care of my message," said the page; "but at present I do not know whither I am bound."

He was about to take the message from his wallet in order to look at the address, when Blackmore checked him.

He did not want Roxburgh to know that the message bore his (Roxburgh's) seal.

"You need not take out your message," he said; "I will inform you where and to whom you have to go. Do you know Wapping?"

"Wapping! Heavens! 'tis a long way off. 'Tis along the Thames, is it not?"

"Aye, 'tis along the Thames; but in your case 'twill be along the road. Listen, and I will tell you your way."

The page listened, while Blackmore gave him minute particulars of the journey, and informed him as to the best inns he was to stop at.

Two *other* persons listened most intently—namely, Stanley and Ronald.

"Now you perfectly understand?" said Blackmore.

"Oh, perfectly, your lordship—perfectly," answered the page. "It is out of all question that I can make a mistake."

"You are right," said Blackmore; "*but*," he added, as he fixed his fierce eyes upon the lad, "should you make a mistake, Heaven help you!"

The page bowed and withdrew.

In less than a quarter of an hour, he was on the road with his message to the assassin, Simon Silex.

"He must be intercepted," whispered Stanley; "and no doubt we shall manage it."

The page having departed, Lord Lionel again left.

Blackmore and his mysterious friends proceeded playing with the cards in the way we have described.

"Our principal stumbling-block removed," proceeded Blackmore (who by that meant the queen), "we can become a little bolder in our operations,

which I shall, of course, direct from beginning to end, and—"

"You are a *liar!*" shouted a voice; "you shall not live to direct any more of the operations which you—vile traitor that you are—and your friends have been at such pains to concoct."

Instantly Blackmore and every man in the room were upon their feet.

Their swords flashed from their scabbards.

Stanley and Ronald, sword in hand, and each holding in his left hand a pistol, dashed through the curtains.

A cry of consternation escaped the lips of the conspirators. Blackmore instantly recognised Stanley, and a fearful cry of rage escaped him.

"Fear nothing, gentlemen!" he yelled. "This youth is the son of the man sentenced and put to death by order of our council—I mean Lord Whitmore. And look ye; I recognise in the other the son of the accursed Hunchback. Gentlemen, I repeat, you have nothing to fear. Cut them down."

Stanley had searchingly glanced at the men, and he saw that neither of them had a pistol.

"Stay!" he cried; "you have *much* to fear. The first who advances one step is a dead man.

"We are here for a purpose, as you may imagine; and that we have not come unprepared, I will show you."

Stanley took out the whistle and blew it.

The wild, ear-piercing blast must have been heard in every corner of the mansion—aye, and far into the grounds.

Barely had the echo died away, ere a loud and startling crash rang out.

This was followed by loud shouts and cries.

And now each conspirator turned deathly pale.

"The meaning of that noise," said Stanley, "is this: You are shut in this house; it means that if either of you attempt resistance, his death will most certainly follow. Behold!"

Stanley pointed to the door.

The men turned their ashy pale faces, and beheld the first of the Avengers enter.

Each of the Avengers had clapped on his mask, so that there was no chance of any of the conspirators seeing their faces.

But the fierce eyes showing through the holes in the masks, the tall, powerful figures, the naked blades, and the pistols they carried in their hands, had the effect of striking terror into the hearts of Blackmore and his bloodthirsty associates.

"By all the incarnate fiends!" shouted Blackmore, "it seems, gentlemen, as if the invitation here to-night were simply intended as a trap. I strongly believe that Roxburgh knows something of the matter."

"You are wrong," said Ronald, sternly. "That foolish young lord knew nothing of our presence."

"Gentlemen," said Stanley, "you will be dealt with anon. It is with Lord Blackmore I would deal now— yes, with Lord Blackmore, one of the vilest and most dastardly traitors with whom the present queen or her predecessors ever had to deal. Stand forth, my lord. You have your sword, I have mine. Here—"

"Perdition on you!" interrupted Blackmore, with a savage growl; "think you that I would cross swords with a boy like you? No."

"I will compel you."

"Gentlemen," cried Blackmore, "if you will take my advice, you will attempt to cut your way out of this."

It was evident that the conspirators were of the same opinion.

Each one had the same thoughts, and they were as follows—

"Here is the son of the murdered Whitmore. He fancies that we are members of Blackmore's council. He may, for aught we know, have a host of men without this house, and if we do not resist, we may be taken somewhere and confined until the circumstances are placed before the queen—if, in the meantime, the dagger of Simon Silex does not find its way to her heart."

Only a movement on Blackmore's part was necessary.

Directly his infamous lordship moved, which he did suddenly, the others, with a loud cry, rallied round him.

The movement was quickly executed, and was unexpected both by Stanley and Ronald.

But no sooner did the Avengers

behold it, than they were at Stanley's side.

So the parties were opposed one to the other.

There was a pause, and during that pause, the sound of a pin falling might have been heard.

Presently Stanley said—

"Were I to give the word to fire, Lord Blackmore, what would be the result? But I will not; it shall be sword to sword. Advance!"

Another second, and the gaming table was hurled aside, and the glittering weapons met with a loud and startling crash.

Never before, in the whole course of its history, had that gorgeous apartment been the scene of such a fearful encounter.

The faces of Blackmore and his confederates wore a most savage expression.

The howls and cries which left their lips as they frantically endeavoured to ward off the steady and determined lunges made at them by the Avengers were absolutely awful.

But no cries left the lips of Stanley or his friends.

Every now and then, high above the clash of steel, rose a terrible cry of mortal agony.

Occasionally a heavy thud denoted that the conspirators were falling before the deadly weapons of the Avengers.

Ronald was to the fore, but our hero had, of course, singled out Lord Blackmore.

His lordship soon became aware of the fact that in Stanley Whitmore he was encountering a swordsman of no common order.

He found that Stanley was not only a skilled swordsman, but a most determined and deadly one.

He was well aware that to expect mercy at the hands of our hero was out of the question.

Again and again Blackmore tried to slink back, but Stanley followed him up.

In the meantime Ronald and his companions-in-arms were dealing death all around them.

Four of the conspirators lay near the table, while two were leaning against the wall, tearing to pieces their elaborate dresses to make bandages to staunch their terrible wounds.

Near the door lay one of the avengers, a jewelled dagger plunged to the haft in his breast.

Two or three others had received ugly wounds, but they showed no signs of giving in.

Since no quarter was asked on either side, it was likely enough that the terrible encounter would not terminate until every conspirator fell to rise no more.

Suddenly, in the very midst of the fight, a loud shout was heard.

As if by mutual consent, the combatants paused and turned in the direction of the sound.

Blackmore and Stanley were missing!

It was quite evident that the two had vanished through the curtains by which Stanley and Ronald had entered.

In that moment's pause the Avengers thought that it would be as well if they followed Stanley.

Ronald guessed what was passing in their minds, and, considering that Stanley would be well able to look after himself, he called upon them, and the dreadful battle was resumed.

And as it recommenced, loud, fierce cries, and the sound as of a number of persons endeavouring to batter down the doors, were heard below.

It was quite evident that the two men on guard were having a hard time of it.

Leaving Ronald and his friends to continue the combat, we return to Stanley.

After a long try, in which he brought all his cunning into play, Lord Blackmore eventually succeeded in reaching the curtains.

"If I can pass through them," he thought, "I am safe, for this accursed youth knows nothing of the entrances or exits above."

Smarting with the pain from two by no means insignificant wounds which he had received, and maddened at the idea of being outwitted by a mere youth, his lordship uttered a cry of thankfulness when he reached the curtains.

Raising his left hand, he snatched them aside, but this action caused him to slightly overbalance himself.

Another instant and Stanley's sword must have passed through his body.

Instantly recognising his danger, Blackmore suddenly dealt Stanley a brutal kick.

Our hero felt this kick most acutely, but no cry of pain left his set lips.

Turning suddenly, his lordship dashed away through the curtains, Stanley at his heels.

To the left his lordship ran, and, ascending the next flight of stairs, he flew along a narrow landing, and, wrenching open a small door, passed through.

But, ere he could close it, Stanley was there, and, wrenching it back with such violence that he nearly forced it from its hinges, he was after his lordship.

But now he found himself in darkness.

"Hold," shrieked Blackmore, "hold! You know not where you tread. Another step and you die! This place is full of secret traps."

"'Tis false!" answered Stanley; "for if it were full of secret traps I should have fallen into one ere now. Come forth, coward! Accursed murderer! I will not leave you until I see you dead!"

"Ha!" yelled Blackmore, "in darkness you cannot follow. I know every step of the way, and if you attempt to follow I will lead you to destruction."

"Your threats have no terrors for me. I *will* follow you, until—"

"Perdition, take that!" screamed Blackmore.

A thundering crash was heard, and a vase fell at Stanley's feet, being shattered to pieces.

Instantly our hero thought of a way of discovering where Blackmore was.

Drawing a pistol, he fired across the room, but not at where he supposed his lordship to be, as he did not want him to die in such a sudden manner.

The flash of the weapon answered his purpose.

He saw that Blackmore was standing beside another doorway.

At once he dashed towards him, and his lordship sped away as fast as his legs could carry him.

This time Stanley found himself in an exceedingly narrow stairway, which he concluded led to the roof.

But such was not the case.

Suddenly he reached a narrow archway, through which the moon's rays were pouring.

Imagine his surprise when he saw that this archway communicated with a narrow bridge, beautifully carved and ornamented.

Now this bridge, which was at the side of the mansion, led to what at one time had been known as the Armoury, but which was now used as a storehouse for oil, links, powder, shot, articles used in the chase—in fact, all sorts of things ; and it was in this house that two or three men were engaged filling and refilling the little lamps with which the grounds were decorated.

From one of the windows one of these men had observed his lordship, as, hatless and breathless, and with a naked blade in his hand, he stepped from the archway on to the bridge.

Directly this man observed him, he, as a matter of course, set up a loud shout of astonishment, the effect of which was to bring his companions to the window, and, as soon as they saw Blackmore and Stanley, who appeared on the scene as they looked, they too yelled as loud as they were able.

The great noise in the front of the mansion ceased as if by magic.

Hundreds of persons rushed to the spot whence the sounds proceeded, and among the foremost Stanley recognised Dacre Deadman ?

Did that young villain recognise our hero ?

He did—instantly, for the moon's rays were so brilliant that the pale but determined features of our gallant young hero were brought out with wonderful distinctness.

Yes, and so were the features of Lord Blackmore.

No pen could properly describe the appearance of the villain at this moment.

By the side of Dacre Deadman stood Lord Roxburgh.

Though this young and profligate lord was in most things a fool, he was no coward ; but observing the situation above, he stood stock still, apparently unable to move.

At last he roared—

" Go on, my lord—go on ! A pistol ! " he said, turning to the crowd ; " who will lend me a pistol ? "

Two or three were eagerly handed over, and while Lord Lionel took one Dacre took two.

Without hesitation both fired at our hero, but fortunately without effect.

Stanley therefore returned the fire.

Lord Blackmore was about to rush on to the end of the bridge, when another and far louder cry than before rose high on the air.

Scared, eager faces were turned towards the storehouse, from the bottom windows of which a bright red light was proceeding.

" The house is on fire ! '

Barely had the awful words been uttered, ere long, fierce tongues of flame shot out of almost every window.

The fire had been caused by one of the men within the house, who, eager to see what was going on between Lord Blackmore and his pursuer, had clambered upon a table, and upset lamp and oils.

On the floor they ignited, and at once such a fierce flame arose that all efforts to subdue it were fruitless.

It was by the merest chance that the men escaped with their lives.

No sooner did Blackmore behold the flames, than with a loud, horrified yell he started back.

He turned as if to retrace his steps, but the young chief of the Avengers stood barring his passage.

Erect and firm our hero stood, his left hand on a pistol in his belt, and his right grasping his glittering blade.

Higher rose the flames, and by aid of the brilliant red glow, the spectators below were enabled to see what was passing above, as, at the present day, a picture or a scene is illuminated by limelight.

A pause occurred—a truly terrible pause.

But it was a pause of only a moment.

Again Blackmore, answering to the cries below, seemed as if about to dash on.

Stanley was instantly on his guard.

Gripping his sword fiercely, he said

in loud tones—tones which had not the slightest tremor in them—

"You cross not this bridge, my Lord Blackmore, unless it is across my dead body."

"You intend to pursue me to the end?" gasped his lordship.

"I do. Here the fight will be resumed, and here it will terminate."

"All strength seems to have left my arm. I feel powerless to renew the fight. If I sue for mercy?"

"I will deal out to you as much mercy as you dealt out to Lord Whitmore and my mother!" was the stern reply.

At this instant a somewhat loud explosion was heard, and millions of sparks shot up into the air, while large splinters came crashing about the ears of the two.

By Lord Lionel's advice, the crowd of guests had withdrawn to a safe distance, and were eagerly watching the awful scene.

Some held their breath with horror as they saw the flames slowly but surely creeping to the edge of the bridge.

And what of Dacre? Did he appear horror-stricken? Nay.

With his arms folded he leaned against a tree, eagerly watching what was passing, but showing no signs of agitation.

True, his face was deathly pale, and occasionally his lips trembled, but this was all.

These were the thoughts of the young scoundrel, who had turned out such an apt pupil of his lordship's—

"Death—certain death for him! Yes. Would I raise my hand to save him if I could? No! And why? Because by his death I become the possessor of all his property. Aye, 'tis not so very long ago that, wanting me to do a ghastly deed, and seeking to please me, he sat down and penned a paper to the effect that, in the event of his death, I should inherit the whole of his property. Oh, little does he think that I am in possession of that paper. But I am. Aye, and no one will be able to dispute its genuineness. Yes, yes," he chuckled, "*Blackmore* dead, *Dacre Deadman* reigns. 'Tis true I cannot inherit the title, but what of that?"

Lord Blackmore looked back.

He saw that the flames were fiercer than ever, and he felt certain that, in a few moments, they would reach the part of the bridge on which he stood.

With a cry of despair he summoned up what courage remained in his treacherous breast, and advanced.

Stanley's blade met his, and the fight commenced, this time with greater fury than ever—at least, so far as Blackmore was concerned.

All the skill he had been credited with in the years gone by he summoned to his aid, but it was of no use.

Again and again he frantically endeavoured to creep past our hero, but that was out of all question.

Like a pillar of stone Stanley barred his way.

Young Lord Lionel fired several shots at our hero, and, incited by him, so did several other persons.

But fortunately not one of the bullets struck the young Avenger.

Every eye was fixed upon the flashing blades, every ear strained to catch the sound of the clashing of the steel.

Presently our hero assumed the offensive, and back went Blackmore—back towards the burning pile.

His lordship had reached the end of the bridge, absolutely forced there by Stanley's steady advance, when another explosion, and this time far louder than the previous one, was heard.

The force of the explosion was so great that a mighty gap in the wall was made, and the interior of the burning pile was laid open to the gaze of the terrified onlookers.

It presented the appearance of a fiery furnace.

Low down was seen a huge barrel of oil.

Round and about it the fierce flames were playing, and it was certain that in a few moments this too would become ignited, and the fire would thus continue to be fed.

Blackmore saw the terrible sight behind him, and he became almost paralyzed with horror.

"Mercy!" he cried. "Mercy!"

"As much as you showed to Lord Whitmore," answered Stanley: "as much mercy as you showed my mother; as much mercy as you showed the woman, Desarge, of whose terrible sufferings my mother told me ; as much mercy as you have shown hundreds of your victims. Villain—cruel tyrant! your end has come."

As Stanley uttered these words Lord Blackmore's sword was struck from his hand ; and the next moment Stanley plunged his blade into his body.

With a series of wild, unearthly shrieks, Blackmore staggered back.

He endeavoured to clutch at the rails of the bridge to steady himself, but the effort was in vain.

Back he went, and amid a fearful cry from the crowd below, he fell head first into the barrel of oil.

Down to its bottom he went, but quickly rising to the surface, he clutched the sdes of the barrel, and shrieked for help.

Help! Such a thing was impossible.

"Stanley — Stanley, come back ! Quick—run for your life !" shouted a loud voice behind our hero, and turning, he saw Ronald at his side.

Ronald seized him by the arm, and hurried him off the bridge and under the archway.

Not a moment too soon.

The flames had seized upon the bridge, and a few moments sufficed to burn away the supports.

Then with a loud crash the bridge gave way and fell.

All eyes were now fixed upon Lord Blackmore.

His end had nearly come.

What little strength remained in his dastardly carcase he exerted to endeavour to drag himself from the barrel.

But what would have been the result had he succeeded in so doing ?

He would instantly have fallen into the flames.

Before many moments had elapsed the flames had eaten away the lower portion of the barrel, and no sooner did it seize upon the oil than the whole of it was a mass of flame.

Blackmore was enveloped in it, and his writhings were plainly visible, and his terrible shrieks distinctly heard, until nothing whatever could be seen but one great mass of flame, which wrapped him round and shut him out of sight for ever.

Then Lord Lionel raised a cry of "Vengeance !"

"Quick to the front," he shouted ; "we shall capture them. Dacre Deadman, do you lead."

"I lead !" answered Dacre, scornfully, as he proudly strutted away. "No, my lord, I do not lead. Lord Blackmore deserved his death, for—"

"What !" exclaimed Lord Lionel, recoiling from him in horror and disgust ; "deserved his death ? "

"Aye, for speaking of me as he did. I owe you a debt, my lord, for what *you* said of me, and I will repay that debt—mark it well. You little fancied that I overheard what was said, but I did. Listen to me. The youth whom you saw above is Lord Whitmore's son, the haughty, insulting young lord who— But no matter—I will be even with him, but not on Lord Blackmore's account. It will be on my own."

"Dacre Deadman," replied Lord Lionel, who was much afraid of this young ruffian, " I assure you that whatever I may have said in reference to yourself was only said in jest."

"*Liar!* Do you imagine that I am such a consummate fool as not to know, by the tone of a man's voice, whether he be in jest or in earnest ? Bah !"

With this Dacre strode away, his black heart rejoicing at the fact that now he could jump into Blackmore's shoes.

He glanced at the valuable jewels on his dress, and smiled as he muttered—

" All mine! All mine! And this is but as a drop in the ocean compared to what I now possess."

Headed by Lord Lionel, the crowd hastened to the front of the mansion.

They found it already occupied by a large number of guests and servants, the latter of whom were bringing out the dead bodies of those who, but a short time ago, had formed the party in the gaming-saloon.

Not a single man had been left alive !

"And where is the son of Lord Whitmore ? " cried Lord Lionel, who was appalled at the sight ; "where is he and his accomplices ? "

" Escaped," avowed one of the guests —"escaped but a few moments ago. He and five others dashed through us, rushed off across the grounds, and rode off on horses which had been awaiting them near the pavilion."

"Blind fool that I have been!" cried Lord Lionel, stamping his foot. "Blind fools that my servants have been. Had they kept their eyes open the movements of young Whitmore and the daring crew he appears to have at his heels might have been detected, and all the horrible deeds which have been done to-night might have been prevented."

"It will be a long time ere you give another gathering, I should imagine," said a voice in sweet, but bitterly satirical tones.

"Aye, aye," groaned his lordship, as the recollection of what Dacre Deadman had threatened rose in his mind; "you are right. 'Twill indeed be a long time."

"You were often warned of the wretch who met a well-deserved fate to-night," continued the voice, which belonged to the lady who had shown our hero how to reach the gaming-saloon by the back way. "Yes, you were often warned as to Lord Blackmore, but you laughed to scorn all warnings. You have *sown* the wind, my lord, and you will *reap* the whirlwind. What has happened will, of course, reach the ears of the queen. Ere many hours all England will be ringing with the news, and—"

"I will at once prepare to leave the country," interrupted Lord Lionel, in agitated tones, "and will stay abroad until this has blown over."

"And thus proclaim yourself a coward?"

"No, no. I—"

"If you leave the country now, you certainly *will* proclaim yourself a coward. No, no, my lord; *don't* leave the country. *Stay* and brave out the affair. Laugh at it!" said the lady, as she scornfully snapped her jewelled fingers. "Laugh at it, my lord, as you have many a time laughed at the tearful eyes and the haggard faces of those unhappy girls you have betrayed. Snap your finger at all inquiries, as you have snapped your fingers in the pitiful faces of the young mothers who, in the midst of one of your wild debaucheries, when you scattered money among your friends as the sower scatters his seed, have raised their hands to you and cried in vain, ' Only a crown'!"

Lord Lionel essayed to reply, but ere he could do so the lady had disappeared.

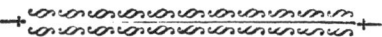

Book II.—Dacre Deadman.

CHAPTER I.

IS OF THE MANNER IN WHICH LORD LIONEL'S PAGE WAS WON OVER TO STANLEY'S SIDE—HOW HE DELIVERS A FORGED LETTER TO SIMON SILEX —AND HOW HE PLACED THE ORIGINAL DOCUMENT IN THE HANDS OF THE HUNCHBACK.

OUR hero, Ronald, and ten of those stern and determined men who had sworn to avenge the deaths of Lord Whitmore and many others who had fallen victims to the power of the dreadful council called the Cowled Eleven, had passed through the gates of Roxburgh House, but of these only Stanley, Ronald, and four Avengers remained.

No less than six had met their death in the house!

It was a dreadful thing to think of, and it was a matter of sincere regret to their surviving comrades that there was no time to bring their bodies away.

Had there been, it is certain that they would have found a last resting-place in the crypt of Old St. Paul's.

The little band took with them all

the horses; but it was decided to dispose of the surplus animals as quickly as possible.

They had little difficulty in this matter.

They were sold to the landlord of "The Fisherman's Arms," a small hostelry standing near the banks of the Thames.

At this house refreshments were partaken of.

Each of the party having refreshed himself with a full measure of wine, they rode off.

Slowly they rode at first, but when clear of the hostelry they broke into a gallop, until they put at least five miles between themselves and Hampton.

Stanley then called a halt, and pistols were reloaded in case of emergency.

"And now," said our hero, "we are well on the road for London. There can be no doubt but that the page who has that important and most damning document in his possession has covered at least ten miles. So at the end of ten miles we must commence our inquiries."

"As you say," said Ronald, "the document is of the utmost importance to my father, as well as to you. It proves how far Lord Blackmore had gone in his schemes against the Crown. And when you have discovered the page?"

"Then you will see how I will arrange matters, Ronald," answered Stanley.

"It is, I suppose, your intention to let the document be placed in the hands of Simon Silex?"

"Not the original—no, because we might not again obtain possession of it. Simon Silex must be handed—a forgery."

"Your plan is excellent. But you, of course, propose that Simon Silex proceed to carry out his instructions?"

"Yes, that is certainly part of my idea. And if your father is warned in time, Providence may place it in his hands to capture the wretch. This will have a most excellent effect on the queen."

"You are right. Pray Heaven all goes as well as you wish. But this has been a night's work which none of us are likely to forget."

"Good blood has been lost," said one of the Avengers, "but it has been in a good cause. For my part, I have a lot to live for, but I would willingly die in the fulfilment of the terrible oath we took in the vaults of Old St. Paul's."

And this sentiment was echoed by the others.

"Stanley," said Ronald, "I am afraid that although Blackmore is no more, you will have a lot of trouble with Dacre Deadman."

"I do not fear the hound," replied Stanley.

"Nay—of that I am well aware. No honest person need fear him in fair fight; but Dacre Deadman is as cunning as a fox, and as treacherous as was Blackmore."

"No doubt of it, and we must meet cunning with cunning. But now let us on."

They resumed their journey, riding slowly this time, the better to converse as to the future.

And that future!

Heaven knows that it looked black enough for our unfortunate young hero and his beautiful mother.

Three miles were thus traversed, and it was almost in darkness.

The moon had hidden herself behind a dense mass of black clouds, and the sudden breeze which had sprung up served to warn the weary travellers that ere long rain would descend.

At last a bright light was seen some little distance ahead.

As they approached this, another, and yet another, sprang into view.

"We are approaching a hostelry," said Ronald.

"Or else the will-o'-the-wisps are thinking of leading us a dance," said Stanley.

"Nay," said one of the Avengers, "we are near a hostelry, and the name of it is 'The Three Merry Men.' 'Tis kept by Toby Tallows, a blind harpist."

"He keeps late hours," Stanley remarked.

"A sign he has company," said Ronald; "and so we had better be careful, for though we have met no one on the road, news travels in the most extraordinary manner."

"Approach the house at a walking pace," said Stanley, "and we shall not be heard."

This was done.

The hostelry appeared to be fairly lively.

As our friends reached the house, the sound of a sweet, boyish voice singing a love song was heard, as also was the sound of a harp.

The blinds not having been lowered, Stanley and Ronald looked into the parlour.

Imagine their astonishment when they beheld Lord Lionel's handsome page standing near the fireplace, his arm about the waist of a remarkably pretty girl of about his own age.

It was the page who was singing.

Seated at his feet was the blind host of "The Three Merry Men."

A small Irish harp was between his feet, and being acquainted with the song the page was singing, he was accompanying him to perfection.

In the centre of the room was a large, rude table, round which a number of villagers were seated, and so entranced were they with the singing, that their measures of liquor remained untasted.

At the farther end, near the door, stood the buxom hostess.

It was the hostess' daughter whom the page was treating in so affectionate a manner, but the hostess did not appear by any means displeased.

"Lord Lionel's page does not lack impudence, at any rate," said Ronald.

"Nay, nor lungs," replied Stanley. "I'll warrant me he pays more heed to a pretty face than to a message, or even a diamond ring."

The song came to a conclusion, "amid thunders of applause," and tankards of ale were eagerly thrust towards the page, but the hostess, bustling forward, pushed them aside.

"No, no," she said, "this cannot be ; a fine young gentleman like him cannot be allowed to drink stale ale."

"True," cried the host; "let the youngster be provided with a measure of the very best the house contains."

"But first," said the page, whose arm still encircled the slender waist of the host's daughter, "I should be allowed to claim a reward as the result of my exertions."

There was a laugh at this.

"And," continued the page, with admirable effrontery, "with the permission of everyone present, I claim, as my reward, a kiss from those pretty lips."

The maiden blushed, and the guests murmured.

"If Alice has no objection," said the hostess, "I am sure I have none."

"Nor I," said the host; "such a sweet singer deserves a sweet kiss."

So the kiss was taken—aye, and given, though, of course, with many blushes and maiden-like hesitation.

"You are the sweetest girl I ever met," said the page.

"Ah," said the hostess, with a shake of the head, "I am afraid that this is not the first time you have said that such and such a girl was the sweetest you have ever met. Lord Lionel Roxburgh is just the very man to set his page a bad example."

"I swear that what I have said is correct, madame," answered the page; "and if you will give me your kind permission, and your beautiful daughter will consent, I shall be only too happy to bestow upon her my undivided attentions. In proof of what I say, I herewith make her a present of a most valuable diamond ring."

Amid cheers, renewed again and again, the page took from his own finger the diamond ring which had been presented to him by Blackmore, and slipped it on the finger of the girl.

The page then took from the hands of the hostess a goblet of wine, and having nodded to all present, toasted the maiden at his side, and took a sip in such an elegant and mock-dainty fashion as to call forth roars of laughter.

Stanley now gave the word, and he and his comrades dismounted.

The sound of their arms and spurs at once alarmed all within the room, which was instantly in an uproar, of which the audacious page took advantage to imprint at least a dozen kisses on the lips of the host's daughter.

The host was led to the door by his wife, who told him that "a number of the queen's officers were without."

"What want ye, gentlemen ?" asked the host.

"Nothing more than refreshment," was Stanley's reply.

"The hour is late," replied the host, "and, if I be not judged too impertinent, what do the queen's officers want on the road to-night?"

"You are mistaken, my friend," said Stanley; "we are not queen's officers, but simply half-a-dozen gentlemen travelling to London."

"Since ye are not queen's officers," answered the host, who had no partiality for queen's or other officers, "ye may enter. Give your orders, and they shall be at once attended to by my wife and daughter. I am of no use, for, as you may observe, I am blind."

"Unless I mistake not, master host," said Ronald, "you are of very great use. You are the first host who has caused us to stand outside a hostelry while we admired his skill."

"Ah, you heard me playing the harp, gentlemen?" asked the host, who was very well pleased at the compliment.

"Aye, and heard yonder young gentleman singing. If the queen were aware of his talents he would soon be at Court."

"Say you so, gentlemen?" asked the page, eagerly.

"Yes," said Stanley; "I am sure of it."

"Well, that is a great consolation to me, gentlemen," said the page; "for I want very much to be rid of Roxburgh House, where I am now engaged."

"You are a long way from Roxburgh House, my friend," said Ronald.

"That is true," replied the page; "I am on the road to London with an important message. But I have time to sing another song if you wish to hear me. I am thinking that, perhaps, one of you might possess the enviable power of speaking to the queen for me."

"We will talk over the matter," answered Stanley. "Will you join us in some refreshments?"

"I thank you, gentlemen, but a very little wine overpowers me, and as my present errand is of vast importance, it is absolutely necessary that I retain full possession of my senses."

"You are wise," said Stanley, with a smile; "such a conscientious and talented young fellow as you appear to be fully deserves to attain some high position."

"I am sure, sir, I fully appreciate your kind remarks. With a recommendation like yours, I fancy I should have little difficulty in obtaining the notice of the queen."

"Well," said Stanley, "if you will not join us in partaking of refreshments, at least you will sit down with us. We will discuss the matter if we can be alone awhile," he whispered.

The page nodded and spoke to the young girl at his side.

In a very short space of time our friends and the page had the room entirely to themselves.

No sooner was Stanley aware of this than, in the most careful manner, he commenced to speak of the matter uppermost in his mind.

So skilfully did he lead up to the subject that the page was, in the manner of speaking, hardly aware of what Stanley was about to say until he was absolutely in the midst of it.

So full of surprise and consternation was the young page, that he never uttered one word until our hero had recounted all that had occurred until they escaped from the house.

Even then it was some moments ere he spoke.

His handsome face had turned ashy pale; his fine, dark eyes actually glittered with fear.

"And you say," he gasped, "that the message I have in my wallet contains instructions to an assassin?"

"Aye," replied Stanley; "on my word of honour I speak the truth."

"Yes," said Ronald, "such is the case. We were behind the curtains at the back of the gaming-room, and heard the message read. So impressed was I with the contents, that I verily believe I could repeat it word for word without looking at the document."

"I believe what you say, gentlemen," said the horrified page, "and am right glad to hear that Lord Blackmore has met his death. As for my master, Lord Roxburgh, I am afraid that he will find a lodging in the Tower ere long. But here, gentlemen, is the message."

And with trembling fingers he opened

the wallet, took out the message, and placed it upon the table, saying—

"I am innocent in the matter. Of the contents, I, of course, know nothing."

"No; of that we are well aware," replied Stanley. "Now, I want to get hold of that message, but I will not take it unless you give it me."

"Oh, most willingly do I give it you, sir," replied the page, as he hastily handed over the document, "and I place myself in your hands. You, I am sure, will advise me. I will never again return to Roxburgh House—never! And yet," he added, somewhat sadly—"and yet by not returning I lose all that belongs to me. 'Tis not much, to be sure, but his lordship owes me fifty crowns, and that—that I sadly wanted."

"To buy a present for your sweetheart?" said Ronald, wishing to cheer him up a bit.

"Nay," replied the lad, shaking his head. "Nay; I have a widowed mother, gentlemen, and in her needy hands I place all my wages. She looks forward to it every year. And this time, alas! she will look in vain. I would rather lose all the money I might ever have, and all chances of future advancement, than lose her good opinion."

"You are an honest and most excellent son," cried Stanley, emphatically; "the words you have just uttered do you infinite credit. May you never have cause to change such noble sentiments. Look you, young sir, what are these?"

And Stanley placed before the lad a roll of paper.

"Goldsmiths' notes," answered the page.

These notes Stanley had received in payment for the horses, and they were payable on presentation at Lombard Street.

"You are correct," said Stanley; "and as soon as I obtain pen and ink, they shall be made payable to you."

"Oh, sir——"

"No thanks," said Stanley; "wait but a little while. Now, what is your name?"

"Mark Mellow."

"Good. Now listen to me, Mark Mellow. You have heard the name of Lord Whitmore?"

"Who left the country in order to escape the queen's troops? Oh, yes."

"No, he did nothing of the kind. Lord Blackmore murdered him. He and his secret council sentenced him to death, and Dacre Deadman acted as his executioner."

"Heavens! is it possible?"

"It is. I am Stanley, Lord Whitmore's only son."

The page bowed.

"And my friend here," continued Stanley, "is Ronald, the son of the Hunchback of Old St. Paul's. You have heard of him?"

"Many, many times. A man held in great dread. I have often wished I might see him."

"Your wish shall be gratified anon."

Stanley then introduced the page to the Avengers, and thus concluded—

"Now, Mark Mellow, though at present I am not at Court—though at present my influence is not very great —yet I offer you the opportunity of becoming my page. If all goes as well as I am inclined to think, I will one day introduce you to the queen, for the purpose of obtaining for you an engagement as Court-page."

"My lord—"

"Nay. Say 'sir,'" interrupted our hero.

"Sir, I accept your engagement with many thanks. I am entirely at your service. Command me."

Stanley took up the letter, and as he beheld the seal a great cry escaped his lips.

"Behold!" he said, holding forth the letter so that all could see. "Behold here, even on this letter, is proof of Blackmore's dastardly treachery; for though his own hand wrote what is within this, he has actually sealed it with Roxburgh's seal!"

"Convincing proof, indeed," said Ronald; "and my advice is, cut open the letter without disturbing the seal."

"Such is my intention," replied Stanley, who then, taking out his dagger, cleanly and evenly cut open the missive.

Stanley spread it open, and read aloud the contents.

Then turning to the page, Mark Mellow, he said—

"You are perfectly satisfied?"

"More—*more* than satisfied," was the reply; "and I repeat that I accept service under you with grateful thanks. I say again, command me."

"In the first place," said Stanley, "let the host supply me with pen, ink, and paper."

The page left the room, and returned with the required articles, including wax.

Stanley took the pen in his hand.

"I know not," he said, "whether any of my own writing has ever been seen by Simon Silex, but no doubt it has not. Still, it will be as well if I write in a disfigured hand."

So in a bold, but cleverly disguised hand, our hero copied the original document.

But he added this on to the postscript—

"An unfortunate accident prevents me from writing with my own hand, and therefore a confidential friend does the office for me."

"You, of course, see the meaning of this?" said Stanley. "Simon Silex is unquestionably familiar with Lord Blackmore's handwriting, and what I have here added will prevent him from becoming suspicious."

The document having been folded up and tied with silken thread, Stanley took from his pocket his own—or, rather, his late lamented father's—seal, and which had a border much resembling the border on the Roxburgh seal.

He melted the wax and took the impression from his own seal; and then, while the wax was still hot, he *blurred the centre* with his fingers.

"On my soul," cried Ronald, "this is an excellent plan. Though Simon Silex is hardly the man to 'hum' and 'ha' over a document ere he opens it, this would surely throw him off his guard if he happened to be in a suspicious mood."

"Yes," said Stanley; "he will be deceived by this. And now, Mark Mellow, prepare to set out."

"To Wapping?"

"Aye, to 'The Wapping Arms.' Hand this document to Simon Silex only. You understand?"

"Perfectly. And you may rely upon it that your instructions shall be carried out to the very letter. And after I have delivered this document?"

"Await the answer; and when you have that, return to us with all speed. Even if you have to change horses once or twice, do not hesitate."

The page took the document from Stanley's hands, placed it in his wallet, and set out.

He encountered the host's pretty daughter on the threshold, and she marvelled much at the change which in so short a time had taken place in him.

His face was now pale, and his eyes wore a serious expression.

However, Mark forgot not to bid the infatuated maiden a most graceful adieu; neither did he, as she held up her face, forget to imprint more than one kiss upon her red lips.

Amid her good wishes and the "Heaven speed ye!" of the blind host and his wife, the page mounted and rode away at a tremendous pace.

It is our intention to follow him to Wapping; and, as nothing occurred on the road, we ask our readers to at once transport themselves to "The Wapping Arms."

Since we last saw Simon Silex, things had gone on very prosperously with him.

Fortune, which for so many years had frowned, now smiled upon him; and with his wife as his helpmate, he was thriving famously.

His "master," Lord Blackmore, did not now require his services so very often, and so he had more opportunities for maturing his schemes.

In less than two hours after leaving our friends, the page was at Wapping.

Not once on the road had he stopped, and when he drew up before the hostelry, his horse's steaming flanks showed the pace at which he had travelled.

"The Wapping Arms" had been closed for two or three hours, and the exterior was in almost total darkness.

The very oil-lamp hanging over the archway which led to the stables, and which generally burned through the night, had either been put out by some roystering gallants, or had been extinguished by the wind.

"'YOU CROSS NOT THIS BRIDGE UNLESS IT IS ACROSS MY DEAD BODY!' CRIED STANLEY.'"

No. 8

The young page looked about him on either side; then he examined the front of the house.

He saw that a light was burning in the first floor.

"Someone is astir, I should imagine," he thought; "perhaps 'tis this dastardly host himself. So that he will—"

Mark Mellow was here interrupted by a loud peal of laughter.

It evidently proceeded from the room in which the light was burning.

The sounds of merriment sounded coarse and vulgar, and as they were accompanied by the loud banging of measures and glasses, the page considered that Simon Silex was engaged in entertaining his friends.

Such indeed was the case.

"If the message was not so important," thought Mark, "I would wait until the morning, for I like not the idea of being brought into a room swarming with drunken gallants and bravos."

Jumping from the saddle, Mark hammered on the door with the butt-end of his riding-whip.

Up, with a tremendous crash, went the window above, and a voice cried out in harsh tones—

"Hallo, hallo! Hang you—*hullo!* What do you mean by it, I say?"

The page stepped back and looked up.

His eyes rested upon the face of Simon Silex.

Mark had never before seen this brutal ruffian.

As he looked upon his face he shuddered, and wondered whether this was the host himself.

"What do you want, my fine-feathered little bird?" asked Simon, as he gazed in wonder at the fine clothes of the traveller.

"I want to see Simon Silex, the host of this house—'The Wapping Arms.'"

"Oh, you *do!*" chuckled Simon. "Then behold him. I am Simon Silex."

"Yes," shouted a voice behind him—"yes, that's true. Behold the *Wapping* host!"

"Silence, gentlemen," said Simon, "and let me hear what this well-painted young buck has to say. Hi, young

sir, I say! *hang* you, I say! I say that *I* am Simon Silex—I say."

"Well," answered Mark, "I want to speak with you."

Simon evidently was about to inform the page that he would *have* to want, when Mark took the document from his wallet and held it up.

"Ha!" ejaculated Simon—"a letter!"

"Yes."

"Who from?"

"Lord B."

"Oh, *oh*, I say! But you are not Lord Blackmore's servant, are you?"

"Nay, I am but Lord Roxburgh's page, and from Roxburgh House I have brought this letter."

Simon knew that Blackmore and Dacre Deadman were at Roxburgh House, but he never expected to be summoned there.

"I will admit you," said Simon, who thereupon shut the window, and descending the stairs, opened the door.

"You had better put up your horse; and, look you—what d'ye mean by staring at me in that fashion?"

Mark, of course, had been looking at the huge figure of the host of "The Wapping Arms."

"I am sure I beg your pardon," he replied, with a mock bow, "but I am bound to have a good look at you, so that, if questioned, I shall be able to describe the person into whose hands I placed this packet."

And he handed over the letter.

"No doubt it was your master, the Lord Roxburgh, who taught you to speak in so pompous a manner," sneered Simon; "but let me tell you that all pomposity is lost on *me*."

"Aye; and everything else, no doubt, thou abandoned, dissipated-looking wretch," muttered the page.

Aloud he said—

"Since I am to return immediately with your answer, it is useless to place my horse in your stable."

"Have you rode all the way on this one horse?"

"I have."

"Then he will never carry you back. You had better have a change."

"Nay; I will manage with this one."

"You are a surly, ill-mannered young man," cried Simon, "and the way you speak does not correspond with the clothes you wear."

"I am sorry I cannot say the like of yourself," Mark promptly replied.

Simon snatched a lamp from a bracket.

"Hold this," he said.

"I am not your servant, and must decline," replied Mark.

Simon looked as if he would throw the lamp at him.

After a few seconds' hesitation, he hung the lamp overhead, and proceeded to open the letter.

Instantly his eyes fell upon the seal.

"Why, what has happened to this?" he growled, as he held it close up to the lamp. "This has been tampered with."

"I know nothing of it," answered the page, coolly. "If it has been tampered with, it was not done by me. It has been in my wallet ever since it was handed to me."

"Hem! then let me— But stay —perhaps you placed it in your wallet before the wax got cold."

"I believe I did."

"Then you are an infernal fool."

"As such I am content to remain," answered the audacious page.

Simon tore open the letter and read. He had to proceed very slowly, for he was no scholar.

When he had finished it, he muttered, as he slowly turned the document over and over in his huge, horny hands—

"Met with an accident, eh? But only to his hand! I wish it had been his neck. So this job has to be done, after all. I was in hopes he and his crew had thought better of it. Esher— 'tis a long distance."

Turning to Mark, he said—

"I will give you an answer to this in a short time. I must first consult my wife. Follow me."

"Where?"

"Follow me," roared Simon.

"I would rather remain here," replied Mark.

"Listen to me, my richly-plumed, saucy young coxcomb," said Simon, now in a towering rage. "If you don't choose to follow me, I shall return no answer at all. Then if Lord Blackmore sends to me, I shall say that I never received any letter from you."

And Simon looked as if he meant what he said.

Mark, after a few moments' consideration, thought it better to do as Simon asked him; so throwing the reins over a hook on the wall, he followed him.

Simon at once led the way to the room above.

Mark quickly found himself almost in the centre of the most depraved-looking crew which could have been scraped together from the four corners of London.

He would instantly have turned and left the room, but Simon said, in loud and significant tones—

"Stay here until I return, my young friend. I have no doubt that you will find the gentlemen present ready and willing to drink whatever you may have the goodness to pay for."

"So I should imagine, by the look of them," was Mark's reply.

The remark, intended as a sneer, was taken the other way, the men being under the impression that he would order and pay something for them.

But they were mistaken.

Mark was no hand at drinking himself, and he never, under any circumstances, paid for other people—unless they were friends of his, or persons absolutely in need of refreshment, and unable to pay for it themselves.

"Well, my fine-feathered little bird," said a bloated waterman, "and what will ye offer us?"

"Sound advice," replied Mark; "and that is—keep a civil tongue in your head."

"Ho! You are a pretty page."

"I am well aware of it, and being a pretty page, I am competent to tell you to turn over a new *leaf*."

"Who taught you to be so sharp?"

"That is my business, master waterman."

"Oh, is it—is it?"

Thereupon the waterman turned and whispered to the men on either side of him.

Judging from the fierce glances directed towards him, Mark came to the conclusion that it was more than probable the men were preparing to give him something which it was likely enough he would not forget in a hurry.

To get into a bother now he knew would be the means of stopping the return message.

He therefore determined to let the men have what they pleased so far as his cash would go.

He had, as we know, the goldsmiths' notes, but he would not have touched them in the presence of these blackguards.

He found that his ready cash consisted of just five crowns.

"I will tell you what I will do, master waterman," said Mark, testily. "I see the dice on the table. Now the one who throws the lowest shall pay for wine or spirits to the extent of five crowns."

The suggestion at once "turned the tide."

"Done!" cried the waterman, seizing the dice.

Mark placed the five crowns upon the table, and the waterman, having shaken the dice, threw.

The number was three.

Mark next took the dice and threw them. The number was five.

"I have won!" exclaimed Mark.

"Of a surety," replied the waterman. "And I must pay to the extent of five crowns. And here is the sum."

Thereupon the thief's horny paw fastened upon Mark's five crowns, amid loud shouts of laughter.

But Mark could well afford to laugh, and laugh he did, and so heartily, merrily, and musically, that the men began to get delighted with him.

Drink to the amount of the five crowns was ordered and brought up, and the first goblet was handed to Mark.

He was about to decline it, but a sudden thought striking him, he took it, saying—

"Now I will make another bargain with you. But this time you will swear to keep it?"

"Aye, aye," was the reply.

"Well, the bargain is this—I will sing you a pretty love-song, and on its conclusion you shall all drink the toast I propose."

"A most fair bargain," replied the thieving waterman.

"Very—very fair," was the reply of the men.

So Mark mounted a barrel, and in rich, ringing tones sang the love-song which he had sung at Hampton.

At the conclusion of the song they greeted him with thunders of applause.

"Now," said Mark, raising his goblet, "the toast."

"What toast?" asked a harsh voice, and Simon re-entered the room; "what toast, I say?"

"You will hear in a moment," said Mark.

He raised his goblet.

The men did likewise.

"Hats off!" cried Mark, with all the effrontery in the world, as he took off his own hat.

The men hesitated; then, laughingly, they complied with the demand.

"*Here's health, long life and happiness to her majesty the Queen, and confusion to her enemies!*" shouted Mark.

"Hold!" roared Simon, striding into the centre of the apartment and stretching forth his long arms; "hold! Drink that toast at your peril."

"They *will* drink it," said Mark. "If they do not keep to their bargain they are cowards."

"Yes, yes," cried the men; "we must keep to our bargain, Simon. Here we have it—Health to the Queen, and confusion to her enemies."

The toast was drunk.

Simon turned to Mark, and in an undertone, said—

"You have destroyed yourself. If I inform Lord Blackmore of—"

"But," interrupted Mark, "is not Lord Blackmore her majesty's faithful servant? Surely he could have no objection to such a toast!"

Simon was confounded at this, but said—

"You have destroyed yourself."

"At any rate," thought Mark, "I have proved that these men know nothing of *your* movements."

"You can now follow me," said Simon; "my wife is now dressed. Gentlemen," he said to his friends, "I bid you adieu for a few days."

"What!" they cried; "are you going on a journey?"

"Yes, I am going to Hampton, and shall remain there a few days. We will resume our jovial gathering when I return."

"*When!*" thought Mark. "*When!* Vile, bloodthirsty assassin, *you will never return.*"

Simon's companions being well furnished with liquor, paid little attention to what the host was saying.

Mark followed him up another flight of stairs, and into the bedchamber, where, on the edge of the bedstead, sat Mistress Silex.

A most repulsive person was the hostess, and her appearance at this moment was that of a person just recovering from a shocking state of drunkenness.

"You are brought to me," said Mistress Silex, in hoarse tones, as she fixed her half-open eyes on Mark's face, "so that I can tell you that Simon will set out for the place mentioned in this letter at once. Lord Blackmore trusts to me to see my husband about his business, you know. Ho, ho!"

"I will return with the answer immediately," replied Mark.

"Are you in so great a hurry, my pretty boy?"

"Aye, a great hurry, indeed," answered Mark.

"This youth," growled Simon, "is not only possessed of the gift of the gab, but he has the audacity of the foul fiend himself. He actually proposed a toast to the queen's good health, and confusion to her enemies."

"And your companions drank it?" queried the hostess.

"They did."

"Well, they could hardly refuse a toast proposed by so handsome a lad," chuckled the hostess.

"Curse his handsomeness, I say," shouted Simon. "Curse him, Blackmore, and you, I say. *That's* what I say."

"Aye—aye, have your say—have your say," growled the hostess; "but whatever you say will not cause *me* to quake."

"Nay, nor keep sober."

"You are right—nor keep sober. But I say, master page, it will go hard with you if Simon mentions this matter to Lord Blackmore."

"How so?"

"Show him, Simon, how Blackmore disposes of those he says shall die."

"It was *not* Blackmore who dis-posed of the men," answered Simon, sulkily.

"Well, it was Dacre Deadman and you, but by *orders* of Lord Blackmore. Heaven!" she cried, clasping her fat, greasy-looking hands together—"Heaven send I may never look upon the like again."

"I shall not show him," said Simon. "If you want him to see the thing, show him yourself."

Mark, as a matter of course, was curious as to what there was to see.

"Would you like to see the show, my sweet page?" leered the hostess.

"Aye; I am fond of seeing shows."

"Well, I cannot take you. But I will summon Grammack, and he will take you. But you will promise to return and partake of refreshment with me?"

"Yes, I promise."

"Fool!" hissed Simon; "fool! idiot! I expect when I return to find the whole place turned inside out. But beware! I hold you responsible for all that occurs. If I fin anything wrong, remember you do not accompany me abroad."

With this he turned on his heel and departed.

After indulging in a coarse laugh, the hostess went on the landing, and shouted out at the top of her voice for "Grammack."

In a short time a diminutive, ill-made man made his appearance.

"Grammack," said the hostess, "you will take this young gentleman to the old wine vault, and show him what is to be seen there."

Grammack opened wide his eyes.

Heaving what sounded like a deep sigh, he said—

"I should hardly have thought that so handsome, and evidently so well-bred a young man, would care about feasting his eyes on so horrible a sight."

"I know nothing whatever of what is to be seen," said Mark, struck by the man's tones, "but if you think 'tis too horrible, I will decline to go."

"I wish him to see how Blackmore can behave to those he sentences to death, even after the breath has left their body."

"Oh, that's it, is it?" replied Grammack. "Then come," he said, touching Mark on the shoulder.

As he crossed the landing, Grammack took a link from a bracket, and lighting it, held it over his head.

"Be careful, young man," he said, "or over you go. A broken neck, or leg, or something of the sort is a common occurrence here."

He led the way down two flights of stairs, and paused at the head of a third.

Turning to Mark, he said—

"How old are you?"

"About eighteen."

"Ah, well, you have just half-a-century to live ere you reach my age; and let me tell you that, when your hair is as white as mine, when your face is wrinkled like mine, when your hands tremble like mine, when, in fact, you are tottering on towards that place whence man never returns, you will think of this night. You will remember what I am now about to show you."

"Is it dreadful?"

"Awful! It will show you what a fiend in human shape is this Dacre Deadman."

"Dacre Deadman!"

"Aye. I often think he must be the Evil One in disguise, instead of—as he calls himself—the illegitimate son of Lord Blackmore. Blackmore, in my opinion, is not half so terrible a man as— But I hope I am not speaking to one of Blackmore's servants?"

"Thank Heaven, no!"

"Amen to that, my young friend. I say that, in my opinion, Lord Blackmore is not half so terrible a man as Dacre Deadman. It was Dacre Deadman who thought of the horrible arrangement I shall show you. Now follow me down this flight of stairs, and go slowly, for they are very rotten."

Down went the pair, and a small vault was reached.

It was crowded with barrels and bottles.

It swarmed with river rats, and the presence of these loathsome vermin was made sufficiently manifest as the pair entered the vault, for they could be heard rushing away, knocking over dozens of bottles in their flight.

"The rats are in a hurry to-night," chuckled the old man, as he led the way across the vault, showing Mark the way by holding the torch low down.

A narrow, oaken door, heavily studded with nails, was reached.

Again the old man turned to Mark.

"I have a small quantity of brandy in my pocket," he said, "and if you care to partake of a little, you are quite welcome."

"I am sure I thank you," replied Mark, "but I would rather not."

The old man opened the door.

"Enter," he said.

Mark entered, but instantly recoiled.

"Ah," he said, "this smells like a grave!"

"You are perfectly correct," was the answer. "But follow quickly, or I feel sure your courage will leave you."

A few steps farther, and a pair of heavy black curtains, fringed with silver, was reached.

Over them hung three glittering daggers, arranged as we have previously described, and beneath them the ominous words—

"Death to Traitors!"

The old man did not allow Mark to study the meaning of all this, but he drew aside one of the curtains.

Mark stepped forward.

What was it he saw?

What? Why, one of the most terrible sights ever witnessed by mortal man.

He found himself on the threshold of a somewhat large, vaulted apartment (it had, in fact, at one time been used as a wine cellar), the walls of which were draped in black, and the drapery, as was evident from the graceful fall of the folds, had been arranged by a skilful hand.

From the ceiling was suspended a heavy silver lamp, the sides of which were of deep blue glass.

It shed a ghastly-looking, bluish light over the apartment, but it was of so indistinct a character, that it was some few seconds ere the wondering young page could make out what was before him.

Suddenly a wild, terrified cry left his lips.

He started back, but the old man laid his hand gently on his shoulder.

"Hist!" he said; "for you may be heard."

Mark now saw before him a large square table, and around it a number of men clad in the queen's uniform.

These men were those whom Dacre Deadman had killed by means of the poisonous fumes of the packet.

Dacre Deadman it was who had conceived the idea of having this room arranged in the manner we have seen, and of placing the men within it, so that by its means they could strike horror into the breast of anyone they showed it to.

Simon Silex had assisted him, though it was very much against his grain; and the men had been placed very much as they died in the apartment above.

They were in various attitudes, and two or three of them had clutched in their long fingers the goblets from which they had been drinking. But some of their faces were turned towards the doorway.

And, oh, what faces!

Mere skulls they looked now, over which a thin sheet of parchment had been spread.

Kneeling upon the floor, his long, bony hands stretched above (they were supported by wire), was the man into whose body Dacre had plunged his dagger.

The dagger was there now (it may not have been the same used by Dacre, of course, but it was a dagger)—it was there now, we say, buried to the haft in the almost fleshless carcase.

The sight was terrible beyond the power of description.

Truly, it would have sent a thrill of horror through the most hard-hearted of men.

The decomposition of the bodies caused the place to smell like a charnel-house.

"Tell me the meaning of this," said Mark, in a whisper.

The old man complied with the request, and in a low, monotonous tone of voice he told the story.

"And," he concluded, "it is Dacre Deadman's orders that that lamp burns day and night. Do you know Dacre Deadman?"

"By sight only. But what is his object in having the lamp alight?"

"So that he can use the room when he thinks proper."

"Use the room! And does he use the room?"

"Frequently."

"But for what purpose?"

"Why, he eats and drinks, and sometimes sleeps here. Yonder, as you see, is a couch. That is where he sleeps."

"Heavens! He must indeed be a fiend—or if not a fiend, he must be a madman."

"Oh, he is no madman!" replied the old man, shaking his head. "No, no—he is no madman. One of these days Lord Blackmore will meet with his death at the hands of one of his victims, or intended victims, and so will Dacre Deadman."

Little did the old man dream that Blackmore had already met with a terrible death.

Mark nearly forgot himself, for he felt hardly able to refrain from crying out—

"A terrible vengeance has already overtaken one of these horrible ruffians."

Turning to the old man, he said—

"I pray you conduct me at once to the exterior of this vile den."

"But will you not return to Mistress Silex?"

"No, no! Not for worlds!"

"Well, I will take you another way, though I am likely to get myself in trouble by so doing. Still, I shall not mind that, so that I know you are out of the clutches of that woman."

Mark took from his doublet the goldsmiths' notes.

"Look you, my friend," he said, "this money is mine. As you see, it only requires changing. When next I come this way I will not forget to reward you handsomely."

"I thank you, my young friend, though if you happened to forget your promise I should not remind you. Money possesses but little attraction for me now."

The man now led Mark from one vault to another, through several passages, and eventually they emerged through a trap-door in the stables.

Thence to the exterior of "The Wapping Arms" was a matter of a few seconds only.

Mark was quickly in the saddle, and, with a parting farewell to the old man, he rode away.

* * * *

Mark overrated his horse's powers. After another five miles he began to show undoubted signs of being much distressed, and therefore Mark was compelled to give him a good rest, and to ride somewhat slowly the remainder of the journey.

He reached the hostelry at Hampton as it was striking six.

Ronald, Stanley, and their companions had retired to rest, but it is a question whether they slept.

As soon as Mark made his appearance the ostler took possession of his tired horse, and Stanley himself assisted the young page to dismount.

Poor Mark looked thoroughly tired out.

"What ails you?" asked Stanley, much alarmed at his appearance.

"I will tell you directly," answered Mark, in low tones.

"You have met with no mishap?"

"No, I thank you; but I have seen such a dreadful sight at 'The Wapping Arms,' that I verily believe I shall never be able to keep it from before my eyes as long as I may live."

Stanley gazed eagerly into the pale face of the youth.

"A dreadful sight, say you?" he exclaimed. "I trust you have not been a witness to any foul murder?"

"Nay—worse."

"You shall tell us the particulars immediately you have partaken of some refreshment."

Mark was soon seated before a table well laden with refreshments of various kinds.

But he could take nothing but a very small cup of wine.

"The old man's words I shall find true," he thought; "I shall never—never forget that dreadful sight."

Amid profound silence Mark told our friends what he had seen in the old wine vaults.

A thrill of horror pervaded the hearts of all as they listened.

"Truly," said Stanley, "this Dacre Deadman seems full of the most diabolical inventions."

"We will hunt him down," said Ronald—"aye, we will hunt down the young villain. But we shall have the greatest difficulty now."

"And why?"

"Because, you see, he will now wield Blackmore's power and his own too."

"No matter; we fear him not. But now, Mark, you require rest. A bed has been prepared for you above, and you may rest till night, when you will take this packet to the Hunchback. He was supposed to go to Windsor, but there is hardly a doubt but that you will find him somewhere at Esher. If you have a good rest you will be prepared for both journeys."

"I go alone?"

"Entirely."

"I fear nothing," said Mark. "You can direct me, and you will find that all your commands shall be most faithfully carried out."

"I have not the least doubt of it. And now to rest."

Of course Mark had informed Stanley as to Simon's reply, but Stanley had expected the answer he brought, hence the packet Mark was to take to the Hunchback was all ready.

We will pause here no longer than to say that as soon as darkness once more stole over the country, Mark set off, bearing the all-important packet in his wallet.

After this our friends set out, their destination being Old St. Paul's.

* * * *

Esher at the present day is a thriving and populous village.

Its outskirts are dotted with pretty villas and ornamental gardens, which give it a most picturesque appearance.

It was picturesque enough at the period of our romance, certainly; but then its picturesqueness was of a wild character.

Then there were no roads and no streets, unless a filthy lane here and there could be so called.

The principal house was that in the occupation of the Earl of Normanton, and called Normanton House.

It was a large, old, embattled mansion, built of stone, and having for its doors, staircases, window-frames, and so on, unpolished oak—the doors generally being heavily studded with brass nails and bars of steel, which were kept most beautifully polished by men specially retained for the duty.

It stood in the centre of a piece of ground forty acres or more in extent, the said ground being just as much neglected as the mansion was attended to.

The residence itself was surrounded by a stone wall twelve feet high, this being provided with platforms on which cannon were mounted.

Beside the walls of the house, and running right round, was a deep moat, in which weeds and rushes of almost every description grew and flourished in wild luxuriance.

The mansion was approached by a drawbridge.

Three or four, at one period of its history, had given access to the mansion, but when the present proprietor inherited the grand old property, he had all destroyed with the exception of one that led to the principal entrance.

The then present Earl of Normanton was a young man of about thirty-five, and a more handsome and daring soldier, or a more graceful and faithful courtier, could not have been found in the kingdom.

The queen openly called him one of her best friends.

When the Hunchback left St. Paul's he, first of all, journeyed to Windsor, and business there detained him some hours.

He made a last call at the house of the celebrated Monkshow, the principal fancy costumier to the Court.

This highly-favoured individual was seated in his counting-house when the Hunchback arrived, busy in his calculations.

In his younger days Monkshow had been one of the principal Court fools to Henry VIII.

At the time we have the pleasure of introducing him he was a man fully fourscore years of age, but there still rested upon his plump, though somewhat peculiar features, an air of comicality.

While he calculated he " hum'd " and " ah'd," and occasionally delivered a crushing volley of abuse to a poor little pug-dog, which sat on the table in front of him.

The Hunchback, who had passed through the passage of the house without the slightest interruption, surveyed him through the glass partition for some few moments.

"How differently we are constituted," thought the Hunchback, with a deep sigh; " here is a man who has met with nothing but good fortune—a man whose long life has been nothing but one long day of pleasure. He has been petted and played with by the highest in the land, and when he could play no longer they made him his own master. I have known him many, many years—I know the whole of his history, and I believe that he does not know what misfortune and trouble are. And, also, how well he knows *my* history! Ah! how well! how well!

"He knew *her* — my wife — yes, knew her when she was— But, ah! where are my thoughts running? I must not think of her—nor of *him*—he who blasted my life—he who snatched my cup of happiness from my grasp, filled it with gall, and compelled me to drain that cup to the very dregs. But," he muttered, as he clenched his huge hands—"but one day I shall meet him face to face! Oh, for that day! Oh, for that hour when the man who ruined my happiness, who caused me to slay her, shall stand before me! But my thoughts must not be of these matters now."

Advancing, he tapped on the window.

"Enter," shouted Monkshow, in tones which, considering his age, were absolutely wonderful—" enter, and be hanged to you! Enter, Paul, and if you haven't brought that wine with you, you shall rue it, you knave, you shall."

" 'Tis not Paul," said the Hunchback, in low, deep tones; " 'tis I, the Hunchback."

Off his seat with wonderful rapidity started Monkshow.

"You !" he said; "*you*—the Hunchback! What, here?"

"Aye, aye, friend Monkshow, I am here."

"Marvellous! It is indeed you, Gil—"

"Silence !" interrupted the Hunchback, raising his hand. "Utter not that name at present. The hour is at hand, Monkshow—I say that perhaps the hour is at hand, but it has not arrived yet."

Monkshow bowed.

"I was born to obey," he said.

"Most true," was the Hunchback's reply; "and by always obeying you have made the journey of life without finding a stumbling-block."

"Aye, I have made the journey of life in an easy manner, sure enough," replied Monkshow. "Would I could say the same of you, old friend."

The two old friends shook hands warmly.

"My life is now fast drawing to a close," continued Monkshow, looking sadly into the dark, stern face before him, "and when Heaven shall call me away, I shall be found ready. I shall die with the knowledge that I never willingly injured a soul."

"Ay, you have a clear conscience," replied the Hunchback, "and that is more than I can say. But I have little time to spare. You no doubt guess my errand here to-night?"

"You require a costume?"

"Two."

"Two! Good. The whole of my extensive stock is at your service, and so is my purse if so be—"

"No," interrupted the Hunchback, with a smile; "I do not require your purse. But listen. The costumes I require are—first, that of a citizen of the highest class; secondly, that of a pedlar-painter. The first you will pack in as small a box as 'tis possible, and in a second box you will pack paints, brushes, and canvas."

"I understand you perfectly. And no doubt you will require various other odds-and-ends in the way of disguises."

"Yes, if you have them."

"I have everything; follow me and you shall choose. But will you not pass a few hours with me?"

"No; 'tis impossible. I must set out directly I have the articles I require. My horse is without, but I beg you to take charge of him until I call for him."

"Willingly; and I am right glad that you will not leave this house again until you are thoroughly disguised, for your arrest is sure to follow."

The Hunchback followed his old friend up the stairs, and from room to room, to select the articles required.

Though Monkshow was fourscore years old, he still had all his wits about him, and did not forget, ere he took the Hunchback into this or that room, to send off his servants so that they should not see the visitor.

In about an hour the Hunchback and his friend descended the stairs.

Heavens! What an alteration in the Hunchback.

His costume was changed for an old rustic one.

His hair was almost white, and so was the heavy beard and moustache affixed to his face.

On his humped back he carried a couple of boxes, covered with leather, and strapped tightly to his body.

In his right hand he carried a staff; in his left, doubled up and tied, an easel.

To look at him one would have taken him to be a pedlar, worn out with age, care, and misfortune, and without a penny in the world.

Certainly not a soul would have imagined that beneath that rustic, travel-stained costume he carried a sword and dagger.

On the threshold of the door he paused. Once more the friends clasped hands, and for some seconds they stood thus without uttering one word.

At last Monkshow, in hushed, trembling tones, said—

"Farewell, old and valued friend —farewell! I will pray that your errand may prove a success. But, oh, I am fearful for you! You are venturing into the lion's den. Oh, if you would only think."

"Think! You mock me, friend Monkshow. I have already thought. I am always thinking. I will go. You have proved yourself a most valued friend, as much now as in the years gone by. With your letter to the countess I need fear no difficulty."

"Only that she may refuse to allow you to paint her portrait."

"I must chance that. Farewell."

"Farewell."

And so the friends parted.

From Monkshow's house the Hunchback journeyed to an hostelry, which was well known to him, and there he was accommodated with an apartment.

He remained until the following

evening, when, by the gift of a sum of money, he obtained a ride in one of the old-fashioned village waggons to the outskirts of Esher.

Having watched the waggon out of sight, he took his way to another hostelry, not so much for refreshment, however, as to learn the news ; for by this time he felt that something must be known as to what had happened at Roxburgh House.

He found the hostelry full of an excited crowd of persons, discussing in loud tones the proceedings of a number of masked individuals who had invaded Roxburgh House when the festivities were at their height, and had *murdered* a number of noblemen and gentlemen ; also how Blackmore had been run through by the son of Lord Whitmore, and how afterwards he had fallen into a barrel of burning oil and been burnt to ashes.

Oh, how the Hunchback gloated over this intelligence!

Who would have suspected in this poor old pedlar, who drank his wine so meekly, the father of one who had been the means of destroying the vile wretches who were so calmly plotting against the life of their queen ?

Yes, he was overjoyed at hearing the news, but he was also overjoyed at the feeling displayed by every person in that hostelry.

"Serves him right !" cried a tall, burly fellow, attired in a costume which the Hunchback recognised as belonging to the Earl of Normanton. "Serves the villain right. He deserved a horrible death. I always thought he was a black-hearted wretch, and the holder of secrets which the queen would have given a round sum to be made acquainted with. And there's that villainous Dacre Deadman; he, if anything, is worse than Blackmore. I know a little, and I feel certain that the Hunchback of Old St. Paul's is at the bottom of this business. If Dacre Deadman can match his cunning with this Hunchback, well, then my name is not what it is."

Everyone present agreed in the most complete manner that Blackmore deserved the fate which had overtaken him, and they also sincerely hoped that the brutal young ruffian, Dacre

Deadman, would have his career brought to an abrupt termination.

The Hunchback shuffled out of the hostelry, and passed through a lane opposite.

At the end of this lane was a stone cross, beside which was a stone seat.

On one side was written—

"London—fifteen miles as the crow flies."

Having halted for a few moments, more for the sake of thinking than resting, the man of mystery again went on, this time across several fields.

At last he reached the outer wall of the mansion, the tall, graceful outlines of which he could easily make out in consequence of the brightness of the moon.

But the lower part was in almost total darkness, for the enormous trees of almost every description completely shut out every ray of moonlight.

Keeping as close against the wall as possible, the Hunchback eventually reached one of the many gates.

Many sounds fell upon his ears, but the principal was the steady tramp, tramp of a sentry.

He looked about for a means of communication, but not finding any, he rapped with his easel upon the wicket of the gate.

In a few seconds the little door was cautiously moved aside, and a gruff voice said—

"Well, sirrah! Thy business, eh ?"

"Is of a somewhat private character, friend, and if—"

"Eh ? Private? Wait," interrupted the man on duty.

Bang ! went the wicket, and presently the ponderous gate was drawn back and the man appeared.

In his right hand he held a drawn sword, and in his left a lantern.

The latter he raised until it was on a level with the Hunchback's face.

Having had a good stare, he said, in tones of most intense astonishment—

"Holy Virgin, guard us ! Your business is of a private character? Private, eh? Ho, ho! Shame! *Shame* on you, old man, to jest at your time of life !"

"I assure you, my good friend, that I am not jesting. I—"

"Are you aware that this is the

mansion belonging to the Earl of Normanton ? "

" Perfectly."

" And that no less a person than her most gracious and highly-gifted majesty, Queen Elizabeth, is at this present moment, within its walls ? "

" Perfectly."

" Heaven's mercy on us all ! " cried the man ; " and— Well, I marvel much at your impudence ! Why, man alive, you are naught but a pedlar, are you ? "

" That is all, my friend. But look you, do you happen to know a person of the name of Monkshow ? "

" Right well. 'Tis the costumier to the Court at Windsor."

" True. But I suppose you do not know his writing ? "

" Nay, I know it not. But why these questions ? "

The Hunchback took a letter from his wallet.

" You can read, I suppose ? " he said.

" Aye, well enough."

" What says this ? "

The Hunchback held out the letter, and the soldier, holding up the lantern, read—

" *To her grace the Countess of Normanton, and to her ladyship only.*"

" Well," he said, " was that written by Monkshow ? "

" It was. And he said that it would, no doubt, be difficult to get it conveyed to her ladyship. 'Yet,' he continued, 'you may chance upon a well-mannered, sympathetic soldier, who, for a small present, would willingly convey it for you.' Now I know you to be a well-mannered young man, who would not turn up his nose at a small present—not so much for himself as for his sweetheart—and behold."

And the Hunchback slipped a ring from his finger.

" What is that ? " queried the man.

" It is a beautiful diamond ring."

" Real stones ? "

" Aye, pure, my son—pure."

" And you mean to say that, if I convey this letter to the Countess of Normanton, you will give me this ring for my trouble ? "

" To be sure."

" Hem ! You must be a very rich old pedlar."

" Nay, that does not follow. But the fact is, my son, I wish to see the beautiful countess."

" Yes, yes ; but—er—hem !—er—you see," said the man, hesitating and turning the ring over and over in his hand, " you see we are bound to be careful, and our instructions are of the most minute and strict description. How am I to know that you are not an impostor ? "

" Young man," replied the Hunchback, in a pained tone of voice, " you are the very first man who has ever told me I might be an impostor."

" Well—er—I am sure I beg your pardon ; but what might be the nature of your business with the countess ? "

" If I tell you, it will not go any farther ? "

" I want to get her commission to paint her portrait."

" Phew ! Is *that* all ? Why, you might have said that in the first place ! And so you are a painter, master pedlar? Well, you don't look it. As to painting the portrait of the Countess of Normanton, I think I may safely say that such a thing is entirely out of the question. As you might imagine, her grace has only to hold up her little finger to be surrounded by some of the leading masters of the day."

" No doubt of it, my friend. But it is notorious that her grace frequently encourages struggling talent ; and in this case I am strongly recommended."

" You are right. Her grace, to my knowledge, is very partial to old Monkshow, and would be willing to render him a service. Enter, and I will take the letter."

The Hunchback entered, and the soldier, placing a stool for him, told him to be seated until he returned.

In less than ten minutes he reappeared.

" You are a lucky pedlar, at any rate," he smiled, " for her grace no sooner read the letter than she said, ' I will see this person ; show him into the fourth summer-house, and I will join him in a few moments.' So come along, master pedlar, and good luck attend ye."

" Thank you. I hope the gift of the ring will make a great impression on your sweetheart."

The man laughed heartily as he said—

"Why, master pedlar, I have been married to my sweetheart these ten years. But, neverthless, the ring will have an excellent effect, I do assure you. It will cause my good wife's tongue to wag in a more peaceful direction."

Through the dark, woefully-neglected grounds the Hunchback followed his guide.

When, some considerable distance from the gate, the sound of music was wafted to their ears.

"'Tis only a State concert, my friend," said the soldier; "a very common occurrence here."

Presently a large, handsome summer-house was reached.

It was a most beautiful place, the carving of the woodwork being simply superb.

But, alas! the whole of it was shamefully neglected.

"Wait here," said the soldier, "and her ladyship will join you. My instructions are to return to my post; and so, if I do not see you again, I bid you a good-night."

"A good-night to you, and thank you," replied the Hunchback.

Away went the man, happy in the possession of a valuable jewel, and the Hunchback stood in front of the summer-house, awaiting the appearance of the countess.

He did not have long to wait. From out the darkness a tall, graceful form emerged, and a sweet voice said—

"Well, sir pedlar, I am here."

The Countess of Normanton stood before him.

She was a splendid creature—one of the most beautiful roses which could have been found among England's garden of beautiful women—and she was not only beautiful, but accomplished and gifted to a high degree, one of her most rare gifts being the possession of a very beautiful, sympathetic voice, which she used to perfection, captivating all who heard her, and especially the queen herself, who was a great lover of music and all that pertained to it.

The Hunchback bowed low, raising his hat as he did so.

"I am your ladyship's humble servant," he said, "and I thank you for this great favour."

"Your friend Monkshow," said the countess, "does not mention your name."

"It is an omission, my lady," replied the Hunchback, who, however, now remembered that he had not told him what name to say—"it is an omission which I will at once rectify. My name is Rosslyn Gilbert."

"You know what your friend wrote?"

"I do not, my lady."

The countess produced the letter.

"I can read it in the moonlight," she said, moving into the rays of the moon. "Listen, sir ped—I mean Master Rosslyn Gilbert. Monkshow says—

"'Your ladyship will pardon the liberty I take'—and assuredly I do—'in addressing a letter to you for the purpose of introducing to your ladyship's most favourable notice a person as insignificant as a pedlar. But, your ladyship, he is most anxious to paint the exquisite outlines of your lovely face'—Monkshow flatters like a young man," her ladyship laughed—"'and I do assure you that he is a very competent person.

"'He is a very old friend of mine—a person who, in the times gone by, when your ladyship was a wee little thing that I used to carry round your father's lovely grounds on my shoulder, was a man well-to-do.

"'Troubles and misfortunes have followed so closely on his heels, that he is now, alas! completely broken down. Yet he is a beautiful artist, and will paint your ladyship's lovely face and graceful figure quite as well as any artist whose name stands high in public opinion. Take compassion on him, my lady, and give him a commission. Knowing the dislike the earl has to pedlars and the like, I ask your ladyship to see the bearer in the grounds and give him your answer.—Your ladyship's most obedient and most faithful servant,   MONKSHOW.'"

Respectfully silent the Hunchback had remained during the reading of this document, but the disguise he wore did not conceal the emotion under which he laboured.

When the countess had finished she folded up the letter, and, turning to the Hunchback, said, in sweetly sympathetic tones—

"Poor old man! Most sincerely do I pity you ; and be assured that in my prayers I shall not forget to address an appeal to Heaven that you may be supported in bearing your heavy burden. I give you the commission, Master Rosslyn, and, in the result, I shall not forget that your hand is not so steady as it must have been in the days gone by. Monkshow speaks most truly when he says that the earl has a great dislike to pedlars. He has indeed. If all England were searched, a man with such bitter hatred towards pedlars could not be found to equal my husband. But I will appeal to him. Follow me."

"Oh, your ladyship, no words of mine could express the gratitude I feel."

"Talk not of gratitude at present."

The countess turned and walked on, the long train of her lovely satin dress sweeping the weeds as she went.

The Hunchback followed her closely.

The magnificent front of the mansion—the drawbridge to which the countess had said was to remain lowered until her return—was crowded with soldiers, officers, and pages of all grades, while to the right and the left scores of horses were in waiting, this proving that a large number of guests were within the mansion.

Through several apartments the beautiful countess led the way, and the Hunchback, as may be supposed, became the object of a vast amount of curiosity and speculation.

Who on earth was this curiously-attired, mud-stained, pack-laden pedlar? each person was asking.

At last an ante-room, communicating with her ladyship's boudoir, was reached.

As soon as she entered the apartment, the countess struck a silver hand-bell.

The summons was instantly answered by a richly-attired young page.

"Where is your master?" queried the countess.

"Still in the state-room, your ladyship," was the reply. "The queen has not yet risen."

"The concert still proceeds ? "

"It does, your ladyship."

"Very good. Go and tell your master that I wish to speak with him at once."

The page bowed and withdrew.

In less than three minutes the Earl of Normanton made his appearance.

He was completely thunderstricken to behold a pedlar, and in his wife's ante-room.

"In the name of all the—" he commenced, but before he could conclude the sentence the little white hand of the countess was upon his lips.

"Hush !" she smiled; "be not so surprised. I wish—"

"Have you taken leave of your senses ? " cried the earl.

"Nay, I have taken an interest in this poor old man, and I want you to do the same, my dear husband."

"Great heavens ! what can you mean ? "

"What I say. My—"

"Knowing my dislike to pedlars," said the young earl, somewhat fiercely, "you yet bring one under my roof."

"I am not in the habit of bringing pedlars under your roof."

"Fortunately, no. Sirrah !" he cried, turning to the Hunchback.

But again the countess checked him. Placing her arms around him, and tenderly kissing him, she cried, in imploring tones—

"Husband—dear husband—for *my* sake, take pity on this poor old man ! "

The earl bent his smiling face, and said, tenderly—

"Generally, my beautiful wife, your pleadings are effectual, but in this instance I—"

"First," interrupted the countess, taking the letter from her bosom, and placing it in her husband's hand, "read this."

The earl took it and carefully read every word.

But while he read his features underwent no change, such as would have shown whether he did or did not feel any compassion for this man.

But the letter had an excellent effect.

"So you are a painter ? " he said.

"At your lordship's service," answered the Hunchback, with a low bow.

"You are a good artist—eh ? "

"So men have said."

"Well, where are your specimens? Have you them in your pack?"

"Nay, my lord; I sell every picture as soon as painted."

"A wise plan, no doubt. But if you have no specimens, how am I to know that you are not an impostor? True, here is Monkshow's letter; but then Monkshow, though good at disguises, is sometimes unable to penetrate one. The letter had a little effect on me, I must admit, but had it not have been backed up by my wife's pleadings, I should have taken no heed of it. You shall paint her portrait, and shall stay here until 'tis finished, but you must first of all prove to me that you are not an impostor."

"Oh, husband!" cried the countess.

"Hist, my love!" replied the earl. "You know I have lived longer in the world than you. Wait."

Down came his hand upon the bell.

The page entered.

"Hasten to the cellars," said the earl, "and procure me a piece of charcoal; sharpen one end to a point. And, at the same time, bring with you a sheet of parchment, on which you will have some flour rubbed."

The page withdrew, but soon returned with the required articles.

After he had withdrawn, the earl, placing the articles upon the table, said—

"Prove that you are an artist."

"What shall I do, my lord?"

"What you please."

The Hunchback laid the sheet on the table, and in a rapid and masterly fashion sketched out a face.

The earl and countess closely watched the rapid and unhesitating movements of his fingers.

When the Hunchback stopped, the earl said—

"Have you done?"

"I have, your lordship."

The earl and countess no sooner looked upon the sketch than they simultaneously uttered an exclamation of astonishment.

"*My father!*" cried the earl.

"It is!" said the countess; "and, oh, how life-like!"

"It is most extraordinary. How do you account for being able to draw a sketch like this? The late earl has been dead many, many years."

"I knew your father well. In my younger days he often gave me a commission."

"Why did you not say so before? And now I come to look at this sketch, it is marvellously like the portrait in the picture-gallery."

"It is, unquestionably," said the countess.

"And that portrait," continued the earl, "was painted by that clever, but extraordinary painter, who killed his wife when he found her with Sir Garnet Glassion—Gilbert Gascony Golding— yes, that was his name.

"Well, sir pedlar, you have afforded us convincing proof that you are a wonderfully clever man, so much so that, despite your misfortunes, I nevertheless wonder that you are a pedlar. Well, you shall paint the countess' portrait, and be well paid and well treated while beneath my roof. It is quite evident that you were well acquainted with my father, or you would not have been able to sketch his portrait so accurately from memory, and any person kindly treated by my father shall be kindly treated by me. I will at once issue instructions respecting you. And now come," he added to the countess; "for both of us have already been too long from the queen's presence."

*   *   *   *

The Hunchback was comfortably installed in a large, lofty apartment adjoining the picture-gallery.

But, anxious to hear if any fresh news had arrived, he requested and obtained the earl's written authority to leave and enter the grounds as he thought proper.

So, as soon as the majority of the guests had departed, he left the mansion and the grounds, and wended his way in the direction of the hostelry.

He found the inn more crowded than ever.

He listened to what was being said, but found it substantially the same as before.

He moved to go, when his eyes became fixed upon a young horseman, who was evidently making some anxious enquiries.

"'I ASSURE YOU, MY GOOD FRIEND, THAT I AM NOT JESTING,' CRIED THE HUNCHBACK."

The Hunchback got close up to the youth, and attentively examined his face and attire.

"Unless I am mistaken," muttered the Hunchback, "this youth bears the costume of young Lord Roxburgh. I must watch his movements."

He saw, from the troubled expression on the youth's face, that he was undergoing some great anxiety.

After a few moments he turned his horse's head and rode down the lane towards the stone cross.

The Hunchback followed him.

When beside the stone cross the youthful horseman, Mark Mellow, paused and looked back.

He had caught the sound of the Hunchback's hurrying footsteps.

"I say, old man," said Mark, "are you familiar with the surrounding neighbourhood, or are you a stranger?"

"I am familiar with the neighbourhood, my son," replied the Hunchback. "Tell me, whom do you seek?"

"Oh, no one in particular. But I should like to meet with a person who would conduct me to the mansion of the Earl of Normanton."

"You were at the hostelry yonder?"

"I was."

"Well, saw you not a number of the earl's servants?"

"I did, and spoke with them. But neither of them would conduct me to the mansion because I am seeking no one in particular."

"No one in particular? A strange errand, my son," said the Hunchback, glancing suspiciously at him. "A very strange errand. With such a tale, is it possible that you would seek *admission* to yonder mansion?"

"Aye."

"You will seek in vain. But you say you want no one in particular—that means, that you seek a certain person, but do not wish to divulge his name, eh?"

"You are a wise man, father pedlar."

"Aye, if I am not somewhat wise now, I never shall be. But list ye. I am acquainted with many who are at present within that mansion. I will not ask you the name of the individual you seek, but if you can describe him, mayhap I can tell you whether such a person is there or not."

"I am unable to describe the person I seek, for I have never yet seen him."

"Holy Virgin! you are a strange youth."

"But," continued Mark, "I can tell you this—in one respect the person I seek resembles yourself."

"Ah! How?"

"He is a *hunchback*."

"Indeed!" was the Hunchback's reply.

Like the lightning's flash the youth's errand occurred to him.

"Dismount, my son," said the Hunchback, after he had taken a good look on all sides to be assured that they were neither overlooked nor overheard, "I have something of importance to whisper in your ear."

Mark hesitated but an instant.

Dismounting, he bent his ear to the Hunchback.

"The person you seek," whispered the Hunchback, "*is the Hunchback of Old St. Paul's.*"

"Holy Mary!" gasped Mark, "how knew you that? Art thou a wizard?"

"Nay, nay; but am I not right?"

"Perfectly. And do you know him?"

"Right well. And you, you say, have never seen him?"

"Never."

"Then behold him."

And the Hunchback snatched the false hair from his face.

"You are the Hunchback, then?" Mark said, in hushed tones. "Yes, yes; I feel 'tis so. Wonderful that I should thus have met you!"

"You are satisfied?"

"Perfectly. As for the disguise, 'tis naught, for I suspected that if I *should* find the Hunchback—and I was beginning to despair of so doing—I should find him disguised."

"I will, in a moment, furnish you with still further proof that I am indeed the Hunchback of Old St. Paul's; but, first, tell me quickly—from whom do you come? My heart tells me that you are a messenger from my son, and from the young Lord Stanley Whitmore."

"You are correct—I am. I was in the service of Lord Roxburgh; now I am page to young Lord Whitmore."

"A wise change, my son—most wise. But they—they are safe?"

"Safe and sound. But here—"

"Wait—look at this."

The Hunchback took a taper and a tinder-box from his pocket, and having kindled a light, he handed the taper to Mark.

Then opening his travel-stained dress, he took out a leathern case, opened it, and turned one side of it towards Mark.

"What see you?" he asked.

"The portrait of your son. And most lifelike it is. But I do assure you that I am satisfied. Here is the packet I was directed to place in your hands, with the intimation that you were to peruse the contents *at once*. Read, and I will hold the taper, and at the same time strain my eyes and ears for travellers."

With trembling fingers did the Hunchback open that packet.

Briefly, but distinctly, everything which our readers know was written down.

Then he came to the projected assassination of the queen.

Was he astonished?

No, he was not; for he and Lord Whitmore long ago had been under the impression that this was what Blackmore's secret council would eventually order.

But he saw that, by the way our hero had arranged matters, he had a splendid opportunity of distinguishing himself, and of gaining a hearing of the queen.

Would Simon Silex really carry out the order given him?

"But I have no doubt he will," thought the Hunchback. "I know his determined character, and, fortunately, he does not know of Blackmore's death. But if he hears of it at either of these hostelries, of course the whole matter instantly falls to the ground. He would return to Wapping, free of the fetters with which Blackmore has for so long bound him. I must wait and watch. It is almost a certainty that he will come this way—disguised, no doubt.

"You will at once hasten to St. Paul's and give my son and those with him particulars of how we met. Tell my son and the young Lord Whitmore that they have done perfectly right. Tell them to wait patiently, and watch for the result. I will now bid you adieu. I thank you for this message ; and fear it not, a large reward shall be yours."

Mark sprang into the saddle.

"Farewell," he said.

"Farewell," cried the Hunchback. "Heaven guard ye!"

In a few seconds Mark had disappeared in the distance.

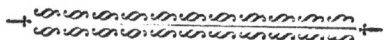

CHAPTER II.

SHOWS THE MANNER IN WHICH SIMON SILEX CAME INTO POSSESSION OF A DISGUISE—OF HIS MEETING WITH THE PEDLAR—AND OF THE EVENTS WHICH FOLLOWED.

IN the first part of this romance, we took occasion to mention that hereafter we should have something to do with the man who sold white mice outside, and even inside, the sacred edifice of Old St. Paul's.

That time has now come. But, first, we must go back to Simon Silex.

He did not go off at once to Esher.

Simon Silex was not a man to rush headlong into anything.

The first thing he did was to take a long rest.

After that he armed himself with pistols, sword, and dagger, and threw a large cloak about his lanky person.

Then, after refreshment, and a fearful quarrel with his wife, he departed.

But ere he had got far, he met a number of companions, and after a little persuasion, he accompanied them to a noted hostelry in Southwark, where he remained drinking and rioting for hours.

Another rest was necessary, and he slept soundly for five hours.

He was awakened by the host, who informed him that the horse he had ordered was ready and waiting at the door.

So Simon at last set out upon his journey.

He met with no adventure until he came to the village of Grattley, at which he arrived exactly at the same time Mark Mellow had met the Hunchback.

Simon, as a matter of course, at once looked about for a hostelry, and after a few moments, he discovered one at some considerable distance from the road.

He proceeded towards it as fast as possible.

"At last!" he chuckled; "at last! Oh, will I not have a huge drink! And I will take care to see that my flask is properly filled. It is a beautiful night; but I feel cold. I wish this job was over."

In the space of two minutes he reached the trough in front of the hostelry.

He was preparing to dismount when his eye rested on the doorway of the inn.

It was closed!

By aid of the moon, he saw that a large piece of parchment had been nailed to the door.

He urged his horse to the doorway, and craned his neck forward to read what was written on the parchment.

This is what it said—

"LOCKSLEY LOVETT,

"Host of this house, 'The Dolphin,' was hanged, June the 11th, after a fair trial, in which he was found guilty of smuggling spirits into this country, against the sovereign will of her most gracious majesty, Elizabeth. His property was afterwards confiscated. Evildoers, take ye heed!

"𝔈𝔩𝔦𝔷𝔞𝔟𝔢𝔱𝔥 𝔕."

"Evil-doers, take ye heed!" sneered Simon. "Pooh! Why, I've smuggled for years! Against the will of her most gracious majesty, eh! Hem! No doubt her reception of this blade will be against her sovereign will. Closed—and I am parched! There—"

"Hallo—hallo!" shouted a loud voice.

At the same moment Simon caught the sound of horses' hoofs.

Turning, he saw three horsemen advancing towards him.

They drew up to allow their animals to drink.

Simon was about to ride away, when one of the men cried out—

"Why, as I live, it is Simon Silex!"

Simon started and turned pale.

"Why," continued the voice, "who would have dreamt of meeting the host of 'The Wapping Arms' in this lonely spot? Well, Simon, what are ye doing?"

"I am on the road to London," was the surly reply. "But who are you?"

"Dan Drocklebury. Why, you don't know your own friends! So you are on the road to London, eh? And you thought you would call here and have a drink? He, he! You are nicely caught, Simon. The house is bolted and barred, and the host is swinging away right merrily at the cross-roads yonder. It's a shameful thing to lock up a house, Simon, when it is full of excellent stuff."

"Full of stuff! Why, it says that the property has been confiscated!"

"So it has; but it has not yet been removed. Well, adieu till we see you at Wapping, Simon. We are off to Windsor."

So saying, the three horsemen— three individuals who certainly deserved to be served in the same way as the landlord of "The Dolphin"—rode swiftly away.

Simon proceeded slowly on his journey, pondering over what the man had said.

"The place full of stuff!" he muttered. "And no one to drink it but the rats—who, there is little doubt, will get as drunk as Tower warders. It is shameful! I wonder whether I could succeed in getting in? Well, it would be worth trying if— But they may be joking. No doubt they were. No; I'll go on."

He urged on his horse, but before he had proceeded a dozen yards, he noticed a man coming towards him.

When he came on a level, Simon drew up.

He was now face to face with a tall, old man, dressed in a tattered, but very picturesque costume—a costume very much resembling those worn by Italian peasants in the days of which we write.

He wore a long, white beard and moustache, and his bald head was entirely uncovered.

He was what would be called a remarkably handsome old man.

Strapped around his shoulders, and brought round in front of him, was a cage, in which were a number of white mice, which little creatures he had taught to perform various tricks.

He took Simon to be a gentleman traveller, and in tones of singular sweetness he said—

"Good gentleman, see my white mice—pray see my white mice. I say, most honoured sir—Heaven's choicest blessings on you!—see my white mice."

"Confound your white mice, Christian Mackay!" growled Simon.

"Eh!" cried Christian—this being the name he had been known by for many years. "Ha! *What!* Can it be? It is—it is Simon Silex."

"Yes, it *is* Simon Silex."

"Lor'! What, here in this wilderness! Wonderful! Is the world coming to an abrupt termination?"

"I neither know nor care. But if you have such a thing as a brandy-flask about you, and will give me the loan of a drink, I will well repay you when next I see you at Wapping."

"I doubt you not. Why, surely I have a brandy-flask; but then 'tis empty."

"Fool! Of what use is that to me?"

"Are you very thirsty, Simon Silex?"

"Very, old mouser."

"Well, 'tis the first time I ever heard a host say that he was thirsty. And you cannot get anything to drink hereabouts? It's very sad! Now I have been in this neighbourhood much of late, the queen being here—and you know I get a good deal out of her train and those who visit her—and whenever I am thirsty I help myself—ha, ha!"

"Oh, you do? What to—water?"

"Water, eh? No, to wine—to wine."

"I will pay you well to let me into the secret."

"I want no pay; but you must swear to preserve the secret."

"I swear."

"Enough—dismount. Leave your horse where he is and follow me."

Simon quickly did as directed, and followed the old man, who turned in the direction of "The Dolphin."

When near the house he turned off to the back.

Pulling aside a few boards which stood against the wall of the house, he said—

"There—look! See that hole?"

"I do."

"I made that, and no one knows of its existence but myself. This house is closed, and the property confiscated to the Crown."

"I know it."

"Well, the property has not been removed. 'Tis here—all of it. Wine enough to swim in; spirits enough to— But enter, unless you are afraid."

"Would not a light be of some service? I have a tinder-box and a taper."

"Light it then when you get within. Here they might attract attention. Get in with you."

Down on his hands and knees went Simon, and he crawled into the house.

Christian followed him, saying—

"Now strike the light, but be careful, for there is a lot of spirits on the floor."

The taper was lit, and Simon, holding it aloft, looked about him.

He saw that he was surrounded with barrels of all shapes and sizes, and that goblets and glasses lay about in every direction.

Christian, having placed his cage on one side, picked up a couple of goblets.

"The names of the wines here that I have discovered," he said, "are many and varied. What is your favourite draught?"

"Brandy," was the reply; "and the stronger the better."

Christian, after many mistakes, found the desired liquor, filled a goblet, and handed it to Simon.

Then he filled himself a measure of wine.

"Now," he said, "let us seat ourselves at the table. A little chat—"

"Nay, nay," interrupted Simon. "I must on—"

"You have important business on hand, eh?"

"Very."

"Ah, all my business has been done

for the day. Soon I shall have ceased altogether to transact business."

"Oh! how is that?"

"I have made enough, Simon—quite enough to enable me to end my days in peace and comfort."

"By the blessed Virgin, Christian, I am right glad to hear it. But I will drain another goblet with you. Come, fill up our measures—and to the brim, since it costs us nothing—and for a little while I will take a seat at the table."

Christian refilled the goblets, and the pair seated themselves at the table.

"A sudden idea—a splendid one, too—has taken possession of me," thought Simon. "It is quite certain that the way I disguised myself, as I thought, is by no means effectual, since that man not long ago at once penetrated it. Who would recognise Simon Silex in the dress of a trainer of mice, eh?"

Aloud he said—

"And so you have actually made enough money to live peacefully and comfortably for the remainder of your days?"

"Aye, I have; but I've had to scrape, and scrape, and—"

"No doubt—no doubt. Why, how many years have I known you at Old St. Paul's? Twenty, I should think."

"No doubt. But I have been there, off and on, these forty years."

"And I suppose you have placed the money you have made with the goldsmiths?"

"No, no," answered Christian, shaking his head. "Oh, no. I do not believe in the Lombard Street disciples. No. My mouse-cage is my bank. He, he!"

"Your *mouse*-cage?"

"Yes; that contains all my wealth, though you would not think so to look at it, would you?"

"Nay, that I should not," replied Simon.

At the same time he thought—

"Here is, indeed, a most splendid opportunity. At one blow I could become the possessor of an impenetrable disguise and a sum of money. I can slay this man, and need never fear being accused of the deed. It must be done. The disguise is an attraction, but the money is a far greater one."

"I always place my money in a secret compartment within that cage," continued Christian, "for this reason. If attacked and robbed, the robbers would certainly leave my little mice alone—and the money."

"It is a strange thing," said Simon, "that, though I have known you for so many years, I have never once looked at the mice. You must have had a good many in that time."

"Hundreds—hundreds! But I never had any half so clever," cried Christian, in delighted tones—for the old man loved his little white mice as a mother loves her first-born. "Do look!" he cried, leaving his seat, and falling on his knees beside the cage. "Do look—do!"

Simon rose.

His right hand stole stealthily beneath his cloak, and his long, bony fingers clutched the haft of his dagger.

"Are they not beautiful?" cried Christian. "They are so clever. They have been the means of procuring me plenty of money, and—"

"And they are the cause of your death," yelled Simon.

Quickly Christian turned.

But it was too late—too late!

Simon drew swiftly back, raised a long, glittering dagger high up over his head, and brought it down.

It was buried to the hilt in the old man's back.

Oh, what an ear-piercing, terrible cry escaped the old man's lips!

For a few seconds he literally writhed in fearful agony at the feet of his murderer.

Again and again he tried to speak, but it was in vain.

His lips moved, certainly, but that was all.

He raised his hand and his eyes above, and the look on his noble face was expressive of the terrible curse he vainly tried to utter.

No sooner had he plunged the dagger into the old man's body than Simon instantly withdrew it.

He held the blade in his hand ready to strike again.

But there was no necessity.

After but a short, terrible struggle, during which the poor old man many times fixed his eyes upon his loved mouse-cage, Christian Mackay fell flat upon his face, uttered a prolonged sigh, and died.

"Well," muttered Simon, "it is certain that I never before saw a man die so hard. And now, if I would don his attire, I had better hasten, or all his clothes will be completely saturated in blood."

With all haste he took the clothes from the old man's body, then slipped off the principal part of his own, and placed them aside.

"I shall know where they are when the queen's job is over," he thought; "and now what shall I do with this carcase? Ah! I have it—down the trap."

On the other side of the table was a large trap leading to the wine vaults. The door was open—perhaps it had been opened by Christian himself at some time or other.

Towards this Simon dragged the body, and without any ceremony toppled it over.

Down the rude ladder went the body, bumping on every step.

"He has been used to *mice* all his life," chuckled the depraved beast; "and now in death the *rats* will get used to *him*."

Oh, how little did this horrid ruffian dream how near he was to *his own* death!

In a few moments Simon Silex had donned the old man's clothes, and a pretty object he looked.

In the back of the doublet was a large patch of blood, and this Simon cut away.

"And now," he thought, "I wonder how I look. That makes me think. No doubt the rooms above have not been disturbed. If that is so, I shall, no doubt, be able to *see* how I look."

Taking the taper, he searched for and found the stairs, and ascended them.

On the first floor he found a bed-room.

Entering it he advanced to the looking-glass, set in a recess in the wall, and critically surveyed himself. So amused was he that he burst out into a loud, hoarse laugh.

With his hands freshly stained with blood, he could laugh, and laugh loudly.

As Simon drew back he noticed a razor upon the dressing-table.

After a little consideration he came to the conclusion that his disguise would be the more perfect if he shaved off what hair there was on his face.

He therefore proceeded to cut it off; but he found it a very difficult matter indeed.

His hair was as tough as wire, and the razor was dreadfully blunt. However, he accomplished it at last.

Having searched about, he discovered an old, short cloak and a battered hat with an enormous brim.

Having donned these, he once again surveyed himself in the mirror.

"The Evil One himself would not know me," he considered. "I am safe from being recognised this time, anyhow."

Descending the stairs, he buckled on his arms, and then turned his attention to the cage.

Kneeling down, he placed the taper on the floor and pulled the cage towards him.

Scores of tiny, delicate white mice immediately came to the bars.

"Very pretty things!" sneered Simon. "Very pretty, by the Virgin! Come here, my little squeakers. I am going to do you all a good turn, for I will set you free, and you can make short work of the wines and the spirits confiscated by the sovereign will of her gracious majesty, Queen Elizabeth."

He tore open the doors of the cage, but the mice came not forth.

They seemed to know that the ugly face and the cruel eyes peering at them did hot belong to the master who had treated them so kindly.

They shrank back into the four corners, and this so exasperated Simon that, picking up the cage, he banged it upon the floor.

At each bang out rushed a number of the little creatures, and, squeaking loudly, they hurried away in every direction.

"By the foul fiend!" growled Simon, "I will make you move yourselves! And now for the hoard."

He placed his hand within the cage, but could feel nothing.

All over the cage, inside and out, he

looked with feverish haste, but saw nothing which could indicate the existence of a secret receptacle.

"Can the old thief have been but joking?" he growled, between his clenched teeth. "Is my only reward for committing murder a filthy disguise? No, I'll not believe it. I'll not be satisfied until I have torn it bit by bit."

Leaping to his feet, he once more looked round the place—this time in hopes of finding an iron bar.

He found a bottling mallet instead.

With this he started on the cage, which was a very pretty, ornamental affair, and made by Christian himself, and in a few seconds had smashed it to atoms.

While hammering on the bottom, which was very thick and weighty, a piece of board fell out, and its fall was followed by a perfect shower of gold pieces.

Simon uttered a perfect yell of joy. His long, bony hands seized upon the gold until he had so much in them that he could not close them.

He placed all the pieces aside, then tore the boards apart.

He discovered three rolls of goldsmiths' notes, and a large packet of diamonds.

It was evident that, having so much gold, and not knowing where to put it as it accumulated, poor old Christian Mackay had exchanged it for these latter.

"Now I have no pockets in this disguise," muttered Simon. "What shall I do? Leave it here until I return, or take it without and bury it? Let me think. Nay, I'll leave it here."

Rising, he stood upon the table and carefully took down a small barrel.

It was full of wine of some sort.

This Simon at once emptied down the trap, and in the empty barrel put the valuables, and replaced it on the shelf.

"When this next job is over," he chuckled, "and Blackmore gives me the amount due, I shall be a man of vast wealth. Ho, ho! I'll leave this country for Spain, and there, for the remainder of my days, I shall be cock of the walk. But my wife don't go with me. No, no! The vixen. I'll be even with her yet."

Having blown out the taper, the wretch returned to the open air by means of the hole shown him by poor Christian.

He made his way to his horse, which he found quietly nibbling the grass by the roadside.

He had placed his foot in the stirrup, when it occurred to him that, if he mounted the horse, it would not tally with his disguise.

"Verily," he thought, "I look more like a beggar than a traveller. My best plan would be to place him behind yonder clump of trees, tie him to one of them, and there let him remain until I return. Yes, that would be the best plan. So be it."

Taking the bridle he led the horse behind a clump of young oaks, to one of which he tied him, and then resumed his journey.

At last, after many inquiries, and after he had had, many times, to retrace his steps, he reached the stone cross.

"Not far now," he thought; "I must, first of all, enter the grounds, and that must be done by scaling the walls in a secluded spot. I must not be in too great a hurry, or the whole plan will fall to the ground. It is certain that the queen does not retire until midnight, and so the deed must be done in the small hours. Ha! who is this? A pedlar? It is. Since the queen is here, the whole place, no doubt, swarms with such people. Hi, ho! master pedlar."

"Aye, aye, my friend," was the pedlar's reply; "what want ye?"

"I say, my friend, master pedlar, what do you— Why, as I live, you are humpbacked!"

"Eh, ah! Did I not know it years ago?"

"Ha, ha! Well, I presume you did. But I say, master pedlar, that I never saw a pedlar who was humpbacked before, I say; and I say—"

"Hold, hold!" interrupted the pedlar —our readers, of course, know that this was the Hunchback—"not so fast. My hearing and my memory are not so good as they were in the years gone by."

Aside the Hunchback muttered—

"His disguise is good, but his peculiar way of speaking—his continual 'I say, and I say,' has betrayed him. It is Simon Silex."

"What the deuce are you mumbling about, you crook-backed old scamp?" growled Simon.

"My son," replied the pedlar, meekly, "your language is somewhat strong—nearly as strong as your *breath*, in fact."

"Ha, no doubt," sneered Simon; "and no doubt you think a very great deal of yourself, old man, eh?"

"Nay, indeed; you—"

"Well," interrupted Simon, "what do you take me for?"

"I take you for one of the poorer sons of society."

"Oh, and pray what is that?"

"A beggar."

"Good. If you are short of hearing, old man, you are not short-sighted. Yes, I am a beggar. Is there anything wrong in that?"

"Nay; all that is good. The profession of a beggar is far preferable to that of a pedlar. For while a pedlar begs and prays, and prays and begs a person he thinks likely to purchase, a beggar *demands*, and is satisfied if it is only for the purpose of getting rid of him."

"Hem! There's some truth in what you say. And I say, old man, that you can preach a sermon so that it looks like truth—*that's* what I say. But what have you done with your pack, master pedlar?"

"Left it at yonder hostelry, so that I might take a walk without it, and by so doing experience the sensation of walking without the inconvenience of a load."

"And what do you sell?"

"Trinkets and the like. And to he or she who buys of me I give sound advice."

"*Oh!* Whether they like it or not?"

"Nay, I do not attempt to thrust an iron bar down a trout's gullet."

"Do you sell books of proverbs?"

"Nay, nor books of foolery, which are intended as wit. But now, since I have told you so much of my business, mayhap you will tell me yours?"

"Willingly; but first, will you take a drink with me, just to show we bear no animosity one to the other?"

"I thank you," and the Hunchback took the flask handed him; "and I drink to your health, and at the same time aasure you that there is no animosity between us."

Simon having taken his share, he said—

"Now as to my business. I have none, except it is to beg of anyone I think likely to dole out a small sum. Perhaps the morrow may prove lucky. I am now in the neighbourhood of the Earl of Normanton's residence, where, I learn, the queen is at present staying, and no doubt I shall get a little from her courtiers."

"I should say such a thing is quite likely. I have done very well with them."

"Indeed!"

"Yes, very well. So pleased were they with the trinkets, that I have several times been into the house with them."

"Eh, indeed! Well, on my word, you are the luckiest humpbacked pedlar, in existence. And I've no doubt you are acquainted with many parts of the old mansion?"

"Oh, yes, with many."

"I say, master pedlar, the queen does not sleep in an apartment by herself, does she?"

"I have heard that she does."

"Humph! I have been told that she never goes to sleep unless she is surrounded by her guards."

"Pooh, it is all fiction! What has she to be afraid of? For my part, I think she is safer in yonder mansion than in either of her palaces. But she is so loved, that no one would willingly do her harm."

"To be sure, master pedlar, you are quite right. Ah, I've no doubt she sleeps in the most beautiful room the mansion contains?"

"As a matter of course. It is a very large and sumptuously-furnished apartment, I have heard say. It is at the back of the mansion, and is called the White Tower."

"The *back!* I should have thought that the queen's apartments were in the front."

"The back is the place—chosen, I

suppose, because some of the windows look out on to a little garden."

We may here inform our readers that what the Hunchback was giving was a description of the place *where he himself had been accommodated.*

"You have been there, master pedlar?"

"No; but I have been at the back and looked at the place."

Simon, as may be supposed, got interested here.

"Here is a man," he thought, "from whom I may get all the information necessary. Of course, the guards are always on duty, day and night; but, if I gain the grounds, I can creep on them in my own fashion, and my dagger will be the means of putting them beyond the power of interference."

Aloud he said—

"Take another drink, master pedlar. Good stuff such as this is cannot hurt you. Here, let us be seated. Soh! Now, take a long drink. It will do you good."

The Hunchback complied.

In a clever, yet apparently unconcerned manner, he learned that Simon knew absolutely nothing of what had occurred at Hampton.

By degrees, Simon, on his side, learned all that he wished to know as to the back of the mansion, in which the apartments of the queen were supposed to be situated.

As a matter of fact, the queen's apartments were situated in the front, and adjoining the apartments of the earl and his beautiful wife.

At last the pair rose.

"I shall betake myself to yonder hostelry," said Simon, "and ask to be accommodated with a bed of some description. And you?"

"I continue my walk for an hour, and then return to the hostelry."

Mighty glad was Simon to hear this. Was it *his* intention to go to the hostelry?

Certainly not.

He knew that he had all his work cut out.

His intention was to walk *towards* the hostelry, and, as soon as he thought the Hunchback had got a sufficient distance, to retrace his steps.

The pair parted with good wishes one towards the other, and the hope of meeting again shortly.

They *would!* But oh, how different would be the next meeting!

CHAPTER III.

IS OF WHAT OCCURRED IN THE WHITE TOWER, AND OF HOW QUEEN ELIZABETH PLUCKED THE DAGGER FROM THE BREAST OF SIMON SILEX.

SLOWLY onwards walked the Hunchback. His brain was filled with conflicting emotions, and his pulses throbbed wildly.

"This man," he considered, "will certainly find his way to the spot I have pointed out. But he is cunning and cautious, and not likely to rush headlong into danger. I know well what he will do. He will glide like a snake to the White Tower, and he will come upon the guards unawares. Ere they have time to recover from their surprise, he will bury his dagger in their hearts. Let me think. Two valuable lives must not be sacrificed. What shall I do? Ah, I have it. I will take some wine in a flask. But I must first drop into it a powerful drug. The guards will partake of it, fall asleep, and Simon Silex, seeing that they sleep, will let them alone. Good! Fortunately, I have a drug powerful enough with me. Now for the wine, and then with all speed to the mansion."

On and on walked the Hunchback, and at a swift pace, but he had to traverse a considerable distance ere he came to a hostelry.

At last he had the wine safely about his person, and before he reached the gate of the mansion it had been drugged.

He was at once admitted, and on presenting the earl's pass, was allowed to proceed—by the back way.

The back of the White Tower, as it was called, presented a beautiful sight.

The glorious light of the full moon flooded almost the whole of it, causing the old walls, with their huge clusters of ivy, to look highly picturesque.

For the first time he noticed that not a single window was secured by a bar.

It was evident enough that, with his guards, the Earl of Normanton considered his mansion secure from any invasion.

The entrance at the back was approached by a broad flight of marble steps, on the right and left of which was an ornamental balcony, and above the windows was another balcony, which was reached by a narrow flight of stone steps, leading from the first balcony.

Just in the shadow of the ponderous door stood two of the guard—tall, grim-looking old soldiers, well-armed, and apparently ready for any emergency.

On the right of them hung a thick rope, the end of which was secured to a staple in the wall.

This rope communicated with the alarm-bell on the roof of the building.

As the Hunchback approached the men, they brought their arms to the charge, and cried—

" Who approaches ? "

" A friend," answered the Hunchback.

" Well, advance, friend," was the reply, " and show your authority for being in these grounds at this hour."

The soldier to whom the Hunchback had presented the ring had spoken to his comrades of the affair, and they at once recognised the old pedlar from the description furnished them.

Having scanned the pass, they announced that all was satisfactory, and one, producing an enormous key, opened the door.

The Hunchback paused on the threshold, and commenced a conversation—a conversation which quickly drifted into the startling things which had occurred at Roxburgh House.

The Hunchback learned that the queen, and everyone within that mansion, was now perfectly familiar with all that had transpired at Hampton.

He learned that the queen was furious at the death of Lord Blackmore,

and had sworn that nothing but the death of the young Lord Whitmore, his mother, the Hunchback of Old St. Paul's, and his son—indeed, all whom she thought had had a hand in Blackmore's death, should satisfy her.

After a conversation, lasting something like half-an-hour, the Hunchback offered the flask.

It was greedily accepted by the soldiers.

" Drink hearty, my friends," said the Hunchback, " for I have more in my pack."

The men did not require to be twice bidden.

One had a drink, and the other a drink, until not a drain remained in the flask.

The Hunchback now entered the mansion, having received the thanks of the soldiers, and the great door was closed.

The Hunchback reached his room, and, approaching the window, listened.

He heard the soldiers conversing in low tones, but what they said he could not make out.

A quarter of an hour went by, and still the men conversed.

But presently the sound of their voices was heard no more.

Then the Hunchback ventured to open the window.

Looking out, he saw both the men seated on the stone steps, one on each side.

Their heads leaned against the stone coping, while their arms lay between their legs.

The drug had had the desired effect, and the men were sleeping soundly.

" So far, good ! " muttered the Hunchback, grimly ; " and now to prepare for the reception of Simon Silex."

*   *   *   *

Simon, after leaving the Hunchback, walked towards the hostelry.

When he caught sight of the lights burning within the tavern, he was strongly tempted to enter and partake of further refreshment, including food, of which he now stood in need ; but after some consideration he thought it better to go on.

On and on he went, taking care to keep out of every well-trodden path, and yet never once losing sight of the walls of the mansion.

Coming to a convenient spot, he laid himself down, partook of what remained in the flask, and carefully examined his arms.

He wore no sword now; that had been left at "The Dolphin;" but he carried his two large pistols and the long, keen dagger.

"Some people would think I was on a wild-goose chase," he thought; "for they would think a man mad who said he was about to enter yonder mansion, and make his way to the queen's apartments. But I no longer think there is any difficulty.

"Chance seems to favour me, for I have got all the information I seek out of that haughty old pedlar. Haughty! Yes, he *was* haughty.

"Humph! That comes of letting him pay visits to the servants in the mansion. Humph! I ought to have served him like I did old Christian Mackay. How quiet everything is, I say, except it is those cursed hares and rabbits, I say, which run about as if the whole place belonged to them. *That's* what I say.

"And what is that yonder? Oh, I can tell. It is the White Tower. Yes; that's plain enough. By the Virgin! that old pedlar's description is exact. Well, I thank him. Humph! here's to his confusion."

And he swallowed what remained in the flask. An hour passed, and once more Simon prepared to proceed.

But he did not rise.

No; on all-fours he went, and this was necessarily very slow work, for his path was beset with thorns and weeds of every description.

In this manner he reached the wall in front of the White Tower.

Again for a long time he listened.

But no sound fell upon his ears.

Several times, as he had come round the wall, he had heard the steady tramp of the guard, but on this side he heard no such sound.

Our readers know the reason.

Simon selected a tree which was easy to climb, and clambering up, he got on a level with the top of the wall.

Again he listened, but hearing no sound, he got still higher.

Now, by aid of the moonlight, he saw that the soldiers on guard were fast asleep.

Clambering down, he gave utterance to a low, joyous chuckle.

"On my soul," he muttered, "everything is certainly in my favour. The guards are asleep! Well, perhaps it is better for them, and better still if they continue to sleep, for if I am interrupted—well, I should stop at nothing. Now to scale the wall."

Yes, it *was* "now to scale the wall."

In front of him it presented such a smooth surface, that to attempt to clamber up was out of all question.

So he kept close against the wall, watching for a convenient spot.

He presently came to a part of the wall which he saw was easy enough to climb.

This was owing to the fact that it was covered with sturdy ivy.

Simon drew his dagger, and placed it between his teeth.

Then he took off his shoes, and commenced the ascent.

He found it quite easy, for the ivy was not only strong enough to bear twice his weight, but it had grown in such a gnarled and twisted fashion, that it afforded him plenty of foothold.

In the space of a few seconds he was on the top of the wall.

Slipping over, he clambered down, and was soon in the grounds.

He placed himself in the shadow of the ivy, in order to take a good survey of the surroundings, as well as to ascertain if anyone was on the move.

Satisfied that all was right, he advanced towards the guards.

His shoeless feet made not the slightest noise.

Reaching the guards, he bent over and examined them.

He saw that they slept soundly, yet their sleep was of a somewhat peculiar character.

But they smelt of the wine which had been given them by the Hunchback, and therefore Simon, as a matter of course, instantly came to the conclusion that they were in a drunken sleep.

Had either of them made a movement, which Simon could have considered preparatory to their waking, the dagger he now firmly clutched in his strong fingers would soon have found its way to their hearts.

Satisfied that no interruption was to be feared from the guards, Simon crept up the steps, and, like a ghost, glided swiftly to the right.

* * * *

The room in which the Hunchback had been accommodated, thanks to the exertions of the old Court Fool, the beautiful countess, and his own extraordinary skill, and which, as we have said, was situated next to the picture-gallery, was indeed a very handsomely-furnished apartment.

It was sometimes called "the Ambassador's Room," owing to the fact that, if the reigning sovereign was staying at the mansion, and happened to be visited by one of the ambassadors, this was the room in which the gentleman was accommodated.

The furniture was of dark oak, except the bedstead, that elaborate and ingenious piece of workmanship —it being constructed to fold up like a cabinet—being of Spanish mahogany.

The window, which was in the French style, being made to open on to the balcony, was shaded with massive dark-blue curtains, with gold trimmings, looped up with silver chains, and fastened with a buckle bearing the Normanton arms.

It was in the shadow of these that the Hunchback concealed himself.

While nothing but the white covering of the bed could be seen from the outside, from the inside the Hunchback was enabled to see everything without.

Long had he waited there. Never in all his life had the minutes seemed so long.

The Hunchback had removed the upper part of his disguise, and, as he now stood, his right hand grasping a long glittering dagger, he looked a terrible, mysterious being—a being to be feared.

His large, keen eyes had watched every portion of the wall which he could see, and he saw Simon Silex clamber up and drop on the other side.

A pause ensued.

A long, long pause it seemed to the Hunchback, yet, as a matter of fact, it was a pause of only a few seconds.

Presently, like a black shadow, Simon stood before the window.

His ugly face was pressed against the glass, and he took a good look into the room.

He at once noted the white coverlet, and a low chuckle escaped his lips as he muttered—

"Yonder is her bed! The Queen of England! Oh, it is a mighty deed! When morning dawns, and her maids-in-waiting discover their royal mistress lying upon that grand bed, with a dagger plunged in her heart—oh, what a cry will ascend to heaven for vengeance on her murderer!

"Quickly, like the fierce prairie fire, the news will be spread, and long ere I can reach Wapping, half England will be ringing with the fatal deed!

"In an apartment such as this there is sure to be plenty of plunder; there must be lots of costly jewels which I can conveniently carry away. For aught I know, the royal crown may be there. Well, if it is, I will make short work of it."

Up to this moment the ruffian felt that he was compelled to undertake the carrying out of Blackmore's order because he feared him, because he was aware of the terrible power he wielded; but now he felt a savage joy in being the one commissioned to slay the Queen of England.

With cautious fingers he pressed the sashes of the window backwards.

They yielded not that way.

He caught hold of the handle and pulled the window towards him.

It opened easily and noiselessly.

The Hunchback had taken good care of that.

"Ha!" chuckled Simon, half aloud, "all obstacles are now removed! I can enter and——"

"Liar!" hissed a low deep voice; "liar! You cannot enter, for *the Hunchback of Old St. Paul's bars the way!*"

Simon, with a wild gasp, moved back several paces.

The Hunchback strode forward, and his face was fully revealed to Simon.

Silex instantly recognised the clothes the old pedlar had been wearing, and he at once saw how nicely he had dropped into the net prepared for him.

There was an awful pause of a few moments, during which both men, each having his dagger firmly clutched in his hand, glared at each other.

Simon knew now well enough that the Hunchback had long ago learned his errand, and had watched for him.

During that brief pause, he thought of turning and running for his life; but he knew well enough that the Hunchback could give the alarm, and that he would be captured ere he could scale the wall.

Suddenly, with upraised dagger, he rushed forward.

But the Hunchback avoided the blow by stepping nimbly aside.

Then, as swiftly as descends a thunderbolt, the Hunchback raised his weapon, brought it down, and buried it to the haft in the body of the would-be assassin.

Simon did not fall instantly.

No; he clutched the sides of the window-frame, and a series of wild, unearthly shrieks of agony escaped his lips.

The tremendous noise caused one of the guards temporarily to recover consciousness.

He partly raised himself, but being powerless to rise, he seized hold of something by which to drag himself to his feet.

That something happened to be the bell-rope about which we have spoken.

Instantaneously the alarm-bell pealed out its ponderous notes of warning.

The din it made was deafening.

Before it had rung two minutes the whole of the mansion, inside and outside, was aroused.

Hurrying feet were heard ascending and descending the stairs, the clash of arms resounded in the courtyard, and loud words of command were issued in all parts.

Quickly the front of the White Tower was crowded with soldiers.

A score of them, headed by their captain, swarmed up the stairs, and stood on the edge of the balcony, appalled at what they saw.

Simon was still alive.

Flat upon his back he lay, the dagger still in his breast.

With sighs and groans he attempted to make the captain understand that it was the Hunchback—who had now resumed the whole of his disguise—who had plunged the dagger into his body.

So petrified with astonishment was the officer at what he saw that he appeared to be quite unable to speak or move.

In a few seconds loud voices and the patter of rushing feet were heard in the direction of the picture-gallery, and then a loud hammering came on the Hunchback's door.

But those without quickly discovered that it was unfastened, and it was soon pushed violently open.

Instantaneously the apartment was most brilliantly illuminated with the glare of a score of links held by male and female retainers, who crowded round two well-known figures, namely, the Earl and the Countess of Normanton.

Both had only partially attired themselves.

But the young earl had not forgotten his arms.

In his right hand glittered and flashed a naked sword.

A terrible look was upon his face—a look of fierce rage.

"In the name of heaven!" he cried, "what means this? Where is this pedlar—where is this man who, if what he said was true, should be in his bed, which, as you see, is untouched? And where—"

"Oh, hush, hush!" pleaded the countess. "Wait but a moment."

"No, no! Wait? *Wait?* No! Where is this accursed pedlar, I say? Where is the man—"

"I am here, your grace," said the Hunchback.

"What is the accursed—"

"Your grace," cried the captain, who had now recovered himself, "your grace, see—here is the man who has been the cause of the disturbance."

And he pointed towards the spot where lay Simon Silex, still writhing and groaning in his agony.

The earl and the lovely countess, followed by the whole crowd of retainers and soldiers, hurried across the apartment.

No sooner was Simon beheld than a

cry of horror escaped the lips of every-one.

"What is this?" gasped the earl; "what — who is this horrid-looking wretch? And a dagger buried to the haft in his breast! Ha! who will explain this?"

"I will," said the Hunchback as he came forward. "Yonder wretch came here to assassinate the Queen of England. I got scent of his intended visit, and I waited and watched for him. See, by his side is the dagger intended for the breast of our noble queen; in his bosom is the blade which I kept ready for *him!*"

If a cry of horror left the lips of the onlookers as they gazed upon Simon's distorted features, what sort of a cry was it which left their lips as the Hunchback made this tremendous announcement!

It cannot be described!

"An assassin!" said the earl in a hoarse, horrified whisper; "a dastardly assassin! Great Heaven! what sort of soldiers as guards have we? Are we——"

The earl was interrupted by a great commotion behind.

All turned. To behold what?

Six stalwart soldiers, each armed with a drawn sword in one hand, and carrying a flaming link high aloft with the other.

Between them, only partially dressed, but looking every inch the strong-willed, brave woman she was, walked Queen Elizabeth.

Slowly she crossed the apartment. There was no hesitation about her foot-steps—she was as calm and collected now as if she was just about to confront her lords in her council chamber.

True it was that her face was deathly pale, and that her eyes seemed to blaze with a fierce, angry light.

The countess started towards her.

"Your majesty," she cried, "I implore you to retrace——"

The queen raised her right hand, and in her somewhat harsh, peculiar tone of voice said—

"Retrace! Elizabeth *retrace!* Ha! by my father's head, I know, or if I know, I recognise no such word. I have overheard something of what has been said. Let me see this *assassin!*"

All respectfully made way as the queen advanced.

Her majesty in a few moments stood looking down at the figure of Simon Silex.

For a brief space she spoke not—her eyes were fixed upon the horrible figure beneath her.

She ran her eyes round the horror-stricken group; then, addressing the earl, she said—

"And this is the man who managed to scale your walls in order to attempt our destruction, my lord?"

The earl bowed.

"Can you account for it?"

"Your majesty, I can only account for it by the fact that the two soldiers on guard at this door were, and are now, insensible. They must have been heavily drugged."

"By whom?"

"Alas! I cannot tell."

"Your grace, you have a traitor within your walls—eh?"

"I am afraid it must be so," replied the earl, who really trembled before the apparently fierce glance of the queen.

"Where is the man who slew this double-dyed villain?"

The Hunchback came forward, and the earl, pointing to him, said—

"This is the man, your majesty."

The queen turned, and fixed a penetrating look upon the Hunchback's strange-looking figure.

"What is he?" she asked.

"A pedlar," was the earl's reply.

"What does a pedlar in your mansion, my lord?"

The earl briefly informed the queen, and also how the Hunchback had heard of the intended assassination at the village.

"No doubt it was foolish to obtain the services of a pedlar as a painter," replied the queen, "but in this instance such a selection has proved beneficial. Master Pedlar, you are a brave old man. We thank you for your timely services. Fear not; you shall no longer have to depend upon your brush for a living. To-morrow, we will grant you an audience, and you shall acquaint us with your history."

Oh, at these welcome words, what a thrill of joy pervaded the breast of the Hunchback!

"HE RAISED HIS HUNTING-WHIP, AND CAUGHT THE OLD MAN A SLASH WITH THE THONG."

No. 10

Once more the queen turned and looked at the fast dying man.

As she looked, she clenched her teeth fiercely together, and hissed through them—

"Vile worm! Abandoned wretch! What is it that I have done that I should be sentenced to death? Tell me," she said, bending over Simon, "tell me—see, I am the woman you came to assassinate—tell me, who sent you on this fearful errand?"

Simon's lips moved.

It was evident that he was trying his hardest to utter the name of Blackmore.

Down on his knees went the earl, and placed his ear to his lips.

But he heard only a confused whisper.

While he listened, Simon, with an agonising gasp, died.

Stooping over, the queen reached out her white hand, and, amid a great cry of horror, plucked the bleeding dagger from the dead man's heart.

"Such a weapon," she said, "used in so righteous a cause, should be preserved. Here, my lord," she said, handing the weapon to the earl, "do you see that a suitable inscription is engraved upon the blade, and have it enclosed in a gold box. It shall ever remain among my most cherished possessions. As for the body of this man," she continued, "let two heavy stones be placed about it, and then let it be flung into the moat."

The earl bowed.

The queen now beckoned to the countess, who ran to her side.

"Come," said the queen; "come with us—we have much to say."

She placed her arm about the countess' waist—more, perhaps, for support than anything else—and the pair took their way across the balcony.

But, after a few steps, the queen stopped, and once more turned to the group.

Everyone now saw that the queen's eyes were full of tears.

After a painful pause, she said, in low, tremulous tones—

"This is the first attempt on our life! Is it possible that we are doomed to die by the hand of the assassin? Heaven forbid it! What can be the reason of this attempt? Not personal hatred? No, no! This man comes from some secret society—some society which, for some reason, has doomed us to death. And yet, since we ascended the throne, have we not always had the welfare of our people at heart? Night and day, day and night, we work body and soul for the people. While our people sleep, our brains are active in their cause. Oh, 'tis hard to think that we are already meriting the attention of the assassin. We do the best we can—but we are a poor, weak woman after all! Heaven guide our footsteps!"

There was such a passionate, touching appeal in these last words, that many a strong man present shed tears.

It can easily be imagined that the body of Simon Silex met with very little respect at the hands of the soldiers.

Two heavy stones were at once procured and tied round his body, which was then carried to the muddy moat and flung in.

Thus it was hidden from sight for ever.

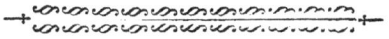

CHAPTER IV.

HOW DACRE DEADMAN OBTAINS SOME INFORMATION—HOW HE ACTS UPON IT—HOW HE SUDDENLY APPEARS IN THE CRYPT OF OLD ST. PAUL'S, AND OF WHAT EXTRAORDINARY EVENTS OCCURRED.

WE must now return to the other and no less important characters in this eventful history.

First, it is necessary to inform our readers that Stanley, Ronald, and the remaining Avengers reached Old St. Paul's in safety, and on the following evening they were joined by Mark Mellow.

It is quite unnecessary for us to say

how overjoyed Lady Whitmore was to once again clasp her son to her breast.

Nor is it necessary to say with what open arms Beatrice Bevan received Ronald Rockley.

As for Swift— well, his continued eccentric and extraordinary movements showed how overjoyed he was.

Lady Whitmore was informed of all that had transpired, and glad was she that such a monster had met a well-deserved fate at the hands of her son.

"Your vow has indeed been well fulfilled," she said.

"Nay," answered Stanley, "only in part. The vow will be completely fulfilled when Dacre Deadman ceases to exist, and our rights are recognised, and we once more occupy that position in society to which we are entitled."

It was resolved that no one but Ronald should leave the vaults until they heard from the Hunchback.

Ronald was only to leave the cathedral for the purpose of procuring food.

And now for Dacre Deadman.

That imp of the Evil One himself, after leaving Hampton, put up at an hostelry far removed from the public road, and there he remained the whole night.

When morning had fairly dawned, he persuaded the host to procure another set of clothes for him, as he considered it important that he should not be recognised.

This having been done, and the costly jewellery with which he had been decorated having been securely placed in his bosom, he bought a horse and set out. Where?

Well, his thoughts were of Blackmore Hall.

"Oh, it would indeed be something splendid," he thought, "for me to at once take the reins forcibly snatched from the fingers of Lord Blackmore. What have I to thank him for? Naught. Smooth and fair he pretended to be towards me, while at the same time he only used me as his catspaw, and waited his opportunity to drive a dagger into my heart. Of everything in his possession I will take command. In London anon I will be the leader of life and fashion. Shall I continue, or attempt to continue, this society? No; I shall shake free of it, for 'tis danger-ous. Let the chiefs continue it themselves, if so they will. But they must go hence from Blackmore Hall. I will drive them forth! But not yet," he mused, "for, on second thoughts, I will not go to Blackmore Hall at present. No, I will make for Wapping. I must once more pay a visit to my *apartment.* He, he! As for Stanley Whitmore, this haughty young lord and his *bosom* friend, the Hunchback's son, I will make short work of them."

Here a ghastly grin overspread his features, and he muttered in bitter tones—

"Humph! No doubt my name is *not* what it is known as. But, fool!" snapping his fingers derisively, "what's in a name? Still, presently, I will change mine from Deadman to something else. *Deadman* is somewhat too suggestive; and, moreover, I am already too well known by that name."

In the course of his journey, Dacre came to a goldsmith's.

To this tradesman, after a long bargaining, he disposed of all the jewels with which Blackmore had decorated him.

They fetched a large sum—far more than Dacre expected; and, with his pockets full of money, he resumed his journey.

Nothing put Dacre in such good spirits as plenty of money, and, as he was in good spirits himself, he indulged in plenty of good spirits at the various hostelries he came to.

The consequence was, that he did not reach Wapping until night had come on; and, as a matter of course, he was more than three parts intoxicated when he reached there.

Imagine his astonishment when he found "The Wapping Arms" closed.

The house appeared to be in total darkness, and not a sign of life was visible inside or out.

So extraordinary and unaccountable did Dacre Deadman consider this, that for the space of at least ten minutes he sat—as firmly as possible—on his horse, looking up and down at the windows and at the door.

Finally, with an exclamation expressive of disgust, he dismounted, and took his horse up the archway leading to the stables.

Here the faint glimmer of a light caught his eyes.

Picking up a shovel, he banged on the door.

This so alarmed the animals within the stable that they neighed loudly.

Presently a night-capped head was popped out of the window of the loft, and a voice asked—

"Who is there?"

It was the voice of the old man who had led Mark Mellow to the fearful chamber below.

"*I* am here," growled Dacre.

"Who are you?"

"Humph! you pretend not to recognise my voice, eh? I repeat that *I* am here, sirrah."

"Stay there then, and be hanged to you, for aught I care! I don't know who you are."

"You can't recognise my voice?"

"I am no hand at recognising voices."

"My name, sirrah, is Dacre Deadman."

"Oh, indeed!"

Of course the old man had recognised Dacre directly he opened his mouth.

"Yes," said Dacre, "it is *indeed* Dacre Deadman, as you will know to your cost if you do not instantly open the door."

"I will do so with all speed," replied the old man.

And he thereupon proceeded to open the stable-door as leisurely as he possibly could.

Directly the old man made his appearance on the threshold, Dacre said—

"What is the house closed for?"

"I am not in the confidence of my mistress," promptly answered the old man.

"Summon her—at once!"

"Who?"

"Your mistress. But, no; summon Simon Silex. Tell him that I demand his instant attendance."

"That is impossible."

"And why?"

"Because he is absent."

"Oh, indeed! Absent! Where has he gone?"

"Can't say for certain, but I heard my mistress mumbling about Hampton and Esher."

"Esher!"

"Aye—Esher."

Dacre considered for a moment.

His brain, consequent on the amount of intoxicating beverages he had imbibed, was somewhat confused.

But, at last, he thought of the errand for which Blackmore had reserved the host of "The Wapping Arms."

"It must be so," he considered. "He has gone to assassinate the queen! And if he does not get assassinated instead, I shall be much mistaken."

Aloud he said—

"And where is Mistress Silex? Is she, too, absent?"

"She is not."

"Well, where is she?"

"Upstairs — drunk. And she has been drunk ever since her husband's departure. I have tried as hard as 'tis possible for a man to try to keep the house open, but I have failed. Nature has got the better of me, and I require rest."

"No doubt. Hence the reason of the house being closed. A nice state of affairs, but nothing to cause one the least astonishment. Here, take my horse, and see to its proper accommodation. There is no one in the house besides your mistress?"

"Not that *I* am aware of."

"I understand you, and will at once seek out Mistress Silex."

"Is it not a liberty to take in a person's own house?"

"Silence!" roared Dacre. "Are you not aware that this house is the property of Lord Blackmore? Or, I should say, *was*, for, since Lord Blackmore is no more, the house is mine."

"Blackmore dead!" cried the old man.

"Aye, he is dead."

"Thank Heaven!"

"How dare you say such a thing? Are you not aware of my relationship to him?"

No answer.

"Suppose I had met my death— what would you say then?"

"Thank Heaven!" replied the old man, promptly and fearlessly.

"Vile lump of humanity!" yelled Dacre; "you shall be taught manners."

So saying, he raised his riding-whip and dealt the old man a fearful slash across the face with the thong.

The ostler uttered no cry, however. No doubt he was used to brutal treatment.

"The mark on your face will cause you to remember me for some time to come," cried Dacre.

"Aye, you are right," replied the old man, in low tones; "you are right."

Dacre raised his whip again, but he lowered it as quickly as he had raised it, and pushing past the ostler, ascended the loft stairs.

He knew his way well enough, and so required no assistance in finding the bedroom belonging to Mistress Silex.

But though well acquainted with the place, Dacre found so great a difficulty in walking in the dark—for he kept on stumbling against this or that object—that he was bound to return and ask the ostler to hand him up a lantern.

The ostler complied, and handed up the light without a word.

"Treachery," muttered Dacre; "he means treachery! But I will be well on my guard; and if he attempts any tricks on me— Well, we'll see."

On through various passages and rooms walked the young villain, and at last Mistress Silex's bedroom was reached.

Like every other room, it was in total darkness, and silence the most profound reigned supreme.

He placed his ear to the keyhole, and attentively listened.

He soon made out that the feminine worshipper of Bacchus was asleep, for he heard her deep, irregular breathing.

Lifting up his foot, he kicked on the door a couple of dozen times without a pause, chuckling aloud as he did so—

"Verily, this noise would wake the dead."

When he left off, he heard the voice of the hostess—

"Who's there?"

"Me," replied Dacre.

"Is it you, Simon?"

"Yes."

"Enter then, and be hanged to you for disturbing my slumbers!"

Dacre pushed the door open, and entered the apartment.

It was quite evident that in this bed-chamber Mistress Silex had been entertaining a large party, for the place was literally strewn with bottles, measures, glasses, and tankards.

The hostess was not undressed— Dacre felt certain that he should find her fully attired, and he was right.

As Dacre entered, she raised herself, and the light from the lantern falling upon Dacre's face, she at once recognised him.

"You?" she said in hoarse tones, fixing her bleared eyes on Dacre's grinning face. "*You?*"

"Aye, 'tis I—Dacre Deadman."

"What made you say 'Yes' when I asked if it was Simon?"

"So that I should be at once answered. Fearing Simon as you do, you would not dare to keep him waiting."

"Fool! You know better. I fear Simon? Pooh! I fear him no more than I fear you. I want to sleep. Go! The ostler will provide refreshments for you if you require them."

"Will he?" said Dacre; "I should not allow him to do anything of the sort. He is an impertinent fellow, and in order to assist him in learning manners I have administered my lash."

"And what did he do?"

"Do! What could he do?"

"I know what I should have done."

"Well?"

"Put a knife through your ugly body."

"Oh, oh! You would—eh? Ah! Listen to me, woman—"

At these words, the hostess, with a wild cry of rage, leapt from the bed to the floor, and stood panting before Dacre, who, however, knew better than to stand before her for more than an instant.

Retreating a few paces, he said—

"Listen to me. Lord Blackmore is dead, and I therefore inherit his property—among other things, this house."

"Can you prove that?"

"I will take steps to do so."

"*That* for you—*that* for you!" yelled the masculine female, as she defiantly snapped the fingers of both her hands. "Go hence, thou miserable, creeping, cringing wretch! Go!"

"Will you do as I bid you?"

"I? I do as you bid me? Holy Virgin! What does the fool take me for?"

"Then you shall be turned from this house, and without warning."

"Who will do this?"

"I, Dacre Deadman, will do it."

Another wild cry left the woman's lips, and, rushing forward, she seized Dacre by the throat with both her enormous hands.

There was no mistake about this woman's strength.

It was absolutely enormous.

And at this moment, having only partially slept off the effects of the shocking debauch, she was a very fiend, a creature who cared not one straw what dreadful deed she did.

But in her blind, passionate rage—a rage so furious that she could not utter the words which rose to her lips—she had overlooked the most important fact, that Dacre was well armed, whereas she was not.

Her fingers twined themselves tighter and tighter about Dacre's throat, and as they closed she pressed his body back.

Suddenly Dacre got his right hand, which had been tightly pressed against his breast, loose.

With the rapidity of lightning he snatched his dagger from its sheath, and plunged it deep into the thick neck of the furious woman.

She knew the blow was a fatal one—that, in a few short moments, her earthly career would terminate, and exerted all her remaining strength in trying to choke Dacre.

The young fellow struggled frantically to release himself.

Hither and thither they dragged each other across the apartment.

It was a horrible sight!

Presently Dacre slipped and fell, the hostess on top of him.

Oh, it was a fortunate fall for him in good truth, for it had the effect of causing the dying woman to somewhat relax her hold.

Dacre drew the blade from the woman's neck, and again and again plunged it into her breast, each time uttering a savage, revengeful yell.

With the last blow the hostess relaxed her hold, and dropped upon the floor.

Dacre instantly started to his feet, his weapon nervously clenched in his hand.

But there was no necessity to strike again.

The hostess' wild eyes—fast becoming fixed with the glassy stare of death—were riveted upon his face: she raised her clenched right hand savagely shook it at him, and ceased to exist.

Exhausted, parched, and trembling violently in every limb, Dacre Deadman leaned against the upset table, by the side of which, having strangely enough escaped being overturned and extinguished, stood the lantern.

Part of its light was thrown upon the distorted and truly awful-looking features of Mistress Silex, and upon them Dacre continued for some few moments to look like one fascinated.

"Dead," he whispered; "aye, she's dead, and I am nearly half dead myself! Lor'! how her vile fingers clutched my throat. On my soul, I shall bear these marks to my grave. I feel as though every spark of life had been wrenched from my body; and my tongue is cloven to the roof of my mouth. Among all this pile, surely I can find something to drink!"

Oh, yes, there was plenty to drink in this chamber; but, had the hungriest of men searched high and low, he would not have discovered a particle of anything to eat.

Dacre found the remains of various bottles of wine, and he drank them.

The vast quantity of drink which, during the day, he had consumed, would have made most men intoxicated, but it had not this effect on Dacre.

He was able to consume an enormous quantity without feeling the effects of it.

But when he reached "The Wapping Arms," he was certainly the worse for what he had imbibed, yet his terrible encounter with the woman-fiend, now lying stiff and nearly cold on the floor, had sobered him.

"And now," he said, picking up his gory blade and the lantern—"now to my apartments. Farewell, vixen. Thou wilt prove a most welcome sight to Simon Silex, who hates thee as the devil hates a paternoster."

Dacre was just about to cross the threshold of the door, when the ostler made his appearance.

"What would you?" growled Dacre.

"Young man," said the ostler, whose face bore the mark of the blow administered by Dacre, "are you going to leave the body of that woman there?"

Dacre uttered a cry of alarm.

"*You* have witnessed what has—what has happened, eh?"

"I have."

"You would give evidence against me if 'twas asked, eh?"

"I have said nothing of the kind. I know that what has occurred was as much her fault as yours. Though I still feel the effect of the lash, and though I will— But no matter. I was about to observe that, though I bear you no goodwill, I am bound to speak the truth. Yes, it was as much her fault as yours. But, had she been sober, she would not have disputed what you said, and she would have done your bidding. I repeat, are you going to leave the body there?"

"I am—at least I— What do you advise?"

"I advise nothing. But, if you leave the body there, it will be quickly discovered, either by her husband or somebody else. I shall be asked questions, and I shall be bound to answer them."

"I see—I see. But you—you will advise me, eh? Think—think! and I will give you a handful of gold pieces to—"

"Don't talk to me of gold pieces," interrupted the ostler; "I would not accept one fraction from your crime-stained hands were I starving. I repeat that I advise nothing, but I would suggest that the body be taken below."

With this the old ostler abruptly turned on his heel and hurriedly departed.

"I know not what to do with the body," thought Dacre. "Why does he make that suggestion? Ah, I see, because he is afraid that if the body be discovered, the blame may be laid on his shoulders! Ah! it would be revenging myself on the old man for his impertinence did I swear that he murdered the woman. I should be believed, especially if I were lavish with my money. But, no; I have thought of something better. By all the fiends, it's excellent! Yes, yes; I know what to do."

Sheathing his dagger, and placing the handle of the lantern between his teeth, he re-entered the apartment, took hold of the dead woman's ankles, dragged her across the landing, and commenced to pull her down the stairs.

Bump, bump went her matted head on the stairs and against the wall. So dreadful was the sound that one would have thought it would have sickened a heart of flint.

But it did not sicken Dacre.

At last "*his apartment*" was reached.

It presented just about the same appearance as on the occasion of Mark's visit, except that the ostler had forgotten to light the lamp above.

Dacre jumped on to the table and soon lit it.

It at once shot o'er the place that strange, ghastly light about which we have remarked.

Going round to the opposite side of the table, and being very careful that he did not knock over the decomposed bodies of the men, Dacre pulled the chair from under one of them, and then kicked the body beneath the table.

Then, returning to the woman, he dragged her round, and after great exertion and difficulty, he succeeded in placing her stiffening body on the chair.

The head drooped forward, and Dacre seized it by the hair, dragged it back, and wound the hair round and round one of the rails at the back.

So it remained—the mouth wide open, the eyes staring and glassy, the great, heavy hands still tightly clenched.

All this was proof of the terrible agony she was undergoing when she died.

Dacre took up a tankard, and forcing open the right hand, placed the handle within it.

Then from beneath his couch he brought forth a bottle of wine, slashed off the neck with his dagger, and poured some of the contents first in a glass, and then into the tankard.

The former he raised to his own lips.

But ere he could swallow the contents he was seized with a laughing fit —a fit of so strong a character that he was nearly doubled.

"Drink!" he yelled, raising his glass on a level with the dead face. "Drink!

Here's to you, vixen—here's to you!
May all the—-"

"Ho, ho! ha, ha! What's all this—
eh? What, in the name of wonder,
does all this mean?"

The question was asked in a loud
and harsh tone of voice.

At the same instant Dacre caught
the sound of footsteps.

Crash went the glass on the floor as,
snatching up the lantern, he rushed to
the door.

"Who speaks?" he cried, holding
aloft the lantern. "Who speaks?
Who is it? Who dares to enter my
private chamber?"

"'Tis I—Rousillion—and three of
my most cherished friends."

And the speaker, a tall, gaunt-look-
ing, ill-clad fellow, advanced another
pace, as did his three companions.

Rousillion was the owner of the well-
known St. Paul's Tavern, one side of
which looked on the cathedral and the
other on the Thames.

Besides this, he owned a number of
wherries, which he let to watermen.

To crown all, he was a very great
rogue—this fact being quickly made
known to everyone who made his
acquaintance.

He was, of course, well-known to
Dacre, who very frequently stayed at
his house.

Dacre was highly displeased with
this unexpected visit.

"Rousillion!" he ejaculated. "Here,
and at this hour—eh? Who admitted
you?"

"We admitted ourselves. We found
the stable-door open, and as no one
answered our summons, we entered."

"A mighty liberty! And do you
mean to stand there, and tell me that
you came to find me?"

"You? No!" grinned Rousillion.
"I had no idea in the world that you
were here. As a matter of fact, I came
here to see Simon Silex, and to ask
where I could find you."

"Oh, indeed! Well, you see, you
have found me without difficulty,
and—"

"And in a strange place. Holy
Virgin, what a horrible sight! And,
by my soul, if that ain't Simon's wife!
Eh? What's the matter—what! Ah!"
he yelled, starting back, "she's dead!"

"Aye," answered Dacre; "you are
right. She is dead."

"Stabbed to death—eh?"

"That is true also."

"Lord! How came she—"

"Ask no questions," snapped Dacre.

"But, at least, tell me who it was who
stabbed her?"

"How should I know?"

"You found her there—do you mean
to say that you found her there, and in
that position?"

"Certainly. I found her just as she
is."

"And the men?"

"I also found them as they are.
What the meaning of it is I neither
know nor care."

"By the Holy Virgin!" said Rousillion; "this must be the work of Simon
Silex."

"No doubt of it," replied Dacre
calmly. "But tell me why you sought
me out? Or did you only come here,
knowing Simon was absent, in order to
get what you could?"

"Nay, nay; I swear I came hither
on purpose to learn your whereabouts.
Master Deadman, I have most important
news for you."

"Out with it, then."

"Be not hasty, my young friend. I
have said that the news is important—
eh?"

"You have."

"Well, then, important news should
always be well paid for."

"I understand. If the news does
prove important I will pay you for it."

"The sum?"

"That depends on the value of the
information."

"Well, it concerns persons whom
you wish to get hold of—that is to say,
young Stanley Whitmore, the Hunchback's son, a young lady whose name
I know not, and Lady Whitmore."

"Oh, indeed!" sneered Dacre; "let
me tell you that I could give you more
information respecting young Whitmore
and the Hunchback's son than—"

And he paused abruptly.

"Nay, nay," he thought, "'tis a day
ago. Ha! this man, then, is evidently
in possession of the information as to
where they are at this present moment.
I would wager the fortune which already
lies at my feet that they are in the

vaults of Old St. Paul's!" Aloud he said : "I was making a mistake ; proceed quickly—where are they?"

"The sum? I must know that first."

"Curse you!—whatever you demand."

"A hundred crowns for the information and our assistance, which, in order to reach them, you must have."

"Agreed! The sum shall be yours. Nay, I will give you double the sum if we succeed in capturing or slaying either one of them."

"The bargain is doubly struck," said Rousillion, tapping his blade; "and my companions are more than satisfied —eh?"

"We are," answered the men.

"Let us all ascend," said Dacre, and, snatching up the lantern, he proceeded to lead the way.

What he was about to do in this horrible chamber of death we know not.

Probably he did not know himself.

Still, it is certain that he seldom entered the chamber until he was three parts the worse for drink, and that there he continued to drink until he dropped helpless on the couch.

He led the way to the public room, and with an air of supreme authority told the men to help themselves from the various casks in the room.

It is hardly necessary to say how eagerly they complied.

Each man filled a couple of tankards of one stuff or another, and they drank success to the errand upon which they were now bound.

"I will tell you how it is," said Rousillion. "One of my men—or, I should say, one of the watermen to whom I lend my boats—was searching for a box dropped by a fare, and in so doing he entered what we have always taken to be a sewer, and which is close to my place. The tide was down, and so he was able to go right under the archway with naked legs.

"After proceeding a short distance, he was struck with the peculiar construction of the place. He found it nothing more nor less than a kind of vaulted chamber.

"Curiosity prompted him to proceed, and he cautiously made his way farther along. The passage proved to be of enormous length.

"By-and-by he touched something solid which was drawn right across the passage.

"While feeling about, he heard voices. He shouted as loud as he was able, and was answered by a voice on the other side of the obstruction, which said—

"'Who are you?'

"My man answered that he had been thrown out of his boat, and had lost his way. He said this because, of course, he wanted to know what was on the other side.

"A consultation was held, after which, when my man had been asked a great number of questions, the obstruction, which proved to be a door, slowly began to move into—so my man said—the very wall.

"He saw several persons behind this door, one of whom he at once recognised as the Hunchback's son. I may mention that it was just as well the Hunchback's son did not recognise *him*.

"Two of the persons he saw were ladies, and from what you yourself told me, there can be no shadow of doubt but that one of them is Lady Whitmore.

"Said the Hunchback's son, 'Whether the account you have given of yourself is true or not, we are unable to form an opinion. It is doubtful, however, but we give you the benefit of the doubt. You wish to find your way to the open streets?' My man answered that he did. 'Then,' continued the Hunchback's son, 'if that is so, you must consent to be blindfolded.'

"There was no help for it, and he submitted to the operation.

"Then he was taken by the arm, and led through long passages, up many flights of stairs, and, finally, the Hunchback's son said, 'Go, and mention not a word as to how you got from the sewer to the street.'

"A huge door thereupon closed. My man took the bandage from his eyes, and found himself beside the vestry door of Old St. Paul's.

"A remarkable and almost unbelievable story," said Dacre. "However, perhaps you can tell me how *we* should be able to gain admission to this subterranean vault? But, first, your man did not see the Hunchback, I presume ? "

" He did not."

"Proceed—how are we to gain admission ? "

" By the subterranean vaults."

" By all the incarnate fiends ! " shouted Dacre, bringing his clenched fist with a mighty bang on the table, " I say *how* ? "

" By aid of *powder*."

" Ha ! Powder ! Humph ! 'tis dangerous."

"How so ? "

" The report would bring down every inhabitant of the place."

" What of that ? I repeat that this vault is of enormous length, and search how they may, they would not discover whence the report came."

" But the report will instantly put those we wish to get hold of on their guard."

"No doubt ; but then there are five of *us*, and only two of *them*. Surely you cannot fear the result with such odds ? "

" Nay, nay," answered Dacre. " Fear it, of course not."

" But," he thought, " I know what those two are, and I will take particular care to keep in the *background*."

Aloud he said—

" And when do you suggest that this attempt should be commenced ? "

" No time like the present," replied Rousillion.

" You are right," said Dacre ; " no time like the present. The attempt shall be at once made by— But what of the powder ? "

" I have it in the vaults of my house in any quantity."

" Good ! Come, let us fortify ourselves with something worth drinking. Look, Rousillion—I pray you look for brandy. These wines have but little or no effect upon me. I must have brandy."

Rousillion and his men searched for the desired spirit high and low, but failed to discover it.

It looked as if it had all been sold, or, if not sold, consumed by Mistress Silex—the drink worshipper ; the fiend in the garb of a woman ; the horrible female whose dead hand, now clutching the tankard containing wine, seemed to mock Bacchus and all his imps.

But, at last, when the contents of no less than twelve casks of various wines had been spilt over the floor, some brandy was discovered.

It was poured out and eagerly drank by Dacre and the men.

Glass after glass they swallowed until, when Dacre imagined that he was sufficiently primed with "Dutch courage," the word was given to move.

Dacre was about to get his horse, but being advised that it would be better if a wherry was obtained, he left it.

We may here take occasion to observe that " The Wapping Arms " now vanishes from our story.

The ostler, on the day after the murder of his mistress, packed up what few articles he owned, and left the house.

First, however, he locked up every door, and flung the keys into the Thames. He divulged nothing until nearly a month had elapsed, when he went to the authorities and informed them.

" The Wapping Arms " was at once forced open, and the dreadful truth of the old man's story was at once apparent.

But, as the reader will see, it was then too late to arrest Dacre Deadman.

The remains of the bodies discovered in the filthy hole were decently interred, the furniture and all effects were sold, and the house was closed for many months.

It was finally partly rebuilt and opened by a blacksmith, named Gwynne, and it was this man's luck to find—when excavating in the vaults of the house some few years after he took possession—a huge pile of gold and silver, deposited there by Simon Silex.

It is needless to say that the blacksmith soon made boxes enough in which to keep the whole of it.

* * * *

It was just about the time when Rousillion reached " The Wapping Arms," that the party in the crypt, which included Mark Mellow, sat down to break a long fast.

Watching and waiting, and the great mental strain, were seriously affecting all present.

Often Stanley wished that something would occur, if it were only to break the monotony under which they laboured.

Lady Whitmore occupied the Hunchback's seat.

How terribly altered she was since first we introduced her to the reader!

The pale, but still beautiful face, now bore tell-tale lines of care, sorrow, and trouble.

The mental sufferings of this poor lady were really and truly of a most agonising description.

Not a day, not a night passed, but what the vision of that horrible and most dastardly tragedy in the "Green Room" of Blackmore Hall was before her.

But, since her stay at the cathedral, pretty Beatrice Bevan had proved herself a very angel.

She devoted herself to this truly unfortunate lady; it was her sweet voice which so constantly sang, in musical tones—

"Hope, lady, hope!"

When, at her own magnificent residence, Lady Whitmore had been surrounded with servants, and with those who many a time and oft professed the greatest friendship; but never, never did she know the true value of a female friend until she knew Beatrice Bevan.

She did not keep this fact a secret.

No, no. Time after time she assured Beatrice, in tones of great emotion and gratitude, how deeply indebted she was to her.

The lot of pretty Beatrice had been by no means a pleasant one.

Her parents were abroad, she knew that—or, at least, the villainous apothecary so assured her—and she had letters which appeared to come from abroad; but whether such was really the case she was not certain.

At any rate, it was almost a certain fact that, now she would have great difficulty in discovering their whereabouts, so that they might be communicated with.

The meal being finished, Stanley and Ronald ascended to the cathedral, and for some considerable time paced the long aisles.

Suddenly a fearful report burst upon their ears.

It was as if a mighty earthquake had occurred just beneath their feet.

The terrible roar was echoed again and again among the many vaulted recesses of the vast edifice.

"In the name of Heaven!" gasped Roland, "what can that be?"

"Hasten—hasten!" cried Stanley, at once leading the way to the vaults; "some terrible accident must have happened."

Reaching the apartments below, they found Lady Whitmore in a half-fainting condition, being supported by Beatrice, while in a panic-stricken attitude stood Mark Mellow.

"What is it?" cried Stanley.

"I know not," replied Mark, in low, horror-stricken tones; "it seemed to me like an earthquake, for the flooring beneath our feet moved."

"'Tis no earthquake!" said Ronald, excitedly, "for most distinctly I can smell *powder!*"

"You are right," said Stanley; "it *is* powder. Ha! I see—I see, Ronald! The man we admitted and passed through the cathedral into the street!"

"Aye," answered Ronald; "I now see it! The man was a spy. He had been sent hither by Dacre Deadman, I will warrant, and it is by him that an attempt is being made to pass the door in the subterranean vault."

"Let us descend," said Stanley, drawing his sword; "but, first, let us see that we are well armed. Mark, my pistols are by your side; hand them here. And do you—— But you are white and trembling. You had better remain above."

"No, no," answered Mark; "now that I know what the danger is I am no longer afraid. I will descend with you."

"Stanley—Stanley!" cried her ladyship, wildly, "do not go; remain here with me. You know not how many desperate men may be below. Descend, and certain death stares you in the face."

"Mother," answered Stanley calmly, as he stuck two loaded pistols in his belt, "you call upon me to dub myself a coward!"

"Heaven forbid, my boy! For forty generations and more the Whitmores can trace their descent. All were men of the sword and entirely fearless of danger. But this is no ordinary danger. You have shown me and Beatrice the vaults, and what was my opinion at the time?—that it was a death-trap."

"And I trust your words will prove correct, my dear mother. I sincerely hope that the subterranean passage will prove a death-trap for those who have had the audacity to enter it in search of us. I must descend."

"And I," said Ronald : "so let us hasten to meet the villains face to face and steel to steel."

The secret spring was moved, the trap opened, and the three commenced the descent, Stanley going first.

Directly the stone of the trap was moved, a mighty volume of sulphurous smoke ascended and filled the apartment.

So dense was it that Lady Whitmore and Beatrice were hidden from sight.

"Will you not take a link?" asked Mark.

"Nay," replied Stanley; "such would be but a mark for the bullets of whoever is below."

Slowly along the passage went the three, being careful to keep a firm hold of the walls, for of course there was no telling what was before them.

Before they had proceeded far, the sound of voices fell upon their ears.

"Hist!" said Stanley, "let us keep close against the wall. Hear you not, Ronald, that they are trying to kindle a light?"

"Yes, I can hear them," answered Ronald, grimly, "and they shall hear us directly."

"Ho!" hissed a voice at some considerable distance from them; "ho! the light, the light, and be hanged to you!"

"By Heavens!" whispered Ronald, "that was the voice of Dacre Deadman, or I stand not here. But oh, for a draught of wind! This sulphurous smoke is unbearable."

Gradually the smoke found its way out, and still further forward pressed the three.

Suddenly a bright light was seen ahead.

Then from this one sprang to or three.

Our friends at once saw that they were lighted links, so of course it was evident that the barrier in the subterranean passage no longer existed.

It was certain that the report came from a charge of gunpowder, with which the door had been blown down.

Ronald was about to suggest something, when Stanley whispered—

"Can you not feel something?"

"Nay," replied Ronald. "What is it?"

"Place your hand on the ground."

Ronald did so.

"Water!" he said. "The tide is rising."

"Aye," replied Stanley, "and that makes the danger all the greater."

High up rose the circling flame from the links, and now the three were enabled to see the faces of the invaders.

There were five of them.

In the centre of them, a naked blade in his right hand and a pistol in his left, stood the abandoned young villain, Dacre Deadman.

Ronald recognised Rousillion, though not his companions.

But it was evident to both Stanley and Ronald that they were all hired men—interested in this movement only for what they would gain in money.

"Rousillion!" shouted Dacre, "let me tell you—"

"Hush! hush!" interrupted Rousillion; "if you make that noise, your voice will be heard, and—"

"Voice heard — eh?" hiccoughed Dacre. "Well, by all the blessed saints! what of the powder? D'ye think *that* was not heard?"

"It has been heard *behind*," growled one of the men, "for I can plainly hear voices. Someone is searching for the cause of the noise."

"Let them search, then," replied Rousillion; "they will never suspect what this sewer is."

"'Twas a wonder we were not all blown to atoms," said Dacre; "for with all your cleverness, Rousillion, you are a blunderer. A little more to the right, and not one of us would have been left to tell the tale. On my soul, the roof of this rat-haunted vault must be as firm as the foundation of the cathedral itself, for I see that only one or two bricks have become loosened. Hold the link here, man," he said to one of Rousillion's men—"hold here—higher, higher! Th—"

Crash!

The report of a pistol-shot resounded through the vaulted passage.

The man holding the link at Dacre's side gave utterance to a loud, piercing shriek of agony, and staggered back, clutching hold of Dacre's arm for support.

But Dacre, with a terrible oath, flung him off, and the man fell shrieking into the mud.

It was Stanley who had fired the shot.

But he had not aimed it at the man. No, you may be sure that he had taken for a mark the figure of Dacre Deadman.

"By all the fiends!" yelled Dacre, "it is as I thought. We have been discovered. I was certain that all this silence would mean something. Forward! Remember, Rousillion, you and your men shall have *treble* the sum agreed upon if either one of these accursed wretches be killed or captured."

It is quite possible that Rousillion's men would have turned and made good their escape, had it not been for the fact that one of their number had been shot down.

This greatly exasperated them, and when Rousillion called upon them they eagerly pressed forward.

In a few moments they came to a sudden halt.

There before them, barring further progress, stood our three friends, Stanley in the centre.

Each held in his hand a drawn sword.

"At last, then, I have you!" hissed Dacre, whose rage, directly he set eyes upon Ronald and Stanley, knew no bounds, "and, by Heaven, you shall not escape me if—"

"You speak as though you were a person of some importance!" interrupted Stanley scornfully, "instead of the illegitimate son of a vile traitor!"

"What—*what!*" yelled Dacre. "A son of a vile—"

"Wait — wait!" again interrupted Stanley. "You have taken the trouble to gain admission by blowing the door down. Well, you have succeeded ad-mirably. And now that we have met, it will be a fight to the death. Just a moment ago I fired at you. But instead of hitting you, the ball struck one of your companions. Well, I am now glad of it—I will not take your life if I can help it—no! If I can succeed in capturing you, your death shall be a terrible death! For think not I forget that it was *your hand* which struck the blow which deprived my father of his life—"

"And it shall be my hand which takes *your* life!" shouted Dacre, who, as he spoke, snatched a pistol from his belt, levelled it at Stanley's head, and fired.

But for the merest chance our hero's career would have terminated.

The man who had received Stanley's bullet in his body had, gradually and entirely unnoticed, worked his way towards his companions.

When near enough, he had raised himself and clutched at the nearest to him, who happened to be Dacre.

Frantically clutching at his cloak, he pulled him slightly back.

The effect of this was to divert his aim, and the ball, instead of striking our hero, flattened itself against the vaulted ceiling.

Unnoticed by Rousillion or his men, Dacre, with a brutal oath, dealt the man a fearful kick, which, taking effect on his temple, sent him reeling back senseless.

In another instant the blades of the combatants met with a ringing clash, and, in less time than it takes to write, the fight waged fast, furious, and desperate.

Ronald became engaged with Rousillion. That blackguard could handle the sword with very fair skill, but he was no match for the Hunchback's son.

Ere a couple of dozen passes had been made, Ronald's sword passed completely through Rousillion's sword-arm, and, with a wild yell, he dropped his blade, snatched a pistol from his belt, and pulled the trigger.

Fortunately it missed fire.

Rousillion then turned to fly. Ronald would, of course, have followed him, but that he found he had to go to the rescue of Mark.

That youth was defending himself

against the attacks of the two men, and in a really splendid fashion.

He had inflicted more than one or two ugly wounds on the men, who, howling with pain, pressed Mark slowly but surely against the wall.

Ronald soon became engaged with one of them.

The man did not hesitate to fight—no; fight he did, and with great fury, uttering the while all the oaths he could think of.

With one of them on his lips he breathed his last, for Ronald's blade quickly found its way to his heart.

In the meantime Stanley and Dacre had been hotly engaged.

Stanley was calm and collected when his blade crossed that of Dacre Deadman; but when he thought of the fact that at his very sword's point stood the black-hearted wretch who had actually struck the blow which had deprived the gentle Lord Whitmore of his life, what wonder was it that his calmness forsook him, and that he almost abandoned himself to the fit of passion which had seized upon him?

"I will wound him only," thought our hero. "I will try my hardest not to kill him, for I will reserve him for a far different death than at the sword's point. In the very house where my father lost his life—nay, in the very room—Dacre Deadman shall lose his—that is, if Heaven guides my hand and furthers my desires!"

In a very short time Stanley received a slight wound in the sword-hand, while Dacre received two severe thrusts in the left arm.

But there can hardly be a doubt as to who would have had the best of the fight.

It was fated not to be concluded.

Suddenly the man with whom Mark had been engaged, and who held the only remaining link, fell, Mark having dealt him such a slashing cut across the head, that his skull was absolutely laid open. And the last link was thereupon extinguished by the filthy water, which, without a sound, had been fast rising.

No sooner had the link gone out, than Dacre dashed upon Stanley. Swords were now useless, and were consequently thrown aside.

With savage fury Dacre clutched Stanley by the throat with one hand, while with the other he endeavoured to snatch our hero's dagger from its sheath.

Not because he had not one of his own.

He tried to get Stanley's so that our hero should not be able to use it.

But he failed, for Stanley instantly fastened his hands on his throat, and a desperate struggle commenced between the pair.

And all this in total darkness!

Ronald's, Mark's, and Rousillion's cries rang through the vaulted passage.

"Stanley!" was Ronald's cry; "Stanley, where are you? Speak—speak!"

"Dacre, Dacre, run for your life!" yelled Rousillion; "run—for the water is rising fast."

For some few seconds, though Dacre heard the warning, he was quite unable to reply to it, for Stanley had hold of the bloodthirsty young ruffian with such tenacity that he could hardly move, let alone speak.

Rousillion stayed not to utter the warning many times.

He had received many severe wounds at the hands of Ronald, and bleeding profusely, suffering intense pain, and filled with terror at the idea of being completely overtaken by the tide ere he could reach the boat by which they had gained the passage, he commenced to grope his way back.

"Stanley, Stanley!" repeated Ronald. "I can hear you, but cannot make out where you are."

"Make your way to the stairs!" gasped Stanley, for by this time our hero had nearly exhausted himself, "and shout for a light. I have my hands upon the throat of Dacre Deadman, and if he attempts to move I will squeeze the life from his body! By Heaven! though to remain here meant death by drowning to both of us, I would not leave go of him!"

"I have found the stairs," cried Mark; "follow my voice—I am touching the stairs, I—"

He was interrupted by the voice of Lady Whitmore.

"Who calls?" cried her ladyship. "Who is it calling? Stanley, Stanley! my son, my son!"

"He is safe!" shouted Ronald. "This way, your ladyship. Descend—in the name of Heaven, descend quickly!"

"Yes—yes," faltered Lady Whitmore, as she endeavoured to force her faltering footsteps down the narrow, slimy steps. "I come! I come!"

In her left hand she carried a flaming link, while her trembling right hand clutched a long, sharp-pointed dagger.

The poor lady, terrified at the shots and the noises of all descriptions below, had at last broken away from the tender embrace of Beatrice Bevan, and, arming herself with the dagger, had commenced the descent, forgetting her weakness—forgetting, in the motherly apprehension for the safety of her loved son, the fact that her poor arm could not now wield a weapon with such effect as it wielded the terrible battle-axe in the Blue Chapel.

Behind her, pistol in hand, came Beatrice, and beside her walked Swift.

Down, down, into the passage, rapidly filling with water—which had now commenced to rush and hiss as it ran along the dark tunnel—went her ladyship.

Ronald greeted her warmly, and, taking the link from her hand, he held it aloft.

Its rays were reflected in the black waters, the sight of which filled Lady Whitmore with undisguised alarm.

And then its rays fell upon two figures at some considerable distance from them on the right.

Two awful-looking figures, truly.

Lady Whitmore looked steadily—fixedly. Did she recognise her son?

She did not at once, and little wonder was there.

Kneeling down, so that the water was nearly on a level with his throat, which was being tightly grasped by our determined hero, was Dacre Deadman.

His partial intoxication, the bravado, which was only partially assumed, had vanished.

The oaths and curses he had been uttering for so long, and which he would continue to utter if he could, were now checked by that vice-like grip upon his throat.

Stanley had not come off scathless.

Beside the wound in his hand he had received one or two slight ones on his face, which was smothered in blood and mud.

His costume, too, was thickly bespattered with mud, and Lady Whitmore, at the first glance, failed to recognise him.

Ronald handed the link to Mark, and made his way to Stanley's side.

"You have him at your mercy, then?" he said.

"Aye," replied Stanley; "and I will take care that he does not escape me. I have had it in my power to slay him, but I have refrained from so doing. But I have doomed him to death! He shall have a little time to repent of his many dastardly crimes. Stand up, thou inhuman monster!"

And our hero, with a sudden wrench, dragged Dacre to his feet.

"By the Virgin!" cried Ronald, "didst ever behold such an ill-looking scoundrel! Dacre Deadman, you are captured at last, and by those who are not likely to lose sight of you, or have mercy on your guilty soul!"

So saying, Ronald seized hold of him by the collar.

Between them they dragged the now thoroughly terrified scamp before Lady Whitmore, who stood on the steps, blessing Heaven that her son was safe.

"Behold!" said Stanley—"behold the one who acted as the masked executioner at Blackmore's mansion! Behold the one who struck the blow which severed my father's head from his body!"

"So this is the wretch?" gasped Lady Whitmore, recoiling in disgust and horror.

"Yes," said Ronald; "this is the murderous villain."

"Let him be well secured, my son," said Lady Whitmore, "for, if the Hunchback's mission prove successful, the queen would order the public execution of this monster."

"Nay, nay," replied Stanley, grimly; "whether the Hunchback's mission proves successful or not, this wretch shall be executed. But not publicly. No; the manner of his death I will determine later on, but it shall be as private as was my unfortunate father's, and, moreover, it shall take place in the same room where he died."

"'SAVE ME! 'TIS I—LOOK! CANNOT SOME OF YOU RECOGNISE MY VOICE?' CRIED ROUSILLION."

No. **11**

Lady Whitmore was too agitated to reply to this; and, moreover, she was only too well aware of the fact that, whatever she or anyone else might say, Stanley would try his hardest to carry out whatever resolution he had formed.

"Cowards that you are!" whined Dacre—"cowards thus to seize me. Let me but get free, and you will see with what effect——"

"Do not alarm yourself," interrupted Stanley; "we shall take particular care that you do *not* get free."

"If I had but a good sword in my hand," groaned Dacre, "I would fight you one after the other!"

"Aye, you would indeed!" sneered Stanley, "especially if there happened to be plenty of room to run away. Ah, Dacre Deadman, you thought to catch us nicely in a trap. But you see you have been caught in it yourself. Congratulate yourself that you are not sharing the fate of three of your wretched companions, whose bodies I can just see from here."

"The man Rousillion," said Ronald, "for I recognised him—has managed to get——"

At this moment a loud agonised voice cried out—

"Help, help!"

And at the same time distant shouts were heard.

"Raise the link!" cried Ronald.

Mark did so, but no one could be seen.

Again came the voice.

"Help, help!"

"Who calls?" asked Ronald in low tones.

"'Tis I—I—the landlord of St. Paul's Tavern, the——"

"Ha!" interrupted Ronald, "it is Rousillion! Speak—is it you, Rousillion?"

"Yes—yes," was the reply.

And now the figure of a man was observed groping its way along by the brick wall.

This was Rousillion.

A most deplorable object he looked, of a surety.

He had lost such a quantity of blood that, becoming weakened, he had, over and over again, fallen into the water, and narrowly escaped suffocation.

As he advanced loud shouts were again heard proceeding from the river entrance to the passage.

"Save me!" cried Rousillion; "the watch are waiting at the other end of the vault. Oh, save me or I perish!"

"Perish you *shall!*" cried Stanley. "Aye, you shall perish here in this vault or fall into the hands of justice! Save you from either alternative—never!"

"Stanley," cried Lady Whitmore, "let your revenge be tempered with mercy!"

"No, no," answered Stanley; "think —only think what would have happened to you and that fair girl by your side had we been taken unawares! No, no; no mercy shall be shown either to Dacre Deadman or those in his pay. Return whence you came, sirrah! for if you advance farther this way your death will surely follow."

With a deep groan of despair Rousillion leaned his back against the wall, and stared blankly at the fast-rising waters.

But as our party ascended the steps the light of the link vanished with them, and Rousillion was alone and in darkness.

Alone, we said. Nay, not alone, for the corpses of his three companions were floating around him.

Again and again he felt their bodies touch his legs, and he shuddered and moaned at the contact.

After a brief pause, Rousillion, more dead than alive, commenced to retrace his footsteps.

He found it slow, laborious, and dangerous work, and at almost every footstep the shouts at the entrance of the subterranean passage appeared to increase.

It was evident that all craft passing up and down the river, every shop-keeper, every apprentice from the bridge who could get away, had gathered round this newly-discovered passage, so many years taken to be the entrance to a disused sewer.

The fact was that a vast crowd of persons in craft of all descriptions had gathered round, and among them were a large number of the very men to whom Rousillion let his boats.

Little did they imagine who was in that passage.

Hundreds of lanterns and links were alight, and their rays served to bring out with striking effect a most extraordinary and novel scene.

It was certain that every one present was under the impression that river-thieves, by them called "Rats"—men who made it a rule to steal whatever happened to be handy in the watermen's boats—were in the passage, and they swore to make short work of the first who made his appearance.

Knowing nothing of the exit at the farther end of the passage, they, of course, concluded that whoever was there would be eventually forced out by the tide, and so they waited.

Presently Rousillion arrived at nearly the end of the passage, where he could see without being seen.

"Maybe there are many who know me," he thought, as he once more leaned against the wall, and placed his hand to his throbbing brow. "I will advance—shout out my name—my voice will be recognised, and I shall be saved!"

Again with great difficulty he proceeded, and at last his figure could be made out by the excited crowd.

Simultaneously everyone shouted out at the top of their voices—

"Here is one! Behold the water-rat! Shoot him down! Shoot him down!"

Rousillion raised his hands, and shouted as loud as he was able—

"Hold! hold! 'Tis I—Rousillion. In the Virgin's name, stay your hands."

But his voice, weakened by the loss of blood, was not heard amid the wild cries with which he was greeted.

A young waterman pushed his boat as far to the mouth of the entrance as possible, and raised an oar over his head.

He, however, failed to reach him, a fact which was noted by the crowd, and another wild yell was raised.

There was an elaborately attired fare in the waterman's wherry, and this individual, taking a pistol from his pocket, handed it to the young waterman.

"Here," he said, "take this. 'Tis charged, and the hammer is raised. You are near enough to the 'rat,' as you call him—see if you cannot make a mark of his head."

The waterman took the pistol, and having assured himself that it was a strong weapon, and not likely to explode in his hands, he raised it and took deliberate aim at Rousillion's head.

Whether Rousillion noticed this we cannot say.

But, at this instant, he again plunged a step or two forward.

"Save me," he groaned. "'Tis I—look, look! Cannot some of you recognise my voice? 'Tis Rousillion."

But again his voice was lost.

The crowd, now that he had come farther forward, noticed his haggard appearance, and they greeted him with loud, ironical cheers, howls, and hisses.

Once more Rousillion raised his hands.

It was the last movement he ever made.

The young waterman, standing in the bow of his boat, fired.

The ball was true to the aim so deliberately taken, and Rousillion fell, shot through the head—fell flat on his face in the water, which quickly became covered with blood.

Cries of "Bravo!" "Well done!" greeted this shot, and the young murderer—for so the law would consider the waterman's deed—suddenly found himself, for the time being, a hero.

The crowd waited for others to come forth, for they thought there were more.

And they were rewarded for their patience, for one by one the dead bodies of Rousillion's men floated out through the archway, and were eagerly seized upon by the occupants of the nearest boats.

The four were taken to the dead-house at the foot of London Bridge steps, there to remain until a jury could be collected to hold an inquest.

In the meantime our party reached the Hunchback's apartment.

Ropes were procured, and Dacre's hands and legs were securely tied.

He knew that to attempt to release himself would be worse than madness.

Oh, how the young ruffian gnashed his teeth, howled, groaned, and cursed.

Had he thought that by so doing he would procure his liberty, he would have begged, entreated, and implored.

When properly secured, Stanley, Ronald, and Mark seized hold of him, carried him upstairs, and deposited him in a side-room or recess.

It had no door, but that was not necessary.

Returning, Stanley said—

"Listen to me. It was agreed that here we should remain until the Hunchback returned. Why he has not returned ere now, neither you nor I can tell. Even Ronald can form no opinion —is that not so, Ronald?"

Ronald bowed his head in silence.

"Well," continued Stanley, "the Hunchback, of course, considered that all of us would be perfectly safe from molestation. Then the subterranean passage was undiscovered. Now that it is discovered, you may depend upon it that as soon as morning dawns, and the tide allows of it, the place will be overrun by persons who, through Dacre Deadman and his friends, have discovered that the passage must lead to somewhere. Under these circumstances, I deem it advisable that all of us should immediately depart."

A dead silence reigned for some few moments.

It was broken by Ronald, who said—

"I am of your opinion, Stanley. Henceforth we are in danger here. For myself I care not, and I know, Stanley, that for yourself you do not care; but we must not forget that these gloomy vaults are honoured by the presence of ladies."

"You speak truly, Ronald," answered Stanley.

"But yet," continued Ronald, "I would brave almost anything to obey my poor mysterious father."

"Of a surety. But I am certain that if he is alive—and most sincerely do I pray Heaven that no harm has befallen him!—he will say that we acted rightly."

"But whither shall we go, my son?" asked Lady Whitmore. "Remember that at present we are homeless."

"Aye, I cannot forget that," replied Stanley, "but I must think. I—"

"One moment," interrupted Beatrice. "The inn-keeper's daughter, of whose heroic conduct you told me, your ladyship—"

"Ah, true," said Lady Whitmore.

"Ruth Ellis would make me comfortable, and you also, Beatrice, if she could contrive to smuggle us into the house. But her so doing might be highly dangerous, for although Blackmore has met his deserts, and his helpmate, Dacre Deadman, is in our hands, there is no telling who occupies Blackmore Hall at this present moment, or whose watchful eyes are upon who comes and goes at 'The Rover's Arms.'"

"The idea is most excellent," said Ronald; "that is my opinion. But, Stanley, from what her ladyship says, it appears evident that she expects us to separate."

"Oh, most assuredly," replied Stanley; "it is out of all question that we can longer remain together. This is what I propose: Her ladyship and Beatrice will at once set out for High Wycombe, having Mark as their escort. About two hours after he has placed them in the care of Ruth Ellis, we will meet him—let me think—"

"We will meet him at Rushton Hill," said Ronald, "at 'The Three Oaks,' at the foot of Rushton Hill, which is about a mile on the other side of High Wycombe. Any person will direct him to Rushton Hill."

"So be it," said Stanley. "Mark, you do not fear to act as her ladyship's escort?"

"On the contrary, I am only too pleased. But perhaps you will allow me to suggest something?"

"Most assuredly. Speak on."

"Since her ladyship is so well known to Lord Blackmore's friends, would it not be as well if both were disguised?"

"Ah, yes, it certainly would. A timely suggestion on your part, Mark. Ronald, can we procure disguises?"

"There are several in the lumber-room of the cathedral—or, at least, there are portions of women's clothes, which might answer the purpose. I will procure them."

He brought down an armful of things in a few minutes, and laid them down.

Truly a most motley collection!

Their strange and eccentric character would have been enough to bring a smile to the gravest face, one would have thought; but neither of our friends were inclined to laugh.

Her ladyship and Beatrice made a selection, and announced that they would retire and don them.

"Your own costumes," said Stanley, "can be made into bundles, and carried with you. You will want them anon."

"I will at once hurry off and obtain horses for them," said Ronald, "and, at the same time, will procure horses and a coach for ourselves."

"But where will you procure them?" asked Stanley.

"Of the Avengers. I shall have to go to Smithfield. When I lay particulars before those to whom I go, they will offer assistance. You are leader of them and can command it. Give me instructions."

"If you can procure the assistance of two or three of them, it will be enough."

"That I can, no doubt, easily do," said Ronald. "And now, Stanley, tell me what it is you intend to do with Dacre Deadman. The coach you, no doubt, require for his conveyance?"

"Precisely. Bound hand and foot as he is, I intend him to be conveyed to Blackmore Hall."

"Aye. And then?"

"I have said that he *dies* at Blackmore Hall."

"You have; but you have not said in what manner."

"No. Of that and of other circumstances, I will consider as we proceed on our journey."

"Good. I, like others, have sworn to do as you say, and I will make no remarks on what you have said. See that her ladyship and Beatrice quickly prepare, Stanley. My absence will be of brief duration."

*   *   *   *

In little over an hour after this Ronald made his reappearance, and announced that three horses were waiting at a little distance from the vestry-door.

Beatrice, having bidden a most affectionate and tearful adieu to Ronald and Stanley, was the first to go.

She, like Lady Whitmore, was attired as a "pew-opener," the clothes Ronald had procured being some of these persons' "cast-off" garments.

Lady Whitmore, sad and sorrowful, weakened with trials and troubles she had undergone, was the next; and Mark, well armed, and carrying the bundles, went next.

Ronald and Stanley did not follow, fearful that too many persons might attract attention.

The "Avengers," three of whom had eagerly responded to Ronald's call, escorted the party.

They were speedily mounted and well on their journey to High Wycombe.

Some quarter of an hour after this departure, two of the Avengers passed through the vestry-door.

They were in the cathedral about five minutes.

When they passed out they carried between them a large box.

A person making an inspection of it would have seen that a portion of the lid was perforated with a number of holes.

This was to admit ventilation to the person within it. And that person?

Who else but Dacre Deadman?

Having waited a few seconds on the threshold of the door, a low but sharp whistle was heard.

It was a signal from the other Avenger that the coast was clear.

The box was thereupon hastily carried across the threshold, and hurried round to the side of the cathedral, where stood a coach.

Harnessed to it in the old cumbersome fashion were two stout horses.

Beside them stood four more saddled and bridled.

From the holsters of each projected the butts of pistols.

Stanley and Swift were the first to leave the cathedral.

As Ronald came forth he halted on the threshold, turned, and cast a lingering look behind him.

"Does this departure mean fortune or *mis*-fortune?" he said.

"Let us hope—fortune," answered Stanley. "Come, for no time must be lost in getting well on the road. The coach will, of course, be the cause of many long delays."

In a brief space they were mounted and on the road.

What were now Dacre Deadman's feelings as he felt himself on the move?

Did he know where he was about to be taken?

Certainly not. Stanley had told him that he should die in the room where he slew Lord Whitmore, but to that he had paid little or no attention, thinking that such a circumstance was out of all question.

So as the coach jogged on, the young scoundrel had ample opportunity for thinking over his past career. All the terrible crimes he had committed rose up before him.

The ghastly spectres of many of his victims seemed to flit to and fro before his eyes, to point their long fingers at him, and shriek "Murderer!"

His brain seemed on fire, his tongue parched, and more than once he yelled for water.

But his voice was lost in the rumbling of the coach.

And here—on the road to High Wycombe, and thence, if fortune favoured, to Blackmore Hall—we leave them, and return to the Hunchback.

CHAPTER V.

IS OF THE MEETING BETWEEN HER MAJESTY QUEEN ELIZABETH AND THE HUNCHBACK OF OLD ST. PAUL'S, AND OF WHAT STIRRING DRAMATIC EVENTS OCCURRED.

An hour after the disposal of the body of Simon Silex, silence once more reigned within and without the noble residence of his grace the Earl of Normanton.

Our readers will think that the Hunchback stood sorely in need of rest.

He did, but his brain was too active to allow him to sleep.

Instead of him retiring, therefore, he proceeded to take out the contents of his packs.

While busily engaged in this task, a gentle tap was heard on the door.

"Enter!" said the Hunchback.

The door opened and in walked the Earl of Normanton.

Gently closing the door, he strode across the apartment and stood before the Hunchback.

"Old man," he said, "I am too disturbed to sleep. The queen is pacing her apartments in a state of great agitation. 'Tis not often that any agitation takes possession of her, but when it does the fit lasts a long time. My wife, the countess, is with her, endeavouring to soothe her. Vain effort, I am afraid. By the blessed Virgin! I shall no doubt suffer for what has occurred."

"You, your grace?"

"Aye—me."

"I don't understand—yet stay. I do now comprehend what you mean. You mean that you fancy you will be called upon by her majesty to answer for the neglect of your guards?"

"Aye. But there is no fancy about the matter. Her majesty never forgets. But now, listen to me. Having discovered the intended visit of this man in the village, how was it that you did not instantly communicate with me?"

"I had already intruded too much on your lordship's kindness and valuable time."

"That answer, old man, will not do for me."

"Ah," exclaimed the Hunchback, "and why will it not do? I trust your lordship is not about to repeat——"

The Hunchback paused abruptly, but his lordship calmly said—

"Go on—go on! You would have said, 'I hope you are not about to repeat that I am an impostor.' Was it not so?"

"Your lordship has correctly guessed what I was about to say, but I refrained from saying so because I have no wish to give offence to your lordship."

"I am neither offended nor inclined to *think* myself offended. No. I was not about to again repeat my suspicions as to your being an impostor, but I *was* about to say that I am not yet acquainted with the facts of this case. I do not think for one moment that you are an impostor in the direct sense of the word, but I believe you are here disguised. You are an artist—that is certain. You leave proved it before my eyes. Now, old man—for such you appear to be—tell me what secret it is that you hide beneath this strange costume. Tell me all—tell me truly, and I will be your friend."

The Hunchback hesitated.

And that hesitation proved to the earl that his suspicions were correct.

"Proceed," continued the earl; "you have naught to fear from me. Speak out, and whoever you are, or whatever you are, I will give you protection while you are beneath my roof."

The Hunchback instantly embraced the opportunity offered him.

"Your lordship will swear to this?" he asked.

"A Normanton never breaks his word!" replied the earl; "but if it please you, I will swear on the cross, if necessary."

"No, no," said the Hunchback in low tones; "the Normantons were ever fierce, but always true. Your lordship here is a seat; take it—so, and I will seat myself beside you, and tell you a story. 'Twill be of great length, and so ere I begin, if your lordship is tired—"

"Tired? No, no! I am anxious for you to go on."

The Hunchback strode towards the door and locked it.

Then he returned, seated himself before the earl, and after a brief pause, he commenced his story.

During the recital of the remarkable history the earl listened with the most rapt and profound attention.

He never once attempted to interrupt, but more than once his starts, his gestures—nay, his tears, for he really and truly *did* shed tears—showed how affected he was. When the Hunchback said, "At present, your grace, that is all I have to tell you," the earl nodded, lapsed into deep thought, and so remained for some minutes.

Rising at last, he held out his hands, and taking the Hunchback's within them and looking into his care-laden face, he said—

"I pity you from the bottom of my heart; I can feel for you as ever any man could feel—you know why?—because *I* am blest with a beautiful wife; because if she were—But no, no! Let me not breathe it! I repeat that I feel

for you and pity you. I heard the story of that strange painter and sculptor—that consummate master of his art; but the story, as I now know, was strangely distorted. Of course my father had it at his fingers'-ends, and it was from him that, piecemeal, I had it. When these terrible incidents of your life occurred I was, as you know, but a mere lad."

"Ay, ay, you were. But, your grace, what think you of the man who wrought all this injury—this man who ruined my life—Sir Garnet Glassion?"

"He was indeed a monstrous villain. And you say that for years you have sought for him—for years you have been so hideously disguised on purpose to meet him?"

"I have."

"But what was your object in calling Old St. Paul's your home? What caused you to live, as it were, within its vaults?"

"Sir Garnet Glassion's father was slain in the aisle of the cathedral—or, rather, 'twas there that he received the fatal blow. And it was one of the clauses of his will that the son, Sir Garnet, should yearly or oftener, make a pilgrimage to the cathedral to offer up prayers for the repose of his soul. But this clause has not been fulfilled, or I should have met him! And then—and *then!*"

"I understand you. The wretch deserves death. Now I can tell you something. Sir Garnet has long ago discarded his own name."

"Ah, he has followed in *my* footsteps, then?"

"Exactly. He changed his name long, long ago, though how long I could not say with any certainty. You have thought him abroad?"

"Off and on."

"To my own knowledge he has not left England for two years."

"Heavens! Say you so? Then, your grace, I implore you, tell me—in what part of the country is he?"

"At this present moment he is on the road to this mansion?"

With a sharp cry the Hunchback recoiled a pace.

"Here!" he gasped. "Here!"

"Aye; let me tell you that the friend of the Spanish ambassador,

Don Salvador Corrozzi—you have heard of him?"

"Often."

"And seen him, no doubt?"

"Frequently."

"Then, by Heaven, his disguise has been as effectual as your own, *for Don Salvador Corrozzi is the man you have sought so long—Don Salvador is none other than Sir Garnet Glassion!*"

Another cry—a cry direct from the heart—left the Hunchback's lips. For a moment he remained stationary, like a man petrified. Then in a wild ecstasy of joy he seized the earl's hands, and frantically rained kisses upon them.

"Thanks—thanks!" he cried, in tones of deep emotion; "you have proved yourself my greatest friend! Don Salvador is the villain! Oh, that I had him here now where I— But I must try to calm myself. I—"

"Yes, yes!" said the earl; "whatever you do, remain calm. It is a matter of the utmost importance. And now let me ask you—from what you have said it is your desire to see the queen alone?"

"It was, but since you have made this startling revelation, it is no longer my desire. Your grace, will you allow me to suggest—"

"Willingly. Proceed."

"No doubt you could prevail upon the queen to listen to my story in the council-room, when all her lords and ladies, her ambassadors, and—and this monstrous, cowardly wretch is present."

The earl hesitated.

He knew not what would be her majesty's humour towards himself.

Then again, Elizabeth, he knew well enough, was not by any means a person given to listening to long stories.

But at last the earl said—

"I think I shall be able to manage it for you. It is hardly likely that the queen can refuse to listen to a story told by an individual who was the direct means of saving her life. Leave it to me, and I will try what can be done. But is it your intention to appear in the council-room in your disguise?"

"Aye; just as you first saw me."

"Good. I sympathise with you so sincerely, that I will not interfere in anything. Be prepared at ten of the clock for the message I will send you."

"At what time is Don Salvador expected?"

"Oh, he and the Spanish ambassador, with the few servants they generally bring with them, are expected here at about nine."

"Good. At ten, my lord, I shall expect your message."

"And you will remember that you must not allow your feelings to get the upper-hand of you? You must, above all things, remember in whose presence you stand."

"Oh, your grace, do not fear; the sacred presence of the queen will be my uppermost thought."

"Well, adieu for the present."

"Adieu, your grace—adieu! If my blessing is of any value to you, then Heaven knows my blessing is yours."

The earl bowed, walked to the door, opened it, turned, bowed again very gravely, and made a slow exit.

"Fool that I have been," thought the Hunchback; "fool! dolt! And often I have actually stood by *his side!* But the hour is at hand. Soon I shall take the revenge for which for so many years I have waited. Then secrecy need no longer be kept. Before men I can once more appear in my own name and my own person, and the world will know the Hunchback of Old St. Paul's no more."

*   *   *   *

As early as eight of the clock the earl was summoned to the presence of the queen.

When he left her and joined the countess, it was evident, from the glad smile on his face that the result of the interview had been far better than he had anticipated.

The whole of the occupants of the mansion were summoned, and cautioned that nothing whatever was to be said of the attempted assassination of the queen until the guests were assembled.

By nine o'clock all was life and activity within and without the mansion.

It being the last day but one of the queen's stay at the earl's residence, guests had been invited from far and near.

These included the whole of the foreign ambassadors then in London, and among the first to arrive was the Spanish ambassador and "his bosom friend and inseparable companion," Don Salvador Corrozzi.

Both reached the mansion on horseback, their animals being a superb pair of greys.

To look at the two men, the most experienced persons would have taken them for pure Spaniards, for not only did their features bear the Spanish cast, but they spoke in fluent Spanish, and their costumes were of the picturesque pattern so notorious of the Spanish nobility.

When they reached the grand entrance, they found it surrounded by an enormous crowd, consisting of lords, ladies, and gentlemen of all positions.

Scores of servants, Court and otherwise, and a host of soldiers filled up the background.

When the Spanish ambassador ascended the broad steps, his hand resting on the arm of his friend, Don Salvador, the crowd on the steps respectfully made way for them.

They were greeted—or at least the Spanish ambassador was—with observations expressive of good-will, which were most courteously replied to by the ambassador, who spoke in tolerable English.

Though Don Salvador was always, or almost always, in the company of the Spanish ambassador, some persons considered "Don Salvador" an uncouth, discourteous, unmannerly bear, and wondered why it was that a man of such refinement and culture as was the Spanish ambassador should tolerate such a companion.

And amongst those who thus thought was Queen Elizabeth herself.

Many times she had refrained from saying what she had intended to say only on account of the presence of this man.

She wondered what influence he could possibly have over the ambassador.

Many times she had felt inclined to ask a few questions respecting him, but she refrained.

The Hunchback's anxiety and impatience increased with every stroke of the clock.

A thousand times he asked himself whether, amid all the worry of receiving his guests, the noble earl would forget his promise of the message.

But the earl did not say one thing and mean another, neither did he forget a promise made.

Precisely at ten of the clock a gentle rap came on the door of his apartment.

"Enter!" said the Hunchback.

The door opened, and in walked a young, elaborately attired and very pretty page.

Walking straight across the room, this individual surveyed the Hunchback with great curiosity from head to heel.

"So *you* are the pedlar painter—eh ? " he asked.

"At your service," replied the Hunchback, with a low bow.

"And 'twas you who saved the queen's life—eh ? "

Again the Hunchback bowed.

The youthful page lifted a white jewelled hand, and dealt the Hunchback a sounding thwack on the shoulder.

"Bravo !" he cried ; "bravo, old man ! Why, you are as good now as many young men, though I must admit that you are far from being handsome !"

The Hunchback was inclined to be amused at the youngster's audacity.

"Well," he said, "I must own I am not so pretty as you, young sir."

"*Sir !*" exclaimed the page, drawing his exquisite figure erect. "*Sir ?* Why, what a funny old man you are ! I am no *sir*—I am a female."

"Well I congratulate you. You have the prettiness of a girl, and the impudence of a boy."

The page placed his—we beg pardon, *her*—hands on her sides, and laughed heartily.

"Why," she said, "so they all tell me. His grace the earl, who is somewhat fond of me, tells me that it was really a pity I was not a boy."

"Why ? "

"Because then I should have all the ladies of the Court at my feet, or at least ready to accept my hand. So then, you see, old man, I might have my choice, marry a lady with plenty of money, and instantly be a person of some importance."

"Humph ! And what of your heart ? "

"Oh," replied the young page carelessly, "that would be a matter of *secondary* consideration."

The Hunchback shook his head gravely, as he replied sadly—

"Don't be so persuaded, my young friend. The *heart* is of the first importance. But you are young yet. Too young to understand much concerning the affairs of the heart. But do you bring me a message?"

"Aye, from the earl; I ask your pardon for delaying it so long."

"Do not mention it," replied the Hunchback.

"The message," said the page, "was a verbal one, and was to this effect—'The pedlar painter will follow you.'"

"Nothing else?"

"Yes; and I was to remind you of the costume which you were to wear beneath your own. This, master pedlar, I considered was a strange and most mysterious message, but I presume it is not so with you?"

"Nay I understand it perfectly. And whither do I follow you?"

"I will show you. Come—that is if you are quite ready."

"Oh, I am quite ready—proceed!"

"Will you not require a pack?"

"I think not," replied the Hunchback.

Off walked the pretty and careless young page, the Hunchback following closely.

He was led through several rooms and passages, strange to say without meeting a single soul, but he could distinctly hear voices in animated conversation.

It was evident that the matter under discussion was the tragic event of a few hours back.

At last the page halted

"We are now," he whispered "in the room used by the earl's secretary when he is well, for, poor fellow, he is nearly always ill, and the room on the right of this is the council-chamber. Observe these curtains; you are to stand by the side of them, and at a given signal I shall draw them aside, and you will at once walk into the presence of the queen."

At this moment a mighty roar from the throats of a dozen trumpets was heard.

"The queen is come!" said the page.

This was soon evident enough.

Now that all expected guests were present, the news of the attempted assassination had gone round and all knew of it.

What wonder was it, then, when the queen, proudly entering the council-room, and walking unattended to the dais, was greeted with loud and prolonged cheers?

These were renewed again and again, until Elizabeth's keen eyes sparkled with joy—until her thin, firm lips trembled with the heartfelt emotion she now took no pains to conceal.

At last when silence was restored, the queen said—

"My lords, ladies, and gentlemen, in the midst of our exultation at our providential escape from a terrible death—for we *might* have been in the room to which this assassin came—we must not forget our saviour. He, it seems, is only a poor pedlar painter, on whom the Earl of Normanton and his countess, with their usual kindness, took compassion.

"Before we proceed with State affairs, we deem it imperative that this man should be summoned to our presence. The noble Earl of Normanton informs us that this poor old pedlar has craved a favour at our hands. It is that he should be allowed to tell his story before us.

"Now, my lords, we think that almost *any* favour should be granted to this man, and when that favour is of so small a character as the earl informs us, we think that there is no cause whatever for the slightest hesitation."

The queen paused, and a murmur of approval ran round that vast hall, crammed as it was with the *élite* of England.

"Your grace," continued the queen, "pray admit the pedlar to our presence."

The earl gave a signal to the page, the curtains across the recess were instantaneously drawn aside, and the Hunchback came forth.

His appearance at this moment was exactly as we described when he left the residence of the old Court fool.

His appearance was the signal for a buzz of wonder.

Was *this* the man who had struggled with a dastardly assassin? *This* old man the individual whose dagger had penetrated the assassin's heart?

Advancing straight to the foot of the dais, the Hunchback knelt before the queen, who at once bade him rise.

Then, fixing her keen eyes on his face, she said—

"Old man, we have granted the request you solicited—that is to say, the authority to tell your story. Proceed, and—mark it well—fear nothing. You are in our care."

The Hunchback, anxious and uneasy as he entered the council-chamber, but now calm and collected, hastily cast his eyes around.

On the left of the dais he saw the Spanish ambassador, and at his side, in a listless, uninterested attitude, stood Don Salvador.

In low, but impressive tones, the Hunchback commenced—

"Your majesty, since I have your permission to proceed, I will at once do so. Your majesty, and all you lords and ladies, are now well aware of the death of Lord Blackmore."

At the mention of this name a great movement took place.

The Hunchback noticed that the face of the queen turned quite pale.

"You wonder what character Lord Blackmore can be in my story—or, rather, my one story, for I have two to tell. Well, he is *first* of the leading characters. The other leading character is poor Lord Whitmore, than whom a truer, a more faithful, and devoted servant to your majesty never drew breath in these realms.

"Your majesty, you are well aware of the circumstances attending the death of Lord Blackmore. You are well aware of the share young Lord Stanley Whitmore had in that death, and also the share taken by those who supported him, and the son of the Hunchback of Old St. Paul's; you—"

"Stay, old man," interrupted the queen, in hoarse tones; "stay! Do not mention in our hearing the name of such a monster as the Hunchback of Old St. Paul's. We mean no slight on you when we say 'hunchback,' seeing that you also are similarly afflicted."

"Monster!" cried the Hunchback; "monster! No—I say no. Your majesty had no greater *slave* than the Hunchback of Old St. Paul's. It was he and Lord Whitmore, with a host of friends, who shall be nameless, who endeavoured to stifle the growth of a dangerous society called the "Cowled Eleven," a society which had Blackmore at its head, and whose head-quarters were at Blackmore Hall. Lord Blackmore saw that Whitmore was gradually collecting evidence, and he, being a favourite of your majesty, gradually spun a web about him. He laid before you forged evidence.

"Your majesty ordered Whitmore's arrest. What was the result? What news reached your majesty?—the news that Whitmore had escaped. That was a most infamous falsehood. But since then your majesty has heard different. Yet, have you—has anyone—believed it? I question it. Yet I know that Lord Whitmore was sentenced to death by the Cowled Eleven, and that his head was severed from his body by Dacre Deadman—Lord Blackmore's illegitimate son."

A murmur of horror ran round the room.

"Yes," continued the Hunchback, "and poor Lady Whitmore, lured to the Hall, was in the same room where the horrible tragedy was committed. She did not actually see the fatal blow struck, certainly, because Heaven willed it that unconsciousness should leave her—"

"One moment," the queen again interrupted. "How comes it that you are so familiar with all this?"

"Because," answered the Hunchback, in tones which thrilled everyone present—"*because I was a witness!*"

"You a witness!" cried the queen.

"Aye, your majesty, I—not the pedlar—but the Hunchback of Old St. Paul's himself!"

The false hair was thrown aside, and the Hunchback thus confronted the queen.

There was, of course, a general stir of astonishment, not to say consternation, for all had heard much of the strange, mysterious being who so constantly haunted the old cathedral.

What of the queen?

Did she appear startled?

Most assuredly, but she tried her hardest not to show it.

She raised her hand and stepped forward a pace, as if to issue instructions, but she paused, and abruptly lowering her hand, said—

"No; since we have promised you our protection, you are safe. Well, and you are the Hunchback of Old St. Paul's, eh? Well, I must say that you have shown your loyalty—eh, your grace?"

"Your majesty speaks most truly," replied the earl, bowing low. "And I believe he will prove to your majesty that Blackmore was the greatest traitor who ever waited on your majesty."

"Eh—ah! Well—well—the proof."

"Is here," said the Hunchback, drawing a paper from his bosom.

"Take it," said the queen to the Earl of Beauchauis, one of her secretaries, "and read it."

"Aloud, your majesty?"

"Oh, yes—aloud."

The Earl of Beauchauis took the document, slowly opened it, stepped forward a few paces, and read the words with which our readers are already acquainted.

We repeat them—

"*Proceed to the house of the Earl of Normanton, prepared to carry out previous instructions. Be careful. Do the deed cleanly, and your fortune is made.*"

For the space of a few seconds after the reading of this astounding letter, a dead silence reigned.

The falling of a pin might have been heard.

The queen was now indeed deathly pale.

"The signature?" she whispered.

"There is none, your majesty," answered Beauchauis, "but the handwriting is undoubtedly that of Lord Blackmore."

"Gracious heaven!" ejaculated the queen, "can it be? You cannot be mistaken?"

"As your majesty is well aware," replied Beauchauis, "I have for years had constant dealings with Blackmore's handwriting."

"Aye, most true. But that document is sealed. Look at the seal. Whose is it?"

"The seal!" answered Beauchauis, evidently thunderstruck. "The seal is that of the young Lord Roxburgh."

"At whose house Lord Blackmore met with his death?"

"Yes, your majesty."

"The spendthrift?"

"Yes, your majesty."

"Heaven's mercy on us!" almost shouted the queen, drawing herself erect and clenching her hands; "it seems as if we are in the midst of a nest of traitors. Where is this Roxburgh?"

"Some say he has left the country," said Beauchauis, "owing to the fact that your majesty would call on him, as he thought, to account for Blackmore's death."

"He is at Hampton still, may it please your grace," said a captain of the guard. "I saw him there yester-e'en."

"Beauchauis," cried the queen, "a warrant for Roxburgh's arrest must be at once executed. Let him be lodged in the Tower. He will find that the affixing of this seal has sealed his own doom."

Turning to the Hunchback, she said—

"You have proved yourself a true friend to the crown. And now once more proceed. We are all attention."

"Your majesty," said the Hunchback, "with your permission I will proceed with my second story."

"Well, well, as you will—go on."

A smile of pleasure passed over the Hunchback's face. But the next moment it faded away, and was replaced by a stern expression.

He cast his gaze in the direction where Don Salvador Corrozzi stood beside the Spanish ambassador, and raising his brows, fixed his eyes sternly, penetratingly, even fiercely upon his dusky face.

Don Salvador's gaze dropped on the floor, and the Hunchback perceived, with a feeling of triumph, the shudder that passed through his frame.

Still keeping his gaze fixed on Don Salvador, the Hunchback continued—

"Many years ago, there lived a certain man who had a high reputation as a painter and a sculptor. His talent was great—proof of that being in the fact that he was patronised by the king himself. And he might have gained a still higher reputation than he did, had he been a fine-looking man. But he was not. Yet that was not his fault.

When his reputation as a painter and a sculptor was completely established, as it was by the assistance of your majesty's illustrious father—when commissions were pouring in from all quarters, this painter took it into his head to get married.

"He looked about—not at Court, but elsewhere—and his choice fell upon his ward. She was a beautiful young girl," he faltered, trying hard to stifle his emotion, " but her experiences of the world were of no account whatever. She accepted this painter much after the fashion that a labourer accepts his wage. He knew she loved him not, but still he loved her—madly, passionately, blindly! He thought that love would soon follow.

"After the marriage they lived fairly comfortably together—that is while they *were* together, for the painter was constantly away on business. Oh, your majesty that was a fatal mistake! While the toiling painter was absent, another stole into his place, and the heart which he thought one day would be his was stolen from him.

"A villain—a depraved and abandoned profligate—a wretch, who had a dreadful reputation in London—a monster whose father was slain by the hand of a man he had robbed of his wife—constantly visited the painter's beautiful wife. He was handsome and gallant—she fell! News in the shape of hints, was constantly sent to the painter by a trusted servant, but little heed did he pay to the hints. By-and-by an urgent message reached him. He hastened home to find his wife in the arms of this villain—this wretch, who had the audacity to stand in the apartment where the painter's tiny infant lay sleeping in its cot!"

The Hunchback paused.

He was no longer calm. No; he was now terribly agitated, and his eyes glittered and flashed after the manner of a tiger before it springs upon its prey.

His story—pathetic in the highest degree, and most pathetically told—had its effect.

Every face betokened a sympathetic feeling.

Down the faces of more than one lovely lady tears were slowly trickling.

Of course all present considered that the Hunchback was telling his own life's history.

And what effect did this narrative have on Don Salvador?

He had turned ghastly pale; he trembled violently, and shifted uneasily and restlessly from side to side.

He felt that the man before him was wielding a hammer, and was driving the nail into his (Don Salvador's) body.

"This Hunchback," he thought, "was evidently a great friend of the painter. There is no doubt that my identity is known to him. But I will brave it out—watch my opportunity, and leave the country."

"Your narrative is interesting," said the queen. " Pray proceed."

The Hunchback bowed, and once more resumed—

"What would have happened, you can easily guess. It would have been the painter's life, or this villain's. But he escaped—yes, he contrived to escape. Blind with rage, his great, his passionate love for his wife turned to hate and a desire for revenge, he plunged his blade into her body."

A cry of horror interrupted him.

"He was too hasty," continued the Hunchback after a short pause; "No doubt he was too hasty, but she deserved her fate—that every honest man and woman will admit. Before her death she admitted her guilt, and in her last moments implored her outraged husband to spare the cause of her murder —for, of course, murder it was. But no; the painter swore on the Cross that he would never rest until he had ferreted out this wretch. But he failed. Years and years have rolled away, but he never saw him—never! But heaven at last took compassion on him. He—"

"He *has* met him, say you?" interrupted the queen. " Where?"

" *Where*, your majesty!" cried the Hunchback in loud ringing tones. " *Here—here!* See, your majesty, yonder! Behold in the person of Don Salvador Corrozzi the wretch of whom I have been speaking—he whose name before that dreadful affair was known as Sir Garnet Glassion. At last he stands face to face with the man he outraged—For I am no pedlar, *I am no*

Hunchback; I am as straight as any gentleman here present. See—see!" he almost shrieked as he loosened his garments and threw them down—"see! *I* am the painter! *I* am Gilbert Gascony Golding!"

The pedlar's garment was off, the doublet beneath it was thrown off, and then the dumb-stricken persons present saw *that the hump was affixed to that garment.*

When it was thrown down the Hunchback stood erect, and was a head taller than before, for as he stood erect his legs became perfectly straight, so all at once saw that his whole appearance had been a disguise.

Don Salvador's face was ashy pale, his eyes had a wild terrified look in them, while every part of his person trembled as with the ague.

Hoarsely he whispered to his friend the ambassador—

"Let us at once retire."

It was not likely!

Lo, the "friend" of so many years was a "friend" no longer.

"Until now," said the ambassador, "I never heard your true history. It is a terrible one. *Diavolo!* you deserve punishment!"

The eyes of the queen were fixed upon Don Salvador's white face.

Stretching out her hand, she said—

"Let that man stand forth!"

Oh, this was a terrible moment for Sir Garnet Glassion, *alias* Don Salvador!

A moment in which he felt that a thunderbolt from heaven was not more dangerous than the queen at this instant.

It was also a moment of supreme triumph for the Hunchback—or, as our readers will now permit us to call him, Master Golding.

With folded arms, proudly erect he now stood, his flashing eyes fixed upon the craven face of the villain who had ruined his life, and caused him to become an outcast and a wanderer on the face of the earth!

"Let the accused man stand forth!" repeated the queen.

All eyes were fixed upon Don Salvador's face.

The wretch moved not.

A captain stepped up, took him by the wrist, and led him forward.

"Are you or are you not the accused man, Sir Garnet Glassion?" asked the queen.

Don Salvador threw himself on his knees, and raising his trembling hands, cried—

"I am indeed Sir Garnet Glassion. Oh, your majesty, mercy! Have mercy!"

"You are the accused man—eh? And so Sir Garnet Glassion has for so many years hidden his identity beneath the Spaniard's cloak. And you cry mercy! By my father's head, what accursed audacity, my lords— eh? Mercy, sirrah? Mercy of us? No! Look, there stands he to whom you should sue for mercy. And a strange man he would be if he granted mercy to such a monster as *you* proved yourself to be. Oh, *shame* on you! *Shame* on you!"

After a brief pause, during which the queen conferred with her secretary, her majesty said—

"This is not a State, but a private affair, my lords, and therefore must be settled in a more suitable place than a council-chamber. My lord," she said to the Earl of Normanton, "the only favour we can do at present for Master —er—eh?"

"Master Golding."

"Master Golding, is to see that Sir Garnet Glassion does not leave the mansion until he has had a *private* conversation with him. So, my lord, let him be arrested, and see to it that he does not escape."

Oh, what a groan of despair left Sir Garnet's lips as these words were uttered.

To have evaded the man he had so deeply wronged for so many years, and then, after all, to fall into his hands, was really something dreadful to think of.

In a few seconds he was led away between a double file of soldiers.

Down into the vaults he was led, and secured in a strong room.

The queen, most likely, would not have thought proper to ask the Spanish ambassador any questions, but that gentleman, coming forward, volunteered a statement.

Having obtained permission to speak, he said—

"Many years ago I met Don Salvador—or, I should say, Sir Garnet Glassion—in Spain. We became somewhat intimate, and to sum up a long story, I became greatly indebted to him. The sum I owe him is large, and I have not up to the present been able to pay him. He told me a story of his flight from England, and of the circumstances, but they were very different to what I have just now heard. Having heard the dreadful story attaching to him, I can, of course, have nothing further to do with him."

"A wise resolve," replied the queen, grimly. "And now, Master Gilbert Golding, be assured that we shall not forget how deeply indebted to you we are. The Earl of Normanton shall communicate our wishes in respect to you."

Master Golding bowed.

The interview so far was at an end, and it was with a feeling of thankfulness that he retired to his own apartment.

He wanted to prepare for his next meeting with "Don Salvador," otherwise Sir Garnet Glassion.

* * * *

Towards evening the earl made his appearance.

"I have come," he said, "because I have just been told that you have borrowed a sword."

"Aye, that is true," was the reply.

"I know your intention without your telling me," said the earl; "you intend to fight with Sir Garnet Glassion. Is it not so?"

"Such was my intention. Has your lordship any objection?"

"None. I applaud your resolve. Though the wretch assuredly deserves a dagger in his heart, it is better he should be allowed to fight. I will see that you are not interrupted. Are you now ready?"

"Quite."

"In ten minutes I will send my page to you."

Sure enough in ten minutes or less the page arrived.

Without a pause Master Golding followed.

The page led the way into the vaults, a series of dark dismal-looking chambers, as cold as charity, and as damp as moss.

To Master Golding's surprise, he found the largest vault occupied by a crowd of soldiers.

They were arranged around the walls, and every other one held aloft a lighted link.

The Earl of Normanton was at the farther end of the vault, leaning with folded arms against one of the pillars.

There rested upon his remarkably handsome and noble features an air of stern determination.

As a matter of fact, the noble earl really considered that Master Golding had wisely determined to allow Sir Garnet to fight for his life.

As to who was the best swordsman—if, indeed, one happened to be better than the other—he had not the slightest idea, for he had never seen either one or the other wield a weapon.

"But," he considered, "Heaven in its sympathy for this ill-used man will give him the victory!"

Master Golding being present, the earl gave a signal, and Sir Garnet was led forth.

Did he know for what purpose he was being led forth?

We have no hesitation in saying that he did not.

When he suddenly found himself in the midst of a large number of soldiers, and saw the earl and Master Golding present, he thought of what was about to happen.

"Ha!" he considered, "I am then to have a chance! Good! In a combat with Master Golding there can be little doubt as to who will be the victor!"

"Sir Garnet Glassion," said the earl sternly, "unknown to the queen—unknown to anyone, in fact, but the persons you see present, a duel is to take place between you and Master Golding. He is a far older man than you, and perhaps not so skilled in the use of the sword. We, therefore, are here to see fair play. So long as fair play continues, we shall not interfere. Now, understand that this will be a duel to the death!"

"THE HUNCHBACK SEIZED THE EARL'S HANDS AND FRANTICALLY RAINED KISSES UPON THEM."

No. 12

"And this you will *also* understand," continued the earl, in tones which there was no mistaking, "if you happen to wound Master Golding in such a manner that he is unable to resume the combat, the fight will terminate. If, on the contrary, he wounds you and you fall, he will be at liberty to despatch you."

Sir Garnet started violently.

"Is this justice?" he asked.

"*Justice!*" answered the earl fiercely. "*Justice!*—a man like *you* to speak of justice! Was it justice to rob that man of his wife? Was it justice to flee from his vengeance? Justice! thou monster! Speak not of justice to *me*, or I shall be tempted to draw my sword on you, and save Master Golding the trouble. Vile caitiff, draw your blade!"

Sir Garnet did so, and his action was followed by Master Golding.

As the bright weapons flashed in the torchlight, a sudden thought struck the earl.

"One moment," he said, addressing himself to Sir Garnet; "in the event of your death, to whom would you leave your property?"

Sir Garnet hesitated.

Then in hoarse tones he said—

"To my wife and child."

"Ah! You have a wife and child?"

"I have."

"Their residence?"

"I refuse to say."

"Very well. What favour do you ask?"

"One only. It is that if it happens that I fall, which is doubtful—*very* doubtful—the only favour I ask is, that I shall be buried *unknown*."

"I understand. Your favour shall be granted. Master Golding, in the event of your death, I treat with your son."

Master Golding bowed, saying—

"If it so pleases you."

Higher up the flaming links were raised; the two men cautiously advanced, and the weapons crossed with a ringing sound.

Now, for the first time, Master Golding spoke to Sir Garnet.

"The moment has come at last," he said—"the moment I have prayed for, dreamed of, when indeed sleep visited my restless eyes. Yes, the moment has come. I will not speak of the past to thee. No; for whatever I might say would have but little effect on such a hardened ruffian as you have proved yourself to be."

The fight commenced.

Slowly at first it proceeded, but it quickly became fast and furious.

The watchful earl and the motionless officer and soldiers quickly saw that both men were expert swordsmen.

It was likely, they thought, that this duel would last a long time, and even then, perhaps, not terminate fatally to either man.

They were mistaken.

Though both were expert swordsmen, Master Golding was by far the most powerful man of the two.

He was an individual capable of great and sustained muscular effort.

This, added to his wonderful activity, had served him well hundreds of times, and it now served him on this occasion.

Sir Garnet found himself severely pressed, and losing his temper, his passes became not only furious but wild in the extreme.

Suddenly the point of Master Golding's blade cut his sword hand.

The sudden sting caused him to hesitate.

True, that hesitation was but momentary, yet in that moment he lost ground, and ere he could recover himself, his weapon was twisted from his grasp, hurled to the farther end of the vault, and Master Golding's blade passed completely through his heart.

He fell on the stone flooring like a piece of lead, and never moved an inch or spoke one word.

Death was instantaneous.

"Thus," said Master Golding, as he hurled his blood-stained weapon from him, "thus my desire of years has been consummated!"

The earl picked up the blade, took it by the point and returned it to Master Golding.

"You should keep this," he said, "and your son, and your son's son should treasure it as a memento of this occasion."

"You speak truly, my lord," replied Master Golding, returning the weapon to its sheath, "I will hand it to my son."

"Let us stay here no longer," said

the earl, casting a look, which was certainly not one of sympathy, on the stiffening body of Sir Garnet; "let us ascend and talk. But, captain!"

"Here, my lord."

"See that that man's last request is at once complied with. Let the stone on which he has fallen be at once raised, dig a grave, and place him within it—just as he is."

"Your lordship's orders shall be strictly carried out," replied the captain.

One last look Master Golding fixed on Sir Garnet Glassion, then uttering a deep sigh he turned, and with bowed head followed the earl.

*   *   *   *

Within an hour the queen was made acquainted with what had occurred.

And what did this remarkable woman reply?

Thus—

"Ah, he has died the death of a gentleman after all, my lord. Had we been left to choose, a felon's chains would have been his portion. Though 'tis a most grievous thing to fight a duel under our very feet, the peculiar circumstances attaching to it enable us to extend our pardon."

Master Golding, now all was over, prepared to depart.

The queen heard of his intended departure, summoned him, learned more particulars, with all of which the reader is familiar, and then assured him that when he had settled his own affairs he was to bring to Windsor his son, Lady Whitmore, and Stanley.

So, at ten of the clock, though urged by the earl and his beautiful wife to remain until the morning, he left the mansion on horseback and made towards London.

CHAPTER VI.

WHEREIN, AFTER MORE IMPORTANT EVENTS AND EXPLANATIONS, THIS ROMANCE IS BROUGHT TO A CONCLUSION.

THE coach, containing Dacre Deadman securely boxed, travelled until the first grey streak of dawn in the eastern sky warned the party that if they would escape detection they must get accommodated somewhere.

This they did, well bribing the landlord and ostlers of an inn to keep their mouths closed.

When night once more came on they again set out.

Our readers must not imagine for one instant that Dacre Deadman was taken from the coach during his stay at the inn.

The upper part of the lid of the box was removed, and a crust of bread and a jug of water was handed to him.

He refused the bread, and at first refused the water.

Finding, however, that if he did not accept of that he would get nothing, he, with many groans, and a curious medley of curses, partook of it.

High Wycombe was reached at last.

Leaving the coach in the safe custody of the grim Avengers, Stanley and Ronald went off at the gallop.

The one mile was covered in a very brief space, and the three oaks reached.

Stanley's and Ronald's joy may be better imagined than described, when a single horseman rode towards them.

They knew it was Mark, and guessed, by his being alone, that Lady Whitmore and Beatrice had been accommodated by Ruth.

"All is well," said Mark, joyfully; "we had but very little trouble. Ruth Ellis is entirely alone at 'The Rover's Arms.' Her father, who, it seems, was smitten with an attack of lunacy, has died raving mad. His body lies in one of the rooms attached to the old mill, and since the fact became known, the house has not been visited by a solitary soul."

"So much the better," replied Stanley, "for they are not likely to be disturbed. They will not be required to stay there long. Now join us, Mark."

Soon the party were once more on their way.

This time there was no halt until well within sight of Blackmore Hall.

"Now, Ronald," said Stanley, "we must dismount. Do you lead the way. I suppose you can find your way into the grounds again?"

"I hope so," replied Ronald, at once springing from his horse.

Mark held the bridles of the horses, while Stanley and Ronald went off.

Our hero gave them to understand that, as soon as his whistle was heard, they were to hurry up to the front entrance.

It will not be necessary for us to say how Ronald gained admission to the grounds.

It will be sufficient for us to say that he did so without difficulty, and that Stanley followed him.

Slowly they were compelled to go, owing to the weeds and bushes which beset their path. And they were cautious lest the least sound should disturb any of the guard—if, indeed, any of the guards were present.

Such a thing seemed doubtful, for no signs of them were to be seen.

Reaching the front, a single sentry was observed to be on guard.

Leaning on his pike he was lost in thought.

Stanley crept upon him, and suddenly laid his hand upon his shoulder.

"Hist!" he said; "make no noise, or you lose your life."

But the man did not even appear surprised.

Simply turning his head, he asked—

"Well, who are you?"

"No matter who we are," was Stanley's reply; "it is our intention to enter this house."

"Very well," grinned the man; "enter, and much good may it do you."

"Who is within?" asked Ronald.

"Only one person."

"His name?"

"That I know not. He is the only member of the Cowled Eleven at present here."

"Is he an Englishman?"

"Nay, a Spaniard."

"In what room is he?"

"In the council-room."

"Listen to me, my man. If I give you a well-filled purse, will you lead me to this room?"

"That I certainly will," replied the man, promptly, as he held out a huge, horny hand,

Stanley dropped a purse into his hand, and the man, turning and picking up a lantern, led the way.

Very quickly the horrible chamber where the dreadful murder of Lord Whitmore was committed — the chamber, the shadow of which was always before the eyes of poor Lady Whitmore—was reached.

It looked much the same as when that awful deed was committed.

True, only one torch was alight, and instead of the many persons about the table, only one was present.

Directly Stanley and Ronald—who had approached with noiseless tread— entered the room, this individual, who wore the cowl, started to his feet, stretched out his hand, and seizing a dagger, cried out—

"Hold! Who are you who thus dares to intrude on the privacy—"

"Hold, yourself," interrupted Stanley, as he boldly advanced towards the man, and drawing a pistol, presented it full at his head; "hold, yourself, I say, and put down that dagger at once."

The Spaniard—for such indeed he was, although some persons might have been deceived, owing to the perfect manner in which the man spoke the English language—seeing that Stanley meant what he said, at once dropped the weapon.

"What is your name?" asked Stanley.

"I refuse to give it," was the reply.

"As you will. We shall see what your reply will be anon, however. Ronald, do you keep guard over this accursed foreigner, and if he attempts any resistance, do not hesitate to put a ball through his brain."

"Do not mention it," answered Ronald, grimly.

Stanley descended with the sentry, and blew a shrill blast upon a whistle. It was instantly answered, and in a short time, Mark, the Avengers, and the coach rolled up to the front.

They were quickly made acquainted with what had taken place.

Dacre was speedily taken from the coach, and the Avengers between them carried him up the stairs.

Stanley first entered the apartment.

Gliding up to the Spaniard, who was now in terror of what was likely to happen, he repeated his former question.

"What is your name?"

"Maravillo," replied the man; "and I implore you to allow me to depart in peace."

"Oh, you *implore* now—eh?" sneered Stanley; "well, we shall see. Look you!" he said, pointing to the box, "who do you think is within that?"

"I know not," faltered the Spaniard. "Is it possible that there is a human being within it?"

He was answered by a deep groan proceeding from the box.

Dacre had recognised the Spaniard's voice, and the groan was followed by the words—

"Maravillo, 'tis I—Dacre Deadman."

"Dacre Deadman!" almost shrieked the Spaniard. "Holy Virgin! what is about to be done?"

"I know not," answered Dacre, with another dismal groan, "but there can hardly be a doubt but that I am brought here to be murdered."

"Murdered? Horror!"

"*Horror!*" cried Ronald; "*horror!* You who have helped to doom so many men to death to cry 'horror'!"

"I am innocent!" exclaimed the Spaniard.

"Innocent! What of—eh?"

"Of crime."

"Of *crime!*" mimicked Ronald.

"Lying villain!" cried our hero; "you—like those of your companions who still remain alive—like those who fell at Hampton—are steeped to the very lips in crime. And the worst of it is that, your victims have been Englishmen and Englishwomen. You have been found in this house, in the garb of one of the Cowled Eleven. We have sworn on the Cross to exterminate the whole of you, and therefore you die."

With a wild shriek down on his knees fell the Spanish coward.

Raising his hands, he implored for mercy.

"Let me think," said Stanley.

He conferred with Ronald for a moment; then, turning to the Spaniard, he said—

"Your life shall be spared on one condition."

"Oh, name it—name it!"

"You remember Lord Whitmore's execution?"

"Yes, yes—I—I do now call the circumstance to mind."

"I should think you did, wretch! You were in this room when it took place."

This was only a venture on Stanley's part.

But the Spaniard took it that those present had been informed of who had been in the room at the time of the execution.

"I was! I was!" he said.

"And you know the name of the monster who acted the part of executioner.

"Yes; it was Dacre Deadman!"

"Precisely. Ronald, bring out what you suppose is behind that stage, and then for justice and revenge!"

Ronald went behind that fatal platform, so well known to our readers, and looked around.

There was the block, and beside it the axe.

He brought out the latter and flung it on the floor.

Dacre heard the crash of the broad blade and shuddered.

"This was the axe with which the deed was done—eh?"

"It was."

"Good! Now, it is by this axe that Dacre Deadman shall die, and on the same block as my father died!"

Simultaneously the Spaniard and Dacre Deadman screamed aloud.

Neither Ronald nor Mark expressed any surprise, neither did the Avengers, who stood beside the box, grim and silent, awaiting orders.

"There is only one way in which you can save your life," continued Stanley, "and that is, that you act as executioner to Dacre Deadman. Do not accept the office unless you like. My friends here are quite ready to do it. But if you do not act as executioner, one of us will act as executioner to yourself."

Here was a terrible alternative!

What were Dacre's feelings now?

The torture he was undergoing was surely worse than death.

His agony was so great that he was absolutely bathed in perspiration.

In a moment or two the Spaniard decided.

The wretch would no doubt have slain his brother to save his own life.

"I will do as you ask," he groaned.

"Curse you—curse you!" yelled Dacre. "My most bitter, blighting curse on you!"

"Release him," said Stanley, "and, Ronald, the block!"

In a few seconds the lid was torn off, and Dacre was pulled out.

Frantically did he endeavour to release himself from the grasp of the Avengers.

His efforts were in vain.

They held him as a vice holds metal, and they quickly strapped his hands behind his back.

His legs, too, were so secured that he could just walk, and that was all.

Certainly he looked a most deplorable object.

The block was put forward on the framework, and Stanley, addressing the Spaniard, told him "To take off his crime-soddened garment."

The Spaniard hastily took off the costume he wore, and which we have so often described.

Then our hero handed him the glittering, but yet blood-stained axe.

"Take it," he said "and mark well what I say. If you make the least mistake—if the head of this dastardly assassin does not fall at the first blow—we shall see how many blows *your* head requires!"

Again did the Spaniard groan.

With trembling hands he took the axe, his action being again greeted with a volley of horrible imprecations from Dacre, who was now hurried forward.

But his struggles were so violent that actual violence had to be used to force him to his knees.

Seeing now that his last moments had really come, his shrieks became awful to hear.

He would not put his head on the block, and so it was held there by two of the Avengers.

"Now," cried our hero—"*strike !*"

The Spaniard raised the axe on high, balanced it over his head, and brought it down with a whirr and a crash on Dacre's neck.

He saved his own life, for the blow was truly delivered, and the head of Dacre Deadman rolled on the floor almost at our hero's feet.

The whole affair was a ghastly, horrible proceeding, but it was unquestionably blood for blood!

"What next?" asked Ronald.

"The next thing," answered Stanley, "is my father's body."

"You then," said the Spaniard, "are the son of Lord Whitmore?"

"I am. Know you ought of my father's body? You remember what my mother said, Ronald?"

"I do, alas!"

"The body," said the Spaniard, "has been decently interred in a deep grave in the Blue Chapel."

"Good. Anon it shall be disinterred and buried in the family vault. I suppose fire could not reach it?"

"Fire?"

"Aye, *fire !*"

"Nay, no fire could reach it."

"Good—very good! Now, sirrah, double up all the papers on that table, tie them up and hand them to me."

This the Spaniard quickly did, and handed the bundle to our hero.

"Now," said Stanley, "I will keep my word as to you. *Depart*, and leave the country at once. That is my advice. If you stay in England, it is likely enough that sooner or later you will be captured, and you may then guess what would happen to you."

The Spaniard did not have to be told twice.

With hasty footsteps he left the mansion, and when clear of the house, took to his heels and fled as if the foul fiend himself was behind him.

"You spoke of fire," said Ronald, "and so I presume that it is your intention to fire the house?"

"It is!" answered Stanley.

"Just as it stands?"

"Aye, just as it stands! Let us disturb nothing whatever."

"Very good. The idea, I think, is excellent. Now that we have destroyed the *birds*, it is but fitting that we destroy the *nest*."

The whole party descended.

Entering the room used as a storeroom, and which was pointed out by the sentry, a huge heap was made and set on fire.

Every window was then opened to admit a free current of air, and the party left the house and grounds, and commenced the return journey.

Before two miles had been traversed, the fire had got a good hold of the mansion, and its reflection lit up the country for miles and miles.

Our party paused not to look behind them, however.

They continued their journey, and without once halting.

High Wycombe was at last reached, and the party made their way to " The Rover's Arms."

No sooner had they stopped in front of the house than Ruth Ellis rushed towards them.

" Safe! " she cried. " Safe! "

" Safe and sound," answered Stanley. " And Lady Whitmore? "

" Is well, but sad! "

" And Beatrice? " asked Ronald.

" She also is well, but likewise very sad."

The whole party entered the old house, and being conducted to the principal room, they found Lady Whitmore reclining on a couch, and Beatrice at her side.

Her ladyship started up directly Stanley entered, and with a cry of joy threw herself into his arms.

Beatrice, as a matter of course, came forward to be caressed by Ronald.

" It is our intention," said Stanley, " to again push on to London. There can be no doubt that——Hush! What is that? "

The noise of the rapid beating of a horse's hoofs was heard.

Ronald hastened to the window, threw it up and looked out.

He observed a horseman galloping up to the house at full speed.

Arrived at the door he dismounted, and shouted out—

" What ho! what ho! Open here! "

" That voice! " cried Ronald, " That voice. It—but no! 'tis not. And yet how like my father's voice! "

" Maybe it *is* the Hunchback," said Lady Whitmore.

" No," replied Ronald; " 'tis not my father. The man who calls is straight as myself."

" What ho! " repeated the voice. " Open—open! "

Ruth, lamp in hand, descended the stairs and opened the door.

" What seek ye, sir? " she asked, as she surveyed the visitor from head to foot.

" Ye know me not, then, Ruth Ellis? " was the reply. " 'Tis because I am so changed—eh? "

" Holy Mary! " screamed Ruth, starting back, " 'tis the Hunchback! "

" The Hunchback? " exclaimed Ronald, rushing down the stairs. " No, no!—it cannot be! "

" It *is*! " was the joyful reply. " But the Hunchback no longer. This, Ronald, is the *second part of the story I told you in Old St. Paul's*. I am no Hunchback; that was merely a disguise—a disguise which was so effectual that my own son could not penetrate it. Ronald, my son—my son! "

With a loud, passionate cry, Ronald clasped his father in his arms.

And his joyful embrace was returned again and again by his now completely transformed father — Master Gilbert Gascony Golding.

Our hero's, Lady Whitmore's, everyone's astonishment can be easily imagined when Master Golding stood among them.

True, the voice of the Hunchback was there, the large eyes and mouth were there, but that was all.

Hastily, but in joyful tones, Master Golding informed them of all that had occurred at the residence of the Earl of Normanton, and of the queen's request that he should bring them all to Windsor.

Then Stanley told the story of what had occurred at Blackmore Hall.

What did Lady Whitmore say to the death of Dacre Deadman?

Well, what *could* she say? What could anyone have said respecting the vengeance taken by a son on the slayer of his father?

Master Golding's opinion was that he could not have been slain in a more just fashion.

" To have put a sword in the hands of such a ruffian," he said " would only have been a mockery. And the house has been burned to the ground? That, then, was the reflection I saw from the hill."

"It was," replied Stanley. "I thought that, since we had punished all the fiends that we could get hold of, it was as well to burn the place where it was likely that others would meet."

"And you did quite right," replied Master Golding. "And now, before we proceed with further explanations, let us partake of some refreshment. And, Mistress Ruth Ellis, can you find sufficient accommodation for all of us until morning?"

"Oh yes," was the reply; "there is room in plenty."

So it was decided that the whole party would stay until morning.

All found good accommodation—horses included—and Swift was not forgotten in the midst of the excitement and congratulations.

* * * *

Little more remains for us to add to this romance.

Her Majesty Queen Elizabeth received our party most cordially, Master Golding introducing them one after the other, Ruth Ellis, whom the Hunchback had persuaded to accompany them, being the last to be introduced; for, of course, it was out of all question for our other character—Swift—to be allowed to romp in the presence of the queen.

Her majesty took under her especial charge Lady Whitmore, and listened to her sad, sad story, the principal part of which she had already learned from Master Golding.

She promised to see her and her son restored to their rights, and we may take this opportunity of saying that she faithfully kept that promise.

Soon no persons were more welcome at Court than Lord Stanley Whitmore, Ronald, and Master Golding.

The latter by-and-by offered his hand to, and was accepted by Lady Whitmore.

The pair waited, and not long after, Stanley fixed his attentions upon a young and very handsome lady, who, strangely enough, was a sister to the beautiful Countess of Normanton.

The courtship proved a happy one, and the wedding-day being fixed, three marriages took place—viz., between Stanley and the lady we have mentioned, Lady Whitmore and Master Golding, Ronald and Beatrice Bevan.

Stanley, of course, took up his residence in the family mansion of the Savoy, and there Swift was once more at home.

Master Golding took a house close by, and Ronald occupied a house in the Strand.

In the declining years of his life, Master Golding had a greater reputation as a painter and sculptor than he had when a young man.

For a special picture of the queen he was knighted by her majesty, and Ronald eventually succeeded to the title.

Ruth Ellis, a few months after the close of our story, married a well-to-do tradesman, and, we have every reason to believe, lived happily with him.

Did Mark ever become a Court page?

No. Such position was offered to him, but he preferred to become our hero's private secretary.

Stanley and Ronald remained inseparable companions; where one was the other was sure to be; and their principal councillor in every matter of importance was the man who for so many years had been known as the misshapen, gloomy, mysterious

Hunchback of Old St. Paul's.